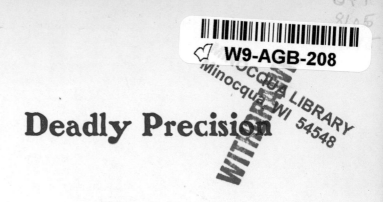

# Deadly Precision

A grating sound assailed her ears. She stopped and listened closely. It was the braying of some kind of animal. She looked up.

A goat-man stood on the summit above her. His goat face wore a gloating, toothy smile. He had seen her.

Impossibly, he began moving down the mountain face toward her, finding toeholds she could not even see. Brie's heart hammered unevenly as she grabbed her bow. She tried to nock the fire arrow to the string, but her fingers were trembling too violently. The goat-man was only a few feet above her, on a minuscule edge of rock. He looked down at her, balanced and steady on his perch. His musky goatish odor wafted down, making Brie's stomach tighten.

Please, oh please, oh please . . . Brie silently prayed for her fingers to work. There. The arrow was notched and ready. The goat-man began to leap down, toward her. Squinting, Brie let the fire arrow fly.

There was a searing, crackling noise. Sparks of light blinded her. Heat on her face, skin. She heard a hoarse scream. Through blurred eyesight, Brie saw the creature fall, its chest split open, flames spewing from inside.

Then it was gone.

# Fire Arrow

# Fire Arrow

## EDITH PATTOU

*The Second Song of Eirren*

MAGIC CARPET BOOKS

HARCOURT, INC.

Orlando   Austin   New York
San Diego   Toronto   London

www.HarcourtBooks.com

First Magic Carpet Books edition 1999
First published 1998

*Magic Carpet Books* is a trademark of Harcourt, Inc.,
registered in the United States of America and/or other jurisdictions.

The Library of Congress has cataloged an earlier edition as follows:
Pattou, Edith.
Fire arrow: the second song of Eirren/by Edith Pattou.
p. cm.—(Songs of Eirren)
"Magic Carpet Books."
Summary: While on the trail of her father's murderers, the young archer
from *Hero's Song* discovers her birthright—a magical arrow—
and the sinister doings of an evil sorcerer.
[1. Fantasy. 2. Revenge—Fiction.]
I. Title. II. Series: Pattou, Edith. Songs of Eirren.
PZ7.P278325Fi 1998
[Fic]—dc21 97-40634
ISBN-13: 978-0152-05530-1 ISBN-10: 0-15-205530-4

Text set in Granjon
Designed by Kaelin Chappell
Map by Barry Age

A C E G H F D B

Printed in the United States of America

*For Vita*

I am a wave of the deep...

—from *The Song of Amergin*
Irish poet, ca. 1270 B.C.
(translation by A. P. Graves)

# What Has Gone Before . . .

On a small farmhold in the land of Eirren there lived a gardener named Collun. He dwelt quietly in the village of Inkberrow with his mother, father, and sister; and his prized possession was a trine with a lucky blue stone embedded in the handle. When his sister, Nessa, went to visit her aunt in the city of Temair, seat of the royal family, she mysteriously disappeared, and it fell to Collun to find and rescue her.

Forging his trine into a dagger, Collun set forth, accompanied on his journey by the aspiring bard Talisen; Brie, a female archer with a quest of her own; an Ellyl prince called Silien; and Crann, the wizard of the trees.

As Collun and his company made their way through Eirren, facing many perils, they learned that Medb, ruler of the evil kingdom of Scath, which lay to the north of Eirren, had kidnapped Nessa and was in pursuit of Collun as well. Medb believed the brother and sister to be in possession of a shard of a great stone of power called the Cailceadon Lir.

Back in the days of the hero-king Amergin, there was an evil sorcerer named Cruachan, who by trickery and murder acquired the Cailceadon Lir. With the stone he created a host of malformed, deadly creatures that laid waste to Eirren; among these creatures was the loathsome Firewurme, Naid, which ultimately turned on and destroyed Cruachan himself.

It was the hero-king Amergin who retrieved the stone and wielded it to subdue the creatures and to trap them inside the very cave from which Cruachan had first summoned them. During the sealing of the cave, the Cailceadon Lir shattered into three pieces.

One shard of the stone was taken safely to Eirren and was guarded well over the years by the reigning kings and queens of Eirren. The other two pieces of the Cailceadon Lir were lost.

In the early days of the reign of King Gwynn and Queen Aine, Medb found one of the missing shards of the Cailceadon Lir, and it became her desire to reunite all three pieces, thereby gaining unlimited power to pursue her evil ends. Believing the girl Nessa to be the link to the third shard, Medb kidnapped Nessa and set the monstrous Firewurme to guard her on the isle of Thule.

As Collun journeyed to Thule, he learned the long-hidden secret of his parentage—that the cold and remote blacksmith Goban, who had raised him, was not his father. Cuillean, the legendary hero of Eirren, was his mother's first husband and Collun's true father. He also learned that the stone in his dagger was the last of the three shards of the Cailceadon Lir.

While Collun and Brie, the archer, made their way across the forsaken land of Scath to rescue Nessa, Medb was mounting a massive invasion of Eirren using Scathians as well as a host of morgs, evil creatures with yellow eyes who dwelled in the island kingdoms of Usna and Uneach.

And so did Collun face the Firewurme, with its lethal ooze that burned like fire. Sorely injured by the creature, Collun finally killed it, using the dagger with the lucky stone embedded in the handle. Finding that Naid was also guardian of Medb's shard of the Cailceadon Lir, Collun took it away with him, and his defeat of the wurme and the taking of the stone caused Medb's planned invasion of Eirren to collapse.

Given the name "Wurme-killer," Collun journeyed back to the dun of his true father, Cuillean, and there had his dagger forged back into a trine. His injuries slowly healed, and he and Brie found a measure of peace as they brought the long-deserted land around the dun back to life.

CRANN'S MAP

# Fire Arrow

# ONE

## The Wyll

"What think you of revenge?" Collun asked the soldier Kled, though his eyes were on Brie. She smiled to herself.

"Revenge? Why there's nothing I like better than a good tale of revenge, dripping with blood and avenged honor and all." Kled handed Collun his cup of chicory for refilling. "Have you one to tell?" he asked.

Collun shook his head, impatient. "No, I am speaking of true revenge, outside of books and stories."

Kled looked puzzled. "Well, I have had no experience with it myself, but certainly if one has been sorely wronged, then revenge is a just and honorable—"

Brie let out a laugh. "Wrong answer, Kled."

"Why wrong?"

"Collun wanted you to say that revenge is a contemptible thing, fit only for cowards and scalawags."

"Why?"

"Because of me."

"You?" Kled's face was a study in bewilderment.

Brie's smile died. "Because I am sworn to revenge myself on the men who killed my father."

"In truth? How many men?" Kled asked, his eyes kindling with interest.

"There were twenty or more, all Scathians, but I would be content with the lives of three."

Collun let out a sound of disgust and threw the dregs of the chicory on the fire, making it hiss.

Brie ignored him. "Two who delivered the deathblows. And a third, whose orders they followed. When the killing was done it was he who came down off his horse to ensure they had done it well." Brie's voice was steady.

"By Amergin," Collun interrupted, "can neither of you see the folly? Ending the lives of these men will change nothing. The only one changed will be you, Brie. Remember the tale of Casiope, the archer? Revenge is as an arrow; it will surely return one day and pierce the one who shoots it."

Brie glared at Collun. She started to say something but bit it back. There was an awkward silence.

Kled cleared his throat. "Perhaps I should brew another pan of chicory, or have we all had enough?" But neither Collun nor Brie responded.

Abruptly Brie's mouth curved into a smile. "An arrow. That was clever."

Kled looked at Brie, then at Collun, uncomprehending.

"I thought you'd like it," Collun replied with an answering smile.

"Very clever."

"Does that mean you agree with him now, Brie?" asked Kled.

"No, not exactly."

Kled gave a shrug and drank off the last of his chicory.

Brie gazed into her own cup, preoccupied. A moment ago, as Collun spoke of Casiope, the archer, Brie had caught something in his eyes; it was beneath the anger, a look of such deep-reaching kindness it had made her heart skid in her chest. No one before had shown her such a look, no one—not her father, nor Masha, the nurse who cared for Brie after her mother died. She could not meet Collun's gaze again and soon after made an excuse and left them.

The next morning Brie rose early, leaving Collun asleep by the campfire. Ever since they had come to the dun of Collun's father they had chosen to make camp outside. The dun had lain empty for almost two years, ever since Collun's father, the hero Cuillean, had disappeared, and the rooms were musty and ill-kept. On the few occasions it had rained heavily, they had sought shelter in the stables.

Brie found the Ellyl horse Ciaran grazing in the forecourt of the dun. The horse ambled over, searching her hand for a sweet. Though they had been companions for many months, Brie was still in awe of Ciaran. The horse came from the land of Tir a Ceol, where the folk called Ellylon lived, out of sight of human eyes. Ellyl horses were smaller than Eirrenian horses, as well as leaner, but they were more graceful. Ciaran was white like foam capping a sea wave, with gray stockings, a patch of gray at her fore-head and another on her cheek. She was a beauty and knew it, but had a gentleness of spirit that made her vanity easier to bear. It was astounding to Brie that Ciaran continued to stay with her. She had expected the horse to disappear back to Tir a Ceol long ago.

Brie swung herself onto Ciaran's bare back, and they made their way west, to the sea and a sandy bay they had discovered a fortnight ago. It was the perfect place for a gallop.

Dismounting, Brie let Ciaran frisk at the edge of the water. Brie dug her toes into the sand and squinted at the horizon of sea and air.

There was an old Eirrenian story—part of the coulin that explained the beginnings of Eirren and included tales of all its great heroes and gods—about the god, Nuadha, who had wielded a magic arrow, or teka. He had stood at the rim of the new world and, to chart a course through the wilderness, had repeatedly shot his teka from a bow and then run to catch up to it. Along the route he followed did appear the first ash tree, the first goshawk, the first flint, and the first hyacinth plant. The ash tree was to make the shaft of an arrow, the goshawk for its fletching feathers, the flint for the arrowhead, and hyacinth for glue to bind the feathers to the shaft. Of course, unlike Brie, Nuadha was a god and had no trouble traveling over the sea with a magic arrow that would not sink beneath the waves. Certainly it was not a journey one could undertake in real life, but...

Impulsively Brie pulled her bow off her back and nocked an imaginary arrow to the string. Ciaran cocked an ear in Brie's direction.

With a grin Brie pulled back and let the imagined arrow fly. With her eyes she traced its invented arc over the waves and pictured it cleaving silently into the water, startling a passing school of fish as it sank slowly to the bottom.

Perhaps if she were an Ellyl, with the Ellyl's fishlike swimming ability, could she chart such a journey. Brie laughed softly to herself and lowered her bow to her knees. It was absurd of course. Such journeys were only for gods and heroes.

As Brie watched the Ellyl horse gallop along the sickle curve of the shoreline and thought back over her time at Cuillean's dun, she felt unaccountably peaceful. It was a new feeling. Indeed, it was the first time within her memory that the hard knot within her—of loneliness and the need to be best in all she did—had loosened. She had never had a brother or sister, but she imagined that this bond between herself and Collun was similar to what a brother and sister might share, and she savored the closeness.

There were moments, however, when she looked at him and a breathless, foreign feeling came over her, unexpected and fierce. Like yesterday when her heart had felt like it was flipping about in her chest. The feeling made her uncomfortable and somehow did not seem quite sisterly. The few times she had felt it, she had fled, going off with Ciaran to gallop in the countryside or on the beach of the Bay of Corran. Collun never asked where she went or why.

Brie gave a long whistle, and Ciaran wheeled around, sending sprays of seawater up around her gray stockings. Soon Brie was astride the Ellyl horse, and they were pounding along the sand.

The night of Midsummer, Collun and Brie climbed the highest tower of Cuillean's dun to view the bonfires that blanketed the countryside.

As they gazed out at the blazing fires, Brie was reminded of a night from her childhood when her father had carried her up to the ramparts of their dun and showed her the Midsummer bonfires for the first time. His strong arms held her as she stood barefoot on the cold stone of the parapet. She had been awed by the sight of all those glowing, leaping flowers of flame, stretching as far as her eye could see. The brightest one blazed at the foot of the hill that bore the White Stag of Herge, illuminating the enormous figure. The Stag had been etched into the hillside long ago by people who cut away turf to expose the white chalk of the cliff.

Brie had told her father she wanted to dance around the bonfire and feel the fire's heat on her face and arms. He had said she was too young. But even when she grew older, Brie didn't dance. She would gaze enviously at the abandoned twirling forms of the dancers, but her body felt hemmed in, awkward. And there was the unspoken word that it was somehow unseemly for the daughter of the hero Conall to join the bonfire dances.

"Brie?" Collun broke into her thoughts. "Where have you been?" he asked with a smile.

"At the bonfire dances, long ago," she said musingly. She shivered slightly. Brie did not often think of Dun Slieve. Her uncle and aunt lived there now. She had left the day after her father's burial—to seek his murderers—and had never returned.

"Perhaps we should go inside?" Collun asked, trying to read Brie's face in the darkness.

"Not yet. I was thinking of the last time I saw the dun where I grew up." She paused. "And the pledge I made when I left there."

Brie felt Collun's eyes on her. "It has been two years, or more, since then..." She trailed off.

Then she turned to Collun with a ghost of a smile. "I have been wondering of late if I oughtn't leave my father's murderers to their own fates."

Collun let out a breath, smiling broadly. "I'm glad," he said simply.

As they made their way down the inside stairway, a loud crack of thunder echoed in the tower. "If we wish to remain dry, we'd best stay inside tonight," Collun said.

They had to rummage about to find bedding, and it took some time to sort out where to sleep in the long-deserted dun. But finally Brie lay on a pallet, Collun in the room next to hers. It felt strange to be separated by walls. She listened to the rain, glad it had held off until after the bonfires. She dozed, thinking again of her childhood in Dun Slieve.

Brie was in the Ramhar Forest, crouching beside her father's body, her heels skidding in the blood-slick grass. Hatred raged inside her, roaring in her ears. The three men stood before her, like ghosts: one with wide shoulders and thick pale arms, carrying a black spear; another tall, with yellowish eyes; and the last, the most evil, with his arrogant, coarse face and black eye-patch.

As she stood to face them, they disappeared. Then there

was darkness. A throbbing, quiet stillness. And suddenly out of the silence plunged a blazing yellow bird of prey. Its talons were extended and it dived at Brie. She raised her hands to fend it off.

There was a pale face hovering over her and the faint sound of a voice speaking. But the features of the face were blurred, black smudges where the eyes should have been, and she could not recognize it. Panic filled Brie, as if she were falling backward into darkness, nothingness. Her hands flailed; she didn't know if she should be trying to catch hold of something or to push it away.

"Brie?" Collun caught one of her fluttering, cold hands in his. She tried to snatch her hand away, hating the feel of his warm skin. But he held fast, keeping his voice low, soothing.

Her racing heart began to slow. She was able to focus on Collun's face, on the comfort in his voice. But for some reason, she still wanted her hand back.

"Let go," she croaked, pulling away, and suddenly her hand snapped loose of Collun's grasp. She cradled it against her chest. Collun drew away slightly.

"A bad dream?" he asked, his voice neutral.

"Yes. My father," Brie replied indistinctly. And a bird, she thought. She didn't understand about the bird. It had been familiar, yet not like any live bird she had seen. Its yellow feathers were overvivid, unnatural. Perhaps she had dreamed it before.

"Can I bring you something? Water or...?"

Brie forced her lips into a smile and shook her head. "I'm better now. It was probably all the peach mead we drank." Collun's face relaxed. They had discovered an overgrown orchard of peach trees and for the past week had eaten little else but peaches: peach pie, poached peaches on toast, guinea hen flavored with peach juice. It was Kled's idea to make several barrels of peach mead for Midsummer.

"It was rich," Collun agreed. He paused. "This is the first of those nightmares you've had in a long time."

Brie nodded. "The first since coming here." They were silent for a moment. "No more peach mead for me," Brie added with a thin smile.

Soon Collun left the room, and Brie rose, crossing to the heavy tapestry that covered the window. She pulled it aside. It had turned into a wild night. Through lashings of rain she could just glimpse the sea.

The next day as she and Collun labored to rebuild a stone wall separating pasture from crop-producing land, Brie felt edgy, her eyes prickly from lack of sleep. She worked hard, hoping to sweat out her unease. Collun tried several times to start a conversation, but Brie's responses were perfunctory. At midday, Kled came by to share their meal. He offered Brie a cup of peach mead, which she refused with a frown. Kled raised his eyebrows, then turned to Collun.

"You'll never guess what Renin came across this morning," he said, munching on a peach tart.

"What?" asked Collun, trying to coax some damp kindling into a fire for brewing chicory.

"A wyll."

"A what?"

"A wyll. A kind of witch-woman or fortune-teller. Haven't you heard of them? You find them mostly in the north, closer to Dungal. That's where they come from. Dungal."

Dungal was a small kingdom north of Eirren, separated from it by the Blue Stack Mountains, a formidable, almost impassable mountain range that began practically at the Western Sea then swept inland, curving northward until it crossed over into Scath and became the Mountains of Marwol. The mountain range provided a natural boundary between Dungal and Scath as well.

To the people of Eirren, Dungal was a place shrouded in myth. Dungalans were said to have more than a little Ellyl blood running in their veins, and it was not unusual to find at least one person in a village with the ability to perform magic of one kind or another, be it the curing of ills or weather-working. They spoke their own language and worshiped their own gods. Traditionally they were ruled by a queen, but in recent years a prince named Durwydd ruled the small kingdom.

"She's a tiny thing, the wyll; Renin thought her a child when he first came upon her. He found her sheltering in that broken-down dovecote," continued Kled. "She knows all sorts of things you can't figure out how she would. The others are all worked up. Renin has already given her his favorite torque because she told him he was going to marry the girl he fancies back in his birth town. The wyll knew the girl's name and everything. You two ought to come, have your fortunes told."

Brie was skeptical and her head ached with fatigue, but Collun was curious, so they accompanied Kled to the soldiers' quarters in what had once been the dairy barn.

When Brie and Collun entered, the soldiers were listening raptly as the wyll told a story.

She was indeed small and had long coppery gold hair. It was woven into dozens of braids that fell past her waist. Her forehead was broad, unusually broad for such a small face, which—coupled with her large amber eyes—kept her from being beautiful. She wore colorful clothing that seemed to consist of many layers, and bright earrings sparkled at her ears. The wyll took note of the new arrivals, but did not pause in her storytelling. She spoke with a lyrical, accented voice, and Kled whispered that her name was Aelwyn.

Despite her sore head, Brie found herself getting caught up in the story. She wished she had been there from the beginning. Then the wyll fell silent, her story finished. She turned toward Brie. A smile curved her small mouth, and she suddenly spoke in a tongue Brie did not know. At Brie's puzzled look, Aelwyn shifted back to Eirrenian. "Are you not from Dungal?"

Brie shook her head.

"I'm sorry. You have a look about you of home."

"They want their fortunes told, Aelwyn," Kled said. Brie started to demur, but Collun stepped forward. Aelwyn motioned for Collun to sit before her, and she took hold of both his hands, shutting her amber eyes. She was silent for several moments, her wide forehead ridged with concentration.

"I see a long journey. A monstrous creature. Burning pain. But then relief and peace." She paused, then opened her eyes. "You have learned something ill of a blood kin, yet where there was honor before, there will be honor again."

Collun stared at the wyll, his mouth open slightly.

"Didn't I tell you she was a marvel, Collun?" said Kled, breaking the silence.

Brie wondered just how much the soldiers had told the wyll of Collun's history, but she said nothing.

"It's your turn, Brie," said Kled.

"I really don't...," Brie began.

"Come," said Aelwyn with a smile. Reluctantly Brie sat before the wyll, who gathered up her hands. Aelwyn started to close her eyes then seemed to change her mind, opening them. She gazed straight at Brie. The wyll's amber eyes were glittery, like faceted gemstones.

Suddenly a shudder went through Aelwyn, and she tightened her grip on Brie's hands. Her eyes seemed almost to spin, and she began speaking in a rasp, unlike the voice that she'd used with Collun. But she spoke in the language of Dungal.

Brie felt cold, as if an icy hand had clamped on to the nape of her neck. She wanted to withdraw her hands but was mesmerized by the wyll's eyes. The wyll continued to speak, the strange words flowing out of her mouth, almost like a melody.

Finally Aelwyn fell silent. Brie heard one of the soldiers nervously clear his throat.

Aelwyn gently released Brie's hands. She blinked several times, then smiled at the assembled group as if nothing untoward had happened.

There was an awkward silence. Kled muttered to Collun, "Haven't seen her do *that* before."

Then the soldier Renin said, "So, did you see anything?"

"I did."

"By Amergin, are you going to tell us or not?"

Aelwyn turned her now-still eyes on Brie. "Do you wish to hear what I saw?"

Brie wanted to say no, but it seemed cowardly. Besides, it was all foolishness anyway. She nodded.

"I saw a brave man hewed down in a forest while a girl"—the wyll looked at Brie—"watched."

She could have learned that from the soldiers, Brie thought.

Aelwyn continued. "There were many, but two struck the most, the deepest. A man with broad pale arms holding a black spear, and another, tall with eyes like saffron, part morg. And last, one who led them, with a dark covering over one eye. Evil." The wyll shivered slightly. She stopped speaking.

Brie drew a deep breath. She had told no one what the killers looked like except Collun, and she knew he would never speak of it. "That was in the past," she said, her voice high and stretched thin. "What of the future?"

The wyll's amber eyes widened. "That which you seek lies in Dungal," she said.

Brie's pulse quickened, and the invisible cold hand at the back of her neck tightened its grip. "My father's murderers?" she asked, locking eyes with Aelwyn.

"If that is what you seek."

The wyll adjusted the torque on her arm. "It has been long since a seeing took such hold of me. Do you yourself have draoicht?" Aelwyn asked, curious.

"You mean magic?" Brie gave a short laugh. "Of course not."

Collun spoke up, his hand on his trine. "I carry a stone . . . ?"

Aelwyn shook her head briskly, uninterested in the cailceadon. "No, it is from her." She turned back to Brie. "What is your name?"

"Breo-Saight. Or Brie."

" 'Fire arrow...,' " the wyll said thoughtfully. "Listen, there is more." She drew Brie closer and spoke softly into her ear. "Shifting water and earth. Sacred standing stones covered with seabirds. A crippled man. And a man of power. Treachery. I saw hatred, the lust to kill. I saw death." Her breath tickled Brie's ear. "And...an arrowhead pointed at your own heart."

Abruptly she resumed her normal voice. "There. That is all." She reached up and smoothed a coppery braid. "Now, does someone have a bauble for Aelwyn?" she asked, flashing a catlike smile.

Brie was too dazed to respond. Kled nudged Collun, who had been watching Brie with a worried frown.

Aelwyn crossed to Collun and said in a teasing voice, "Didn't you say something about a stone?"

"Uh, no...I mean..." He stumbled over his words, reluctantly tearing his gaze from Brie. "That stone is, uh, too precious..." He trailed off.

"Not the cailceadon," laughed the wyll. "I have no interest in so potent a stone. I mean the one in your other pocket."

Puzzled, Collun felt in his pocket and drew out a chunk of rock he had found while plowing several days ago. It had several large saphir gems embedded in it, and he had thought to dig them out and make a bracelet or hair clasp for Brie.

Kled gave him another nudge, and Collun offered the rock to Aelwyn.

She took the chunk of rock with a look of pleasure, holding it up to the light coming through the dairy door.

Brie had been sitting very still, unaware of the conversation around her. Abruptly she rose, a flash of blue from a saphir banding her cheek as she began to move across the barn.

"Will you go to Dungal?" Aelwyn called after Brie.

Brie paused. "Perhaps," she said, her voice sounding muffled.

Startled, Collun gave Brie a sharp look.

"Be warned, Breo-Saight," said Aelwyn, rummaging in her colorful layers of clothing for a soft leather pouch. As she slid the rock into the pouch she continued, "Once you go to Dungal, it is not easy to leave."

"You left."

"Because I like pretty, shiny things, and your people will pay well for the skills I have. But the hiraeth, the heart-sickness from being away, it is with me all the time, like a knife in the heart. Farewell, Breo-Saight."

"Farewell, Aelwyn," Brie said, and left the barn.

There was a roaring in her ears and her breath came short as she moved away from the barn. Her father's killers. In Dungal. She would have her revenge.

TWO

Dun Slieve

In the room next to Collun's, Brie was stowing her things
in her pack.

Collun entered. She glanced at him, then back at her
pack. She did not want a quarrel but could read the mood
in his eyes.

"What are you doing, Brie?"

"I am resuming my quest." She spoke tonelessly.

"Because of the words of a wandering fortune-teller
with a weakness for shiny things?" His face held disbelief,
as well as anger.

"As I recall, you were more than ready to believe in the
wyll."

Collun's eyes flamed. "Even if she spoke truly, I cannot

believe your blood lust so strong that you do not see the folly of such a quest."

Brie felt her own temper flare up. "I made a vow over my father's body. It is no folly to act with honor."

"It is no honor to seek death over life."

"I seek revenge, not death."

"And how will your *revenge*"—he said the word as if it were a foul thing—"profit you or your father?"

"Leave me," Brie said, her voice becoming quiet. "Before we say words we wish we had not."

Collun looked away, silent. When he spoke again, there was a stillness about him. He took a step closer, his eyes kindling as if from an overfull heart. "At least wait. Stay here at Cuillean's dun a few days more. Brie, I fear..."

Brie felt a rising panic. She could not hear what Collun was about to say. It frightened her. She closed her pack with a snap of the leather thong. "No."

"But..."

"I am not like you." She looked him full in the face. "I do not *fear* to act."

Collun whitened at the words, his expression hurt, but then his jaw hardened and the brightness in his eyes went cold.

There was a long silence. Then Collun spoke. "You have made your choice. I will not journey with you, since it is clear you do not seek the companionship of a coward."

"Collun, I—"

He interrupted, giving her an odd cold salute, his face still transfigured with anger. "May you find what you seek, Brie."

And he was gone.

Brie was in the stable with Ciaran when Kled appeared. He carried something in his hands. "Collun asked that I bring you this," Kled said, holding something out.

Brie took it. It was the wizard Crann's map. Brie caught her breath. The map was one of Collun's most treasured possessions.

"I can't accept this," she said.

"He said that I mustn't bring it back." Kled's eyes were alight with curiosity.

Reluctantly Brie stowed the map in her quiver.

"Please thank him."

"I will. Do you journey forth for vengeance?"

"Yes," she said dully, thinking of the cost. "Kled, watch over Collun."

The young man nodded. "And good luck to you on your quest, Brie."

On the evening of the first day of Brie's journey, she spotted a rider heading toward her. As he drew closer, Brie recognized his saddlebags as those of a messenger.

He was a thin young man with a thatch of shiny sienna hair and, like most of the travelers Brie had come upon, he couldn't help gaping at the Ellyl horse. Reluctantly tearing his gaze away from Ciaran, he asked Brie if he was headed in the right direction for Cuillean's dun.

"Yes. I've just come from there. Who do you seek?"

The young man drew a parchment from his saddlebag. "Let's see...Someone by the name of Breigit."

Brie was about to say she knew no one of that name when she stopped, startled. Breigit was her own childhood name.

"I am Breigit," she said.

The letter was from Brie's uncle at Dun Slieve. Masha, the serving woman who had helped run Brie's father's dun for him and was the nearest thing to a mother Brie had, was dying. Her uncle requested that Brie come at once. Masha was asking for her.

Masha. Brie realized with a pang of guilt that it had been some time since she had thought of the silent, gaunt woman. Masha had been wet nurse to Brie after Aideen, Brie's mother, died in childbirth. Masha had been with child at the same time as Aideen, but the serving woman's baby had been stillborn. Masha had been doubly laden with grief when, shortly after, her husband died in a hunting accident. As Brie was motherless and Masha childless, they were paired. When she recovered from childbirth, Masha put on her black clothes and became silent, though she watched over Brie diligently. The girl knew Masha was always there, solid and silent as a stone, but hard, too, with little in her of affection or laughter.

In the letter, Uncle Amrys said the sickness had come on Masha suddenly, and no manner of treatment had helped.

Brie felt a spasm of impatience. She did not want to delay her quest. Then she was suddenly uneasy. Was Collun indeed right? Was this thing, this hatred, poisoning her? Of course she must go to Masha.

Bidding the messenger farewell, Brie urged the Ellyl horse into a brisk trot. "Well, I guess we're going home, Ciaran."

At least, she thought with another pang of guilt, she would not be drawn far off course. Dun Slieve lay on the same northern road she had chosen to travel to Dungal.

When the fortifications of Dun Slieve came into sight, Brie felt a mixture of pleasure and apprehension. She knew that her aunt and uncle disapproved of her and felt that roaming the countryside was ill-befitting a highborn maiden of Eirren. Brie no longer affected the appearance of a boy, at least, having let her hair grow and return to its natural golden color, instead of staining it with black walnut leaves as she had before. She did, however, still wear breeches, finding them more comfortable than dresses.

After Conall's death, Brie's uncle Amrys had taken over Dun Slieve. Amrys and his wife, Rainne, had urged Brie to stay and make her home with them, but Brie had refused, explaining that she would have no ease until her father's murderers were dead. Periodically she had sent word through messengers to her aunt and uncle, letting them know she was well.

She could see the dun now, rising above the trees. She felt a twisting in her stomach at the sight of it.

Brie's had not been a happy childhood. She had lost her mother at birth and had been raised by a father who would have preferred a son. But here she was, and it was an odd feeling to be once more at the entrance to the home where she had grown from infant to girl. She guided Ciaran to the gate.

Brie was met by one of her uncle's serving men, who escorted her to her aunt. Rainne gave Brie a quick, affectionate hug, then hurried her along to Masha's room. "She's been asking for you, every day."

"What happened?" Brie asked her aunt as they strode through the halls.

"It was sudden. I found her lying on the floor of her room, clutching at her stomach and throat, in terrible pain. I thought she was dying. I got her to bed and called the healer.

"He worked over her and the crisis seemed to pass, but instead of healing, every day she seems to get a little worse. She does not speak—at least not in words we understand. Except your name, which she calls out insistently." Aunt Rainne opened the door to Masha's room, letting Brie go in ahead of her.

Masha's face had always been thin, but now, as she gazed down at it, Brie felt if she were to lay the palm of her hand over it, the whole of Masha's face would be covered. All of her body was shrunken, caved in on itself.

Masha's eyes burned bright in the wasted face. They stared up at Brie.

Not knowing if Masha was aware of her or not, Brie took the woman's emaciated hand in hers. Masha's eyes suddenly closed and she appeared to drift into sleep, a look almost of relief on her face.

Leaving Masha in peace, Aunt Rainne showed Brie to her old room. It felt strange to Brie: small and lifeless. And suffocating. As Rainne bustled about, stripping the bed of musty linens and calling to a serving maid for fresh, Brie crossed to the small window and pulled aside the tapestry. She wondered with a grin what her aunt and uncle would think if she slept in the dun gardens.

꩜

"What does the healer say? Can he not discover the cause of Masha's sickness?" Brie asked as they sat down to dinner.

Aunt Rainne shook her head. "I fear he is not as experienced as he might be."

"How long does he think she has to live?"

"He is surprised she is still alive at all," answered Aunt Rainne. "I wondered if she was waiting for you."

"Rainne has it in her head Masha has something to tell you," said Brie's uncle, "although it seems highly unlikely to me." He cleared his throat. "Now, Breigit, you have been away from Dun Slieve for a long time, and I hope now that you have returned you will settle in and make your home here. I fear your education has been sorely neglected, and I should be happy to take on the task of tutoring you in the many..."

Brie stared into her bowl of barley-mutton soup, her stomach tightening.

"Not now, Amrys," said Aunt Rainne, her eyes on Brie. "There is plenty of time to discuss Breigit's future. Let her eat in peace."

"But I was only suggesting that—"

"Did you know, Breigit," Rainne said, firmly interrupting her husband, "that Corwin, the daughter of Lord Darrfed, has married the boy Dalmen of Dun Treane?"

"Not that skinny fellow with the squint?"

"The very one."

"And whatever became of the maidservant Verena who had such a lovely voice?"

"She married a bard and they travel together now."

A disgruntled Uncle Amrys called for more soup while Brie and Rainne exchanged gossip. Finally, as they were served dessert, Rainne took pity on him, saying, "Amrys, tell Breigit of your newest acquisition."

He brightened immediately. "Ah, yes, it is an exceedingly handsome leather-bound edition of a lay from the second cycle of the coulin, as rendered by the poet..."

Tired from her travels that day, Brie stifled a yawn, trying hard to appear interested in her uncle's words. Amrys was a scholar and an enthusiastic collector of books. It was said that he had the finest collection outside Temair, especially of books on bird lore, which was his special area of interest.

As he droned on about a book on purple martins, Brie thought longingly of her bed.

Brie went to Masha the next morning, and again the bright eyes seemed to focus on her. A ghost of a smile appeared on the thin lips. Brie took Masha's hand.

Gradually the sick woman's eyes drifted shut and her breathing grew regular. Thinking Masha asleep, Brie started to withdraw her hand, but Masha's thin hand held hers with surprising strength. Masha muttered something sounding like "caroo teeth."

Brie squeezed Masha's hand. Soon after, Masha slept.

At the midday meal Brie asked her aunt and uncle about her mother's family. After Aideen's death, Brie's father had been too torn by grief to speak of his wife and her people to the daughter she had left behind. The only relative of Aideen's Brie had met was a distant cousin, a boy, who had spent a year with them as a sort of squire to her father, Conall. At first Conall had been ill-pleased at the unannounced appearance of this cousin, but he was soon impressed with the boy's athleticism and his self-confidence. His name had been Balor, and Brie remembered looking up to him. She also remembered feeling grateful that this handsome cousin distracted her father, however briefly, from pressing Brie in her endless lessons in archery, swordplay, and all the rest he would have expected from the son he did not have. After he left Dun Slieve, however, Balor had not kept in touch, and Brie knew of no one else in Aideen's family.

"Aideen didn't have much of a family," Uncle Amrys told her. "Just her mother, Hudag—your grandmother. Hudag was a widow, lived in a village not far from Temair. She didn't visit much, and not at all after Aideen's death. I don't think they got on well."

Brie's aunt laughed. "Aideen always said her mother bored her to tears. The only things she cared about were needlework and that little dog of hers."

"Is Hudag still alive?" Brie asked.

"No. We got word several years ago that she had died," Uncle Amrys said. "They sent along her things. The dog died a few days before she did."

"Your mother had a grandmother; I think Aideen was closer to her than to Hudag," said Aunt Rainne.

"What was her name?"

"Seila," Uncle Amrys said. "I recall that my brother did not care for her."

"Wasn't there some kind of scandal?" asked Rainne.

"What sort of scandal?" Brie asked, curious.

Uncle Amrys cleared his throat. "Oh, well, I can't quite remember. Conall preferred not to speak of it. Anyway, it's all in the distant past."

"She showed up at Aideen and Conall's wedding," Rainne said.

"Much to Conall's displeasure," put in Uncle Amrys.

Aunt Rainne said, "You know, Breigit, there are some things stored in the tower room that belonged to your parents. Mostly to your father. There is also a box of your grandmother Hudag's things. I doubt that will be of much interest; it seems to consist mainly of little china statues of dogs. Anyway, you ought to go through it."

Uncle Amrys laughed. "Rainne's been wanting to clear that room out for a long time."

Brie was suddenly eager for the meal to be over. "Perhaps this afternoon...?"

Her aunt shook her head. "I've some matters to attend to this afternoon. Best wait until tomorrow. And anyway, that room's been shut up for a long time. We'll need to air it out; everything is covered with dust."

❧

Brie was up early the next morning. Her aunt did not keep her waiting. Together they wrestled open the shuttered windows of the tower room and dusted and wiped until Brie's arms ached.

"Were you at my mother and father's wedding?" she asked Rainne as they worked.

"Oh yes. I remember it well." Rainne paused thoughtfully. "Your uncle and I had been married several years by then. It was a lovely spring afternoon. Your mother was always beautiful, but she was particularly beautiful that day. Radiant. She wore a dress of many colors, with matching flowers in her yellow hair.

"All of Conall's family was there, but Hudag was the only one from Aideen's side—that is, at first. Halfway through the ceremony a woman rode up on a white horse. She was quite remarkable, you could hardly keep from staring. She must have been ninety years old or more, but her face was almost as luminous as that of Aideen herself.

"Of course, her arrival caused quite a stir. Hudag was clearly horrified and Conall looked thunderous, but Aideen ran over to the woman and gave her a great joyful hug. Seila stayed through the vows, then afterward presented Aideen with a gift, whispering in her ear for some time." Rainne smiled. "We all wondered what that amazing woman was saying to Aideen, and I kept glancing over at Conall, who looked ready to burst. Then all of a sudden Seila departed on her white horse. Now," Rainne said briskly, casting a critical eye over the room. "I think we've done enough. I will leave you in peace."

Brie began to sort through her father's belongings first, though her patience quickly wore thin. His things were a jumbled mess. Her father had had little skill at organizing. He was a man of action who preferred being outdoors, hunting, competing in tourneys, or, best of all, riding to battle. Brie could see from his papers that Aunt Rainne must have had a difficult time putting the affairs of the dun in order.

She moved to other boxes but found only old clothing

and weaponry. Finally Brie came to a small trunk that was clearly her mother's. Inside was a dress of many colors that Brie guessed to be Aideen's wedding gown. It was musty, but the light coming in the window caught the colors and made them almost sparkle.

There was an assortment of odds and ends—jewelry, biorans for Aideen's hair, half-finished tapestries, old books. Then, at the very bottom of the trunk, Brie found a long, thin, pale blue box. It was made of wood, and painted on its surface in pale, opalescent colors were images of suns and fish and breaking waves. They were wrought in a distinctive, almost primitive style. Brie tried to open the box, but the lid was stuck. The wood had warped slightly over the years. Brie worked her fingernail around the edges, then rapped it gently against the side of the trunk. Still, it remained stuck. She dug her nails under the lid and pried as hard as she could. Finally the box opened with a rasp.

Brie let out a small sound of disappointment. The box was empty. Or not quite. She lifted the box to her nose. There was a faint powdery smell, as of ancient dust, and of something else, something faintly familiar. A soft, abrupt sound made Brie look up. The door stood several inches ajar; hadn't Aunt Rainne closed it all the way when she left? She got up and closed it, wondering why she felt the need.

That afternoon as she helped Aunt Rainne take down and fold some freshly washed linens in the outer ward of the dun, Brie suddenly asked, "Do you remember anything of the scandal you mentioned, about my great-grandmother Seila?"

"I'm afraid I don't. It may not have been all that scandalous, you know. Your father was, uh, traditional. It runs in the family," she added with a flash of a smile at Brie.

Brie smiled back, then said offhandedly, "The gift Seila brought my mother, do you know what it was, by any chance?" She realized she was holding her breath.

"No, I never knew." Rainne folded a damask tablecloth. "But I do remember it was in a long blue box. Very thin."

Brie let out her breath with a feeling of wonder. So the blue box was from Seila; somehow she had known that.

Rainne was still speaking. "I was beside a young cousin of Amrys's when Seila presented it to Aideen. We made a little game of trying to guess what such a long thin box could hold. Came up with a few outlandish ideas. But we never learned what it was."

"Why not?" Brie asked.

"It was put away, not shown about the way the other presents were. I heard that Conall was offended by the gift for some reason."

As she entered the kitchen that evening to make up a posset for Masha, Brie spotted a man in ragged clothing scuttling out a door at the other end of the room. He limped heavily, one leg shorter than the other. She had caught sight of the ragged man once before and had asked Rainne about him. Rainne said he had come begging at the dun several months ago, and, feeling sympathy for him, they had found him some odd jobs. He turned out to be especially helpful in the kitchen, and the head cook had suggested hiring him on permanently. He went by the name of Crin, but Brie had yet to see him face-to-face.

The yellow bird hurtled down at her. She saw its face as it swooped in, eyes wide, black pupils dilated, its curved beak open and shrieking with a strange, high-pitched, human sound. Brie woke with a scream.

Her heart pounding, Brie gazed wildly around the darkened room.

It was only a dream, she said to herself. She was safe. But still she was having trouble breathing. Had no one heard her? Her room was remote from the other bedrooms. She suddenly felt a great aching loss as she thought of Collun. She wished she were lying by their campfire, listening to the sound of his breathing as he slept.

She rose and crossed to the long thin blue box. Listening to the rain beat thickly against her small window, Brie traced the patterns of fish and suns and waves with her finger. What did they mean? she wondered. And what had they meant to her mother?

# THREE

# The White Stag

**F**eeling jumpy from the sleepless night, Brie descended to the kitchen for the morning meal. Rainne told her tersely that Masha had taken a turn for the worse in the early hours of the morning. The dun healer could not explain it. Brie went directly to Masha and spent the day at her bedside. The older woman's breathing was labored and her words incoherent. She spoke again those strange words, which sounded this time like "caroo tree ra eeth."

The words sounded faintly familiar to Brie, and as she listened to them, repeated again and again, she suddenly thought they sounded Dungalan, like something Aelwyn would say. But that was absurd; she was beginning to see Dungal in everything.

When Brie heard the gong for dinner, she realized she had not eaten all day. She left Masha with the dun healer and went down to dinner.

"Uncle Amrys, have you a Dungalan dictionary by chance?" Brie said abruptly, as she helped herself to some minted red potatoes.

Surprised, he replied, "Why, yes, I do. It is very old and very valuable, one of the prizes of my collection, in fact. Traded for it with an old vendor from—"

"May I look at it sometime? Tomorrow, perhaps?" Brie interrupted.

"Well, I don't know...I suppose so, but—"

"Thank you, Uncle Amrys."

After dinner Brie stopped by the kitchen for a fresh basin of hot water to take up to the sickroom and was surprised to see the dun healer there. "Who is with Masha?" she asked.

"The man Crin. I needed some herbs—"

Without knowing why, Brie was suddenly alarmed. She bolted out of the kitchen and up the stone stairs. The ragged man was just leaving Masha's room, his face hidden. He spotted Brie and scurried down the hall in the opposite direction.

"Stop!" Brie called. She swiftly caught up with him on the winding stairway and grabbed his arm. He kept his face averted, pulling away from her, but Brie held fast to the fabric of his sleeve. The man then deliberately turned his face toward Brie.

It was a ravaged face, ridged with scars and gaunt with suffering. Brie stared. She knew the face. Then the ragged man violently wrenched his arm from her. There was a tearing sound and he catapulted away, down the stairwell.

Brie stood still, looking at the torn fabric in her hand. It was stained and dull with wear, threads unraveling, but once upon a time it had been velvet, from a lustrous scarlet cloak. And she knew whose cloak it was; it belonged to the traitor Bricriu, who had been responsible for the kidnapping and torturing of Nessa, Collun's sister.

Masha. Brie ran back to the sick woman's room. Masha was in her death throes, her back arched up off the pallet, her face distorted by pain.

"Masha, it's all right. I'm here," Brie murmured soothingly in Masha's ear.

The wild eyes turned toward her. "Breigit. From Aideen. Caroo tree ra eeth," she said one last time, then died, her body rigid and contorted. Brie took Masha in her arms and awkwardly tried to lay her down. She felt something wet. A brownish liquid had run out of Masha's ear onto Brie's hand. Brie raised it to her nose and sniffed. Bitter, like a root: mandrake perhaps. Bricriu had murdered Masha by pouring poison in her ear.

Brie recalled Collun telling her about mandrake, how in small doses over time it can take away a person's wits, and how a large dose is lethal, squeezing the heart until it stops beating.

Brie drew a blanket over the dead woman and then went downstairs to raise the alarm. A search for Crin was quickly mounted. Brie wanted to go with the search party, but her aunt reminded her of Masha and of the night-vigil. Aunt Rainne was a strong believer in the old traditions, so Brie sat with her aunt in Masha's darkened room, lit by a single beeswax candle. In contrast to the still body lying on the pallet and the quiet of the room, Brie's thoughts were like a stream rushing headlong, veering from the ruined figure of Bricriu to the prophecies of Aelwyn the wyll to Masha's strange final words.

Sometime before dawn, the two women left the room. They joined Uncle Amrys at the morning meal. He told them that the searchers had found no trace of the ragged man. Then Brie related to her aunt and uncle all she knew of the traitor Bricriu. They listened, horrified, to Brie's tale.

"No one knew what happened to Bricriu after his attempt to destroy us failed. But we thought perhaps he went to Medb. If so, she must have dealt with him harshly," Brie said, thinking of the once handsome nobleman's shattered face.

"But why here? Why Masha?" Aunt Rainne asked in confusion.

"I do not know," Brie replied. "Uncle Amrys," she said abruptly. "May I see that dictionary of Dungal?"

"Now?"

"Yes."

"You must be exhausted."

"Please."

"It is very delicate, one of a kind..."

"I will be careful."

Aunt Rainne was giving Amrys a direct look. He sighed. "Very well."

Uncle Amrys led Brie to his library. It was located halfway up one of the dun's highest turrets. Silently he lit several oil lamps.

The last time Brie had been in this room it had been her father's. Gone were the animal-skin rugs, hunting trophies, and sundry bows, arrows, swords. Instead, the floor was covered with woven rugs of muted colors and shelves crammed with books lined the walls.

Uncle Amrys found the Dungalan dictionary, took it off

its shelf, and handed it to Brie with an expression of profound reluctance.

"I promise to treat it with the greatest of care," Brie said.

Looking only slightly reassured, and with several backward glances, Amrys left Brie alone with the fragile volume. It was bound in blue leather, and on the cover, embossed in gold, were the figures of a fish and a bird. Brie gingerly leafed through the brittle pages.

"Caroo tree ra eeth," she muttered under her breath. And laboriously she pieced the gibberish together. She had been right. The words were Dungalan. One by one she found them. *Carew* was "stag." *Tri,* "three." And *rhaidd,* "horn" or "antler." Stag, three, antler. Stag of three antlers.

Brie closed her eyes. Stag. Memory washed over her: a memory from many years ago—she and her father at the top of Dun Slieve, her father holding her up, looking down at the bonfires, the white stag lit by the flames. Abruptly Brie stood, leaving the book on her uncle's desk.

She ascended the winding stairs of the turret, taking them two at a time, and came up into the battlements. A steady rainfall hampered her vision, but peering through the castellations she could just make out the White Stag of Herge. And the stag had three horns.

She turned and descended to her uncle's study. Carefully she put the Dungalan dictionary back in its place and blew out the oil lamps.

Brie exited the dun, pulling her cloak over her head against the rain. She began climbing the slope of the hillside on which the stag lay.

The wind blew rain into her face and the grass was slippery. Finally she came to the top of the moor, where the stag's antlers crested. Not knowing why she was there or what she was looking for, Brie gazed down at the wet grass and white chalk-stone. Three antlers. Slowly she walked along the length of the first antler, then, rounding the top, walked back down to the head. She did the same with the second and third antlers. When she got to the tip of the third antler, Brie noticed a jagged gray rock sticking up out of the grass. She knelt beside it, then dug her fingers into the soggy earth around it. Despite the cool rain her skin felt hot, and there was a faint humming in her ears.

The piece of rock was firmly embedded in the ground, going down the length of a forearm. Brie kept digging. The rock finally came loose and she pulled it out. It was an ordinary bit of stone, though long and narrow. Brie put her hand into the hole and pressed her fingers further into the earth. Her fingertips hit something solid.

Using the rock as a shovel, Brie enlarged the hole and worked her way around the buried object until she could grasp it. It wouldn't budge. She dug and loosened soil for some time, rain saturating her cloak until water dripped through to her neck and trickled down her back. Finally, tugging hard, she pulled the object out of the ground.

It was a long thin packet, wrapped in some sort of waterproof material that reminded Brie of the material used by fishermen to line their curraghs, the small boats they went to sea in.

Her fingers shaking, Brie started to unwrap the packet.

Suddenly a hand reached out and grabbed it from her. Brie jumped up, but she slipped on the grass and fell awkwardly on her side. Rising, she took off after the hobbling figure of Bricriu as he scrambled up the hill. He was headed toward the nearby forest. Brie could see a horse tethered at the edge of the trees. She ran faster. Then her foot hit a mossy patch and she slipped again. Letting out an oath, she clumsily regained her footing. She was slathered with mud and grass but kept slogging toward Bricriu. He was just mounting his horse when Brie reached him.

Bricriu savagely whipped the gray horse. Brie thrust out a muddy hand and caught him by the leg and stirrup as the horse began to bolt. She was dragged several yards before the horse halted, unnerved by the extra weight. Bricriu again beat the horse's flank with a leather whip. This time the horse reared. But Brie held fast.

Bricriu let out a grunt, trying to pry Brie's hand loose while he continued to flail at both Brie and the horse with his whip.

Keeping her head low to avoid the lashes, Brie lunged up. She grabbed Bricriu by the neck and pulled him off the horse.

They landed hard in the muddy grass and for a moment neither moved, the wind knocked out of them. Then silently they began to struggle, face-to-face. Bricriu's ravaged face was distorted by a look of naked desperation; Brie almost felt pity for him. All of the man's strength was concentrated on getting free of Brie and he barely seemed to see her, though her face was inches from his own.

But because of Bricriu's ruined body, Brie was the stronger of the two, and inexorably she gained the advantage. She deftly pinned him facedown in the mud, his hands twisted behind his back. Then she quickly dislodged the packet from his grasp. Bricriu let out an animal-like howl. Brie rolled him over onto his back.

"Who sent you?" Brie asked. "Medb?"

Bricriu's body shuddered and a look of fear creased his face. He shook his head violently.

"Then who? And why?"

Bricriu's hollow eyes stared up at her.

Brie heard a noise from the dun and, distracted, slightly eased the pressure on Bricriu's arms. Swiftly he twisted away from her and leaped up. With a berserk speed that astonished Brie, Bricriu darted into the forest. She heard a shrill whistle and saw Bricriu's horse plunge after him through the trees. She could just make out Bricriu swinging himself onto the animal, then they vanished from sight.

Several of Amrys's men rode up. Two went in pursuit of Bricriu while the third bore a muddied, drained Brie back to the dun.

Aunt Rainne took one look at her and ordered hot water and clean towels sent to her room immediately.

Blissfully Brie lowered herself into the large tub of hot water. She sat there, eyes closed, savoring the sensation. When she opened her eyes she caught sight of the packet, still unopened, lying on the table where she'd placed it. Quickly she finished her bath.

After she had dried herself and dressed in clean clothing, Bric reached for the packet. It, too, was caked with mud and the oilskin material was several layers deep. She peeled off the layers until she came to a stiff leather case. It was tooled with a graceful spiral design and was fastened with a leather cord. With some difficulty she untied the cord and opened the case. Inside was a pristine white velvet cloth. Amazed at how well the waterproof material and leather case had protected the cloth, she washed the mud off her hands again; then, carefully, she unwound the cloth, marveling at its whiteness.

Inside several layers of the soft, rich material was an arrow. Brie stared at the slender, perfectly straight object. For a moment she was afraid to touch it. Then she wrapped her fingers around the shaft. A sudden strong heat pulsed against her hand, going halfway up her arm. She let out a small cry but did not drop the arrow. Slowly the heat faded to a gentle, barely perceptible warmth.

Gingerly Brie held the arrow up into the faint light coming in the window. The shaft was ringed by dozens of colorful bands. She peered more closely. It seemed to her that if her eyes could see differently, if they were somehow stronger, she would be able to see tiny pictures on those bands, pictures that told a story. As it was, the designs were too small, just a blur of color and line. The arrow was fletched with deep golden feathers.

It was an extraordinary arrow and Brie suddenly felt a keen desire to notch it to her own bowstring and let fly. But she wrapped the arrow back up in the white cloth, discarding the tarred oilskin fabric. She pulled the blue box to her and placed the arrow inside. A perfect fit.

Then she took the arrow back out of the box and unwrapped it. She stood, flinching slightly at the stiffness in her legs, crossed the room, and slid the arrow into her quiver. For some reason it looked right, as though it belonged there. Brie suddenly recalled Aelwyn's words: "An arrowhead pointed at your own heart..."

There was a knock on Brie's door. One of the serving women entered, saying that Aunt Rainne would like to see Brie as soon as it was convenient.

"The burial will be at midday today," said Rainne in her practical dry voice. Brie nodded. "The man Crin...that is, Bricriu, has disappeared without a trace."

"I believe I know what he was after, perhaps even why he killed Masha." Brie held up the bundle of white linen cloth.

"What...?"

"Masha told me where to find it before she died. It is an arrow," she said unnecessarily as the cloth fell away.

Uncle Amrys took a step closer. "May I?" he asked, holding out his hand.

Brie handed him the arrow, watching to see if he felt the same heat that she had when she had first held it. But his expression did not change as he took the arrow.

"I believe my great-grandmother Seila gave this to Mother on her wedding day," Brie said.

"The blue box!" exclaimed Rainne. "An arrow; now that's one we didn't think of."

"And no wonder Conall was displeased," added Amrys.

"Why?" asked Brie.

"It is unlucky to receive a sharp object, such as a knife or a sword—or even an arrow—as a wedding gift. It is believed to be an omen that the union will be severed. Interesting design," Amrys commented, examining the shaft of the arrow. "Can't quite make it out. Almost Ellyllike..." Then his eyes narrowed. He brought the arrow closer to his eyes. "Curious..."

"What is it?" asked Rainne.

"May I take this to my study?" Amrys asked Brie abruptly.

"If I may come with you."

"Of course." Brie followed her uncle out of the room, while Rainne stayed behind to attend to the plans for Masha's burial.

Amrys set the arrow down on his desk and crossed to his bookshelves. Taking out a large dusty book, he thumbed through the pages.

He replaced the volume, then took out another. Bringing the book back to the desk, he set it down next to the arrow. He riffled through the pages and began muttering, "No, it's not a peregrine..." Then he retrieved yet another book. "By Amergin, this is most fascinating..."

Impatiently Brie circled the desk and peered at the open books. They were books about birds.

"There it is, a goldenhawk," he said finally in triumph, stabbing at a picture with his finger. The bird was a deep gold color with dark markings on its outstretched wings and had the curved beak and proud stare of a bird of prey.

"The fletching feathers?" Brie asked.

Her uncle bobbed his head excitedly. "Extremely rare. And found only in Dungal. Quite extraordinary."

Brie felt a quickening of excitement. Dungal again. Seila had brought the arrow from Dungal. And Aideen had told Masha where it was hidden, so that one day it would come to Brie.

"Uncle Amrys," Brie said suddenly, "when you first touched it...did the arrow feel hot to you?"

"Eh? Hot, you say? No, not particularly. Why?" He looked at her with a puzzled expression.

"Uh, no reason."

That afternoon Brie helped her aunt prepare Masha's body for burial. They wrapped her in an ivory linen cloth. The border of the cloth was woven in brown thread and depicted the three faces of Solas, the goddess of birth, death, and rebirth.

Dun Slieve had its own burial ground, a traditional passage grave built on a nearby hilltop. Carved inside the hill was a large vaulted inner room, which was entered through a long cruciform passage. Masha's conra, the wooden box in which she was placed, was interred beside that of Aideen.

Brie stayed behind in the passage grave after the others had returned to the dun. Standing silently beside the graves of her father, her mother, and now Masha, Brie tried to think of some last words to say to them, but she could not. Her breathing loud in her ears, she abruptly turned and left the burial place.

"I go tomorrow," Brie announced that evening at dinner.

Her aunt and uncle looked stunned.

"Where?" said Amrys.

"Why?" Rainne asked simultaneously.

"I go to the Blue Stack Mountains and from there, most likely, to Dungal, in pursuit of the traitor Bricriu," Brie replied calmly. And my father's murderers, if he should lead me there, she thought to herself.

"This is absurd! I will not have my niece wandering about the country on foolish and dangerous missions," sputtered her uncle. Brie saw her aunt shoot him a warning glance.

Brie's gaze fell to her plate. Uncle Amrys continued to speak, his cheeks flushed. "No one in their right mind would even think of venturing across the Blue Stack Mountains. I will not allow it."

Brie's chin went up and she gazed defiantly at her uncle.

"Amrys, would you please pass me the bittergreens?" interrupted Aunt Rainne. Brie's uncle turned to Rainne with a look of irritation. Then he glanced around the table vaguely. Finally locating the platter at his elbow, he handed it to Aunt Rainne.

Before he could resume his lecture, Rainne spoke, her tone direct and gentle. "Breigit, you lost your mother before you even knew her, and then, at a young age, witnessed the murder of your father. And now Masha. If this man Bricriu murdered her, then it was a vile act and he should be punished. But it is not up to you to render justice."

Brie opened her mouth to speak, but Rainne continued. "I know you wish to pursue your father's killers, but do you not think it better to return to the business of living your own life? What good can such a journey do you?"

"I do not wish to speak of this anymore, Aunt Rainne," Brie interrupted, her voice implacable. "I leave tomorrow."

"It is preposterous!" exclaimed Amrys.

But Rainne bowed her head and said softly, "Very well. I understand that you are seeking answers, Breigit, and your uncle and I want you to know that if you discover that these answers lie at home, at Dun Slieve, we are here and always will be."

"Thank you," Brie replied, her own voice softening.

"But Rainne—," interjected Uncle Amrys.

"My dear, do you not have a map of Dungal somewhere about? I remember you telling me you found it among those documents you purchased from that vendor in Temair."

"Why, yes, I do believe you are correct. Got it at the same time I received the Vetigullian manuscript. I'm quite sure the vendor had no idea of its true worth." Amrys's eyes brightened at the memory, his anger at Brie vanishing. "Indeed, it was quite an extraordinary find..."

That night Brie had the dream again. This time the bird came so close she could almost feel the powerful yellow wings beating against her face. When she woke she was gasping for breath and covered in sweat. At least I didn't scream, she thought grimly.

She rose, still shaky, and crossed to a small basin of water. She rinsed her face in the cold water. Wiping her face with a towel, she glanced at her quiver. Suddenly she wanted to see the arrow.

Quickly she pulled it out. The arrow was warm; it gave off a reassuring warmth that felt good against her skin. She ran her fingertips over the soft feathers. A goldenhawk, she mused, then her body went rigid. Was it possible...?

She put the arrow back in the quiver, donned a jersey for warmth, and exited her room.

Brie impatiently ascended the stairway to her uncle's study, thinking she must be losing her mind. She entered, lit an oil lamp, and began scanning the shelves. Finally she found the book with the picture of the goldenhawk. She stared at the bird. Except for the coloring, it was exactly the same as the bird in her dream.

# FOUR

# Goat-man

That morning as she readied herself for the journey, Brie thought how good it would be to sleep out in the open again. She was not sorry to leave the room of her childhood.

Aunt Rainne had packed food for Brie, and Uncle Amrys gave her his favorite skin bag filled with spring water. Brie gratefully accepted the provisions, although she declined the map of Dungal her uncle offered. She could see that he was exceedingly reluctant to part with it, and besides, she had the wizard Crann's map, the one Collun had given her.

At the entrance to the passage grave, Brie paused for a moment to say a final farewell. "I have the arrow. Thank

you, Masha," she whispered into the cool gloom of the chamber.

Then she whispered to Ciaran, "I'm ready," and the Ellyl horse burst into a powerful canter. Brie leaned into the horse's neck, her fingers twined in the soft mane.

Just before twilight Brie stopped by a copse of rowan trees. She gave Ciaran a brisk rubdown then ate a small meal. Leaving the Ellyl horse munching contentedly on a patch of clover, Brie walked a little way into the trees, carrying her quiver and bow. As she tested the string, she noted that the light in the sky was growing dim.

"Well, why not?" she said with a reckless grin. Brie fixed her sight on a barely visible knothole on the lower trunk of a far distant rowan. "Let's see what you can do." She reached into her quiver for the arrow from Dungal. It felt warm to the touch and hummed lightly against her fingers.

With a sudden feeling of great joy, Brie nocked the arrow to her bow. Then she let fly. There was a whishing, sizzling sound, and she felt as if the tips of flames were licking at her face. Her string snapped in two, and the fingers that had held the fletched end of the arrow blistered.

She had squinted at the last moment and realized it was a good thing she had. As it was, her vision was blurred by burning white dots as if she had been gazing too long into the sun.

She didn't move for several moments, waiting for the dots to fade. Ciaran was beside Brie, nosing the girl's burnt fingers with her soft muzzle. When Brie was able to see again, she went to retrieve the arrow. The arrowhead was lodged directly in the center of the knothole, and the bark all around it was charred black.

Brie pulled the arrow out of the tree. Holding it lightly in her hands, she gazed down at the arrow from Dungal.

*Fire music,* said a voice next to her. Brie jumped, almost dropping the arrow. She swung her head first to the left and then the right. But no one was there. No one but Ciaran.

"Who's there?" Brie said nervously.

*The arrow. It has tine draoicht. Fire music.*

Brie looked carefully around her. Then she looked at Ciaran. When their eyes met, Brie knew; the Ellyl horse had spoken the words inside her head. She gaped at Ciaran.

Brie remembered Collun telling her that he and his Ellyl horse, Fiain, had been able to communicate wordlessly. But up until now, Ciaran had given no sign of talking or making contact with her in any way other than the usual ways one communicates with a highly intelligent horse.

Brie felt a little shy. What was she supposed to do now? she wondered. Could Ciaran read her mind, or did she need to speak out loud, or...?

*Salve. On your fingers.* Ciaran lowered her head to tear up a mouthful of grass, then casually walked away. The conversation was over.

With several backward glances at the Ellyl horse, Brie slid the arrow back into her quiver. Then she turned her gaze on the blackened tree. Clearly this arrow isn't for felling a guinea hen for dinner, Brie thought wryly, unless one prefers it cooked to a crisp.

After Brie rubbed bayberry salve on her fingers and bandaged them, she restrung her bow. She had carved the bow herself in Tir a Ceol, the land of the Ellyl. It was fashioned in the image of a flame-bird, or a tine ean as the Ellylon called it. A fire arrow for a flame-bird, she thought with a smile. And, in fact, her own name, Breo-Saight, meant fire arrow. Why so much of fire? she mused. Perhaps Talisen had been right when he dubbed her Flame-girl, she thought, grinning at the memory.

Breigit was her birth name, so where had the name Breo-Saight come from? She could not remember. She distantly recalled someone promising that one day her arrows would fly so high and so fast they would set the clouds on fire. Perhaps her father, though he was not one given to fanciful images. It sounded more like her mother, Aideen, what little she knew of her; but Aideen had died at Brie's birth.

At first Brie would startle whenever Ciaran's words came into her head, but gradually she got used to it, until it began to feel as if it had always been so. She found it felt most natural to speak out loud to Ciaran, though she sensed the Ellyl horse often knew her thoughts without her saying them. Ciaran rarely spoke more than a few words at a time and seemed to have an innate sense of politeness. She never barged into Brie's mind at an inopportune moment, except occasionally to let Brie know that it was time for a grooming session, or that Brie's own face needed washing or hair required tidying.

As Brie rode north, Dungal was ever in her thoughts. She felt she was being drawn there, for good or ill. First the wyll, and now Bricriu, for surely Dungal was his destination. And when she found Bricriu, she felt certain he would somehow lead her to her father's killers.

Even her great-grandmother's arrow seemed to have something to do with it; ever since leaving Dun Slieve, Brie had had the sense that the arrow wished to return to Dungal.

Late in the afternoon on the eighth day of the journey, as they navigated the foothills of the Blue Stack Mountains, Brie realized that she had not felt Ciaran in her thoughts since early that morning. The Ellyl horse was moving at a normal pace, but Brie thought she was holding her head just a fraction lower than usual.

"Ciaran?" she said out loud.

There was no response. The Ellyl horse kept moving ahead. Brie reached her hand up along the animal's neck. Ciaran's skin felt hot.

"Hold, Ciaran," Brie called, and the horse obediently stopped. Brie dismounted and moved to Ciaran's head, stroking her muzzle gently. The Ellyl horse's eyes looked dull to Brie.

"Are you ill?" she asked softly. She thought she heard a faint *No* at the edge of her mind.

"You do not look well," said Brie.

Ciaran raised her head and flicked her long tail. *Impossible,* Brie thought she heard, though again it was faint.

"Just the same, I think it's time for a rest." She led Ciaran to a shady spot beside some trees, gave her water to drink from Brie's depleted skin bag, and proceeded to rub down and groom the Ellyl horse thoroughly. Usually

Ciaran loved grooming sessions, but she continued to be listless. "We need to find water soon," Brie said as she teased the last burr from Ciaran's tail. There was no response. Ciaran lowered herself onto the grass and shut her eyes.

Brie watched the horse, her worry mounting. How did one take care of a sick Ellyl animal? she wondered. She remembered that Silien, the Ellyl prince who had taken her to Tir a Ceol, was sensitive to certain herbs; some could make him very ill at even the sparest dose. What if in trying to help the horse she were to give Ciaran the wrong thing?

Shortly before twilight, the Ellyl horse woke. She gracefully got to her feet and began cropping the green grass at the base of the trees, her long tail slowly twitching from side to side. The horse seemed refreshed by sleep. *Thirsty,* Brie heard in her thoughts. Brie hurried to supply the skin bag.

*Almost empty,* came Ciaran's voice.

"I know. We need to find a stream. On Crann's map it looks like there's one not far ahead."

*I am ready.*

"Are you sure you're feeling—"

There was a high-pitched whinny of impatience that made Brie's ears ring. She swung herself onto Ciaran's back without another word.

It was dark now, with clouds muffling the brightness of the almost-full moon. They had been traveling for less than an hour when Ciaran suddenly halted.

"What is it?" Brie asked softly.

*Ahead.*

"What?"

*Morgs.*

Brie stiffened.

*Something else. Evil.*

Brie sensed the puzzle in the horse's thoughts. She dismounted and began walking cautiously forward. Ciaran followed, her Ellyl hooves silent on the ground.

In the wake of Medb's failed invasion of Eirren, Scathians and morgs, even scald-crows, had almost completely disappeared from the land. King Gwynn and Queen Aine still sent out scouting parties and occasionally sightings were reported, but they were rare.

Brie could hear voices and then she saw the flickering light of a campfire. Keeping well hidden behind a bank of gorse bushes, she peered out at the figures clustered around the fire. There were two hooded morgs listening to the guttural sounds coming from a third figure, which stood with its back to Brie. At first she couldn't make out if it was man or beast, but then it shifted slightly and she saw it had the legs of a man, though they were unclothed and shaggy with whitish gray hair. The head was shaggy, too, and narrow, with a beard wisping down from a long chin.

There were two horses tethered a short distance from the other side of the campfire, and draped across the back of one of them was what looked to be a body—a small body, like that of a child. It was either unconscious or dead.

Brie sat back on her heels, her mind working fast. If the child was alive it must be set free. The beastlike figure was large, as was one of the morgs, but the other looked small, smaller than Brie. Ciaran nosed her arm.

Suddenly the one who was not a morg brayed, gesturing with his arm toward the north, then strode across to the tethered horses. Brie tensed, but the creature mounted the one not carrying the body and rode away, heading north. The morgs began breaking camp.

Brie spotted a thick branch on the ground nearby and lifted it silently, testing its heft for a makeshift club. *Shall we?* she mouthed to Ciaran, who replied, *Yes.*

Brie began circling around toward the remaining horse. The bushes shielded the girl and the Ellyl horse for a short way, but as they drew closer, the morgs' horse began to move restlessly, as if sensing their presence. They had just emerged from behind the gorse bushes when the horse suddenly lifted its chin and let out a loud, harsh sound.

The morgs whirled, instantly spotting Brie and Ciaran. Hissing, they rushed forward. Ciaran reared in front of the larger morg while Brie met the attack of the smaller one. As it reached for her with its clutching poisonous fingers, Brie abruptly swung out with the branch she carried, landing a lucky blow directly on the side of the morg's head. It reeled away with a hiss of pain, dropping to its knees.

Brie turned and saw the large morg moving in on Ciaran, brandishing a long curved knife. Brie quickly reached back for her bow and felt in her quiver for an arrow. It flew from her bowstring, and the large morg fell, an arrow in its shoulder.

But before she could reach for another, damp gray fingers closed over her wrist. She looked into the smaller morg's slitted yellow eyes. A poisonous cold torpor began traveling up her arm; she had felt the sensation before, when morgs had ambushed her and Collun. The touch of morg skin was poisonous, paralyzing one with an icy numbness that spread throughout the body. Brie struggled, fear rising in her throat, but she could not muster the strength to break free.

The morg began dragging her toward the campfire. When they reached the fire, the creature paused to kick a pile of kindling and dried gorse branches onto the embers. The fire flared up, hot and blue. The yellow eyes flicked back to her, and the morg's mouth curved into a cruel smile. Brie realized the morg meant to burn her alive.

Suddenly Ciaran's hooves shot out of the darkness and, catching the morg under the chin, lifted it off the ground. The damp fingers were wrenched off Brie's wrist as the morg staggered back into the center of the fire.

Brie collapsed. She lay for a moment, winded and half-paralyzed, until the heat of the flames warmed her body. With a great effort, she rolled away from the campfire. The morg's cloak had ignited. Feeble and half-conscious, it tried to scrabble out of the fire, but the flames were consuming the creature too quickly. It let out a high-pitched hiss. Willing herself to move, Brie struggled to her feet and grasped the morg by the bottom of its cloak. Even as she pulled it out of the fire, she knew it was dead, but she halfheartedly tried to extinguish the flames. Finally she sat back, scorched and exhausted. The rank smell of burnt morg filled the air. Ciaran nuzzled her blackened forehead.

"Thank you, Ciaran," Brie said out loud, lifting a hand to the horse's forehead. "Where's the other morg?"

*Dead.*

"How are you?"

*Tired,* came the word faintly. And indeed the Ellyl horse's head was drooping and her eyes were bloodshot.

"Rest a moment. I'll be back," said Brie, rising stiffly. Slowly she crossed to the horse that was still tethered by the trees. Close up she was startled to see that it was not a horse, or at least not like any horse she had ever seen. It had the head and face of a goat, yet had the broad back and musculature of a horse or large donkey. Brie approached the animal, and it kicked at her savagely with its hooves. She jumped back.

Brie tried offering it a bit of honey cake, but it bared its jutting teeth at her and kicked out again. Cursing, Brie lunged for the ropes tying the unconscious child to the goat-horse's saddle. The beast tried to reach back and bite her with its jagged yellow teeth, but Brie dodged the thrusting head. She cut the ropes with her dagger, nearly slicing her hand in the process, then caught the small figure as it slid off the animal's back and into her arms. The goat-horse reared, incensed, and let out a grating bray.

Brie carried the body a safe distance away and set it down carefully. There was a large hood covering the child's face, and when Brie pulled it away, she gasped. It wasn't a child at all. It was Aelwyn, the wyll.

The wyll was very pale, but when Brie put her ear to the girl's chest, she could hear a heartbeat. Cuts and bruises covered Aelwyn's broad, ash-pale face.

Ciaran approached with a morg skin bag dangling from her mouth. *Water,* Brie heard, as if from a distance.

"The morg's? Is it safe to drink?" Brie asked.

The horse wearily jerked her head to indicate assent.

Brie bathed Aelwyn's face. As she did, the wyll began to revive, her heavy eyelids flickering. They abruptly opened wide, revealing the wyll's startling amber eyes. She did not appear surprised to see Brie, but smiled a welcome with her catlike mouth.

Soon she was sitting up and drinking the water.

"Lovely smell," Aelwyn commented, with a gesture toward the crumpled figure of the morg by the campfire.

"It clears the head, anyway," Brie responded. Aelwyn stared at her for a moment, then she laughed out loud. Brie smiled back.

"Thank you for rescuing me," said Aelwyn.

Brie shrugged. "It is Ciaran who deserves your gratitude. It would have been my roasted hide you'd be smelling now if it weren't for her."

Aelwyn gazed at Ciaran. "Then thank you, Ciaran." The wyll paused. "She understands me, doesn't she?"

"I shouldn't be surprised, though she is tired."

"I haven't seen many Ellyl horses. She's a beauty."

"Now I'm sure she understood that. She's a vain one. Aren't you, Ciaran?" Brie said affectionately, ruffling the Ellyl horse's forelock. Ciaran whickered faintly in protest.

"We have that in common—or so I've been told," said Aelwyn, unconsciously fiddling with a glimmering necklace of opaline and amber at her neck.

"How did you come to be prisoner of morgs?" asked Brie. "And what was that creature with them?"

Aelwyn raised a small hand to her bruised face. "When they first came upon me, I thought I was seeing a phantom. In Dungal the goat-men are creatures more of legend than of fact, evil beasts that mothers use to scare children into minding, especially in the hill country, because the goat-men are said to dwell in the mountains. I grew up in a village in the hill country."

"It is called goat-man?"

"Or gabha. He stood on two legs like a man, with a face roughly in the shape of a man, though the mouth was large and the eyes bulged out at the sides of its head. And he was covered with hair, even his face, forehead and all, and it was the long, coarse hair of a goat."

"With a wispy goat beard," interjected Brie.

Aelwyn nodded. "He smelled of goat; I never could abide that odor. And his voice had a 'baa' sound like a goat. I couldn't understand his language, though the morgs seemed to."

"They ambushed you?"

Aelwyn nodded. "After I left Cuillean's dun, the same day you did, I believe, I began making my way north. I have a friend, from my village in Dungal, who now lives in a town at the foot of the Blue Stacks. There are a handful of Dungalans scattered throughout the few villages and farmholds that lie in the foothills of the mountains. I think it is because they cannot stand to be too far from Dungal." She paused. "My friend is expecting a bairn, and I had pledged to come when the child was due, to help with the birthing, as well as afterward, for she already has a young son and daughter. I was traveling east through the foothills when I spotted them, the morgs and the goat-man. They came after me, killed my pony, and knocked me unconscious. I am not certain," Aelwyn said matter-of-factly, "but I believe they were headed toward Lake Or. To throw me in."

"For what reason?"

"They said nothing, at least nothing I understood, but I sensed it was because they knew I was Dungalan and did not want me traveling to Dungal."

"Why not?"

Aelwyn shook her head. "I do not know. In fact, I had been thinking of returning, after helping my friend, before the winter snows come to the mountains. Now I certainly will," she said with an obstinate smile. "And you, Brie?"

"I am on the trail of a man."

"One of your father's killers?"

"No. But one who may lead me to them, I hope."

"Who is this man?" asked Aelwyn.

Brie described Bricriu. The wyll nodded in recognition. "I met such a man, before the morgs and goat-man ambushed me," she said. "He asked the way to Beirthoud's Pass in the Blue Stack Mountains."

Brie's interest quickened. "Then he was journeying to Dungal?"

"Most likely. No one chooses to travel over Beirthoud's Pass unless they go to Dungal." Aelwyn frowned at the eager look in Brie's eyes. "Remember what I saw, Flame-girl," the girl said with a warning glint in her eye. "Bog Maglu is a dangerous place."

"Bog Maglu?"

"Maglu is a large, treacherous wetland that lies in the center of our country." Aelwyn paused, shaking her head. "I do not know, but the stones I saw, the standing stones, looked as I have heard the stones of memory look. The stones of memory lie in the heart of Bog Maglu. Yet it is confusing because I saw seabirds as well and the Bog is far from the sea..." She trailed off. "But there was shifting earth and water, and the arrow. You do not forget the arrow I saw?"

"No, I do not forget. Pointed at my heart. So I will journey with great care. Are you up to traveling, Aelwyn?"

Aelwyn shrugged. "I am well enough."

"Then we ought to move on. The goat-man may return," Brie said, rising and looking for Ciaran. The Ellyl horse had moved away from them as they talked.

The night had deepened while Brie and Aelwyn spoke. At first Brie could not see Ciaran, but then found her lying down behind the gorse bushes. Ciaran's skin was even hotter than before and her manner listless. She did not respond when Brie spoke to her.

"What is wrong with her?" asked Aelwyn, who had followed Brie.

"I do not know. I'm worried..."

Aelwyn crouched beside the horse. Gently she laid a small hand on the horse's neck. Ciaran tensed for a moment, moving her legs as if to rise, but then she settled, her body relaxing into the tall grass. Gradually the large eyes closed.

Brie watched, anxious.

Then Aelwyn rose and moved toward Brie. Ciaran was sleeping. "How long has it been since Ciaran was in Tir a Ceol?" asked the wyll.

"A long time."

"Three moon cycles? Four?"

Brie thought. "Eight or nine perhaps."

"I am getting a strong feeling of hiraeth, the heartsickness I told you of. Perhaps there is something similar for those from Tir a Ceol. I also felt a very strong longing for something green, soft, with sweet-smelling white flowers..."

"Seamir," murmured Brie. "It is what the Ellyl horses eat in the cavern of the horses in Tir a Ceol," she explained.

"It must be very good. I believe that if Ciaran doesn't have some quite soon she may die."

# FIVE

# Monodnock

Then she must return to Tir a Ceol at once," Brie said without hesitation. "Is she strong enough to journey there?"

"I believe so. I know of a porth—or a portal as you call it—into Tir a Ceol that is not far from here, by Lake Or. But she does not want to go."

Brie looked puzzled. "But you said..."

"She needs to go, but she will not leave you."

"She must."

After swiftly dressing Aelwyn's cut face and cutting loose the disagreeable goat-horse from its tether (for which kindness Brie received a glancing blow to her shin), they

set out on foot for Lake Or. Ciaran walked slowly, head down.

They walked until the moon was directly overhead. By then Ciaran was barely able to raise her head, and Aelwyn said her own head was pounding as if from a thousand blacksmith hammers. Brie spotted a small stream and suggested they rest there.

She lit a campfire and went to fill the skin bags. When she returned Aelwyn had already brewed a pan of brownish liquid she called cyffroi. She offered Brie a cup.

Brie tasted it and grimaced.

Aelwyn chuckled. "If you go to Dungal you will get used to it. It is what we drink instead of chicory. I am slightly mad in the morning until I've had my cup of cyffroi. Of course, there are those who say I am mad most of the time, being a wyll."

"What's it like?" asked Brie.

"Being a wyll?" Aelwyn smiled her cat-smile at Brie. "It is not so very different from not being a wyll. Eirrenians think that we are always being bombarded with visions and portents. But seeings come only when I ask for them, when I deepen my thoughts, turn inward. In Dungal they say of us that we have a fire in the head, and I suppose it is so, although it is a fire we kindle ourselves— it is gentle, and, for the most part, without fear. I find it rather pleasant, a hearth fire, if you will." She took a sip of cyffroi, looking thoughtfully at Brie. "I should not be surprised if there was a little of wyll fire in you."

Brie laughed. "That's absurd."

"Why?"

"Because I am Eirrenian and have shown no particular

gift for fortune-telling in all my years. No, I have fire in my bow, my arrow, even in my name. That's quite enough fire for me."

"Perhaps, but perhaps not. I have not had a trance that took such hold of me since I was in Dungal, with a fellow wyll who sought the heart of an unbending fisherman."

"Would I not have felt it, if I did have magic or draoicht of some kind?"

"It is usually so. But there have been cases when it lay dormant for many years..."

"Well, I have no wyll fire, nor any draoicht, and that is that." Brie took another sip of the cyffroi. As she got used to the Dungalan beverage, she was noticing that under the bitterness was a subtle taste of nuts and vanilla. "Are there many wylls in Dungal?"

"Not so many as there once were. There used to be at least one in every village. But now many villages have none. The coastal villages had their own kind of wyll; they are men, called Sea Dyak sorcerers. There are also only a very few of these left in Dungal.

"In fact, there is a Sea Dyak sorcerer in Bog Maglu. Perhaps he is the man of power I saw, which could account for the seabirds..." Aelwyn paused as though to examine this train of thought. Then she continued. "He was once the most powerful sorcerer in Dungal; Yldir is his name. I cannot tell you how old he is for no one knows, but there are stories of him alongside heroes who lived hundreds of years ago. Before my parents were born he became a hermit, went off by himself to live in Bog Maglu. There are a few who have made pilgrimages to see him there, and they say he is quite mad, but still powerful. He lives near the stones of memory."

"Why are they called stones of memory?" Brie asked.

"Because they are thought to hold the entire history of Dungal inscribed on their surfaces. Only one of great power, such as Yldir, can read the ciphers and pictures etched in the stones." Aelwyn paused. "I see a Dungalan arrow in your quiver. Is this the arrow of fire you spoke of?"

"Yes. How did you know it to be Dungalan?"

"The fletching feathers are goldenhawk."

"It was my mother's. The man Bricriu tried to steal it. It has bands of color I cannot make out. Perhaps you..." Brie reached for the arrow.

"No," said Aclwyn definitely, raising her hand to arrest Brie's movement. "I prefer not to hold the arrow. Fire magic can be unpredictable."

Brie nodded, thinking of her blistered fingers. "Yet it is cool most of the time." She paused. "Sometimes I feel it is drawing me to Dungal."

"It could be," answered the wyll, smiling. "Take care it does not kindle in you more than you bargained for."

Brie uneasily asked what the wyll meant, but Aelwyn ignored her, saying her head was still pounding and she needed to rest. She finished her cup of cyffroi and settled herself on the ground, pulling her cloak over her face.

When dawn came, Brie woke a cranky Aelwyn. Ciaran was already awake, grazing nearby.

While Aelwyn brewed more cyffroi, Brie consulted her map.

"That looks to be a wizard's map," observed Aelwyn.

"It belonged to Crann, the wizard of the trees."

"I have heard of him."

"Where is the village where your friend lives?"

Aelwyn leaned over the map. "Here," she said, pointing to a spot a short distance east of Lake Or. "And this is the way to Beirthoud's Pass." The route through the mountains lay directly north of the lake.

Aelwyn suddenly laughed, her good spirits restored by the cyffroi. "A fire arrow and a wizard's map. And you say there is nothing of wyll fire in you."

As they came to the top of a ridge, they saw Lake Or stretched out below them. It was a large lake that glowed golden in the late afternoon light. The lake was bordered on its right side by a gentle rolling terrain of grass and heather, but its left side was dominated by a large fell with sheer screes of loose rock plunging straight into the water. Beyond Lake Or a fertile green valley with a scattering of farmholds could be seen, and beyond the valley loomed the Blue Stack Mountains. So high did they rise that some were peaked with white, though it was late summer.

Aelwyn led them down the ridge and onto a path leading toward the scree side of the lake. They followed the path until it ended, directly at the foot of a slab of stone. Aelwyn laid her two palms against the rock face and a handful of pebbles cascaded down, splashing into the water. Then she turned to Brie. "Now we wait."

"What did you do?"

"The draoicht equivalent of knocking. I let him know there was an Ellyl here. They don't usually open porths for anyone but Ellylon. They don't mind us Dungalans in general, especially wylls, but they still do not choose to invite us into Tir a Ceol."

They waited in silence. Aelwyn made herself comfortable on a boulder, while Brie stood beside Ciaran, her hand resting lightly on the horse's warm flank.

Suddenly there was a person standing at the foot of the path.

He was tall for an Ellyl, and his body was long, sitting atop two gangly, storklike legs. He had long, skinny arms from which dangled two large hands. His hair was more orange-red than gold, and instead of curling down his neck like the hair of most Ellylon, his was cut short and stood up straight, giving him a slightly demented look. But the eyes were unmistakably Ellyl, a startling silver color that gleamed at Brie and Aelwyn in the twilight.

"I beg your pardon, fair maidens, but I understood there to be an Ellyl at the porth," he said in his thin, somewhat reedy voice.

Ciaran raised her head at the sound of the Ellyl's voice.

"Oh, yes, I see. Come," the Ellyl said. He beckoned and they moved toward him, though Brie did not see where there was a doorway of any kind. Then the Ellyl was gone, and as Brie watched, Aelwyn moved right up to the scree wall, where the path ended, and she was gone, too.

Ciaran suddenly broke into a trot and disappeared as neatly as the others. When Brie came to the end of the path she saw a sliver of a crack in the rock face, and while she was thinking that she would never fit through it, a bony hand closed over hers and she was through, standing in a large, dimly lit cavern.

The Ellyl dropped her hand and strode to Ciaran. He

laid his head beside Ciaran's and seemed to be listening attentively.

Aelwyn was moving about the cavern, closely inspecting their surroundings. The Ellyl stood up, running his hand through his spiky orange hair. "My dear young lady," he said, "you will find no gems or trinkets here. Indeed there is little of value here at all. I am afraid this is a remote porth. A lonely posting, especially for one as fond of society as I, yet I endeavor to do my duty with a stout heart. But first things first. Which of you is called Brie? The wyll perhaps?"

"No. I am Brie."

"The horse Ciaran must proceed to Tir a Ceol at once. Will you journey with her?"

Brie hesitated. She felt Ciaran nudge faintly into her thoughts. *Come.* Brie was suddenly filled with a sharp yearning to revisit the land of Ellylon: to see Ebba, the artist with brindled hair; to visit Slanaigh, who had brought Brie back to life with the healing waters after Brie had been bitten by the demon creature Nemian; and to see Silien, the Ellyl prince and a companion to Brie and Collun when they had traveled to find Collun's sister.

"I cannot," she heard herself say. She crossed to Ciaran, resting her cheek against the horse's warm skin. "Our paths must divide here, Ciaran," she said softly.

There was a buzzing sound in Brie's ears that sounded almost like tears, then the words, *Your face needs washing.* Brie smiled broadly, saying, "I know."

*Fly high and true, Breo-Saight.* Ciaran abruptly reared up on her hind legs, broke into a gallop, and was quickly lost to sight.

"Well, very good then, that's done. Allow me to introduce myself. Monodnock is my name, and I am at your service, exceedingly kind damsels." He bowed low from his long waist.

"I am Brie, as you already know," replied the girl, suppressing a smile, "and this is Aelwyn."

"Charmed, without a doubt. Now I hope you fair maids will do me the honor of being my guests for a simple repast at my oh-so-humble dwelling."

Brie and Aelwyn exchanged glances. Then the wyll spoke, her expression demure. "You are very kind."

The Ellyl flushed with pleasure. "Not at all. This way, if you please." He led the way through a dimly lit tunnel.

"Pray do keep in mind that we are at the very back of 'beyond' here. If you are the Breo-Saight of whom even I have heard tell out here in the hinterland, then you have had the pleasure of being entertained by King Midir himself. Most certainly my abode will seem quite squalid in comparison."

But when the Ellyl ushered them into his suite of caverns, Brie saw that they were quite comfortable, even elegant. Monodnock sang softly in his thin voice and several lights kindled in their golden wall sconces, revealing deep pile rugs and a scattering of soft pillows. A large tapestry dominated one wall, depicting a knight in the act of slaying a formidable red-scaled dragon. Shelves of books lined the walls.

As they gazed about in appreciation, Brie noticed that Monodnock's long nose was twitching, and he was darting sidelong glances at the two travelers.

"Well now," he said in a high, rather artificial voice, "perhaps you fair maidens would enjoy a nice hot bath? It must be simply ages since you have been able to pause in your travels to enjoy, uh, the pleasures of, uh, abluting." Monodnock pressed bars of sweet-smelling soap into their hands, his upper lip contorted from the effort of keeping his nose stopped up. He led them to a chamber, where he sang up some hot water in a large and elegant porcelain bathing tub.

Brie and Aelwyn again exchanged looks, but lost no time in availing themselves of the Ellyl's facilities. Each had a long luxurious soak and, after drying with feathery soft towels and dressing in fresh clothing, they rejoined Monodnock in the central chamber. His nose no longer twitching, the Ellyl greeted them with glad cries. "Isn't that ever so much better! Why you both smell—uh, I mean— look perfectly refreshed and splendid."

Then he served them Ellyl tea, which he poured from an elegant white teapot with gold-leaf trim into delicate white teacups of the same design, along with airy white cakes frosted with rich clotted cream and fresh strawberries.

"Now, ladies, pray tell me of your exploits. Nothing of import ever happens here." He sighed. "It is a terrible trial for one who yearns so to answer the call to adventure." Monodnock ran his hand over his upright hair in a gesture meant to smooth, but the orange spikes only stood up straighter. "I fear you have been ill-used, Miss Aelwyn," he said, eyeing her face.

The wyll raised her hand to her cheek. "Oh, I'd forgotten. Have you a mirror by chance?" she asked with a trace of anxiety.

As Aelwyn critically studied the bruises on her face in a gilt-edged mirror, Brie told the Ellyl of the wyll's ambush by the morgs and goat-man.

"Ah yes. The gabha."

"You have seen them?" asked Brie.

Monodnock nodded. "I saw the first several moons ago. And since then there have been more. I do not know their business. So far they have not made themselves known to the people living along the Blue Stack Mountains, save for the occasional loss of a farm animal, which the Eirrenians attribute to wolves. The gabha have a disgustingly voracious appetite for uncooked flesh." Monodnock shuddered.

"They did not seem to want me to go to Dungal," said Aelwyn, adjusting one of her braids.

"There are not many travelers through the Blue Stacks to Dungal, but I've noticed that the gabha are keeping a close eye on those who do travel there. Still, I have not heard of any attacks on travelers before now. Oh, my dear ladies! The more I ponder the prospect, the more I am convinced that you must not even *think* of journeying on to Dungal."

"I will go to Dungal," Brie responded firmly.

"And I, too, though not right away," said Aelwyn. She finished the last of the cakes and drained her cup of tea. A mischievous look appeared in her eye as Monodnock refilled her cup.

"I have a splendid idea," she said. "Why do you not journey with Brie to Dungal? She could use a stalwart and brave champion such as yourself." Monodnock's face took on an expression that was half swaggering and half unsure. "Brie is headed on a quest of vital importance, which may even take her deep into the heart of Bog Maglu."

"Ah, to travel," Monodnock began, his eyes wearing an exalted look, "to sally forth, to...to Bog Maglu?!" He sputtered, raising a trembling hand to his mouth. The Ellyl's face had gone a distinct shade paler, making his hair look even more orange. The hand holding his teacup was shaking so that the cup rattled in its saucer.

"You, uh, didn't actually say 'Bog Maglu,' did you?"

Aelwyn nodded.

"Why, uh, of course, quest and all...It sounds perfectly, immeasurably thrilling of course...Bog Maglu, are you sure? I am sure I should be delighted, under other circumstances, but there are penalties for deserting a post, rather severe and all. Desperate as I am to come to the aid of a damsel in distress, it is a terrible crushing disappointment to have to decline...More cakes, ladies?" he finished brightly.

After that Monodnock seemed to hurry them through the rest of the meal, looking quite pink around the ears. He brought out several fur-lined blankets and more feather pillows, made sure Brie and Aelwyn were quite comfortable, and bade them an abrupt good night. Then he disappeared into his adjoining room.

Brie and Aelwyn took one look at each other and were overcome with giggles. They desperately tried to smother their laughter so Monodnock wouldn't hear. Fatigue soon overwhelmed them, however, and they nestled into their luxurious bedding and fell fast asleep.

Brie woke suddenly, something hard digging into her back. She opened her eyes to find herself sitting on the lake path, her back against the hard rock of a scree. Her pack, quiver, and bow were placed neatly beside her. Aelwyn was nearby and she, too, was just waking up.

"We seem to have been rather unceremoniously dismissed from the porth," Brie said.

"Perhaps Mr. Monodnock is not at his best in the morning," said Aelwyn, stretching her body.

"You shouldn't have teased him like that," Brie grumbled, rubbing her back.

"I suppose you're right, but wasn't his expression priceless?... 'To sally forth, to Bog Maglu?!' Still, I wish he had saved us some of that strawberry cream cake."

But when they opened their packs they discovered that Monodnock had indeed given them each a hefty portion of cake, as well as a piece of medlar fruit and a big hunk of cheese. They also found that all their clothing had been freshly laundered. And tucked discreetly in with the rest were two bars of sweet-smelling white lilac soap.

"At least his heart is in the right place," said Aelwyn, biting into a strawberry. "You know, I've been meaning to tell you what a great fool you are."

"Oh?" Brie raised her eyebrows.

"To leave behind that handsome young man who cares for you at Cuillean's dun."

"Indeed." The color rose in Brie's face.

"I saw the way his eyes stayed on you. Collun, that was his name, was it not?"

Brie nodded. "We are friends."

"Of course." Aelwyn yawned, then gazed critically at Brie. "It is not as if you were pretty."

Brie was surprised into laughing out loud.

Aelwyn ignored her. "Although if you took a little trouble..." She reached under several layers of her colorful clothing and retrieved the soft leather pouch that contained her treasures. As she removed her hand, Brie saw something sparkling in her fingers. The wyll leaned over and fastened a pair of earrings to Brie's ears. They were spiral mosaics of differently colored iridescent stones. Aelwyn then unplaited Brie's hair and caught it loosely with a bioran that also glimmered with iridescent gems.

Aelwyn settled back into her place and gazed critically at her handiwork. "Yes. You could do better with what you have."

"Thank you," Brie responded with a smile.

"Still, it is not often one wins that kind of loyalty, especially from one so fair."

Brie's forehead furrowed in puzzlement. "It is Collun we are talking of?" she asked.

"Of course. He must be powerful, as well, to live in such a large dun."

Brie almost laughed again, but refrained, removing the wyll's ornaments from her hair and ears. "It was his father's dun. Collun is a gardener, not a lord."

"So you say," responded Aelwyn, accepting the shiny things from Brie. "But you ought to think about taking more care about your appearance, perhaps wear a skirt every so often; that is, if you do not wish to end up old and unwed."

"Unwed?" Brie replied with some measure of astonishment in her voice.

"Surely the prospect is not an appealing one?"

"I have never thought of it, one way or another," Brie responded. And indeed she had not.

Aelwyn gazed at her with a look of incomprehension. "I believe you speak truly."

"Of course."

Aelwyn stood, shaking out her skirts. "Well, you reap as you sow," she said briskly. "It is time for me to go. My friend's time is near."

They walked back the way they had come, and Aelwyn pointed out a path that followed the lake's edge on the opposite bank. "In the first farmhold you come to beyond the lake lives a Dungalan woman married to an Eirrenian farmer. I do not care for the farmer, but the girl is kind. She will give you a welcome, as well as fresh supplies. They can direct you to the path leading into the mountains and Beirthoud's Pass. And, Breo-Saight, if you should journey into Dungal, to the hill country, and your way takes you near the village Cerriw, know that you will receive a welcome at the home of my family. I may be there as well by then. Farewell."

It was midday when Brie arrived at the first farmhold. A heavy, soaking rain had begun to fall, and Brie was welcomed into the snug farm kitchen, where a fire burned cozily on the hearth. Bread was baking and a large well-fed cat rubbed against Brie's legs.

The farmer Ladran was warm enough in his welcome, though Brie thought there was something sly in his eyes. It was his wife, Rilla, who urged Brie to stop with them for the rest of the day and overnight, as well.

"We get so few visitors," she said with a shy smile.

Rilla was a small, pale girl, with copper hair cut short and a voice as soft as ash. When the farmer gazed at his wife, his slyness disappeared; to even the least observant it was plain he was devoted to her.

Brie described Bricriu and asked if the farmer and his wife had seen such a man. Ladran quickly shook his head. "No, no travelers through here, not in a long while."

Rilla looked at Ladran, puzzled. "I thought I saw you talking to a man a few days ago."

"Ah, no," Ladran responded glibly. "That was Farmer Gluhn. You haven't seen him since he shaved off his beard. He had a sheep go missing, second one in a fortnight, and was asking if I'd seen it about."

Rilla nodded, though said nothing.

She invited Brie to share their meal and served a soup thick with corn and potato, along with bread that was crusty on the outside and melting-soft on the inside.

During the meal Ladran asked Brie where she journeyed. When she replied, "Dungal," a look of the most appalling emptiness came over Rilla's face, the look of one who has lost a part of her body and can still feel the ache of it.

Ladran, paying no heed to his wife's discomfort, advised Brie against the journey. "It's a nice little place," he said, "but there's nothing on that side of the Blue Stacks that you can't find on this side, and then some. And who in their right mind would want to go to all that trouble getting over Beirthoud's Pass? That's my opinion, anyway. And I say that even though I found the treasure of my own life there." His eyes softened as he gazed toward Rilla.

Brie said she was set on going, and Ladran replied that in that case he'd be more than happy to show her the best way through the Blue Stack Mountains.

After dinner Rilla took out a box of paints. She began painting on small circles of wood. "Panners, they're called," explained Ladran. Each was no bigger than a small locket. "No one makes a lovelier panner than my Rilla. It's a craft native to Dungal."

Brie went around behind Rilla and saw that she was painting a miniature portrait on the small wooden disk. The face was that of a man, with a beard and keen blue eyes.

"My father," Rilla said softly. It was extraordinary, Brie thought, how the girl used tiny dots of color and hatch marks to create a face so alive it looked as though it might speak.

"It's exquisite," Brie said.

Rilla flushed slightly then smiled.

It rained through the night and into the next day. Rilla shyly invited Brie to stay on with them for the day and, as it was not the most inviting weather to travel in, Brie found herself accepting. Rilla offered her a pallet in the farmhouse, but catching a frown on Ladran's face, Brie said she preferred to sleep in the barn.

Ladran was gone on an errand to a neighboring town from late morning until sundown. As she helped Rilla with chores around the farmhold, Brie found the young farmwife to be very reserved, but then she asked her about Dungal and Rilla's reticence evaporated. Her soft voice became animated as she spoke of her family in the fishing village of Ardara; of the fishing boat called Storm Petrel, on which her father would go out every morning; and of the times, remembered with an acute longing, that Rilla had joined her father on the boat. As Rilla spoke, Brie could almost feel the rough wooden planks of the Storm Petrel under her bare feet and the spray on her face.

"Why did you leave?" Brie asked.

Rilla's face closed. "I married Ladran. He has been a good husband to me," she said tonelessly, and after that she would not speak more of Dungal.

Later, as Brie swept the hearth and Rilla made preserves out of gooseberries, Brie felt as though she was being watched. She turned to find Rilla gazing intently at her. The look on her face was strange, as if she were watching a story unfold. Then she gave a little nod and a smile, and returned to the stirring of the simmering berries.

When Rilla took out her panner work that night, she set aside the one of her father and began a new miniature. She worked on it with great concentration, seemingly unaware of the conversation going on around her. And she placed her hand over it whenever anyone came near.

Ladran also seemed distracted that night, though he made a great commotion about giving Brie directions through the Blue Stacks. After making sure the wooden table was free of crumbs, he laid out a square of muslin. Carefully he drew a map of Beirthoud's Pass on the cloth. His directions were clear, and he went slowly to make sure Brie followed as he traced the way through twisting mountain paths.

He didn't offer to walk Brie to the barn as he had the night before. Brie thanked the couple for dinner, saying she would stop in to bid them farewell in the morning before she left.

As Brie crossed to the barn she was startled by a sudden loud bray. It sounded like a goat. She couldn't remember seeing goats among the animals in Ladran's farmhold. Apprehensively, she looked around in the darkness but saw nothing.

Brie slept fitfully. After several hours she woke. The animals in the barn were restless; a cow lowed uneasily. Brie was filled with a strong desire to see the fire arrow. She pulled her quiver toward her and encircled the shaft with her fingers. It was warm. She fell asleep again, her hand still on the arrow.

She awoke suddenly what seemed a few minutes later. The arrow was white-hot on her fingers.

# SIX

# The Mountains

**B**rie let go of the arrow with a cry of pain, realizing at
the same moment that she smelled smoke. She heard
crackling and was aware of a wild unnatural flutter of light
in the barn. The hayloft at the other end of the barn was
aflame. Brie leaped to her feet, shoving the arrow into her
quiver.

The barn was filled with the grunts, yelps, squeaks, and
howls of terrified animals. A squealing pig slammed against
Brie's legs and she was almost knocked flat. The fire had
snaked its way along the hay-strewn floor, cutting Brie off
from the door. Although Brie had purposely left the barn
door ajar before going to her pallet, it was now shut tight.

The heat and smoke thickened. Coughing, she rum-

maged in her pack for a kerchief, which she quickly clamped over her nose and mouth. Then she scanned the wall behind her. There was a small open window set just above the top of her head.

Brie shoved a bale of hay under the window, and climbed onto the straw; she lifted her pack and stuffed it through the opening. The heat of the fire beat against her skin and smoke clogged her throat. Maddened animals jostled against the bale she stood on as they tried desperately to escape the flames.

As Brie hoisted her body to the window, the bale underneath her feet ignited. Kicking out at the burning hay, she swung her body up and through the window. She dropped heavily, then darted around to the front of the barn to let the animals out. She had just lifted the wooden bar and begun to pull open the large door when a large, foul-smelling creature sprang on her from behind. Its fur-matted arm wound around her throat, jerking her head back in a choke hold. Gasping, Brie desperately groped for the quiver slung across her back. The arm was like iron around her neck, immovable, and Brie felt herself weakening. Suddenly a swarm of animals burst out of the flaming barn, and the creature's arm was knocked loose. Brie reached into her quiver and grabbed hold of the red-hot fire arrow.

The painful heat on her fingers startled her, but she held fast and swiftly plunged the arrow into the creature's neck. Her attacker let out a scream, falling heavily to the ground. There was the rank smell of burnt flesh. Brie pulled the arrow out of the creature's neck and quickly thrust it back into her quiver.

Brie had a fleeting glimpse of the goatish face and dead

bulging eyes before she heard Rilla's voice calling her name. The girl was running toward her, blood flowing down the side of her face. When she reached Brie, Rilla's eyes rolled up under her eyelids and she collapsed. Brie dropped to her knees beside the farmwife. Rilla's copper-colored hair was soaked with blood. Brie found the wound and laid her hand on it as she tore off her tunic. Wadding it up, Brie held the cloth to the girl's head.

Rilla gazed up at her. "When you ... go to Dungal ... tell my father good-bye." Rilla's small hand pressed something into Brie's palm. "Pob hwyl," the girl said, smiling. Rilla's eyelids closed. She began to speak softly. "Ladran ... the mountains ...," she whispered, then stopped. Brie leaned closer; Rilla was dead.

Suddenly Brie heard guttural shouts and, hugging her pack to her chest, she sprinted across the yard. She spotted a large bag of feed leaning up against a feeding trough and she dropped to her stomach, squeezing herself into the small space between the bag and the trough. She could just barely see three figures run into the yard. They found their fallen companion and immediately separated to search for his killer. Brie's heart thudded unevenly against her ribs. Clutched in her hand was the small object Rilla had given her. It was a panner. Without looking at it, Brie stuffed the wooden disk into her pocket and made herself as small as she could under the bag of feed.

One of the gabha found Rilla's body. It leaned over the fallen girl, gave the body a kick to make sure she was dead, and then turned toward the house.

As the goat-man came closer to Brie, she could see its features clearly for the first time. Its face was a horrible mangled blend of man and goat: man-lips, jutting goat-teeth, and a long black tongue that flicked in and out. The eyes were almost fishlike, set on the sides of its head, but they protruded, oval shaped and malevolent, with an enormous black iris and a clear white dot of a pupil in the center. And while most goats' faces are stupid, almost grandfatherly, this one bore a cunning and brutal expression. On its lower body the goat-man wore the skin of a goat; its arms, shoulders, and neck, as well as its face, were thickly covered with hair. Swinging from a belt at the creature's waist were what looked to be parts of a real goat— feet, ears, even an organ that could have been a heart. Brie shuddered. The goat-man walked past without seeing her.

Then she saw Ladran emerge from the house. Catching sight of Rilla's body, he let out a high keening sound and ran at the gabha.

The creature knocked Ladran down with a single blow. Bric watched as the farmer lay on the ground, tears running from his eyes. The goat-man put a foot—or was it a hoof?—on Ladran's neck and seemed to ask a question. Ladran shook his head. The gabha drew a blade and swiftly, brutally, stabbed Ladran through the heart.

The gabha was soon joined by his companions, and they proceeded to torch the remaining buildings, including the house. Brie lay very still under the bag of pig feed. She closed her eyes as the gabha chased down and slaughtered the terrified farm animals. Finally they rode off on their goatlike steeds, animal carcasses draped over the beasts' hindquarters, each gabha braying in triumph.

Brie rose and crossed to Rilla. Under the girl's arm was a small bundle. Brie gently removed it, and, carefully untying the strings, she looked inside to see hundreds of the little panners. The colors glittered jewel-like in the light of the burning buildings. Retying the bundle, she thrust it into her pack. The flames around her were getting higher and more fierce, so she swung her pack onto her back and ran.

Later, by a small stream, Brie splashed her face with cold water, shivering though the night was warm. She left her tunic soaking, Rilla's blood washing away in the clear flowing water.

Brie reached into her pocket and drew out Rilla's panner. Pictured on the small disk was a bow stave that was plainly Brie's, and flying from it, in an arc over what looked to be water, was the fire arrow.

Brie caught her breath. She had not shown Rilla the arrow. She had never left her quiver unattended, and, even if she had, she did not believe Rilla was the sort to look through her things.

Was Rilla perhaps a wyll? Aelwyn had not said so. But then why the picture on the panner? Was it a dream? Or a prophecy?

A faint rustling caught Brie's attention, and she looked up. Two gabha were not fifty yards downstream, running toward her.

Brie grabbed her wet tunic, pack, and quiver, and ran. The goat-men were swift, but Brie managed to keep ahead of them. She found herself pounding back along the path that bordered Lake Or, moving away from the mountains.

There was a tremendous boom and the ground under her shook. Just ahead a column of blue flame exploded upward, sending plumes of light into the still-dark sky.

Brie rounded a corner and there was the scree, behind

which lay the porth into Tir a Ceol. Against the face of the scree danced large tongues of blue-white flame.

Then Brie stumbled, tripping over the bodies of two dead goat-men. Their faces were blackened as if from the fire. She jumped to her feet and continued to run.

The gabha who pursued Brie burst onto the path. They let out brays of rage on seeing their fallen comrades and lunged after her. She ran hard toward the place she had entered the porth, praying she would be able to slip through without Monodnock's help. But even as she came to the slit in the rock, a bony hand closed over her wrist and pulled her through.

"Stand away," came the Ellyl's whisper. His face looked even paler than usual in the gloom, and his limbs seemed to be trembling.

Breathing hard, Brie sank to her knees. She watched as the gangly Ellyl leaned toward the entrance. He rested his hands and face against the rock wall. Then there was another booming sound and Monodnock fell back onto his rear with a small whimper, his skinny legs flailing. Brie quickly crossed to him.

"You are most kind, dearest maiden," Monodnock said, in a voice that shook, his hand fluttering in Brie's direction. He drew out a large floral handkerchief to wipe his brow, but his hand was trembling so hard that he almost missed his face altogether.

"Dreadful creatures," he said. "Do you know what they sought to do?"

Brie shook her head.

"Seal the porth."

"Seal it?"

Monodnock nodded vigorously. "It is unheard of. And where they got the draoicht...! Gabha aren't supposed to have any draoicht. Well, I can't be expected to fight off hordes of goat-men with draoicht."

"I saw only two. And the two after me."

"Just the beginning."

"Perhaps you ought to send word to King Midir."

"Of course." Monodnock brightened a little. "And he will send reinforcements, though goodness knows I haven't the room to accommodate very many Ellylon in my humble dwelling..."

Brie crossed to the crack in the rock and tried peering out to see what had happened to the gabha who had pursued her. She thought she saw two more bodies lying on the path.

"Monodnock," she said, interrupting the Ellyl's ruminations on how he would house Ellyl reinforcements. "I must get to Dungal."

"Oh, no, most lovely maiden, you must not think of going to Dungal, not now, with the foothills crawling with those vile creatures. And I just had word yesterday, from a passing Ellyl, that there is something odd going on in Dungal. What was it? Oh dear, all this excitement has quite driven it out of my mind. Something to do with fish." He squinted his silver eyes shut in an effort to remember.

"Fish?"

"Yes, fish. I'm sure of it. Oh, oh, now I remember. It appears that something is killing off the fish in Dungal. No one knows what. And I have to say this is indeed a calamity. From what I've heard, fish is the only thing they know how to cook there. The rest is all quite hideous: meat with no sauce of any kind, potatoes, and stringy, limp vegetables.

And then there are those enormous mountains to get through. So, please, do not think of going to Dungal, not for one more moment."

"I'm afraid I must." She looked up at Monodnock hopefully. "I don't suppose there is a way to Dungal through Tir a Ceol?"

"As a matter of fact there is."

Brie's expression brightened.

"Though you would need to be a decent swimmer. It is all underwater. A hundred miles or so."

"I see."

"Now if that doesn't suit you, there is, at least, a very pleasant shortcut through the first mountain. Inside it, in fact. It is a bit cramped, but it takes you all the way through into Sura's Gorge, and well past those gabha I've observed watching the pathways into the Blue Stacks. But please, most charming, graceful, and highborn lady, rethink this absurdly dangerous quest."

"I would be very grateful for your help, Monodnock."

The Ellyl sighed. "Very well. Follow me."

To call this a "bit cramped," Brie thought some time later, was far too generous. She had been in small spaces before and had not thought of herself as particularly uncomfortable in them, but never before had she been crushed between two walls of cold, jagged rock. She tried to breathe slowly and evenly, convincing herself that there was sufficient air to keep her alive a little while longer. After all, Monodnock wouldn't take her where she would be likely to suffocate. That is, if he did not forget that Eirrenians need more air than Ellylon.

They inched forward. Brie willed herself not to ask if they were almost there. Better, perhaps, not to know.

There came a time, though, when she could not push down the panic any longer, when Brie realized that even if she turned back she would still be trapped, flattened between enormous slabs of crushing rock for hours to come. A cold sweat broke out on her skin.

"Monodnock," she whispered to keep from screaming. "How much longer?"

"Not much. Relaxing, isn't it? Nothing I enjoy better than feeling this good solid rock right up against me. Just look at the texture..." He held up a dim light. Brie tried to concentrate on the whorls and ridges of the rock surface. Her chest felt ready to explode.

"Uhp...Here we are." Monodnock stepped down into an open space and Brie followed, sinking gratefully to her knees. She closed her eyes and took several deep draughts of air.

"Oh, my dear lady, you look quite peaked," Monodnock said with concern. "Shall we rest?"

"Perhaps a moment or two," Brie replied dryly.

"Very well. I could do with a snack." Monodnock pulled out a small wedge of brisgein—an Ellyl delicacy made of stalks of heather and silverwood—and offered one to Brie. She took it, her hand shaking only a little.

"Oh, dear maiden." Monodnock pressed a hand to his heart. "It makes me quite ill to think of you, with danger pressing on all sides. If only I were free to journey with you, be your champion, vanquish the devils who beset you!" Then he stood straight up, pulling his lanky frame into a heroic pose and rubbing his orange hair into a frenzy of spikes.

"Alas, you are not free," said Brie, casting her face down to hide the smile. "But I will always be in your debt for your many kindnesses."

"Ah, 'twas nothing, nothing at all," he said mournfully.

"You are needed here at your post. There may be further attacks on the porth by the gabha."

Monodnock's heroic pose suddenly sagged and he began muttering, "I must send word right away to King Midir. I wonder how many reinforcements he will send. I could fit no more than three and even then it would be quite cramped." He began walking away. "And what of my food stocks? Oh, I do hope they won't have large appetites…"

"Excuse me, Monodnock," interrupted Brie, "but how do I get out of here?"

"Oh, just go down that tunnel; it will lead into a cave, and out the cave's entrance lies Sura's Gorge. Now, I could fit two Ellylon in the parlor, provided they are small… Oh, but will I have enough coverlets? The last time I checked…"

Brie watched him disappear into the rock and then turned and made her way down the tunnel.

She emerged into Sura's Gorge through a narrow rectangular passage, almost stumbling down a steep pitch that ended in a creek. Carefully she began to descend, but she ended up sliding most of the way down on her backside, landing with a splash in the creek.

Rising, she gazed back at the mountain through which she had passed with Monodnock. It was steep and forbidding, though she wasn't entirely sure the shortcut had been worth it. Ahead stretched a jagged mountainscape. According to Crann's map, the tallest peaks were called Beirt, or the Twins, and she could just see them in the far distance.

Aelwyn had told her that Beirt was really two spires standing side by side, like twins, almost identical in shape. Between the Twins lay Beirthoud's Pass. Taking a deep
breath, Brie set out, following the creek through the gorge.

By twilight she had ascended the first mountain that lay
between her and Beirthoud's Pass. The path had been an
easy one, ascending in zigzags to the top. But the descent
was trickier and steeper, and again she spent much of it
sliding in a downpour of loose stones and scrub.

When she reached the valley, Brie made camp and spent
the night there. So far she had seen no sign of any goat-
men.

During the next few days, as she traversed a smaller range
of mountains dense with pine trees, Brie occasionally looked
at Ladran's map, comparing it to Crann's. As she had sus-
pected, the farmer's map was a lie. He had sought to mis-
direct her; without Crann's map she would almost certainly
have gotten hopelessly lost in the vastness of the Blue
Stacks.

Brie quickly found that hiking up and down mountains
taxed leg and back muscles she had used but little before.
And she developed blisters the size of coins on her heels.
But the grandeur of the mountains, their wildness and dig-
nity and beauty, filled her with awe.

As the days succeeded each other, Brie found herself
getting stronger, able to travel farther in a day. Still, it took
her two days of backbreaking exertion to reach Beirthoud's
Pass. She had several terrifying moments when she had to
scale almost-sheer stretches of rock face, made even more
treacherous by the occasional patch of icy snow, which at

this high altitude never completely melted. But finally Brie reached the summit.

There was a small rock marker with BEIRT BEALACH faintly inscribed on it; "Beirthoud's Pass" in the old language. With a fresh mountain wind blowing across her face, Brie felt a surge of exhilaration. She gazed at the two snow-capped spires rising on either side of her—the Twins—and beyond, to the north, she could see the kingdom of Dungal, the sea glittering alongside it. After Beirthoud's Pass, she had only two summits of significant size to cross, and then she would be in the foothills of Dungal.

Two days later, Brie had just crested the second of the two peaks and was gazing down in some despair at what looked to be a sheer wall of rock when she was struck by an enormous blast of wind. She had been vaguely aware that the wind had picked up, but was unprepared for the strength of the gust. The force of the wind pushed her to the edge, her feet skidding off into open air. She grabbed at the path, but the weight of her body pulled her down and she was over the side of the ledge. One hand caught hold of a protruding rock and she hung against the face of the cliff, terrified. Gazing down over her shoulder she could see another ledge, perhaps thirty feet below. The toes of her boots scrabbled against the rock face. The wind tore at her. Suddenly the piece of rock under her fingers came loose and she lost her handhold.

She fell.

# SEVEN

# Fara

Plummeting downward, Brie clutched at the cliff face, scraping off skin and breaking her fingernails. She landed heavily on the ledge below, crushing her right leg beneath her. Pain exploded through her body and she screamed. Then she clenched her teeth and lay still. Barely conscious, she spotted a small crevice in the rocky cliff and burrowed into it, dragging her leg. She was able to fit only half of her body into the opening, but it gave her some protection from the lashing wind.

Brie lost track of time, her leg throbbing with a pain beyond any she'd known before. Her thoughts became disconnected, dreamlike, and she grew warm with a tingling rushing under her skin. Collun was there, at their campsite,

an arm's length away. They had spent the day planting rutabaga and were exhausted, drowsing peacefully by the embers of their fire. Then Brie's father bent over her, telling her it was time to get up and practice with her bow and arrow.

The arrow. Brie came alert. Where was the arrow? She shifted her body to reach for the quiver. Her leg moved and pain knifed into her. She began to panic, then her fingers brushed the leather surface of the quiver. It had stayed on her shoulder as she fell, along with her bow and pack. But to get to the arrow she would have to move her body again. She couldn't. Her fingers dropped from the quiver.

> *Cross your heart,*
> *Then to die;*
> *Shoot an arrow in your eye.*

The singsong bit of doggerel repeated several times in her ears, though she didn't know if it was her own voice or someone else's. She needed the arrow. If she didn't hold the arrow, she would die. As she reached for the quiver, the pain again coursed through her, worse now. She pulled the quiver to her chest. With numb fingers she found the arrow. It was ice-cold to the touch. She had been expecting warmth, comfort, and the shock of the cold made her numb fingers flinch away. The arrow fell.

Brie felt a whirling dizziness, as if she, too, were falling. Then she was somehow looking down from above at the crumpled body of a girl. She saw blood and a white tip of bone sticking out of her leg. But the arrow...It was falling slowly through the air, and as it fell, tiny pictures unraveled like thread off a spool. A thin streamer spiraled away from the arrow; it was long, longer than she would have believed possible. The wind played with the colored picture streamer, teasing it into great looping coils.

Brie reached for the streamer, thinking to reel the arrow back in like a fish at the end of a line, but the wind was mischievous, whipping the streamer out of her grasp just as she thought she had it. She sighed. She was so tired. It was easiest just to close her eyes....

"Brie."

Someone had spoken her name. A voice with melody and strength. A woman's voice. Brie's eyes flicked open. Then she saw a face. Unlined, beautiful, yet old, very old. White hair—or was it a cloud?—surrounded, flowed all around the face. Seila. Brie smiled, closing her eyes again.

"Brie, wake up." The voice was insistent, even urgent.

"I'm tired, great-grandmother."

"You can sleep later. Now you need to get up. Here." Something was being pressed into her hands. It was the arrow, no longer cold, with just a little warmth humming along its shaft. Brie wondered if all the pictures were gone, unraveled.

"Look," said the voice.

Brie opened her eyes and looked at the arrow. The pictures were still there. For the first time she could see one of them. The little pictures were like pictures in a book, only they were moving, telling a story. There was a young girl with yellow hair skipping along a seawall, carefree. Then water rising, rising. And a light bursting from the girl as she held back the water. Brie watched the pictures unfold, avid, waiting to see what would happen next.

"Get up, Brie."

She jerked with surprise. The pictures faded, disappeared. She wanted them back.

"Get up, Brie."

"It hurts."

"Get up."

"I can't."

"The arrow, Brie."

Brie closed her eyes, but she held tightly to the arrow. It was getting warmer. She concentrated on the warmth, felt it seep into her hands, up her arms.

"Seila?" Brie called out, pulling herself up. But she knew even before opening her eyes that Seila was gone. Brie almost sank back onto the rock; the feeling of loss was so overwhelming. But she stayed upright.

The wind had died down. Brie looked around her, taking stock.

The ledge she was on jutted out of the cliff, narrowing away to her right. Below her the cliff face plunged straight away. Brie could not see a way down.

Then she steeled herself to look at her leg. She could see the whiteness of the bone where it protruded. It was bleeding badly. If she didn't get help soon she surely would die. The warmth of the arrow beat against her fingers.

The first thing to do was to set the bone back into her leg and then stanch the flow of blood. She laid down the arrow and, painfully, slowly, shrugged the pack off her back. Brie felt a sudden, unexpected surge of self-pity. It wasn't fair.

But, hardening herself, she reached down and took hold of the white knob of bone. With her other hand, she felt under her leg for the opposite end. Taking a deep breath, she pushed them together. A scream tore out of her throat and she battled against losing consciousness. For a few moments she teetered in grayness, then the miasma began to clear.

Again she pressed together the two ends of shattered bone, and again came the unspeakable pain. Brie looked at her leg. It wasn't good enough. But she could do no more. Reaching into her pack she found a spare tunic. She tore it into strips and tightly wound the largest around the bleeding wound. Then she took out one of her two remaining arrows and, breaking off the arrowhead, used the shaft for a splint, tying it in place with strips of jersey. She did the same with the last arrow; only the fire arrow remained in her quiver.

After that Brie lay still, letting her pounding heart rest briefly. Then she shifted onto her stomach and began to drag herself along the ledge to where it tapered off. Perhaps if she could see around the corner there would be a way off the ledge.

A grating sound assailed her ears. She stopped and listened closely. It was the braying of some kind of animal. She looked up.

A goat-man stood on the summit above her. His goat face wore a gloating, toothy smile. He had seen her.

Impossibly, he began moving down the mountain face toward her, finding toeholds she could not even see. Brie's heart hammered unevenly as she grabbed her bow. She tried to nock the fire arrow to the string, but her fingers were trembling too violently. The goat-man was only a few feet above her, on a minuscule edge of rock. He looked down at her, balanced and steady on his perch. His musky goatish odor wafted down, making Brie's stomach tighten.

Please, oh please, oh please ... Brie silently prayed for her
fingers to work. There. The arrow was notched and ready.
The goat-man began to leap down, toward her. Squinting,
Brie let the fire arrow fly.

There was a searing, crackling noise. Sparks of light
blinded her. Heat on her face, skin. She heard a hoarse
scream. Through blurred eyesight, Brie saw the creature
fall, its chest split open, flames spewing from inside.

Then it was gone.

Brie listened. Some time later—it seemed an eternity—
she heard a far-off thud. Then she slipped into uncon-
sciousness.

She woke to the feeling of something soft rubbing against
her eyelids. Slowly she opened her eyes and saw a blurry
white ear. As she blinked several times to ease the blur, a
pink tongue lapped her eyebrow and Brie found herself
looking into the silvery eyes of a faol, an Ellyl animal from
Tir a Ceol. Dumbly she wondered what a faol was doing
in the Blue Stack Mountains, then the animal purred a
welcome and rubbed her white furry face against Brie's.

"Fara," she whispered in amazement. And the faol lov-
ingly gave Brie's cheek a lick with her coarse tongue. Feebly
Brie lifted her hand and ran it down the animal's back.
"Well met, friend," she said, gazing at Fara. Faols were an
odd hybrid of wolf and big cat, and this one had a gleaming
white coat with a gold star burst on her forehead.

Then Brie remembered the goat-man and her fire arrow
splitting his chest with fire. The fire arrow was gone. She
felt a wave of desolation.

Sensing Brie's grief, Fara licked her again several times.

But then the faol moved away, down the ledge to the end where it tapered off. She stopped, waiting expectantly.

"I cannot, Fara. My leg is broken," Brie said almost apologetically.

Fara didn't budge.

Brie sighed, then began dragging herself toward Fara. Finally she reached the end, and—sweating and raw with pain—she peered around the edge. Approximately ten feet away was a moderately steep slope, made up of mostly loose pebbles and small patches of scrub grass. It was not as steep as the cliff face, but it didn't look particularly navigable, certainly not for one with a broken leg. Between it and the ledge she was on lay one narrow outcropping of rock. The rest was sheer.

Fara ever so slightly beckoned with her head.

"Now that is a very fine stepping-stone," said Brie to the faol, "*if* you happen to be a goat-man. But for a one-legged girl who has lost a fair amount of blood..."

Fara sat on her haunches, waiting.

"No." Brie shook her head. She could not.

Fara began cleaning her whiskers.

Brie closed her eyes. Then she opened them again. Because of a thick patch of taznie plants and the way the slope angled off, she could not see where it led. Even if she could get there, she might easily be dashed on jagged rock at the bottom. With two graceful leaps, the faol effortlessly glided to the top of the slope. She settled herself and waited.

Brie suddenly smiled recklessly. She dragged herself to the end of the ledge and slowly, excruciatingly, pulled herself into a standing position. Then she tried putting all her weight on the broken leg. She almost screamed out loud. Trembling, she gazed at the empty space between her ledge and the narrow one, trying not to look down to the valley below. Clenching her fists, she again put her weight on the injured leg and pushed off, jumping to the small ledge. She landed on her good leg, swayed a moment, teetering on the edge of consciousness, but she stayed on the outcrop, her breathing shallow, sweat thick on her skin. She opened her eyes. Fara was sitting unruffled, watching her from the top of the slope. She cocked her ears forward, then rose, as if to say, "Stop dawdling."

Thinking she would much rather stay where she was, Brie limped the few steps to the far edge of the rock. This jump would be shorter, but it still took all the courage Brie possessed to fling herself once more into the air.

She lay where she landed, and squinted at Fara, who had already begun loping easily down the incline.

The slope was too steep for Brie to walk down, so, with several muttered curses, she lifted her injured leg so that it rested on top of her good one. Then she pushed off, sliding on her backside down the slope. She quickly picked up momentum. Pain overwhelmed her as her shattered leg was jarred by the motion. Then she hit bottom, her leg collided with something, and she lost consciousness.

When she woke it was nighttime. She had no sense of where she was. Her body was sore and battered, and her leg throbbed. She could feel Fara's rough tongue on her face. It brought her into focus.

She was lying beside something large. At first she thought it was a boulder, but then the odor assailed her and she gagged. Goat.

She recoiled, pulling away from the still body. Pain from her leg shot through her and she gasped.

Hands shaking, Brie felt for her pack. With a great

effort she shrugged it off her back and fumbled inside for a lasan stick. Letting out a groan, she struck the tip against rock. Light flared. The first thing Brie saw was the fire arrow. It was sticking straight out of the goat-man's gutted, blackened chest.

Relief washed through her. Then she thought, But now I have to take it out of the goat-man. She felt weak, weaker than she'd ever been.

She heard Fara burrowing in her pack, then watched as the faol used her teeth to drag out Brie's skin bag. "Thank you," Brie whispered, taking the water. As she drank she realized how hot she was and how thirsty. She felt as though she could drink the entire contents of the bag, but she did not.

Then she gritted her teeth and, closing her nostrils against the smell, reached over and took hold of the arrow lodged in the goat-man's chest. She gave a tug and it slid out, catching only a little. Brie took a deep breath and began pulling herself as far away from the corpse as she could manage. Finally, bathed in sweat, she lay still, holding the arrow.

Fara curled up by her shoulder and they both slept.

When the sun rose, Brie woke and pulled herself into a sitting position. While Fara cleaned her fur, Brie gave herself a thorough examination. Miraculously, the makeshift splint had held and, except for cuts and scrapes, her leg at least did not look worse than before. And the bleeding had abated. She was lucky, but she could tell that the break was a bad one, and she was weak from all the blood she'd lost. According to Crann's map she was far from any of Dungal's villages.

The first thing she must do, she decided, was to get as far away as she could from the evil dead thing that lay nearby. The smell still filled her nose, and the summer sun would soon make it worse.

Brie pulled herself to her feet and tried hopping on her good leg, but it immediately buckled beneath her. So, dragging her broken leg behind, she began to crawl across the ground. It took half the morning to reach the small creathan tree she had made her goal. She rested for a time in the shade of the tree, then set about making herself a rough crutch out of a branch she had found nearby. When she finished, she ate the last of her meat strips and drank water from her skin bag. Then she set out. By late afternoon she collapsed, sleeping where she lay.

She woke shivering in the dark. At least the smell of goat was gone, but she was burning with fever. The wound on her leg was swollen, festering with pus. She gazed up at the stars, thinking about Collun, wondering if he had finished tilling the north field.

"Plant in rows, straight and long. Temper them with care and song," they had sung by the fire at the end of the day. Collun's voice always went off-key on the next-to-last word, and he would be the first to laugh. Once that same off note had coincided with the cry of a nightjar and had been in perfect harmony. They had both laughed until tears ran down their cheeks.

Brie dozed.

She woke to a raucous barking noise. Fara let out a long sibilant hiss.

"Dyfod, Jip!" commanded a distant voice.

There was another torrent of barking. Fara stood beside Brie, her back arched high, her tail swollen with outrage.

"Easy, Fara," Brie whispered. She was too weak to sit up.

"Dyfod!" called the voice, impatient and still far away.

Brie tried to cry out, but her lips were cracked and dry and she could barely move them.

The voice continued to speak, but it seemed to be moving away. Tears of frustration pricked Brie's eyes. She struggled against her weakness.

But the dog kept coming toward Brie. It got as close as Fara would allow and, planting its legs stubbornly, continued to bark, loudly and persistently. Fara's eyes were slits and she looked ready to hurl herself onto the large brown-and-white dog. "No, Fara," Brie whispered.

Then Brie heard footsteps moving toward her. Abruptly they stopped, and Brie could see the outline of a person standing over her. It appeared to be a woman, though a tall one.

Brie felt a dry, cold hand on her forehead. "Poeth," said the voice tersely. Strong fingers gently probed her leg. Brie groaned. Suddenly she was being hoisted onto a strong back.

# EIGHT

# The Havotty

The next thing Brie was aware of was lying on straw. A firm hand held up her head, and warm liquid was ladled into her mouth. She managed to swallow a little, then fell back.

She was so cold, shivering until her jaw ached from chattering. Then she was hot, burning up, and trying to rip all the coverings off her body. Throughout, the woman was near, often speaking to her in a matter-of-fact way that, though Brie could not understand the words, was oddly reassuring. The woman's face was a blur, but her voice was sturdy, like a well-built home.

Fara stayed at Brie's shoulder, occasionally hissing at one or another of two dogs when they came too close.

Brie was in and out of consciousness. Once, she was aware of the woman resetting her leg.

That was the only time Brie screamed.

Brie woke to the smell of cooking. It was just past dawn. A black cooking pot hung from a chain over a hearth fire. The woman was dozing in a chair beside the hearth, an open book facedown in her lap. The brown-and-white dog slept at her feet, the other, ebony with gray markings, slept on the flagstones of the hearth. Fara, too, lay asleep at Brie's hip.

Brie studied the woman's face. It was a strong face, roughened by weather and framed by short thick hair the gray of a campfire burned to ashes. The woman wore long brown trousers and a bulky knit jersey. Her body looked strong, too, lean and muscular.

They were in a stone hut, unfurnished save for the rough wooden chair on which the woman sat and the two primitive beds made of straw on either side of the hearth.

Brie put her hand to her cheek. It was cool to the touch, but she felt frail, her limbs inert, lifeless. She reached down to pull off the quilt that lay over her leg and the effort made her head spin. Fara awoke and stretched, flexing her claws.

Brie looked at her leg dispassionately. It had been carefully, even expertly, set and throbbed only a little when she tried to move it.

"It will heal straight," came a voice. Brie looked over at the woman, who was now awake. Her eyes were the same light gray as her hair. They revealed little.

"Thank you," said Brie. There was a brief silence. Then Brie asked, "You know the language of Eirren?"

The woman nodded. "During the fever you spoke. I recognized the tongue." Then she picked up a small clay pipe and, tamping its contents down with a broad thumb, lit it. "Hungry?"

Brie realized suddenly that she was very hungry. "Yes."

The woman drew on her pipe and exhaled a stream of perfect circles. Then she rose and crossed to a pot on the hearth. The dogs rose, too, tails wagging. When the woman lifted the lid, the smell of simmering oat porridge made Brie's stomach rumble.

The woman handed Brie a half-full bowl.

"Don't eat fast. Your stomach hasn't had much in it except broth these past seven days," she warned.

"Seven days?!" Brie stared at the woman.

"You had a bad fever. Almost took you, but I guess you're stubborn, like me."

Brie gave a thin smile, then took a spoonful of the porridge. It was hot and delicious. Brie gazed at the woman. A beam of early morning sunlight came in the window, and Brie saw that the woman's eyes were blue, not gray.

"What is your name?" asked Brie.

"Hanna."

The woman spoke Eirrenian with an accent, a Dungalan accent, which made the words sound more interesting, even musical. Rilla had spoken with the same sort of burr.

"I am called Brie."

The woman frowned, then said Brie's name, but in her mouth it sounded like "Biri."

"No, it's Brie," the girl repeated.

"Biri," the older woman said again. She shrugged. "I shall call you Biri," she said.

They sat for a time in silence while Brie ate small bites of porridge. Then the woman said, "I saw a dead goat-man, not far from where I found you. Did you kill him?"

"Yes."

"With what?"

"An arrow."

The woman arched an eyebrow, but said nothing.

Brie thought of the split, burnt chest of the dead creature. Fara rubbed against Brie's shoulder and the girl absently fed the animal a fingerful of porridge, then another. Hanna watched.

"This is a faol? One of the Ellyl animals?" she asked.

"Yes."

"I had not known they could be tamed."

Fara's eyes went into slits, and she fastidiously began cleaning her whiskers of porridge.

"Fara is not tame. Is this your home?" asked Brie, to change the subject.

The woman shook her head. "This is a havotty. It is where we bring the sheep in the summer, to graze the flocks in the foothills."

"You are a shepherd?"

"No, a Traveler."

Brie gave a questioning look.

"A Traveler is a sort of gypsy, one with no set home. I range throughout Dungal, sheepherding in the summer, harvesting in the fall, and," she added with a slight smile, "during the dark months I am a teller of tales."

"I see." Her stomach comfortably full, Brie set the bowl

down, and Fara licked it clean of porridge. "By chance, have you seen a man come out of the mountains, a ragged man with a bad leg?" Brie asked.

"I did see such a man, perhaps three days ago. It was from a distance. I noticed him because he was the first to come through in a long time. Except for a few goat-men. I expected him to stop for food or water, frail as he looked. But he did not. He was headed north."

"Toward Bog Maglu?"

Hanna arched her eyebrow again. "That direction, yes."

"How far a journey is it to Bog Maglu?" asked Brie.

"A distance. More than a week by horse."

"I see. And to Ardara from there?"

"The same, more or less. You go to Ardara?"

"Perhaps. I bear ill news for one who lives there."

"Who?"

"A fisherman named Jacan."

"I know Jacan. What news?"

"His daughter Rilla is dead. Killed by goat-men."

Hanna's face darkened. "This is ill news indeed." She refilled her pipe. "I have seen bands of gabha. Have even lost a sheep or two, and I thought it might be them. But I have not heard of them attacking people." She lit the tobacco with a worried frown. "There has been a mist over the stars to the north. I knew it boded ill for Dungal."

The older woman's eyes suddenly turned dark, almost black. Brie stared. "Are you a wyll?" she blurted out.

Hanna turned her black eyes toward Brie and gave a short laugh. "Not exactly, no," she said shortly. "Why do you ask about Bog Maglu?"

"I seek to go there."

"No one seeks to go to the bog."

"I am on the trail of a killer. More than one, I hope."

"This man you follow?"

Brie explained as briefly as she could about the traitor Bricriu and her belief he would lead to her father's killers.

Hanna's eyes seemed to grow darker yet as she listened. But she said nothing for a time. Then she rose and crossed to the hearth.

"At any rate, you will not be able to travel anywhere, not for a time."

She scraped what remained in the porridge pot into two rough wooden plates and set them on the floor for the two dogs.

Brie stayed at the havotty while she regained her strength. Hanna was gone a fair amount, moving the flocks around the grazing land of the foothills, accompanied by Jip and Maor, the Dungalan sheepdogs. But when she was at the havotty there was an ease between Brie and Hanna, almost a recognition, and a friendship grew between them. Hanna was taciturn, even gruff at times, but she had an active, seeking mind. She loved books, though her wandering life kept her from owning them. But she always took one book with her when she came out to the havotty at the beginning of the summer. By the end of the summer she had the book memorized. Consequently there were dozens of books, she said, in her mind that she could call up at will. These book stories were only a small part of the repertoire of stories Hanna held inside her; there were innumerable oral histories and tales picked up from all the places in Dungal to which she had traveled. There was a great demand for Travelers such as Hanna during the dark months, when the nights were long and much of the time was spent indoors.

Hanna asked Brie many questions about herself, and about Eirren. She was curious about Brie's great-grandmother, Seila, though Brie could tell her little.

In turn Brie asked Hanna about Dungal. She had a deep curiosity about the small kingdom so close to Eirren, yet so apart from it and so unknown. If her great-grandmother was from here, it meant that Brie herself perhaps had Dungalan blood.

Brie asked Hanna how she knew the Eirrenian language so well, and if this was true of all Dungalans. Hanna shook her head. "Travelers often do," she said, but did not elaborate.

"Would you teach me Dungalan?" Brie asked.

"If you wish."

And as they roasted meat or cut vegetables or baked bread together, Hanna began to teach Brie to speak Dungalan.

Hanna was a gifted wood-carver, something she did to pass the time while watching over the sheep. She fashioned a crutch for Brie, sturdy and quite beautiful, with the semblance of an ivy vine climbing the stem.

One morning while Hanna was out, Brie retrieved her quiver from the corner of the havotty where Hanna had placed it. Gingerly she removed the fire arrow. She had not looked at it since yanking it out of the goat-man, and there were still traces of charred skin and blood on it. Again she remembered the goat-man's chest splitting open and the smell and the flames.

The arrow felt cool and dull in her fingers, almost as if reproaching her for neglecting it so long. She carried it outside with a bowl of soapy water and a clean rag. As she washed away the blood and hair, the arrow, very faintly, began to hum against her fingers. Brie smiled. "You're welcome," she said, then looked around in embarrassment. Only Fara was nearby, lying in the sun with her eyes shut.

When the arrow was clean, Brie gazed closely at the picture bands. She found that by squinting she could just make out the one she had seen in the mountains, the one that had unraveled, showing the girl child with yellow hair and the seawall. But the rest were just as blurred as before.

"You're a fickle one, aren't you?" she said in a teasing voice.

"Talking to arrows now, eh?" Hanna said, crossing to Brie, her dogs at her heels and a bleating lamb in her arms.

Brie flushed slightly but retorted with a smile, "And this, coming from one who spends her days conversing with dogs and sheep..."

"That's a Dungalan arrow, isn't it?" Hanna said, setting down the lamb. She lifted one of its back legs and began to pry out a small stone that had lodged in the hoof.

"So I've been told."

"It wouldn't be the one killed the goat-man, would it?" Hanna said, glancing up from her task.

"It is."

The stone popped out and the lamb struggled out of Hanna's arms, bleating furiously. Jip quickly herded it back in the direction of the flock.

Hanna sat back on her heels. "May I?" she said, holding out her hand.

Without hesitating, Brie handed her the arrow.

"As I thought. Saeth-tan. Fire arrow," the older woman said softly.

Brie started, hearing Hanna say the name she herself had been calling the arrow. "What is a fire arrow?" she asked.

"Rare thing, never seen one myself, except a picture drawn in a book. Goldenhawk fletching, story bands, and the arrowhead made of black flint. How did you come to acquire a fire arrow?"

Brie explained about the wedding gift and Masha's last words. "The man I followed here sought to steal it from me."

"I shouldn't wonder. Fire arrows are extremely powerful."

Brie smiled wryly. "Indeed. And I've had the blistered fingers to show for it."

"Pardon me, Biri, but if all you've suffered are blistered fingers then either you are extraordinarily lucky or you yourself have something of draoicht in you."

Brie shook her head decisively. "I spoke of this with the wyll Aelwyn. I have no magic."

"No? You travel with an Ellyl animal; most would find that unusual."

"Fara and I are old friends."

"Perhaps the Dungalan Seila was a wyll, or had Ellyl blood."

Brie suddenly remembered the hatred her father had for Ellylon. Perhaps this was why he had disliked Seila so.

She said absently, "I thought I saw her in the mountains,

when I lay near death. Her voice kept me alive. And she found the arrow for me when I thought it was lost. But she did not have silver eyes. At any rate, I have no draoicht." Brie's tone was final, signaling an end to the discussion.

Later that day, when Hanna had gone off with the dogs to check on the flock, Brie set about making a cord out of an old piece of leather Hanna had found for her. She had decided to string Rilla's panner and wear it as a necklace.

When she had finished whittling a hole at the top of the small disc, Brie stared at the image of the arrow. Were all the women of Dungal possessed of magic powers? she suddenly wondered. And if Brie's great-grandmother had indeed been some kind of wyll, then perhaps Brie herself did have a trace of draoicht thrumming along in her veins. The thought made her uneasy.

She slid the homemade necklace over her head, and the panner settled against her chest as if it belonged there.

On her eleventh day at the havotty, though she was still weak and her leg ached, Brie grew restless, frustrated by the forced inactivity. She decided to hike up to Simla's Tor, where Hanna had taken the sheep for the day.

Fara stalked along beside Brie, occasionally loping off to chase down an unsuspecting squirrel. The sun was warm on Brie's hair, and at first she felt good, glad to be doing something and pleased that her strength seemed to be coming back. She would be able to continue her journey soon.

But as the morning wore on, the uphill walk grew more

difficult and she began to falter, leaning more and more heavily on the crutch Hanna had made. By the time she reached the tor, her breathing was labored and her face pale and clammy.

"That was a fool thing to do, to come so far," Hanna said, frowning at Brie, who had settled thankfully on a large, flat rock. The dog Jip bounded up to greet Brie, then backed away when he saw the faol. Fara had not yet decided to trust the two sheepdogs.

"I needed the exercise," Brie gasped.

Hanna only snorted. "Where's your skin bag?"

Brie felt at her side. "I forgot it," the girl replied shamefacedly.

"Here," Hanna said gruffly, thrusting her own at Brie. "Now, drink. And stay put."

The older woman moved away, shouting at Maor, who was enthusiastically redirecting a large sheep that had strayed too near an incline.

Brie made herself comfortable on her rock and watched Hanna and the two dogs move among the longhaired, black-faced mountain sheep. Like Brie, the animals seemed restless. She closed her eyes and listened to the sounds of barking, bleating, and Hanna's calling voice as they blended and wafted back to her on the warm wind. Brie dozed.

She woke to a flash of light. Confused, she gazed around. The sky had darkened and small splinters of lightning danced among the looming clouds. But there were only faint rumblings of thunder and no rain. Brie could not see Hanna or the dogs.

All of a sudden a small shaft of lightning knifed the air not twenty feet from Brie. She let out a cry and had started to her feet when another crackling dagger of light struck the ground on her other side. Startled, Brie was knocked off balance and she fell, landing on her injured leg. The jolt of pain stunned her and she rolled into a ball, cradling her leg with her arms.

Hanna appeared, at a run, and leaned over Brie. Flashes of white light continued to dance about them.

"Blasted summer storms," Hanna growled. "Can you walk?"

Brie nodded, but it was a struggle just to sit upright. All the sheep seemed to be bleating at once, making a deafening noise.

"Uffern!" Hanna exclaimed. Brie recognized the word as a particularly potent Dungalan expletive Hanna had taught her. The older woman's eyes were the color of the gray-black clouds above.

Brie tried to get to her feet. Suddenly Hanna put a restraining hand on Brie's shoulder, holding her in place. Then she closed her eyes and, standing very still, began to move her lips, though no sound emerged.

The flashes of lightning abruptly disappeared and, with an astonishing swiftness, the gray-black clouds rolled across the sky, fading in the distance and leaving bright blue skies in their wake.

# NINE

# Bog Maglu

**H**anna opened her eyes. They were now mirror images of the sky, brilliant blue. Her face, though, was drawn and etched with pain. She lowered herself into a sitting position on the flat rock.

"You did that," Brie said in amazement.

Hanna did not reply.

"I thought you said you were not a wyll."

"I am not."

"Then . . . ?"

"Weather making and unmaking is different from the wyll's hocus-pocus of trances and seeings," Hanna replied in a gruff voice. Then she got heavily to her feet, letting out a faint groan.

"Are you ill?" Brie asked, concerned.

"Headache," Hanna replied curtly. "Blinding thing. Comes from lightning. Either making it or getting rid of it."

"I see. Can I help?"

Hanna glowered at her. "Next time you can stay put until you are ready for a hike to Simla's Tor."

"I'm sorry." Brie pulled herself painfully to her feet.

Hanna grunted. "Just look at the pair of us. Well, I'd best check on the flock, then the dogs can bring them in. I'm hoping we lost none during the lightning storm."

Somehow they made it back. At the havotty Hanna immediately lit a fire and brewed some wood betony tea, her face screwed up with pain.

"Helps the headache," she muttered. She drank off a full cup and then sank into her pallet of straw. She was soon asleep.

"We've been having strange storms this summer," Hanna said as she sliced a loaf of brown bread. Brie sat by the hearth, stirring the mutton stew. "Either sudden wind squalls like the one you met in the mountains, or lightning only, with dozens of small bolts and no rain and very little thunder. There's not been much rain at all since early spring. Unusual for Dungal. Likely as not there'll be a big fire one of these days, things being as dry as they are."

"Have you always had weather magic?"

"Yes. Thought it was quite a splendid thing when I was young. But I quickly found out it was not without its price." She gestured at her head, her face still pale. "Interesting thing is, each kind of weather I make or unmake has its own distinctive aftereffect, none of them pleasant. Lightning causes headache. Bringing on rain gives me a bad cold. Making a day warm and sunny invariably brings on fever. At any rate, I don't use it much, the weather making and unmaking. Only in emergencies. Most of the time the weather does a fine job all on its own."

"Don't you get people coming to you, asking for rain for their crops and such?"

"Not many know, these days. I prefer it that way."

Brie spooned stew into their bowls. "Hanna," she began, "the pictures on the fire arrow, you called them story bands?"

Hanna nodded. "Each one, unraveled, tells a story of Dungal's past. Only a wyll, or a sorcerer, can unravel the bands."

"In the mountains, during the storm, I saw one unravel."

Hanna raised her eyebrows.

"I was ill, half-dead, probably hallucinating. It does not mean that I have draoicht," said Brie defensively. "At any rate, what I saw was a girl with fair hair on top of a seawall and the water rising."

"That would be Fionna. There are many tales of Fionna. She was queen not so very long ago, perhaps fifty years. One of our greatest queens, in truth." Hanna paused, looking thoughtful. "The story band must have been about the great flood."

"Do you know the story?"

Hanna gave a look of disdain. "Every Dungalan knows that story."

"Will you tell it to me?" Brie asked humbly.

Hanna slowly lit her pipe. "Fionna was the middle of

three sisters; their mother was Queen Ilior. Dungal is traditionally ruled by a queen, though if there is none alive,
as now, then a prince may rule. Golden-haired and beautiful, Fionna was the most headstrong of the three sisters.
After her elder sister, she was next in line to be queen, but
she was little interested in her royal heritage. As a child she
was a wild one, always off somewhere getting into mischief.
She had a particular fascination with the sea, loved to mess
about in boats and was always pestering the fishermen. As
is true of most with royal blood, she had draoicht."

"She was a wyll?"

"Not exactly. The royal draoicht is more like that of a
Sea Dyak sorcerer."

"All these different kinds of magic; I don't know how
you keep track of them all," Brie said with a smile.

Hanna ignored her, intent on her tale. "Fionna was just
six years old when the bad rains came. It was during the dark
months, and it seemed that it would never stop raining.

"Now, the royal seat, or Sedd, as we call it, lies on the
coast. Sedd Brennhin. That part of Dungal, in the center
of the country, consists mainly of low-lying flatlands, rich
farmland. There is a network of dykes and sluice gates that
protect Sedd Brennhin and the nearby town of Mira from
high water.

"Fionna loved rain and storms, as she loved all manner
of wild things, and no matter the weather she would roam
the land and seaside by herself. That was why she was out
that day when most were snugged up warm in their houses.
The watchman who was supposed to patrol the dyke was
asleep in his armchair, his feet soaking in a bucket of warm
water, for he had a bad chest cold.

"All around the town of Mira and the royal Sedd the creeks were swollen, and the River Caldew had risen beyond the top of its banks.

"Fionna saw the first crack in the dyke. She watched in fear as the thin web of lines grew thicker and longer. She knew at once there was not time to run for help, and she was frightened. But Fionna remembered a time she had made the earth open up when she wanted to see where a busy mole had gotten to. She wondered if perhaps she could close the crack in the dyke the same way.

"She concentrated very hard and quite soon the crack closed. Her head ached, but she felt very pleased with herself. Then she noticed another crack snaking along the wall farther up. She concentrated again and it worked again, but cracks kept appearing, faster than she could close them. By then her head was pounding until she thought it would burst, like the dam, but she kept all her energies focused on the cracks.

"Water had begun spouting. Fionna felt panic rise in her. She was too young, she should never have tried; she should have run for help. But it was too late. She began to picture the dam giving way and all the water she could feel pressing against it on the other side would pour through and the village of Mira would be overwhelmed and all its villagers drowned. And Sedd Brennhin, even that could well be washed away, with all her family: sisters, mother, and father...

"Fionna took a very deep breath and put all of herself, body and spirit, into holding, building, strengthening the dam. Light exploded in her head and she felt herself very near death, but she held on. And then the dam was whole and strong and unbroken. Fionna let out a small sigh and collapsed at the foot of the dam.

"They found her there after the storm, half-dead and half-witted. They took her to the local Sea Dyak sorcerer. He brought all his healing power to bear. Worked over her for fourteen days and nights. But it still took her a full year to recover.

"All her hair fell out, they say. When it grew back it was pure white, the gold was gone. She stayed inside her room at Sedd Brennhin for one entire year. After that, she did not use draoicht. No one knew if it was because the effort of holding back the flood had drained it all out of her, or if she simply chose never to use it again."

Brie was silent. "What happened after? How did she become queen?"

They had finished their meal, and Hanna moved to the fire, removing a coal to light her pipe. She pressed the hot ember into the tobacco with a calloused thumb. A perfect smoke ring emerged from her mouth.

"Well, as I said before, Fionna was beautiful, too beautiful for anyone's good, even with her pure white hair. When she grew older it was the kind of beauty men make fools of themselves over, fighting each other and such nonsense. Fionna hated all that. Tried to hide her beauty, wore plain clothes, shawls half over her face, once she even cut her white hair close to the head like a man's. None of it did any good. Finally she got fed up and ran off. Disappeared for more than five years. No one knew where she went. Some guessed Eirren. Others thought she'd disguised herself and actually become a Traveler, roaming about Dungal.

"She never told anyone where she had been during those

five years. When she returned she seemed to have settled down a bit. She was still beautiful, but she didn't have that same wild beauty. She took a Dungalan husband before too long. A fisherman. They had a son—a wild lad he turned out to be. No one could rein that one in."

"But when did she become queen?"

"Oh, that was later. Her mother ruled for many years, but then was taken by a fever that also took Fionna's older sister, so the crown fell to Fionna. She lived a long life and was said to have been more than one hundred years old when she died.

"When she got too old to rule, she handed the crown to her nephew Durwydd; her own son had long since disappeared, run away to sea and was presumed to be dead. She retired to a small fishing village up north."

Innumerable smoke circles were spinning among the rafters. Hanna watched them with an air of satisfaction.

"She was a great queen, revered by the people of Dungal. I'm afraid her nephew Durwydd takes after Fionna but little."

"How is that?"

"He's weak-minded, afraid to make decisions. This summer there've been problems with drought, and the fishing is poor. Prince Durwydd sits in Sedd Brennhin, wringing his hands and hoping the problems will go away." Frowning slightly, Hanna refilled her pipe. "Ah well, I suppose there could be worse rulers. He is a good man at heart."

The following day as Brie made new arrows for her quiver and Hanna fed a bottle to a newly born lamb that had lost its mother, Hanna said, "When you were sick, Biri, you called out a name, several times."

"What name?" asked Brie.

"Collun."

"Oh." She colored slightly. "He is a friend."

"Is he also Wurme-killer?"

"You know of the wurme?"

"Even in Dungal, songs have been sung of Wurme-killer. Remember, the Isle of Thule is not so very far from the northern tip of Dungal. There is a strong current and whirlpool, called Corryvrecken, which keep Scathians from our shores. But we did not know if even the strongest whirlpool would hamper the progress of Naid should it have chosen to leave Thule." She paused. "There was also word of a woman warrior who rode with the son of Cuillean." Hanna was looking straight at Brie.

"It was Collun who killed the Wurme," Brie said. "And bears the scars."

Hanna was not listening. "You have come to Dungal bearing a fire arrow. I wonder..."

"What?"

"I do not know. Perhaps you have come here for something beyond your own vengeance."

Brie shifted in her chair, uncomfortable. She leaned over to set her bowl of porridge on the floor for Fara to finish, wondering if Hanna, like Collun, disapproved of her quest.

Fara finished the porridge and went to the hearth, where the dogs lay. Brie was surprised to see her stalk over to Jip. With the air of one bestowing a great favor, she settled beside the dog. Jip stirred, lifted an eyelid, then returned to sleep.

The day came when Brie could wait no longer. Hanna frowned, saying her leg needed more time to heal, but Brie shook her head. She said it was because she feared losing Bricriu's trail, but, in truth, she did not; she was certain she would find him in the bog with her father's killers.

Because Hanna was a Traveler, she had journeyed through the bog and its surrounding area and so was able to tell Brie what she would find there. She also told Brie of the powerful sorcerer, Yldir, who lived as a hermit at the center of the bog.

"I am half-inclined to journey with you," said Hanna reflectively. "I have always wanted to lay eyes on the sorcerer Yldir. But I cannot. The farmer Tharda will be coming at the end of the moon cycle with his two sons and their dogs to guide the flock back to his sheep farm. I must stay until then. Then I go to the coastal village Ardara."

"Where the fisherman Jacan lives."

"Yes. And though as Traveler I have no home, I have a soft spot for Ardara for it is where I spent part of my childhood."

"Hanna, if I should not..."—Brie paused—"make it to Ardara, will you bear the news of his daughter to Jacan?"

"I will. You have done well with your lessons," Hanna added with an approving look. "You are beginning to sound almost like a native Dungalan."

"You are a good teacher," replied Brie, pleased with the compliment.

"But as for going into Bog Maglu, well, I've known sheep with more sense than that."

"I must."

Hanna shrugged. "Then we may or we may not meet again."

Brie nodded, but she could not see beyond Bog Maglu. She suddenly reached over and hugged Hanna, surprising the older woman. "Thank you, Hanna," she said softly. The dogs wagged their tails wildly, licking Brie's face as she bent down to give them an affectionate farewell pat. Fara touched noses with both dogs with an air of queenly for-bearance, then flicked her tail in Hanna's direction. Brie and the faol left the havotty.

Hanna had told Brie that Bog Maglu was not one bog but many, stretching many leagues across the lower belly of Dungal. At the heart of the vast bogland did lie a single bog, which was called Maglu, its many layered blanket of peat covering ancient waters. The standing stones called the stones of memory thrust out of the water at the very center of Maglu.

Brie had left the crutch Hanna carved for her at the havotty, and during the early days of her journey her leg ached; by the end of a day's walking she was exhausted, with barely the energy to start a fire. But with each day her strength began to return, and by the time she came to the bogland she limped only slightly.

She came across an occasional sheep carcass, the flesh mostly gone and the bones bleaching white in the summer sun. But though she kept a vigilant eye out for gabha, she saw no one.

She had been traveling almost a fortnight when Brie noticed the ground beginning to change. At first it grew softer, spongier. Then damp patches started to appear. The farther she went the more waterlogged the ground became, until she was sinking to her ankles in a combination of water and mud. The terrain was flat, treeless.

Brie could not imagine a more forsaken place. There was no animal life; indeed, the only sign of life at all, aside from herself and Fara, were the midges, clouds of them hovering around her face. They did not bite but made a low humming sound that began to prey on Brie's already taut nerves.

In the Blue Stack Mountains, Brie had felt alone, but there had been life all around: soaring kestrels, small brown hares emerging from their holes, an occasional deer, vibrantly colored wildflowers, and stately pine trees. Here in the bogland was nothing but the reek of death and decay.

There was nowhere dry to sit, so she ate her meals crouching on the soggy ground, her boots almost completely submerged in water.

Nor was there anywhere dry enough to make camp, so Brie slept little, catching brief catnaps in that same crouching position. She was continually bedeviled by a thorned plant with black berries, which tore at her damp leggings, and she often blundered into deep patches of brackish water, once sinking all the way to her waist. Fara was able to stay on the bog's surface, barely dampening her paws.

One night Brie was startled by occasional flashes of light from will-o'-the-wisps—small clouds of bog gas that would spontaneously light, burn a few moments, and then disappear. Brie had seen will-o'-the-wisps back in Eirren, but never so many and on such eerie terrain. Fara made a game of leaping at them and once almost slid into a large pool of water.

By the time dawn came, Brie was covered with mud and her nerves were strung tight. In the pale light she spotted a small cluster of buildings some distance away. The hamlet of Muckish, she supposed. Hanna had told her of this small enclave of farmers who harvested the delicate yellow cymlu-berries that thrived in bogs. Brie heaved a sigh of relief. She had begun to doubt the possibility of ever coming across human habitation.

Fara, who had loped ahead, let out a sound. Wearily Brie squelched over to her and saw that the faol had found a raised wooden walkway. In one direction the walkway stretched ahead of them toward the buildings and in the other it snaked away to the north. Brie clambered up onto the track.

It was a great relief to be able to raise her legs without the bog sucking at each footfall. She was sorely tempted to curl up on the wooden planking and go to sleep, but she kept moving, her eyes fixed on the nearest building.

She stumbled to the small wooden door of the house, and before she could knock, it was opened by a gaunt woman in a berry-stained overall. The woman's eyes widened, but she silently guided Brie around to the back of the building, gesturing toward a wooden screen, behind which stood a tub filled with water. She spoke several sentences in Dungalan.

From her lessons with Hanna, Brie recognized the word for wash, and she gratefully began stripping off her mud-encrusted outer clothing.

"I do not speak your language well," Brie said.

The woman shook her head, indicating she did not understand Brie. She handed Brie a clean cloth with which to dry herself and then disappeared.

Sleepily Brie washed off as much of the mud as she could. Dressed in clean clothes from her pack, she emerged from behind the screen. The woman reappeared and gestured Brie into the house, where she was given a simple meal of bread and cheese, followed by a small bowl of cymlu-berries and cream. Brie had never tasted the fruit before and found it delicious. She used her halting Dungalan to express her pleasure in the meal as Fara leaped into Brie's lap and finished the cream at the bottom of the bowl.

When Brie had finished, the woman pointed to a pallet in a corner of the room. Brie crossed to it and, placing her quiver, bow, and pack next to her, was asleep almost as soon as her head reached the small woven pillow. Fara settled herself at Brie's shoulder.

When she woke, Brie saw that the woman's husband had returned. It turned out that he spoke a little Eirrenian, and using an awkward mixture of the two languages, Brie was able to convey her gratitude for their hospitality. Then she asked about Bricriu. The man nodded and described an abandoned hut some distance from the berry farmers that had been occupied by five men. They were Scathians, the man thought, and he said he had seen a man fitting Bricriu's description join them at the hut.

With barely suppressed excitement, Brie described her father's murderers, the three Scathians she sought. Though the berry farmer said he had not seen them up close, he said none of the men wore an eye-patch, but two of the Scathians roughly matched Brie's descriptions.

"We know not why they came here. But they did not bother us, and we did not bother them," the man said in broken Eirrenian.

"How long have they been here?"

"Many moon cycles. Five perhaps. But they are gone now. With the man with bad leg, they left."

Brie rose, her body tense. "When?"

"Two days maybe, they go."

"What direction?"

"To the center. To Maglu."

Shouldering her pack and quiver, Brie was already at the door when she remembered herself and tried to offer silver coins to the couple for their hospitality. But they would not take them.

Brie made her way on the wooden planking for some distance, passing through the farmholds of the berry farmers. Stretching on either side of her were vast tracts of brilliant yellow cymlu-berries floating in water. Brie could see the farmers wading through the berries in their black hip boots.

When the berry fields were behind her, Brie had to leave the walkway. She plunged regretfully back into the mud and water.

She knew Maglu when she came to it. It was different from the bogland she had been traveling through. This was a raised bog, with a carpet of peat and humus that floated on top of deep water. The mat of peat was thick, an arm's length deep in some places, and it easily supported a man's weight. Dwarf larch and spruce trees grew out of the mat, reaching no higher than Brie's shoulder. It was like a floating miniature forest.

Following Hanna's advice, Brie tied a blue scarf, the brightest bit of clothing she owned, to a cinnamon fern marking the place where she was entering the bog. As Brie stepped onto it, the mat tilted crazily, and when she walked between them the dwarf trees also tilted.

The bog stretched before her, a mosaic of trees, hillocks and hollows, ferns, sedges, mosses, and occasional pools of tea-colored water. She could dimly make out the shapes of the stones of memory in the distance, pushing their way up into the gray sky.

It was humid in the bog, and though the sun was not very hot, Brie quickly began to sweat. After her foot broke through the mat a few times, drenching her leg with bitter-cold water, she learned to recognize the signs of thin patches—standing pools of water and a lack of shrubs or trees.

When she had first entered Maglu, Brie had seen a few birds, a white-throated sparrow and a marsh hawk, but the deeper she journeyed, the less she saw of any kind of wild-life. The only sound she heard was the perpetual hum of midges and other insects.

The sorcerer Yldir was standing by the larger of the two stones of memory, his palm flat on the surface. She walked toward him, nervous. He was not as she had expected, wizened and elderly, but rather was erect and muscular, with broad powerful shoulders. He had long, burning copper hair tied back with a leather thong. As she drew closer, she saw his age on his face, not in lines or clefts, but in his eyes. They were brilliant and depthless and clear. Meeting his gaze was painful.

"Breo-Saight," he said, and his voice, too, surged with vitality. He somehow did not seem real to Brie. "Come. We will break bread. Then you will show me saeth-tan, the fire arrow."

Brie followed him meekly to a primitive one-room wooden hut. Indicating with a gesture that Brie should wait outside, Yldir stooped and entered the hut. He reappeared soon after with a thin loaf of bread.

"Missenbread," he explained. "Foul to the taste, but it strengthens." He sat cross-legged on the quaking mat, and Brie followed suit, facing him. Fara settled at Brie's side, alert. Yldir broke off a piece of the thin dry bread.

"The others are here. The time will come for meeting them."

Warily, Brie looked around her. It was late in the afternoon and a mist had come up, sending the dwarf trees into shadow against the murky sky.

"When I came here from the coast I sought quiet. The sea can be a noisy place. It teems with life. But there is life, too, in the bog. You have to look for it. Birth, decay, death—it is all here."

Brie sat before the Sea Dyak sorcerer, her legs crossed, eating bread that tasted of mold. Somewhere in the mist around them were perhaps six men, two of them her father's murderers, and yet she felt completely at ease, as though there were no other place she could be.

As she sat, chewing, all her senses became keener, and she was suddenly aware of the life of the bog. The bog turtle emerging from one hiding place and slowly making its way to another. The copper butterflies fluttering brown wings burnished with a purple gloss. There were damsel-flies and green frogs, spiders and bees and insect-eating plants that grew in abundance—butterwort and sundews—each carrying out the endless cycle of life, death, and decomposition.

Abruptly the Sea Dyak sorcerer spoke, seeking her eyes with his. "Your father was brave, but he made mistakes. They were not your mistakes. You were only one in Ramhar Forest, and it was *necessary*," he said, laying a powerful, broad hand on her arm, "that you live."

Brie blinked back sudden tears.

Then he said, "May I see the arrow?"

Brie began to reach for her quiver, but the sorcerer held up his hand with a small shake of his head.

Brie looked past Yldir and saw a Scathian materialize out of the fog. He was tall and had a yellowish cast to his eyes: Brie recognized the Scathian who was part morg. Once more she heard the clang of swords, smelled the stench of blood as it soaked into the roots of the trees in Ramhar Forest. A dull pounding thudded in her ears.

"So," Yldir said, rising. "They are here."

# TEN

## Yldir

**F**ive others slowly appeared, with Bricriu in the lead. They formed a ring around the sorcerer and the girl. Bricriu grinned at Brie with broken teeth; his hollow eyes held a look of something like victory. And Brie understood now that he had led her here purposefully, slowing and waiting while her leg healed at the havotty, making his trail obvious so she could not fail to find him.

The thick-armed killer, who had tortured her father with a black spear, walked just behind Bricriu. Brie could see the black spear in his hand. He also carried a box strapped to his back. It was a worn, crudely made wooden box, as long and as wide as his back. The three remaining

men were Scathians Brie had never seen before; all were large and brutal.

Yldir looked undisturbed. He had expected them. The Scathians would not meet his eyes, but one of the largest pulled a sword and advanced on the sorcerer. He got within a foot of Yldir, then the sorcerer held out his hand, palm up. On it were what looked to be three small black seeds. He tossed them at the feet of the Scathian. A fine gray dust burst from the seeds, wafting into the man's face. He coughed once, then toppled over, dead.

Bricriu let out a cry of fear and backed away, but the four remaining Scathians began to close in. Yldir squatted and struck his fist against the peat mat, bursting through the surface and thrusting his arm down until it was submerged to the shoulder. Quicker than thought, he withdrew his hand, which was caked in slimy black mud. Calmly he rolled the mud into a snakelike shape, his hands deft and almost invisible they moved so swiftly. The snake lengthened and became a rope of mud. With his powerful arms Yldir lifted it high and flicked it like a whip. It hit a Scathian at chest level with a wet, cracking sound and wound around his neck, growing tighter and tighter. The Scathian clawed at the slimy black thing, but he, too, was quickly dead.

The Scathian carrying the black spear and the box on his back had halted in his tracks, as had the Scathian-morg, but the other Scathian jumped on Yldir, a dagger in his fist. The sorcerer met the charge and, without seeming to strain a muscle, flipped the man around and broke his neck, dropping him gently to the ground.

Bricriu screamed and backed farther and farther away,

his eyes darting between Yldir and the two remaining Scathians. The killer with the box dropped it on the ground, and Brie felt the mat quake underfoot. Yldir gazed at the box with curiosity.

As the Scathian wrestled with the rusty latch, symbols appeared and writhed across the wooden surface. They were unintelligible to Brie, weird, runelike. She looked at Yldir's face and saw surprise there. It frightened her. It did not seem possible that anything could take those knowing eyes by surprise. But before she could move or speak, the killer had succeeded in unloosing the latch and threw open the lid of the box.

A mass of white moths flew up and bore themselves directly to Yldir. They swarmed around his head. Through the swirling whiteness Brie glimpsed the sorcerer's startled face, then watched his expression change to one of utter bafflement. Brie felt sick seeing the knowledge and power seep out of his magnificent eyes. He stumbled about heavily, his powerful arms swatting ineffectually at the spinning moths.

Yldir's faltering steps led him toward the standing stones, and soon he had bumped up against the taller of the two. Like a drowning man, he wrapped his arms around the stone and abruptly the moths left him, spiraling upward. They were soon lost to sight. Brie started toward the sorcerer, but heard a grunt behind her.

The killer with the black spear held it upraised, pointed directly at her. Brie stood still. He made no move to throw the spear and, looking over at the Scathian-morg, Brie saw that he, too, held a spear in his hands. He had just ignited it with a small torch.

Brie watched in horror as the Scathian-morg launched the spear at Yldir. It cleaved the air and pierced the sorcerer between his shoulder blades. Yldir's mouth opened, but no sound came out.

Flames traveled quickly along the spear shaft, dropping embers on the quaking peat mat. Yldir's tunic caught fire. Brie let out a cry and, despite the spear still aimed at her, ran to the sorcerer. Burning her fingers, she pulled the flaming spear from his back and began beating out the flames on his clothing with her arms.

Fire flared up from the dry sedges on the mat. Smoke was everywhere. The two Scathians moved slowly toward Brie and Yldir. There was no sign of Bricriu.

Brie took the sorcerer in her arms, pulling him around to the back side of the stone. For a moment, as she held him, his eyes were radiant with the last of his power. He spoke. "Golden head. Eye like sea foam. Looking over the sea. Great evil. The arrow. Queen Fionna..." Then his eyes emptied and he was dead.

Brie gently laid him down, feeling suddenly bereft. But she forced herself to stand and cautiously peered around the stone.

She could not see either of her father's murderers. Thick smoke obscured her vision. Brie remembered what Hanna had told her about the dry summer and she realized that even the bog was vulnerable; despite the water underneath, all that grew on top was overdry.

Suddenly the thick-armed Scathian with the black spear leaped toward her from out of the smoke. He tripped over a dwarf spruce, and Brie dodged around the stone and ran. The mat tilted crazily, making it hard to move fast. She almost collided with the wooden box, the runes still glowing, evil and eerie, in the smoke. Behind her the Scathian was back on his feet and gaining on her.

Brie veered toward Yldir's wooden hut. She ducked behind it, the Scathian close on her heels. Then the hut was suddenly ablaze, and they were showered with live motes of flame and burning wood. The Scathian's cloak ignited and he dropped to the ground, rolling back and forth to smother the fire.

Brie ran. The smoke choked her and made it nearly impossible to see. With a pang, she realized she had lost track of Fara. She ran blindly, occasionally stumbling over shrubs and small trees. Finally, overwhelmed by smoke, she sank to her knees, coughing violently.

She crawled forward, one hand tearing through the ground and sinking into water. A thin section of the mat. She abruptly backed up, still coughing, her heart racing.

Then the mat tilted slightly and a pair of legs appeared beside her. She looked up into the yellowish eyes of the Scathian-morg. He smiled and savagely kicked at her. His boot caught her on the forehead, hard, and she reeled back, ears ringing. But as she fell she flung out her hand, catching the Scathian around his ankle. She yanked with all her strength and he fell heavily onto his back, landing directly where the mat was its thinnest. He broke through with a splash. The Scathian surfaced for a moment and gasped, shocked by the cold of water that hadn't seen the sun in untold years. He struggled to pull himself out, but the mat crumbled away around him and he sank down again. Brie could hear him thrashing as he was engulfed by the slimy black mud of the bog's bottom.

Bubbles formed on the surface. For a moment Brie sat

frozen where she was, blood dripping from her forehead. Then she inched forward, but the mat in front of her started to give way. She froze again and, as she watched, the bubbles grew fewer, then were gone.

Smoke billowed around her. Overcome by another fit of coughing, Brie stood and floundered away from the gaping hole in the peat. She had no idea of direction now. But she kept moving, trying to keep ahead of the fire. She could not think; she could only move, coughing and wiping away the blood from the wound on her forehead as it trickled into her eyes.

And then he was there, a tree-length away, the killer with the black spear. His back was to her, his cloak in charred tatters and his hair singed. Brie swung her bow around, snatched an arrow from her quiver, and pulled back the string. She thought of her father, and a sob rose in her throat.

She wanted to let the arrow fly, pierce the killer through the heart with no mercy, as he had shown her father no mercy.

She could not do it. Not with his back turned.

"Scathian," she called, her voice raw.

He pivoted, saw Brie, and for a moment froze, then his arm came up and she could see the black spear gripped in his right fist. Smoke filled her nose and throat.

"Father," she whispered. She could not breathe. The Scathian was drawing back his arm. Tears standing in her eyes, she started to release the arrow, faltered a moment, then let fly.

The arrow sliced a path through the smoke and pierced the Scathian in his right shoulder. He staggered, then surged forward, running headlong toward Brie. The mat under Brie's feet pitched with his footfalls. She reached back for another arrow but had lost the distance; he was too close. Dropping her bow, she seized her dagger.

With a roar, the Scathian thrust his black spear at Brie. She dodged the blow, but he was quick and lunged again. The sharp point grazed her cheek.

She kicked his arm away, and the black spear went whistling to the side, lodging point first in the mat. Then the Scathian tackled her, his thick body pinning her face-down on the mat's surface. Brie had a horrible image of the two of them plunging through into Maglu's ancient waters, but the mat held.

His body holding her down, the Scathian stretched forward for his spear. As he pulled it from the peat, Brie shifted her weight and drove her elbow up into the arrow that protruded from his shoulder. The Scathian let out a harsh cry of pain. In that moment, Brie plunged her dagger into the Scathian's neck.

Blood gushed forth and Brie watched as the killer's eyes emptied of life.

She had sought this man's death, but the feeling of triumph she had expected did not come. Pushing his body off hers, she lay still beside the Scathian. His blood was everywhere—on her clothing, in her hair; she could even taste it in her mouth. She rolled onto her knees and vomited until her stomach held nothing.

She lay quiet for a time, then sat up, feeling a hundred years old. A thin windless rain began to fall.

"Father," she whispered, "you are avenged." But the words were as empty as the dead man's eyes. All was ashes and blood in her mouth. She swayed as if she were weeping, but no tears came; not for the man who had drowned in brown water, not for the man who lay dead beside her, and not for herself, for the thing inside her that had died as well.

The arrow had come back, as Collun had said it would, piercing her own heart.

Her body quaked with tearless grief until finally she let her head fall to the mat. When she rose, she purposefully set to work. She cut a hole in the mat and, taking the man's body by his large shoulders, slid him into the water head-first.

She found a branch and, with her knife, whittled it into a flat piece of wood. In Eirrenian she carved the date and the words "Five Scathians died this day in Bog Maglu."

She stuck the piece of wood upright into the mat. Then she walked away.

Brie did not know where Fara was. She hadn't seen the faol since the sorcerer Yldir's death. Brie trudged on, her eyes probing the wafting smoke for any sign of the white animal.

Then she spotted a dash of blue. The scarf she had tied to the cinnamon fern. She had come to the edge of Bog Maglu.

There was a movement near the fern. Someone was crouching in the sedge. Then the person stood and came toward Brie. It was Hanna. Jip and Maor burst out of the grass and shrubs, greeting Brie enthusiastically.

The older woman's eyes widened when she saw Brie. Silently Hanna held out her arms. With a sigh, Brie let the woman enfold her. Slowly, tonelessly, she told Hanna of Yldir's death. The older woman closed her eyes in sorrow.

"We must go back," Hanna said, "and bury him."

"I know."

Hanna cleaned Brie's blood-streaked face and bandaged the wound on her forehead. Then they went back into Maglu, Hanna, Brie, and the two dogs. The rain had reduced the fire to a smoldering blanket of thick gray smoke that smelled of burnt chicory. They passed the wooden marker Brie had fashioned for the Scathians. Hanna saw it but said nothing.

They found Yldir's body beside the stones of memory. Using few words, Hanna instructed Brie in the Dungalan burial ways, and by day's end they had fashioned a small rough-hewn boat for use as a casket. They spoke little as they worked. Hanna once asked Brie if she had found the crippled man she sought. Brie replied that he might have perished in the bog. After that, Hanna did not ask Brie any more questions.

Gently they placed the sorcerer's body in the boat, a skin bag of cymlu-berry wine at his elbow. As they did, Brie noticed birds circling above. They were seabirds—kittiwakes, gannets, guillemots, fulmars, and cormorants. The seabirds were uncharacteristically silent, and one by one they began settling on the stones of memory. By the time Hanna and Brie had cut a large hole in the peat, the stones were covered with birds. And as they slid Yldir's boat-casket into the ancient water of the bog, the birds gave tongue, each to their own individual song. It was loud, even harsh, but somehow beautiful.

Brie thought of the other two bodies that lay in the same waters, the men she had killed. Then her gaze fell on the wooden box. It was charred, but the runes on it still faintly glowed. As she watched, they flickered out.

Meanwhile, Hanna approached the stones of memory. The seabirds on the larger of the two stones lifted off, almost as one, and hovered above. Hanna kneeled by the stone and, using a sharp-pointed piece of iron she had found in the remains of Yldir's hut, began carving Dungalan words at the base of the stone. It took her much of the night, but when she was done she read aloud to Brie, " 'Yldir of the sea did die this day in Bog Maglu/So shall his tale be told as long as the stones of memory stand.' "

The seabirds suddenly rose up and with a whoosh ascended to the sky. They were soon lost to sight. Then Brie felt something brush against her legs. It was Fara. Crouching down beside her, Brie ran her hand over the faol's back. Fara arched against the girl's hand. Her white fur was scorched and damp. Brie guessed she had swum under the peat mat to escape the fire.

Then Hanna, Brie, the two dogs, and the faol left Bog Maglu.

"Will you come with me to Ardara?" Hanna asked.

Brie was silent, threading the panner thong through her fingers. She knew not what to say; it mattered little to her where she journeyed.

"Or do you return to Eirren?"

Still Brie did not answer.

"When the snows come to the Blue Stacks, you will not be able to travel through, not until the spring thaw. But the snows will not come for two moon cycles, so there is time for you to visit Dungal, if that is your wish."

Silence.

"Biri," Hanna said, her voice gentle, "come with me to Ardara. You will find a welcome there."

And so Brie went to Ardara. She had a message for one who lived there. And who better to deliver tidings of death? she thought grimly.

During the journey, Brie remained silent. She did all that she had done before Maglu, walking, eating, sleeping, but she felt like a shadow, lost and without mooring, as though the thread that connected her from one day to the next had snapped. She set one foot ahead of the other, but knew not why.

For so long she had sought this one thing: the death of her father's killers. Now that she had achieved it, or nearly so, the deed stuck in her throat. Before her father's death... what had directed her steps then? She could barely remember, but it seemed she had always been thrust forward, like a small boat driven by a great wind, to be the best at whatever she undertook—the best archer, the best trail finder, the best at building a stone wall. Except for those few months with Collun at Cuillean's dun, she could remember no time when she had known peace.

And Collun. What would he think of her now? Would he pity her, or would he recoil from the blood on her hands? She could not think of Collun now. Better to think of nothing at all.

Bogland gave way to rich farming land. Cozy, whitewashed farmhouses were scattered here and there along the way, and the people were friendly to the wandering Traveler and her silent companion.

Hanna and Brie arrived in Ardara at midday. The town was bright and bustling and full of vigor. But Brie felt like a specter moving among these people with their active, certain lives. Ardara was a well-cared-for town, if not a very prosperous one. The buildings were solidly built, and though many of the boats bobbing in the harbor or pulled up on shore could have used fresh paint, they still looked snug and seaworthy. There were all sizes of boats, from curraghs—rowing boats with turned-up prows to help them in the surf—to two-sailed ketches forty feet long or more, for handling the deep water of the sea. Dogs were everywhere on the streets of the village: intelligent, strong dogs like Jip and Maor.

Dungalans either were fair-haired with dark eyes or had hair which bore that distinctive copper hue, like Rilla's and Yldir's, with matching coppery eyes. Most of the men (and a few younger women, though not many) wore the distinctive garb of the Dungalan fisherman: trousers of homespun tweed held up by a multicolored, braided belt called a criosanna, and thick flannel shirts, dyed indigo.

Hanna and Brie did not stop in town but traveled on until they came to a large farmhold to the north of Ardara. The farmhouse stood on a rise. Looking back from the door Brie had a clear view of the sea and fishing boats, in miniature, stretched out toward the horizon.

The farmer's wife, Lotte, greeted Hanna warmly. She spoke fast, in Dungalan, and Brie understood only a few words. Hanna introduced Brie as Eirrenian, translating the woman's words. Lotte looked a little surprised, her eyes caught by the faol. But she was welcoming to Brie and tried to speak more slowly so that Brie could follow what she said.

Her husband was out in the barley field, Lotte said, and had just been saying this morning that he wished the Traveler would come soon. "It seems as though harvesttime comes earlier every year," Lotte commented. "And Garmon believes there will be an early frost." She pressed warm buttered bread into their hands, and together they made their way to the barley field.

Farmer Garmon was a prosperous-looking man with gray side-whiskers and an open smile. He embraced Hanna warmly, said his crops were well nigh bursting. Then he welcomed Brie, saying that any friend of the Traveler was a friend to him, and did she know any good tales from Eirren?

"How is your daughter in Dungloe? And your son in Mira? And my friend Lom?" asked Hanna.

"They are all well. I have another grandbairn, Sophe's second son. And as for Lom, he is spending more and more time working on that boat of his. I'll be lucky to tear him away come harvest day," Garmon said. Hanna explained to Brie that Lom was the youngest of Garmon's sons and daughters and the only one still living in Ardara.

"A fine son he is, too, though I lost him to the sea long ago." Brie could see disappointment on the man's face, but acceptance as well.

"You will like Lom," said Hanna to Brie. "He works with Jacan and his son on their fishing boat until his own is built."

Garmon showed them to the barn where they would sleep. "But treat the farmhouse as your home," he said.

"Shall we call on Jacan?" Hanna said when the farmer had left them.

Brie nodded.

The fisherman Jacan had a lean, weathered face, dark copper hair and beard, and the keen blue eyes Brie recognized from Rilla's panner work. He wore a leather fishing apron and smelled of fish.

His son, Ferg, was almost the duplicate of Rilla—copper hair, pale skin—but Jacan's other daughter, Hyslin, had fair hair and rose-colored cheeks. She had been paring potatoes, her sleeves pushed up over her elbows, when Brie and Hanna arrived.

They greeted Hanna warmly, but were wary of Brie, and of Fara, who sat on her haunches by the front door, eyes half closed. When Brie entered the cheerful, comfortable room with its smells of fresh bread and fish, she felt like an ill dark wind blowing cold through the house.

"There is bad news," Hanna said in Dungalan.

"Go on," replied Jacan, his face suddenly taut.

"Rilla is dead."

Hyslin let out a cry, dropping her paring knife. Ferg's pale skin went a shade paler.

"How?" asked Jacan.

"By goat-men. Murdered." Brie stepped forward, speaking low in halting Dungalan.

"The gabha?" Jacan looked disbelieving.

"I was there," Brie said. "I saw. She bade me bring you the news. And I brought her panners as well." She handed Jacan the leather pouch.

He stared down at it. "What of Ladran?"

"Dead, too. He...died going to Rilla."

"She never should have married that raff," said Ferg, anguished.

Jacan was silent. Hyslin lifted her apron to her face and cried into it.

"We stay with Farmer Garmon until harvest," Hanna

said to the fisherman, then added, "I am grieved for you, Jacan."

Brie, Hanna, and the faol left the house. Brie touched the panner around her neck.

"There is another I would have you meet," Hanna said as they walked along the harbor.

"Who?" asked Brie without interest.

"Sago. He is a Sea Dyak sorcerer, like Yldir. He is not as powerful as Yldir, though perhaps he is even older. With Yldir gone, I believe Sago is the last of the Sea Dyak sorcerers in Dungal. Some say he has little draoicht left and even fewer wits. But they still come to him for advice on fishing. Indeed, there is none better."

The Sea Dyak sorcerer lived south of Ardara's harbor in a secluded inlet. His home was a small, round, one-room building, called a mote, made of white stone and seashells. At the top were lodgings for seabirds.

Sago stood waiting in the shell-lined doorway, as if he was expecting them. He wore a tunic the color of seawater, and Brie was struck by how thin he was: His arms and legs looked to be no more than bone with skin stretched over them. The dome of his head was covered by a close-fitting cap of the same seawater color as his tunic; feathery wisps of white hair protruded from the cap. His skin was worn by weather and age, but his green eyes were unclouded, and they watched intently as Brie and Hanna approached.

"So," the sorcerer said to Brie with a wink, "the arrow finds its mark."

# ELEVEN

# Ardara

**B**rie gave a start, her hand going to the panner at her neck. The sorcerer had spoken in Eirrenian. Brie looked sideways at Hanna. The older woman shrugged.

"Come." Sago led them inside.

After the brightness of water and sun, the inside of the mote seemed dim, but a window of green glass provided some light. Brie had the sensation of being underwater: Green-hued light rippled on the surfaces of things. The walls of the mote were lined with shelves made of driftwood, and each shelf was jammed with flotsam cast up by the sea—shells of all shapes and sizes, feathery sprays of seaweed, frosted sea-glass, smooth sand-coins, brittle sea stars, and many other oddments.

Inside the mote were several seabirds. One tern settled onto Sago's shoulder and ate bread crumbs from his hand.

"Some sepoa?" asked the sorcerer, holding up an empty cup encrusted with bits of many shells.

"It's a kind of tea made of seaweed, sweetened with honey and cinnamon," explained Hanna. "It's actually very good."

"Yes, please," Brie said.

They sat on cushions and drank the seaweed tea. Sago did not speak, but gazed steadily at Brie. She began to be uncomfortable under his scrutiny, and yet, as had been true with Yldir, she felt an odd rightness about being here in this cluttered, dim mote. She sipped the sepoa tea thinking it tasted almost like ginger cake.

"Yldir is dead," said Hanna.

The bird on Sago's shoulder let out a cry, sounding almost human, and beat its powerful wings.

Sago's eyes were bright, staring out the dim green window. "The water went dark, almost black, as if a cloud had passed overhead. But there was no cloud. We knew it was Yldir." His eyes suddenly twinkled, and he said,

> *"There was an old man*
> *And nothing he had,*
> *And so this old man*
> *Was said to be mad."*

Hanna gave Brie a look, then asked Sago how the fishing was today. He did not reply, just hummed the melody to the rhyme under his breath with a benign smile.

When they had finished their tea, Sago took them to a bucket hidden in the shadows at the corner of the room.

"Sumog," he said, carrying the bucket closer to the window so they could see its contents more clearly.

Coiled in the wooden pail a dead snakelike sea creature lay. It looked greenish brown in the wavery light, and its staring eyes were large and bulging, rimmed with a delicate line of orange. There was evil in the blunt snout. Brie shivered.

"What is sumog?" she asked.

"Eats all the little fishies, heigh-ho," Sago sang.

"Sago," Hanna said sternly. "Is this true? Is that why the fish supply has been poor of late?"

Sago bobbed his head several times. "Oh, yes, and yes, and yes. This is only one, but there are many more. Out there." The seabird on his shoulder squawked.

"Do the fishermen know?"

"They don't believe."

"Why not?"

"Crafty, the sumog are. Kill at night. Swift and silent. Almost invisible." Sago carried the bucket back to the shadows.

"What can be done?"

"Kill the sumog. Hunt and kill them. But only old Sago believes in sumog." He grinned. "Enough of dark. I want the sun." He led them out onto the beach.

Brie breathed in the sea air. She looked out over the sun-sparkled sea. Again she felt Sago's eyes on her. She turned to him.

"You have come home," said Sago.

"What?"

He reached over and laid his thin fingers on her breastbone. "Here."

A petrel wheeled overhead, then dived low, its feet skimming the surface of the water.

As she and Hanna made their way back to town, Hanna said, "You will get used to Sago. He has his good days and bad. But," she added with a grin, "which of us does not?"

Hanna took Brie to an inn called the Speckled Trout for their evening meal. The inn was full and noisy, with a cluster of men around the ale barrels. A gow, Hanna called them, and she signaled to one, a large-boned young man with a thatch of gorse-colored hair. He was Lom, Farmer Garmon's son, and he joined them at their table. Lom was only a few years older than Brie, but he towered over her.

"So the Traveler has returned." He grinned. He had the same open, enveloping smile as his father.

Hanna lifted her glass of ale.

"And what book did you take to the havotty this season?" Lom asked.

"The tale of Gydwyn and Cessair."

"Ah, the jeweled wings and snow-white bear cub...I look forward to hearing it during the dark months."

"How goes your boat?"

Lom's eyes lit up and he launched into a rapid description of which Brie understood almost nothing. Her eyes wandered, taking in the Ardarans as they drank and ate and talked. The innkeeper, a round-faced man with a sunken chin, was staring at Brie, a scowl thinning his lips. He looked away quickly when their eyes met.

"...in a day or two, if you'd like," Lom was saying, with a shy glance at Brie.

"Uh, I'm sorry..."

"Lom has invited us to see his boat."

Brie politely said she would like that, then turned her attention to the mutton and potatoes the unfriendly innkeeper was placing in front of her.

"We've been to Sago," Hanna said to Lom.

The innkeeper overheard and let out a snicker. "Did he caper about and sing of fish that dance and talking birds?"

"No," replied Hanna, annoyed. "He spoke of something more serious."

"Oh, and what would that be? Ladybugs in petticoats?"

There were a few guffaws from a nearby table.

"Sumog," Hanna said loudly.

"You mean that phantom fish of his that's supposedly devouring all the fish between here and Mira?"

"I saw it," Hanna stated matter-of-factly.

Silence greeted her words. Most of the people at the inn were listening to the exchange.

"Was it bigger than a whitebelly, have large horns, and breathe fire at you?" the innkeeper persisted, his lips in a sneer.

"No. It was dead, in a wooden pail. But it had the stench of evil about it."

The innkeeper opened his mouth, but Hanna continued. "I would not underestimate the Sea Dyak sorcerer, were I you, innkeeper. He is not the half-wit he would have you believe. Now, I, for one, am ready to eat."

Shutting his mouth, the innkeeper moved away to a table of his cronies. They muttered back and forth, casting sidelong glances at Brie and Hanna.

Very early the next morning, Hanna went off with Farmer Garmon to discuss plans for beginning the harvest, and Brie, finding herself at loose ends, directed her steps toward the harbor.

Leaning against a stone wall, she gazed out at the bustle of activity. Many boats were already out, though some were still preparing for the day's fishing. Yldir had been right. There was so much of life around the sea: the constantly moving water; the birds wheeling and calling overhead; the fishing boats with the men aboard heaving, hauling, tightening, spooling, mending.

She felt outside it all. As if her soul were somehow back in the bog.

Watching, she stayed at the stone wall through the morning. Then she caught sight of a trim, whitewashed boat returning to harbor. It had a familiar look to it, as if she had seen it before somewhere. As it came closer she was able to make out the words *Storm Petrel* in black paint on the prow. Of course. Rilla had spoken of the Storm Petrel, Jacan's boat. She watched the craft with pleasure as the four men aboard, Jacan, Ferg, Lom, and another man Brie did not know, pulled the boat into the dock. Jacan caught sight of Brie and gave her a nod of recognition. Though she had no certainty of a welcome from them, Brie found herself walking down to the Storm Petrel. She had to see it up close.

Jacan's keen eyes watched her come. He must have read her face, for without being asked he invited her aboard. He introduced her to the fourth man on the boat, a spry older man named Henle, and she exchanged greetings with Lom, though she barely was aware of doing so, so caught up was she in her up close look at the Storm Petrel.

She drank it all in—the clean lines of the prow, the way the deck boards fit snugly together, the symmetry of the mast and yard, the finely proportioned hull. And all Brie could think of was that she must sail on this boat, out on the sea.

"It was a poor day for fishing," Jacan was saying. "We'll try again tomorrow. Perhaps you—" He stopped, almost as if he was surprised at himself. Ferg glanced over, also surprised.

"If you will have me, I would come with you tomorrow," Brie said loudly.

"Do you know anything of fishing?" asked Ferg.

"No."

"We leave at dawn, Biri," said Jacan. "You are welcome."

And so it was that Brie found herself on the Storm Petrel at dawn the following morning. As Jacan, Ferg, and Lom instructed her in the ways of a Dungalan fishing boat, she had an odd sense of familiarity. She learned quickly; in truth, it was almost not like learning at all, more like remembering. She got her sea legs at once. Both Jacan and Ferg were impressed with her adaptability and asked several times if she was sure she had never been on a fishing boat before.

Indeed, it felt as if she had done this all her life— scratchy hemp in her hand, bare feet on sun-warmed wooden slats, the wind in her face, the dancing blue of sea waves all around her.

Fara came along. At first the Dungalans were leery of the faol. And they gaped when the wolf-cat dived gracefully into the water, surfacing some distance ahead, her sleek wet head skimming the surface like some kind of seal. Fara then dived down and reappeared with a flapping fish in her mouth.

Lom gave a hearty laugh.

"The creature is a better fisherman than I," said Jacan in amazement. They soon got used to the faol, who alternated between playing in the waves and basking on the foredeck.

The fishing turned out to be good that day, and Ferg called Brie and Fara good-luck charms. They went out on the Storm Petrel the next day and the next.

Brie found that as she grew increasingly at ease on board the boat, so grew her ease with the Dungalan language. And she quickly picked up the language of the sea as well—the words for the parts of the boat, for the different kinds of fish they hauled in with their nets, and for the seabirds circling overhead. She learned of dowsing a sail (lowering it), and of craffing a net (mending it), and that a brusker was an energetic fisherman not easily deterred by bad weather. All of the fishermen on the Storm Petrel were bruskers, Ferg told Brie with great certainty.

As the days passed, Brie eagerly drank in everything they taught her. She learned to set the nets and to haul them in; to hoist the sail and make fast the ropes. She became familiar with the many knots used by sailors and how to splice, coil, and throw rope. She discovered that a good sailor knew his position on the water at all times, and that when the captain gave an order it must be repeated and obeyed at once. She began to understand the moods of the sea, from friendly and playful to dull and unresponsive to an outright and cruel indifference. Jacan introduced her to the cross-stave, an instrument of wood and iron used to navigate by measuring the altitude of the sun and stars. She pored over Jacan's charts, one in particular called the table of the airts, which showed the different names for the directions of the wind. She started to get a feel for reading the weather and what different cloud patterns portended; and she learned of the tides and how the moon cycle affected them.

After almost a week of going out on the Storm Petrel, Jacan invited Brie to join them in their evening meal. Hyslin greeted her kindly, though Brie saw the grief still in her face. That night Brie learned Hyslin was betrothed to a fisherman named Gwil, and would be wed the following spring. To celebrate the good catches of the past few days, Hyslin donated a bottle of homemade lemongrass-and-rose wine from the cache she had already begun to stockpile for her wedding feast. They ate a delicious meal of fresh fish, roasted red potatoes, and tender white corn. Hyslin politely filled a plate with fish and a bowl of sweet cream for Fara, who gave it a careful inspection then set to with regal pleasure.

When Brie returned to Farmer Garmon's barn that night, she found Hanna smoking her pipe and reading one of Lotte's books by oil lamp. The older woman gazed on Brie then smiled.

"What?" Brie asked, curious.

"You have come back," said Hanna.

"Of course," responded the girl with a puzzled look.

"No. From Bog Maglu. I was not sure you would." Hanna blew a smoke ring, then added, "One day perhaps you will tell me of the bog."

Brie curled up in the hay, drowsy, content, Fara nestled at her side.

"Harvest day is the next full moon," Hanna's voice came. Less than a fortnight away, Brie thought. Hard to imagine that the summer was almost over. Something nagged at her, something she ought to remember, but she was too tired and was soon asleep.

The fortnight passed quickly. There were good days of fishing and bad. On the bad days Brie learned how to weave and craff the nets.

She also visited Lom and helped him with his boat. She liked Lom, as Hanna had predicted. In him she found a willing audience for her newfound love of the sea. He listened to her indulgently, as one who has been through the same early throes of passion.

From Lom, Brie learned of designing and constructing a boat. Proudly he showed her a model he had whittled, the size of his open hand; he would talk on and on, childlike in his enthusiasm.

The boat was a living creature to Lom, a bairn to which he was slowly and surely giving birth. Indeed it had the anatomy of a person, Brie thought, with a backbone and ribs; the rigging was its muscles and the planking its skin. Lom had yet to name the boat, though there was no question as to its sex. All boats, he said, were female. Incongruously, though, there were few fisherwomen in Dungal, a tradition that a handful of the younger women were trying to change.

Then it was harvest day. Brie had been hearing much about Cynheafu, the day the harvesting was finished. Even the most industrious fishermen left their boats in the harbor to participate in the festivities. Hyslin had been busy baking the borrog, large, round, moon-shaped cakes, in honor of the moon's influence over crops and harvests, and on the days when the fishing was poor and they came back early, Brie would help Hyslin with the baking. They grew to be friends.

The night before Cynheafu, Hyslin gave Brie a bright yellow dress and told her she must wear it the next day. "No one is allowed to wear anything drab or dark on harvest day," she said, eyeing Brie's gray tunic and leggings meaningfully.

"But I will be helping with Farmer Garmon's harvest," objected Brie. "I cannot be wearing a dress."

"We all help with the harvest, and all the women wear dresses," responded Hyslin. "You will stick out like a pilchard in a basket of cod if you do not." So Brie took the dress, thinking to hide it under a bale of hay back at Farmer Garmon's barn, but Hanna caught sight of it and nodded her approval. She showed Brie the brightly covered vest and long skirt she herself planned to wear. "Lotte loaned them to me. 'Twould be an insult not to wear them," she said.

As she took her place alongside the other reapers in the field the next morning, Brie felt so irritable in her yellow dress that she didn't notice the admiring glances cast her way. The last time she had worn a dress was in Tir a Ceol, and that had been a simple white shift that fell straight to the floor. This dress was cinched at the waist, with flaring skirts made even wider by the red flannel petticoat Hyslin had insisted she wear. It was the custom, she assured Brie.

Brie quickly forgot about the dress as she worked. Harvesting went quickly with so many hands gathered. Farmer Garmon was a particularly popular farmer, known to be generous, and so had no shortage of able-bodied workers. Even the elders and children of Ardara participated, following behind and tying the harvested grain into sheaves. Everyone was indeed dressed in their most colorful clothing, and it was a splendid sight—bright bursts of color weaving in and out among the rows of barley and, later, in the fields of golden wheat.

The day went quickly and it wasn't long before the shout went up. "We've got the grainne!"

"The grainne, the grainne!" Other voices echoed and a knot of women rushed forward and busied themselves; Brie could not see with what. Finally they stepped aside, to cries of "the grainne maiden, the grainne maiden," revealing the last sheaf of wheat dressed in a white flowing gown belted with a criosanna and colored ribbons.

The effigy was attached to a pole and the tallest and strongest of the reapers hoisted the grainne maiden high. Meanwhile, a gaily decorated wagon, pulled by horses with flowers and ribbons plaited through their manes, was filled to the top with sheaves of wheat. Then a procession formed, led by the men carrying the grainne maiden, followed by the decorated wagon, which was in turn followed by the brightly dressed harvesters.

The procession made its way into town and was met by many such processions. Then all the wagons and grainne maidens converged on a large grassy bluff overlooking the sea. The grainne maidens were set up along the bluff looking like a promenade of finely dressed, highborn ladies, their ribbons blowing in the sea wind. Tables were swiftly set up and almost as swiftly covered with food.

After all had gorged on the harvest bounty, the dancing began. It started with the drol, a traditional Dungalan dance in which a human chain is formed by linking hands and the dancers weave in and out in complicated patterns, never breaking the chain. It was led by Sago, the Sea Dyak sorcerer, his paper-thin legs following the ancient patterns easily and surely. Gradually, though, as more mead was consumed and twilight fell, the group of dancers split into pairs.

Contentedly munching on borrog, Brie had watched the drol, thrilled by the graceful, colorful patterns made by the dancers. Then Lom stood before her, flushed and smiling.

"Will you dance?" he asked.

Brie looked out at the whirling skirts and capering feet and felt a longing to join them. But she shook her head. She saw Lom soon after dancing with a tall, slender girl with coppery red hair.

Brie suddenly remembered herself as a child watching the Midsummer bonfires, wishing to dance. She strained to spot Lom in the diminishing light. Occasionally she caught a glimpse of the indigo shirt he wore. He was still with the red-haired girl. Brie found herself trying to remember if she had ever seen Collun dance. And then for some reason she thought of Aelwyn's words of Collun's comeliness. She flushed, irritated with Aelwyn, and with herself.

Jacan and Ferg came to sit with her. Jacan talked of the next day's fishing, but Ferg was distracted by a saucy girl named Beith, who took great delight in teasing him.

The dancers began to disperse; Jacan drifted off to talk

with some fellow fishermen, and Ferg went running after Beith, who had stolen one of his shoes. Brie could no longer see Lom. A knot of fiddlers began to play a lilting ballad about Fionna, the queen.

Brie sat peacefully, gazing up at the three-quarter moon.

Lom suddenly appeared, saying, "I cannot stay on my feet a moment longer," and sank down beside her on the grass.

"You do not like to dance?" he asked.

"I have never danced."

He looked at her in surprise, but said nothing. Then he followed her gaze upward. "They say," Lom spoke, "that on harvest night a shower of beautiful flowers falls from the moon."

Brie smiled. "I can almost believe it will," she replied dreamily.

Suddenly Lom lifted his hand into the sky, and when he brought it down, he unclosed his fingers to reveal the delicate blossom of a sea pink in the palm of his hand. Brie laughed, and with a grin Lom reached over and carefully plaited the stem into Brie's yellow hair. Brie felt an odd stirring. She flushed again, unsmiling, and looked down at her hands.

Then Ferg ran up, his shoe restored, and Jacan returned with Hyslin, as well as Hanna. Jacan asked if Brie would be joining them on the Storm Petrel the next morning.

"Of course," she replied, standing.

Lom spotted his mother and father and went to join them, giving Brie a quick salute as he left.

As she walked along in the darkness with Hanna, Brie reached up to touch the pink flower plaited into her hair. She thought of Collun, sitting by the fire, drinking chicory with Kled, but his face wavered and she had trouble summoning it back again.

That night Brie dreamed of Collun. She was running toward him. He stood on a rise, his back to her, and although she was running very fast, with each step he seemed farther away instead of closer. She pushed herself until she was almost flying over the ground. Finally she reached him and put out her hand to touch him. But where her hand brushed against his skin, red appeared, dripping red, and she realized it was blood. She looked down at her own hands and they were covered with blood.

Brie woke. Shaking, she lit a candle. Closely she inspected her hands. They were clean; nonetheless she crossed to a bucket of water and scrubbed and scrubbed with honey lye soap until her skin was raw.

# TWELVE

# Sumog

A week after the harvest festival, Jacan told Brie he had decided to take the Storm Petrel out to the deep water. He was beginning to worry that there would not be enough fish to hold them through the winter when bad weather and storms kept them ashore for weeks at a time. There was also Hyslin's wedding celebration to think of; it would take place on the first fine day after the dark months.

Sometimes, he said, when the catches had been poor nearer in, they had more luck on the deep water, far out to sea. It was time-consuming and dangerous, especially now as the weather became more unpredictable. He and Ferg would go, as well as Lom, Henle, and a fifth fisherman called Stulw. Brie asked to be included and Jacan agreed,

though he warned her that they would stay out for at least two nights, perhaps three, with little time for sleep.

They set out well before sunset the next day. As they headed out on the open sea, Brie noticed Jacan's lips moving. When she had occasion to pass him, she heard something that sounded like chanting or singing. She had noticed Jacan humming before, but not singing.

By midday they had been out of sight of Ardara for some time, farther out than Brie had been before. As she gazed at the vastness of sea and sky, Lom came to stand beside her.

Brie gestured at Jacan, saying, "I didn't know Jacan liked to sing."

Lom smiled. "Jacan is singing the cerdd-moru, the traditional Dungalan songs of navigation."

"Cerdd-moru? Is it magic of some kind?"

Lom shook his head. "They are the songs of the sea. Everything Dungalans know of the way the sea moves was put into the songs. For thousands of years we have sailed on these waters, and the songs have guided us. At night there are also the stars, but it is the song that shows us where we are on the water."

Brie watched Jacan in wonder. His lips moved constantly, sometimes imperceptibly, but always with the rhythm of the sea. "Do you know them?"

"I know some, but there are many. I have only begun to learn the songs for the deep water," Lom answered.

Then Jacan gave the call to lower the nets, and after that they all worked feverishly, lowering, hauling, and hoisting nets; scooping the flipping, whirling fish into the holds. All through the day and night they worked, into the next day and even the next, with only brief breaks for sleep.

Before dawn of the third day, Jacan's boat could hold no more fish and he turned the ship back toward Ardara. On the long journey home, they took turns sleeping, except for Fara, who made a game of racing with the Storm Petrel, and Jacan, who remained at the helm, quietly singing the cerdd-moru though his eyes were glazed with exhaustion and his throat hoarse.

During her turn to rest, Brie lay on the bow gazing at the stars, numb with fatigue. She recognized many of the star patterns, though their places in the sky were different than they were back in Eirren.

Lom came to sit beside her, yawning. "Do you have stories for your serennu in Eirren?"

"Serennu?"

"The star clusters."

"We call them patterns or realta. And yes, we do. The bright band there"—Brie pointed—"with the two points above it, that is Amergin's Crown."

"For us it is Sandyman's Hat. Sandyman is a Dungalan sand monster, sometimes comic, sometimes frightening. The children enjoy being scared by Sandyman."

Brie smiled. "What do you call that one?" she asked sleepily. "There. It looks like a large cup. We call it Ea's Cup."

"Unnla's Spoon," Lom replied.

As the Storm Petrel skimmed over the sea waves, Brie and Lom continued comparing names for the constellations: the Wheel of Light and Bootes, the Dragon and the Ox, the Harp and the Eagle, and so on. Few were the same. Brie loved hearing the Dungalan stories behind the star clusters and kept asking for more. Finally Lom threw up his hands, saying, "Enough! It is Hanna you should ask for serennu stories. She knows them all." Brie apologized and they fell silent.

Brie was half asleep when Lom broke the silence. "Do you see that serennu, the one there in the far western corner of the sky?" Brie raised her eyelids with an effort and looked in the direction he pointed.

She saw the star pattern called Casiope, the archer.

"We call it Hela," said Lom, "or the Huntress. Hela was an archer; she had great prowess with bow and arrow."

"Ours is an archer as well."

"Who is your archer?"

"Casiope," Brie replied, then went on, her voice tone-less. "He was a man who sought to destroy one who had wronged him, but instead he killed his own son with an arrow." Brie's eyes glittered with unshed tears as Collun's voice echoed in her ears, *like Casiope...an arrow that will surely return one day and pierce the one who shoots it.*

Lom gazed at her sideways. "Biri?"

She swallowed hard, then smiled falsely. "Tell me of Hela."

"There are several tales. She was brave and kind and...beautiful." He paused, then added shyly, "You remind me of her."

Through the haze of her sadness and exhaustion, Brie felt a wave of astonishment and looked at Lom to see if he was joking, but his face was composed. He was looking at her with a curious expression.

"Biri, there is a sadness in you," he said, haltingly.

Brie stared at Lom. And suddenly she found herself telling Lom of the bog and the two men she had killed. The words spilled out, unchecked, and as they came, Brie felt a sort of easing inside her, like that of a spring wound tight that was letting go at last. Lom listened closely. When she had finished, he said quietly, "You killed those men to keep from dying yourself. Choosing to live is no dishonor."

"But I had sought their deaths."

"It matters not. You could have killed one when his back was turned, but you chose not to, risking your own life. It is a brave thing you did, Biri."

Brie looked into Lom's face and knew he spoke the truth—his truth, at any rate. For herself, it was not so clear, but some of the pain had seeped away with the words she had spoken. Soon she slept.

Dawn was just breaking when Ferg, who was on watch, let out a cry. The tone of his voice jerked Brie awake and to her feet. The boy was pointing at the water. Brie left Lom, who stirred but remained deep in slumber, and went to the side of the Storm Petrel. She peered down.

There was a dark shadow passing under the boat. It spread out over the sea a good distance.

As Brie stared, her eye caught a movement. Something detached itself from the dark mass and came closer to the surface. Brie got a glimpse of the long undulating form and protruding round eyes rimmed with a line of shining orange. "Sumog!" she cried out. Fara, at Brie's legs, let out a hiss. Then the creature dipped down into the thick swathe of darkness.

Lom had awakened, as had Henle and Stulw, and they joined Brie at the side.

"Did you see?" Brie said, her voice urgent. The fishermen said they had not. Jacan had seen only the darkness from his place at the helm.

They watched the dark band until it was far out to sea and they could no longer see it. Brie's throat was dry. To make up that wide band of darkness there would have had to have been hundreds and hundreds of sumog.

"Are you sure it was sumog?" asked Lom.

"Yes. And look." Floating on the surface were fish bones, tails, fins, and bits of flesh. The Storm Petrel sailed over the grisly trail as they made their way back to Ardara.

Too tired to hike up to Farmer Garmon's barn, Brie stayed the night in a small shed behind Jacan's house, as she had done a handful of times before.

Brie dreamed of Collun again. It began as a peaceful scene, Collun bent over his mother's garden, staking some white cosmos that had grown as tall as his shoulders. Then a light snow began to fall. Collun looked up, puzzled, then afraid. Brie woke.

She remembered as if from long ago a day at Cuillean's dun when she had come across Collun sitting silently beside an overgrown patch of weeds. He had been very still, with a blank look on his face. She had knelt beside him.

"Cosmos and briar roses," he had said, a tangle of winding roots and stems clutched in his hand. "They were Emer's favorites. This was her garden." Brie could see unshed tears in Collun's eyes.

"Can we help it to grow again?" she had asked softly.

"Yes." And they had spent the rest of the day weeding, watering, and staking the neglected plants. When they were done, the blank look in Collun's eyes was gone.

But in her dream he had been afraid.

Still exhausted from the deep-sea fishing, Brie could have easily slept through the rest of the day, even into the night. But she quickly got to her feet and dressed. She must go to Collun. She had postponed it too long. Pulling on her boots, Brie flinched as she remembered her bitter parting words to him.

She checked on the fire arrow. It hummed against her skin, but not with warmth. It seemed faintly displeased.

As she stepped outside, Brie breathed in the morning air. Something was different, she thought. There was a tang, a chill that had not been there yesterday. Sharply she turned her face toward the mountains. Snow. And clouds heavy with darkness hovered over the highest peaks.

It was too late. She sank to the stone steps in front of the hut. Everyone had told her that once the snows came to the Blue Stacks, no one dared travel through. "Think of the storm you met, Biri," Hanna had said, "and imagine ice and snow mixed in with the wind. Not to mention drifts of snow as high as your shoulders."

She could try anyway. Or perhaps...perhaps she could go by sea. It was possible, she thought, her face lighting for a moment. She could borrow a cross-stave and a table of the airts; she had Crann's map, which clearly marked Dungal's coastline. Yet she had no boat.

She would go to Sago. Perhaps he knew of a boat.

But when she got to Sago's mote, he was just setting out with a canvas satchel slung over his chest. "Sago's amhantar," he said with a looping smile, pointing at the satchel. "For treasures," he added in a dramatic whisper, finger to his lips. And he wandered down to the shoreline peering closely at the sand. Occasionally he stooped to pick up a shell or a tuft of seaweed. Brie watched him, frustrated. Then she followed after.

"Sago," Brie called. "I must return to Eirren."

"Too late, too late," he chirped. Brie frowned began to sing,

> *"I wish I were*
> *where I could not be*
> *and that where I could be*
> *I was not at all."*

Sago finished his doggerel with a cheerful smile, then dived upon a bright purple starfish that was missing a leg. He placed it in his amhantar.

"I was thinking I might go by sea...," said Brie, reining in her temper.

"The sea, the salty old sea. And shall old Sago teach you the cerdd-moru, the songs of the sea? 'Sing hey ho, the life of the sea,' " he trilled.

"I *must* go," Brie almost shouted.

Sago turned to face her, still grinning, but his words were spoken softly. "Perhaps, but not to Eirren. And not yet."

Brie searched his face for meaning. Then he chuckled again and, wagging his forefinger at her, recited,

> *"One little fish bone*
> *went to see the queen;*
> *when the bone came back*
> *nothing had it seen."*

After that she could get nothing of sense from the sorcerer, who skipped down the beach, occasionally crouching low to inspect something in the sand. Brie sank to her knees, numb with disappointment.

to leave. Sago suddenly doubled back,
...ld of her wrist.
...en a ghost anemone?" he asked.
...e.
...her across the sand, then onto a large rocky
...op. He stopped in front of a sheltered basin of water
within the rocks and pointed down. Brie moved forward,
stepping on a bronze-colored plant that let out a wet, pop-
ping noise. Sago told her the plant was a bladder wrack.

"But here, look," said Sago.

Brie peered down into the still pool of water and saw a
slender column from which emanated dozens of delicate,
swaying tentacles of a whitish, translucent color.

"It's beautiful," said Brie.

Sago nodded. "But when it is disturbed, the ghost anemone releases white stinging threads that paralyze. It uses its
ghostly little arms to pull anything edible down to its
mouth. You see the mouth? In the center there."

Brie gazed at the oval lips, which undulated with small
sucking movements.

"There are two kinds of predators: those who set forth
to hunt and kill, and those who sit still and wait," the Sea
Dyak sorcerer said matter-of-factly.

Sago stirred the water in the basin with a long piece of
driftwood. The tentacles of the ghost anemone contracted
slightly, and Brie saw several threads of white shoot out
and coil around the stick; then they drifted slowly away.

"You saw the sumog on the sea?" Sago asked unex-
pectedly.

"Yes."

"Come," said the sorcerer, dropping the driftwood and
moving away from the tide pool. He bent down and picked

up a shell. "Moon shell," he said with a smile. It was fan-shaped with whorls and ridges corrugating the opalescent, milky white surface. Brie gazed on it with pleasure, then she suddenly noticed Sago's thumbnail. It was long and thin and it hooked under, curving in toward his thumb at a sharp angle. Sago smiled and held up his other thumb for Brie to see. It was the same.

"It is the mark of a Sea Dyak sorcerer. They are said to be fishing hooks that catch the souls of the departed so they won't be washed out to sea."

Brie stared stupidly at the hooked thumbnails.

Sago raised both thumbs and wiggled them, wearing his looniest grin. "Showy, aren't they? But of no use whatsoever. Not these days. Not because there is no death, may the gods forbid, but because souls have a way of finding their own way to where they belong. No assistance is needed from a pair of brittle old thumbnails.

"Flora, dora, bora, bite," the sorcerer suddenly chanted, counting out on his two thumbs, "bimini, jimini, reena, mite." Sago wiggled the thumbnail he ended up on, said, "You can never have too many moon shells," and deposited the shell in his amhantar.

They walked on, following the curve of the seacoast. Sago occasionally paused to point out some new wonder— sea spiders, pipefish, blood stars, and two dainty arrow crabs.

The sorcerer suddenly turned to Brie and said, "Have you the stomach for hunting sumog with old Sago, I wonder."

"What do you mean?"

"Next full moon. You will come?"

"I suppose so," she replied, uncertain.

"Nothing better, nothing better. Hunt the hunter." He fluttered his thumbnails at her again.

They walked back to Sago's mote and found Hanna there, waiting for them. The dogs and Fara were with her, and she carried a loaf of fresh bread and a flagon of new honey wine. Sago dug a pit in the sand in front of the mote, and Brie helped him start a small fire with pieces of drift-wood and dry seaweed. While she and Hanna built up the fire, Sago wandered off and returned with several handfuls of clams. He threw them on the flames.

It was a warm night, and the three ate companionably, the animals ranged around them. The broiled clams, the fresh bread, Sago's sepoa tea, and the honey wine were all delicious. Brie lay on her side on the sand, feeling peaceful, her stomach full. Then Hanna broke the silence. "I leave tomorrow," she said. "The dark months are soon upon us and it is time I journeyed north. I will return to Ardara by the winter solstice."

"Breo-Saight and I will have stories to tell you, of hunting beasties in dark waters," said Sago, winking at Brie. Hanna raised an eyebrow, then called to Jip, who was trying to get at a hermit crab.

Brie and Hanna said their good-byes the next morning, and, after thanking Farmer Garmon and Lotte for their kindness to her, Brie moved her few belongings to the stone hut behind Jacan's house. Then she headed for the Storm Petrel.

The night of the full moon, Brie set out for Sago's mote. Fara was not with her, having disappeared at twilight as she occasionally did. When Fara reappeared the next morning she would no doubt have a sleek, well-fed look, and Brie guessed that hunting forays accounted for her absences.

It was a warm night and the moon hung in the darkness, swollen and heavy. Brie walked quickly, feeling jittery.

Sago was readying his boat, a small one-masted ketch he called Gor-gwynt or Western Wind, after the wind direction that all right-thinking fishermen favor. The sorcerer worked quickly and with easy skill. He brought aboard his fishing pole, a lantern, a small basket, and a handheld landing net. Brie saw no weapon of any kind.

They cast off, and Brie took the tiller while Sago raised the sail. The night wind was fresh and came from the east. "We are lucky," Sago said, making fast several ropes in quick succession. "Dwy-gwynt means we don't have to row out of the inlet." Brie recognized dwy-gwynt as the name for the east wind on the table of the airts.

They came out of the harbor into the long waves. Sago took over the tiller, and, though the moon was bright, he bade Brie light the lantern. Then Sago had them change places again, and, as she gripped the straining tiller, Sago lay belly-down on the bow of the boat, holding the lantern just above the surface of the water. He stayed motionless for a time, then rejoined Brie.

"It is early yet" was all he said. The boat, poised and eminently sure of herself, skimmed over the rippled surface of the ocean.

"Where do the sumog come from?" asked Brie as she rehung the lantern on the iron forkel at the bow.

"Oona, moona, mollopy, mite; show me little fishies that bite!" chanted Sago gleefully.

"Sago," Brie said, impatient. "Truly, tell me what place they come from. The north?" she said, thinking of Scath, and of faraway Usna and Uneach, where the morgs lived; even the north wind on Jacan's table of the airts wore the face of a viper.

Sago made his face serious and shook his head. "There is much of value that comes out of the north. The corals of Usna. The bearded yellowfish of the Grissol Sea. The mountain sheep of Sola. No. Not the north. It is from man that evil always comes."

"But man did not make the sumog."

"Did he not?"

"Then are the sumog from the Cave?" Brie asked slowly.

Long ago an evil sorcerer named Cruachan had unleashed a horde of malformed, deadly creatures on Eirren. They were caught and contained in a vast cave by the great hero-king Amergin and his allies. Henceforth it was called the Cave of Cruachan. But in recent times Medb, Queen of Scath, had found a way to unseal the cave, using the cailceadon stone, and from the cave she released Naid, the Firewurme; Nemian, the black-winged creature that had nearly sucked the life out of Brie; and Moccus, the eyeless boar.

"There was an evil man who walked an evil mile...," Sago began. "No, not Cruachan; not this time."

"Medb?"

"Riddle me this, and riddle me that," Sago said with an air of finality. He stood and lowered the sail, letting the boat drift. Then he reached for his fishing pole. As he baited the hook with a mudminnow, he said mildly, "The sumog is a beaked fish and beaked fish always circle bait before swallowing it. And we will need something large to catch the eye of a sumog." He cast the line, and a few moments later it jerked. Sago pulled in a small chub, then threw it back. He caught several more small fish and threw them back as well. Finally he hooked a good-size mullet, and he set down his pole. He proceeded to kill the fish, slice it in half, and remove its spine. After inserting a hook in its head, he deftly sewed the fish back up using a thin clear thread. Then he set the whole thing aside, floating the dead fish in a bucket of seawater. He passed Brie a skin bag filled with tepid sepoa tea, and several of the small fish-and-potato cakes called taten-pisc.

They ate in silence in the rocking, drifting boat, the moonlit sea whispering around them.

Halfway through her second taten-pisc, Brie saw Sago's body go still. He slowly set down the skin bag and took up his fishing pole.

Sago moved silently to the bow and looked across the water. Then, with a set face, he cast his line, the dead fish shining silver in the moonlight as it arched through the air, dropping into the sea with a small splash. Brie joined Sago at the bow. She caught sight of a blur of darkness moving swiftly toward the bait fish. Sago gestured at the lantern, and Brie quickly took it from the forkel. She held it up over the water and saw a school of five sumog converge on the dead fish.

Teeth flashed and powerful jaws tore, and in a matter of minutes there was nothing left of the fish. Sago quickly pulled in the line and the iron hook was bitten in half.

Suddenly there was a thudding sound from the hull.

Sago looked surprised, but he gave a manic grin as the boat lurched. Then another thud and the boat rocked violently. Brie was thrown off balance and clutched the side of the boat to keep from falling. A sumog cleaved out of the water, slicing at her fingers with its knife-sharp teeth. She let out a cry and pulled in her hand, several drops of blood falling into the water.

A pair of sumog threshed around in a frenzy where Brie's blood had spilled, and she caught a glimpse of their round, bulging eyes rimmed by shiny orange. Then she spotted more dark shapes flowing toward the boat.

Brie crouched in the bottom of the rocking boat, cradling her torn fingers. She looked over at Sago, who stood, holding on to the mast, still with that wide, reckless smile on his face. The boat pitched from side to side as the sumog continued butting against the hull.

They were trying to capsize the boat.

"Raise the sail!" Brie cried out.

Sago shook his head, smiling, his eyes fixed on the water.

"Sago!" she shouted.

"A sailor sailed the sea, sea, sea, to see what he could see, see, see...," Sago sang.

*Thump* went the sumog.

Brie turned cold. What had possessed her to follow this ancient wraithlike man out into the middle of the sea, to hunt sumog? She must have been as mad as he.

The tilting boat suddenly seemed very small in the vast dark sea.

# THIRTEEN

# The Wedding Dance

**B**rie rose and took a step toward Sago, thinking to push him aside so she could get to the sail, but she stopped and stared. Some kind of light was coming from the Sea Dyak sorcerer, a golden glow from under his skin. His face, his hands, even his stalklike legs, were lit with a fiery radiance, burning brighter than a hundred lanterns. Then he gestured with a golden hand toward the sumog.

Brie turned her gaze on the writhing, undulating mass under the boat. There must have been fifty or more sumog in the water. She could feel the evil pulsing from them.

Turning to look back at Sago, she had to shield her eyes, for bursts of light began to appear on the surface of the water all around the boat, like tongues of flame. As she

watched, transfixed, the movements of the sumog began to slow. The bright shafts of light were widening and thrusting down under the water, spreading like some kind of undersea wildfire. The sumog had gone still, and as the light lapped over them, they too began to glow, the brown serpentine bodies becoming suffused with light.

Brie was just about to avert her eyes when, with a flash, one sumog near her burst into pinpoints of light, and then there was nothing left except tiny phosphorescent specks floating in the water.

Hypnotized by the sight, Brie watched as one by one the sumog exploded, like so many iridescent soap bubbles. Then the sumog were gone, and the water around the boat sparkled with thousands of tiny motes of light.

Brie wheeled around to look at Sago, suddenly, irrationally afraid he, too, was going to burst. But the light was already fading from his body, and he gave her a smile.

Then he crossed to her. His arm was glowing only faintly as he took her injured hand. Wiping the blood off her hand with a cloth, he looked closely at the jagged cut across the backs of her fingers. Abruptly he lifted them to his mouth and sucked. Brie winced.

Then he spat into the twinkling water. For a moment he looked almost otherworldly, his pale face still radiant, with the red of Brie's blood around his lips. At last he wiped his mouth with the cloth.

"There is poison in the sumog tongue. I got most of it, but you may be sick for a day or two."

Brie stared at him in a daze. Then she sagged onto the bench, suddenly exhausted. Sago raised the sail and, as he took the tiller, Brie's eyelids closed. She slept all the way back to Ardara.

For the next few days, Brie was feverish and her head ached. When she tried to stand, everything had an annoying tendency to spin, so she stayed close to her pallet. Lom brought her books of Dungalan lore, which she read until her head pounded, then she slept again. When Sago had left her at the door of Jacan's hut that night, he had asked Brie not to tell the villagers of the sumog hunting expedition. "Life is more peaceful for an old Sea Dyak sorcerer if the people come only for fishing advice." So Brie told Lom and Jacan she must have caught a chill.

Sago did not visit during her sickness, but Lom reported that mysterious flickering lights had been spotted out on the water each night, and Brie knew what occupied the sorcerer.

When the sumog sickness had mostly passed, she went to see Sago at his mote. She found him a little paler than usual, but otherwise unchanged. He sang her a nonsense song about taten-pisc and custard, showed off a highly prized parrot fish he had caught that day, and said offhandedly that the fishing should be better now in Ardara. And it was.

The Ardarans credited their good fortune to a change in the current and wind direction. Later, when Brie heard the innkeeper and his cronies deride Sago as a useless, witless old man, she wanted to tell them of the radiant sorcerer who had turned a monstrosity into innumerable, beautiful specks of light.

But she did not.

The days grew shorter until the sun was winking below the horizon only a few hours after the midday meal. Brie was unused to the shortness of winter days in the north, and the perpetual darkness began to weigh on her like a full basket of dead fish, except that there were no full baskets; there was little fishing at all. During the dark months, Dungalans turned to storytelling and music to pass the time, and Brie could now see why Travelers were so highly valued.

When no Traveler came to Ardara, homegrown storytellers presided over the long nights, along with fiddlers and singers. There was also dancing, though Brie continued to demur when asked. At first she told herself she was weak from the sumog poison; for a long time after the sumog hunt, just the thought of moving in any direction resembling a circle made her head spin. But after the sickness had finally worn off, Brie still remained òn the side of the room, watching. It became a standing joke between Brie and Lom; he swore that by spring he would have her up and twirling on a dance floor. And she swore, equally adamant, that he would not.

Although Brie had become part of the weave of life in Ardara, she was yet held at a distance by many of the townspeople. She was most comfortable with the fishermen, who had come to respect and accept her.

Brie wasn't quite sure how it happened but word had gotten around of her skill with bow and arrow. And one day a young village boy named Dil appeared at the door to her hut and shyly asked if she would teach him. He was a slight fellow, though tall for his age, with a head of unruly coppery yellow hair.

Though it was a windy day with the threat of rain, Brie took Dil to a sandy bay north of the harbor and immediately began his lessons. They started by fashioning a bow out of a piece of driftwood. Then Brie loaned him an arrow and a piece of bowstring, saying that arrow- and string-making would be part of their next lesson. Dil nodded eagerly.

As she guided his hands and directed him how to aim the arrow, Brie remembered herself long ago with her father. "Open your stance, Brie. Back straight, head upright. I said up, not down!" And "What are you trying to do, strangle the bow?! Don't grip so hard, relax your fingers."

At the end of the lesson Dil's eyes shone, and Brie found herself promising to meet him again the next day.

That night there was a gathering at Farmer Garmon's barn to hear the tales of the latest Traveler who had come to the village. The Traveler had an unpleasant face, long with a small oval of a mouth and red lips, which he licked often. But his stories were captivating, if a little frightening. Several of the children had to be taken, crying, from the barn by their mothers.

After readying herself for sleep that night, Brie took out the fire arrow. She had begun doing this in the past week, at the end of the day. At first she told herself it was because the arrow really ought to have a daily cleaning and polishing, but she was coming to believe that, for some reason, the arrow wanted her to hold it in her hands. At any rate she found it comforting, in a peculiar way, to feel the arrow humming under her fingers. After a while it was almost as if she needed to touch it. As the wyll Aelwyn needed her cup of cyffroi in the morning, Brie needed to feel the arrow humming against her skin before she went to sleep. And as this became a nightly ritual, she noticed that her dreaming changed, became more vivid, more acute.

Brie had not dreamed of Collun since that night when

she had realized it was too late to cross the Blue Stacks, but several days before the winter solstice she did. It was a brief, terrifying dream; Cuillean's dun was deserted, and the soldier Renin lay dead in the forecourt. Brie woke, shaking and wild-eyed. She had been right; Collun did need her. Once again she tried to think of some way to get to Eirren. The sea was her first thought, as before, but she knew now, firsthand, that the winter sea was as dangerous to navigate as the Blue Stacks, if not more so. She felt useless, frustrated, and promised herself that she would begin her journey back to Eirren, to Collun, the day after Hyslin's wedding.

The next day, as Brie helped Lom on his boat, she was preoccupied and accidentally splintered a trunnel while hammering it into place. Then she broke off the handle of Lom's broadax and, later, hammered her thumb instead of a nail. She let out a howl of pain, and Lom wound his handkerchief around her thumb, muttering that she was more hindrance than help to him today. "If I am to finish by Hyslin's wedding day I can't be losing precious time carving new trunnels and mending tools."

"I'm sorry," Brie said, contrite. "I'll do better."

"Perhaps you would do better to take the rest of the day off."

"It's the darkness. It wears on me."

"Aye. But after winter solstice the days will start to get longer. And before you know it, it will be spring and time for Hyslin's binding ceremony."

Brie looked unconvinced.

"And if I don't finish this boat in time, I won't be able to dance you across her deck," he teased. "So get off with you. Take a walk or go help Hyslin."

As Brie made her way to Jacan's house, Fara loping along at her side, she thought of the promise she had made herself that morning.

Winter solstice was a time for celebration in Dungal. Spring was still distant, but the solstice marked the turning of the sun and the lengthening of the days.

Three Travelers had arrived in Ardara for the sun-return festivities; Hanna was one, as was the severe-looking man with the red lips and an elderly man with a crystalline voice and a pure white beard.

Brie was glad to see Hanna. They spent a peaceful afternoon walking the coastline with Fara and the two dogs, who frisked together like old friends.

That evening they gathered, along with most of the townspeople, in Farmer Garmon's large barn. There the storyspinning, dancing, eating, and singing would continue until dawn on this, the longest night of the year. At sundown the families arrived, each bringing with them the greatest delicacy left from their rapidly dwindling stores. They ate at long tables amid much chatter and high spirits, and afterward the tables were moved away and everyone settled onto blankets or hay to listen to the storytellers.

During a break between stories, Brie and Lom got into a friendly quarrel about Lom's boat.

"Truth is, you wouldn't know a hawsepiece from a deck beam if it wasn't for me," Lom said with a rather superior air.

"Oh, and who was it measured the sternpost three inches too short?"

They continued to trade jibes, then finally dissolved into

laughter at the absurdity of the quarrel. As Brie laughed, she happened to glance over at Lom's mother, Lotte. The innkeeper of the Speckled Trout was speaking softly in her ear. Lotte's eyes grew uncertain and darted to Lom and Brie. Brie averted her own gaze just in time. When she looked back at Lotte, the innkeeper had moved away and the older woman was clutching her husband's arm, talking urgently. Farmer Garmon listened, then shook his head with a quick definite motion and returned to the chocolate tart he was eating. But Brie could see the uncertainty still in Lotte's face.

Several days later, on a dark, cool afternoon, Brie and Lom were working together on the hewing of the mast, a fine fir Lom had carefully selected for its clear, straight grain.

Abruptly Brie turned to Lom and asked him if he knew of any gossip that the innkeeper might be spreading. Lom frowned and his nose twitched slightly as though at a bad smell.

"It doesn't bear repeating," he replied tersely, hewing downward with the rasel, using long sure strokes.

"Tell me," Brie said.

"The innkeeper is a sour old miser."

"Tell me, Lom."

Lom set the rasel down and brushed wood shavings from his arms. "He has been calling you a leannan-shee."

"What is that?"

" 'Tis an evil creature, female always, who attaches itself to a man and sucks the life out of him."

Brie was so astonished she nearly laughed, but because of the anger in Lom's face she did not.

"And is it your life I am supposed to be doing this to?" she asked.

He nodded, a hint of color in his cheeks. "And the boy Dil, who you're giving the bow lessons to, and some of the lads in the village as well, ever since you wore that yellow dress on harvest day..." He trailed off.

Brie had forgotten about the uncomfortable yellow dress. "Well, I am a busy little leannan-whatever it is, aren't I?"

Lom's face relaxed into a smile.

"You don't think I am, do you, Lom?" Brie demanded.

He laughed. "No proper leannan-shee would go around stinking of fish and arguing with a fellow about how to lay a keel."

"I do not stink!" Brie rejoined, laughing along with him. "And even you have to admit that keel was the slightest bit off center..."

The days and weeks following the winter solstice were hard ones. Spring was still a long way off, and there was little to break the desolation of dwindling food supplies, howling wind, and bitter cold. Other than working on Lom's boat and continuing Dil's bow lessons, the only thing that provided Brie a diversion was preparations for Hyslin's wedding ceremony. Brie learned that there was almost always a marriage ceremony at the end of winter as a way to celebrate the end of the dark season.

Hyslin had taught Brie how to use a weaving loom, and Brie was working on a piece of cloth. She had not decided what it would be when she was done, but she enjoyed the weaving of it. Hyslin, with her deft, experienced fingers, was making a luminous, pearl-colored cloth for her wedding cyrtel, the traditional flowing gown used for the binding ceremony.

For weeks the Storm Petrel did not leave the harbor. And constant driving rain or, more often, sleet meant no boatbuilding or archery lessons. Brie could hardly contain her restlessness. When she was not weaving or preparing food, she took long walks on coastal paths, occasionally pausing to stare up at the Blue Stacks, willing the snow to melt.

She began to experience a growing sense of unease, of something left undone. Every night as she lay in her pallet, after stowing the fire arrow safely in her quiver, she would go over the day's activities in her mind, few as they were. She tried to think of something she might have over-looked—mending a tear in one of Jacan's nets, some ingredient she might have left out of the lemongrass-and-rose wine she was helping Hyslin make, a missed thread in the cloth she was weaving—but she always came up blank.

Her dreams grew more vivid. She began to have the nightmare of the yellow bird again—the rapacious beak, the large, suffocating wings, the pulsing black sky. She dreaded going to her pallet at night and stayed up reading until she could keep her eyes open no longer.

There were other dreams as well, but two in particular that kept repeating. In the first she was approaching a lake, very still and gleaming like a mirror. From the center of the lake rose a bell tower. Coming toward her was a goat-man, dragging something behind him. When he drew close, she could see that the goat-man was dragging Collun, his head bloodied and raw. Then Collun's face blurred and changed, and became the face of Brie's father, streaked with blood and still contorted from his death struggle.

In the second dream she was watching the fire arrow flying through the sky, away from her. But where her eyes should have been, there were flames. The pain was terrible, a white-hot burning into her skull. She would awaken with a scream, hands clawing at her eyes, and later, when she looked in the mirror, there were scratches on her face from her fingernails.

She asked Jacan if she could sleep on the Storm Petrel; he told her she was daft and refused outright. So she slept with the windows of her little hut wide open, and that seemed to help, though more often than not she woke shivering, her blankets drenched with rain and, occasionally, snow.

Slowly the storms began to be less savage; the boats could go out more often and for longer periods of time. Brie rejoiced in the return to work, though was still troubled by the occasional dream of bird or bell tower. Lom's boat suddenly stopped looking like a skeleton as it neared completion. Brie was there when Lom, Jacan, and Ferg hoisted the mast into place.

"She's yar," said Jacan tersely, squinting up, and Brie thought Lom looked like one of Hyslin's roosters, preening, a wide foolish grin splitting his face. She told him so, and he let out a great laugh and got her to admit his boat was one of the finest she'd seen.

"Not that I've seen all that many," she said, getting in the last word.

The day Lom's boat was taken down to the water, Brie was late getting up. She'd had the bell tower dream during the night and hadn't fallen into a sound sleep until the early hours of the morning.

She grabbed an oatcake and hurried to the shore. From a distance she could see a knot of men gathered around Lom's boat. There were woven garlands of sea grass and seaweed draped around the prow, and the men were bending their shoulders to her newly painted sides. Brie paused, holding very still. The boat slid into the water, and it was as if life had been breathed into her as she bobbed and dipped on the sea waves.

Lom jumped on board and quickly turned the boat into the wind. The sail filled, and Brie grinned as she watched the ketch skim over the water.

Lom caught sight of Brie making her way down the path to the harbor and waved. She waved back.

Lom had been very secretive about what he would name the boat, holding off until the last minute to paint the name on the prow. Brie strained to see. There it was: Hela. The name of Lom's favorite star cluster. Brie's cheeks reddened slightly as she remembered their conversation on the deep water.

Lom soon brought the boat in, and all had a turn sailing her.

The signs of spring were everywhere; in the cuckoo's repeating refrain, and in the fragile blue silla blossoms that pushed through the muddy soil. Even on the water, Brie could see the difference, from the larger flocks of vocal seabirds to the somehow friendlier hues and rhythms of the water itself.

Then it was the day of Hyslin and Gwil's binding ceremony. It dawned clear and bright, and the smells of grasses and newly sprouted spring flowers were carried on the breeze.

The finished cyrtel had been delivered the night before by the seamstress in the village who did the fine embroidery on the bodice and sleeves. That morning Brie helped Hyslin put it on. It was a wonder of a gown, all light and glowing, and with her rose-petal cheeks and sparkling sea blue eyes, Hyslin was radiant.

Brie wore a dress made of the cloth she had woven during the dark season. It was a soft glowing green, and though she was all too aware of the places where her hand had been less than deft, she was pleased. She also wore a pair of featherlight slippers that Hyslin had helped her fashion; they were made of cowhide and dyed green to match the dress. Before braiding her hair, Brie went to show Hyslin.

"Why, Biri, you are more beautiful than Fionna herself," Hyslin said earnestly.

"Fionna?! Your happiness must be affecting your eyesight," responded Brie with a laugh. "In truth, it is you who dims the sun's light today."

Hyslin laughed with her, catching Brie's hand in hers. "There is something I wish to ask of you, Biri."

"Yes?"

"During the binding ceremony, there is an arrow, a

ceremonial arrow, which is sent aloft. It was to have been done by a friend of Father's, but he's not keen on the job because of a bout of sickness he's recovering from. I was wondering if you would do it."

"Of course. I would be honored."

"I have a necklace that would go well with your dress," Hyslin said. "That is, if you wanted something a bit, uh, prettier than..." She trailed off, blushing a little.

Brie's hand went to her panner. "You mean you don't think a leather thong is quite right for the occasion?" she asked with a wry smile. "You know, Rilla made it for me. Have I ever showed it to you?"

Hyslin shook her head and her eyes seemed to mist.

"I miss Rilla," she said. Blinking back her tears, Hyslin leaned forward to peer at the panner. " 'Tis an arrow," she said thoughtfully. "Perhaps it is the arrow of binding."

Brie looked incredulous.

"No, it is possible," Hyslin said. "Rilla used to see things. Father would always say she might turn out to be a wyll one day, but then Ladran came and..." Hyslin trailed off, her eyes again bright.

"I'm sorry," Brie said awkwardly, wishing she had never brought the panner to Hyslin's attention.

"No, I'm fine. In truth, I am glad to be thinking of Rilla on my binding day." Hyslin smiled. She quickly pinned a gillyflower behind each of Brie's ears and told her to leave her hair as it was; in Dungal, she said, unmarried maidens wore their hair loose on wedding days.

The food and drink had been conveyed in many trips to the Storm Petrel over the past few days. The night before, the children of the village had gathered cannyll-pryf, or candle flies, which came to Ardara when the weather began to warm. They captured them in clay pots with loosely woven linen tied over the top. These pots had been carefully stowed in the hold of each fishing boat.

By the time the sun was directly overhead, the fishing fleet of Ardara, with most of the village aboard, had arrayed itself in a wide circle in the center of the bay. Their sails were furled, and each boat had sent ribboned nosegays of crocus, bluebells, and silla up the mast. The boats were lashed very closely together, and the anchors were lowered. From her place on the starboard side of the Storm Petrel, Brie could see Lom's boat bobbing on the water several boats down, with Lom and his parents and several others on board.

Sago stood by the mast of Jacan's boat. He looked more ethereal than ever in his ceremonial singing robe, a long white garment decorated with sparkling, beaded pictures of fish, dolphins, and whales that glittered in the midday sun.

Earlier that morning, as they had set bottles of wine into the hold of the Storm Petrel, Jacan had muttered to Brie that he hoped the Sea Dyak sorcerer would not forget what he was about and break into one of his nonsense songs instead of the song of binding. But when the time came, Sago gently and clearly led the couple through the words of union. And he sang the song of binding, the cwl cano, with great solemnity.

The sorcerer's voice filled the bay—an astonishing, bursting sound from such a frail source, thought Brie—accompanied by the sound of waves slapping against the boats' hulls.

Brie watched the serious, radiant faces of the two young people as Sago wove their fingers together to form the symbolic rhwyd, or fishing net. This lacing of hands, Ferg whispered to Brie, would ensure bounty and joy in the years to come.

When the song finally died on Sago's lips, a pair of fiddlers standing on the stern of the Storm Petrel began to play a lively air, and Gwil joyfully gathered Hyslin in his arms. He danced her across the deck of the Storm Petrel and back again. Hyslin's eyes were as bright as the sunlight glittering on the waves. Musicians on the other boats took up the melody, and the fisherfolk began stamping their feet and clapping their hands in rhythm with the dancing couple.

Suddenly Gwil danced Hyslin to the starboard side of the Storm Petrel and, twirling her feet up into the air, he tossed his bride across the water to the next boat in the circle. She was deftly caught by the sturdy bearded fisherman whose boat it was, and he in turn danced Hyslin across the deck of his fishing boat. After their brief dance, the bearded fisherman tossed Hyslin to the next boat in the circle. And on and on, until Hyslin had danced on each boat and come full circle to the Storm Petrel.

Ferg told Brie this, too, was an old custom, and that it bestowed good fortune to have a newly married woman dance on the deck of your fishing boat. He made Brie laugh by telling her a story about one year when a bride, whose girth was twice that of her husband's, had wound up in the sea when one fisherman had bobbled the toss from deck to deck. It was said that that particular fisherman had a very poor yield of fish that year.

By the time Hyslin had completed the circle her legs

were wobbly, but her smile was no less radiant, and she returned to Gwil's arms for more dancing.

Thereupon all commenced to dance, and before she had time to figure out how he'd gotten from his boat to the Storm Petrel, Brie found Lom at her side. Without a word he swept her into his arms and they were dancing.

# FOURTEEN

# The Bell Tower

For a moment Brie panicked, her legs feeling as stiff and unbending as the legs of an oystercatcher. But her feet somehow found the rhythm of the music and she relaxed. Brie closed her eyes, a smile curving her lips. She was dancing.

Brie and Lom danced until the setting sun turned the sky orange, then purple, then a dark, deep blue. Just before the sun went down, Brie looked up to see Sago standing at the mast, gazing at her as she danced.

Then, on an impulse, Brie looked Lom full in the face and for the first time saw his true feelings for her. She did not look away.

Lom was a kind man. Perhaps Hela could be their fish-

ing boat, together. And perhaps she need not ever dream of yellow birds and bell towers again. Brie's feet spun and twirled and flew over the wooden deck.

It was dark now and the music slowed. The children ran for their jars of candle flies. The dancers moved forward, lining the rails of the boats. As a lone harper played, the children let loose the cannyll-pryf. Hundreds of the insects scattered, flying upward. They glowed like golden pearls hanging in the air, their lights pulsing on and off.

As Brie and Lom watched the candle flies dance in the night sky, Lom's large, warm hand enfolded Brie's, and she left it there. She was unaware of the knowing glances and the whispers that went around the circle of boats.

Brie loosed her hand from Lom's only when Hyslin appeared before her, bearing the arrow of binding. Brie gazed at it. Where the arrowhead would have been was the skeleton of a fish head, and the fletching had been worked in sea roses, with ribbons trailing from the ends.

Jacan brought Brie her bow from the hold, and she stood at the very tip of the prow. She nocked the ribboned, flowered arrow to her string. Fara, who had disappeared during the dancing, materialized suddenly at Brie's side. Brie glanced down at the sleek, wet head of the faol and smiled. Then she let fly. The arrow soared through the pulsing lights of the cannyll-pryf and cleaved the water almost directly in the center of the circle formed by the fishing boats.

As a cheer went up from the fisherfolk, Brie remembered Rilla's panner. An arrow flying over the water. Perhaps Hyslin was right, Brie thought. She plucked the panner from the bodice of her dress and peered at it. In the flickering light of the torches, she saw that what she had taken for the fire arrow might easily be the arrow from the binding ceremony, with candle flies flickering around it.

Brie closed her fingers around the panner. A candle fly brushed her cheek.

The music started up again and there was more dancing. Brie danced with Ferg and Jacan and a few of the other fishermen, but mostly she danced with Lom. Gradually, though, the ropes between boats were untied, and one by one the fishing boats began making their way back to shore. Snatches of song and laughter could be heard floating over the water.

Hyslin and Gwil departed in a small horse-drawn cart gaily decorated with seaweed, flowers, and ribbons. It took them to their new home, a cottage on Gwil's father's farmhold.

Brie stood with Lom on the shore watching the last few flickering candle flies and listening to the sounds of a fiddle coming from the few boats still anchored in the bay.

Lom turned to Brie with an earnest expression. "Biri, I—"

"Lom!" Lotte's voice came, sharp and nervous. She and Farmer Garmon rode up in their curricle. "Come, quickly."

"What is it?"

"Your father and I would speak with you," Lotte said loudly. Brie caught a glimpse of Farmer Garmon's face in the moonlight. He looked uncomfortable, his eyes fixed on the horse's reins.

Lom hesitated.

"It's news from your sister in Dungloe," Farmer Garmon said reluctantly after a nudge from Lotte.

"But cannot Biri...," Lom began.

"Go on, Lom," said Brie. "I will meet you in the morning."

Reluctantly Lom swung himself into the back of his parents' curricle and was soon out of sight.

Brie made her way home, Fara gliding alongside. Brie found herself humming a melody she had danced to on the Storm Petrel. When she arrived at the hut, she poured Fara a bowl of milk, then took out the fire arrow and sat on her pallet, still wearing the green dress. She held the arrow loosely in her hands. There was something different about the humming on her fingers tonight. It was urgent, like Lotte's voice through the darkness.

"What is it?" she said softly.

And suddenly she saw Sago. He lay on the beach, face-up, waves foaming around his spindly legs. His singing robe was crumpled, crusted with sand, and his eyes were closed.

Brie dropped the arrow, frightened. She had not been asleep or dreaming, and yet it was like one of her dreams. Could it be true? Was Sago hurt? She tried to remember when she had seen him last. She thought she remembered seeing him leave on his boat, Gor-gwynt, soon after Brie had shot the arrow of binding. Brie blinked. Her eyesight was blurred and her eyelids felt heated. Fara licked her hand. It took several minutes for her sight to clear.

Brie ran most of the way to Sago's mote, Fara alongside her. When the water came in sight, Brie spotted a small boat making its way north. She recognized the markings on the sail as those belonging to a fisherman who was one of the innkeeper's cronies. She did not remember seeing him or the innkeeper at the binding ceremony. Then the moon came out from behind some clouds, and Brie could make out three men in the boat: The innkeeper and the fisherman, and the third looked like the Traveler with the red lips. Almost reflexively Brie ducked into the cover of some bushes. Soon the boat rounded a bend and was out of sight.

When Brie arrived at Sago's mote, she found it deserted. She thought things looked out of place, but it was hard to tell in all the clutter. The seabirds were quiet up in their aerie. Brie went out onto the beach. The moon was obscured by a thick layer of clouds. She looked both ways down the coast, but could see little.

She went back into Sago's mote for a lantern. She lit it and began to run down the coast, Fara still at her side.

Brie ran and ran, slowing occasionally to catch her breath. A mist of rain started falling, growing heavier as she went. She told herself she was a fool, running on a wet night along the coast because of a briefly glimpsed picture in her head. Her green dress was soaked and slapped against her legs. She had not even stopped to put on her boots, and the thin leather dancing slippers grew sodden and slipped on her feet. Finally she kicked them off.

She and Fara had been running steadily for a long time when Brie spotted something white and shining on the shoreline. Fara reached it first.

It was Sago. As in Brie's vision, he lay on his back, but now the waves were washing up over his shoulders. When they receded, Brie could see his legs like two pale bones sticking out from under his crumpled, waterlogged singing robe. Rain pelted his exposed face and limbs. For a moment she thought he was dead, but as she came up alongside him, she saw his eyes were open. They blinked. Fara let out a sound and a large wave came and crashed over them, knocking Brie off balance. The undertow was pulling Sago to the sea, but Brie grabbed one of his arms and pulled him onto dry sand.

She crouched next to him, peering anxiously at his wet, pale face. Fara made another low sound, and Sago blinked again. He attempted to whisper something through barely moving, cracked lips.

Brie saw that one of his hands was swollen to almost twice its normal size and was an ugly purple-yellow color.

"A stonefish. In my amhantar."

Brie could see Sago's amhantar nearby, its contents spilled out on the sand. The stonefish, dead, lay faceup, its flat staring eyes gazing at nothing.

"How did it happen?" Brie asked.

"Back at the mote. A visitor, a villager put it there. Afterward, they brought me here, in a boat." The whispery voice paused, then resumed. "Rig a jig, jig; three men in a gig." His cracked lips curved into something that was meant to be a smile.

Brie remembered the boat she had seen. Then she hurriedly put her hands at Sago's armpits and lifted. He weighed little more than a small child. Indeed, most of the weight came from his sodden singing robe. Carefully Brie cradled him in her arms, carrying him like a baby, and began the long walk back to the mote through the rain.

When they arrived, she laid Sago on his pallet while Fara settled in a wet mass by the door. Numbly Brie followed Sago's whispered instructions, peeling the wet robe off him, rubbing his gaunt body with dry cloths, and covering him with blankets. Then she brewed a broth, using ingredients from jars Sago indicated. She poured the sour-smelling liquid into a shallow cup and held it to the sorcerer's lips. He drank and then closed his eyes. Exhausted, Brie sank down on the floor next to his pallet and slept.

She woke, sneezing. Her clothing stuck to her skin and her hair was still damp. Amazingly, a ragged piece of gilly-flower was still pinned behind one ear. It seemed a lifetime ago that she had danced with Lom on the deck of the Storm Petrel, a flower behind each ear. She looked up to see Sago sitting on his pallet, smiling. His fingers were weaving something small out of strands of a red-orange seaweed called carragheen.

"Dry clothes are in the chest there," Sago said, his voice no longer a whisper.

Brie stood, her limbs stiff and aching. When Sago lay back again, his fingers still wove the seaweed, but he closed his eyes. Brie stripped off the green dress, now clammy and discolored with seawater, and put on a pale blue tunic that was soft to the skin but too long for her.

"Shall I make more of the healing drink?" she asked.

Sago shook his head. "It is time for you to leave Ardara."

"And go where?" she asked dryly.

Sago grinned. "Kesca too fay, kesca too fee, which is the way to go to sea?"

"What if I don't go?" Brie asked, sighing.

"Many will die," Sago answered calmly.

Brie drew in a sharp breath. "Why? What is it you know, Sago?"

"He knew a little, he knew a lot, he knew enough to stir the pot," the sorcerer responded, his expression birdlike, alert.

"Stop it!" Brie said loudly. "Enough of riddling. What villager put the stonefish in your amhantar?"

"The innkeeper, with the help of his friends. Rig a jig, jig..." Sago's eyes were still bright, but he had answered solemnly enough.

"Why?" Brie cut him off.

"They serve a dark master."

"Who?"

"Go," Sago said, suddenly severe. "There is little time. And none at all for good-byes."

"You speak of Lom."

Sago nodded.

Reluctantly Brie stood.

"Here..." The sorcerer held up the thing he had been making with his fingers. "It is a travel charm. To put in your boot, near the anklebone."

Brie took the charm and crossed the room. After all the dancing she had done, the long run along the coast, and the walk back carrying Sago, her legs felt as substantial as a pair of feathers, and her knees gave way for a moment. She had to grasp a chair to steady herself. Shaking her head, Brie whispered, "I cannot."

Sago said nothing.

Straightening, Brie forced her feather legs to move, one foot in front of the other. She looked back at the gaunt, pearl-colored face, the fey smile of the Sea Dyak sorcerer. Tears came unbidden to her eyes. Blinking them back, she whispered, "Farewell, Sago." And quickly she left the mote, Fara at her heels.

Dawn was just breaking as Brie passed the harbor. She caught sight of the Storm Petrel pulled up on the sand. No one appeared to be about, but she kept in the shadows, not wishing to be seen. As she moved away from the harbor, up the cobbled streets, Brie suddenly remembered standing barefoot on the sun-warmed planks of the Storm Petrel's deck, sea wind on her face. With a certainty that bewildered her, she knew she would never sail on the sturdy fishing ketch again. This time the tears fell unchecked, hot and wet, mingling with the rain on her face.

After a brief stop at the hut behind Jacan's house to change clothes and gather her belongings, Brie made her way through the streets of Ardara. She had seen no sign of Jacan or Ferg, and there was something different about the village this morning. Something unsettled, nervous. The villagers she saw walked with jerky movements, their faces shuttered, voices hushed.

She spotted a fisherman she knew hurrying along. "Is something amiss?" she asked after exchanging greetings.

"Aye. Been an attack down by shore. Old Ewsko and his son, both dead. Some kind of killer fish they're saying."

"Sumog!"

The fisherman looked at her sideways. "Mayhap. Some have gone down to the mote, but the sorcerer be half asleep, singing his nonsense songs." He soon hurried off.

Brie stood, irresolute. Perhaps she ought to stay, help the villagers somehow with the sumog. But Sago had told her it was time for her to go, and somehow she knew it to be true.

She stopped that night to make camp. As she lay on the ground, sleep eluding her, a bone-chilling loneliness overcame her. She rolled onto her back and, looking up at the sky, found the star pattern Casiope. She could hear Lom's voice, telling the story of Hela; then it mingled with Collun's, "The archer Casiope...the arrow that doubles back..." Brie found herself reaching for the fire arrow. It was pleasantly warm to the touch. She closed her eyes and there, etched on the dark canvas of her eyelids, was the bell tower, the one she had dreamed before. She held very still, straining to make out the details; she thought she could just make out a figure standing beside the bell tower. Then the image faded.

Brie opened her eyes and, though she could not see, she sat up. *The bell tower.* That was where she journeyed.

The next morning, fording an ice-cold river, Brie thought that it was all very well to know you wanted to get to a certain bell tower, but it wasn't much good if you hadn't the least idea where the bell tower was. Or what awaited you there.

So Brie continued to head north. Sago's travel charm, lodged firmly inside her boot, seemed to make her feet ache less at the end of a long day's tramp. Fara, as always, was tireless, bounding along at the same pace at the end of the day as at the beginning, occasionally vanishing for short periods of time to reappear with a well-fed, smug expression on her face.

Once Brie caught sight of a band of gabha in the distance, heading north like herself. They did not see her, but she veered east to stay well apart from them.

One night, after a particularly long day of hiking, Brie dreamed of the bell tower again. This time the figure beside it was moving toward her. To her relief she saw it wasn't a goat-man, and it did not drag anything behind it. But otherwise she could not make out its features, not even if it was man or woman. "I am waiting," it seemed to say.

She woke suddenly, uneasy, a smoke circle wafting over her head, and jumped to her feet. Hanna was sitting by the campfire, smoking her pipe and gazing calmly at Brie. The two dogs, Jip and Maor, lay peaceably on either side of her. Fara was nestled next to Jip. Another large smoke circle drifted lazily out of Hanna's mouth, followed by another smaller one, which sailed through the center of the first.

"Well met, Biri," Hanna said.

"Good morning," Brie responded with a yawn, and went to sit beside Hanna. Brie set about rekindling the fire and brewing a pan of cyffroi.

"I would have started the water boiling, but I didn't want to wake you," said Hanna.

"I must have been sleeping soundly."

"Indeed. It is a good thing I was not a goat-man."

Brie nodded, then said, "I thought to travel alone."

"Think again," said Hanna with a grin.

"I am glad." Brie smiled back.

"I arrived in Ardara just after you left. I saw Sago, and Lom as well."

Brie flushed slightly.

"The sorcerer was ailing and not in any condition to aid the villagers with the sumog that infest their waters."

"Is it bad?" Brie asked.

"Aye. They're scared. No one will go out on the water, and yet they need food." Hanna shook her head. "I got Sago to talk sense long enough to learn you'd left. Said you'd be heading north."

"That was more than he'd tell me," Brie grumbled.

"I gather there was some urgency in your departure," Hanna said. "Lom was little pleased, but he insisted I bring Araf for you." She gestured behind Brie, who turned to see two horses tethered a short distance away. The white mare she recognized as one Hanna used when she was at Farmer Garmon's; the other was indeed Araf, Lom's bay.

"That was kind of him."

"He wishes to wed you."

"I know."

"And?"

"I am afraid I am ill-suited to be Lom's wife. Anyone's wife, for that matter," she added with a trace of bitterness.

"No one? What of the boy Collun?" asked Hanna.

Brie shook her head. "I doubt whether he even calls me friend." She swallowed the rest of the hot cyffroi.

As they broke camp Hanna said to Brie, "Where do we journey, Biri?"

She told Hanna about the bell tower.

"And where does this bell tower lie?" asked Hanna as they mounted their horses.

"I have no idea," Brie answered, her good spirits restored.

But each night Brie dreamed the bell tower again. And each time the figure came closer, though its face was yet obscured. It appeared to be moving across water, on top of it, and she thought it was a man.

They had turned inland, heading east as well as north, at a diagonal. It was familiar terrain to the Traveler. They stopped in only two villages, preferring to keep to the countryside. The Dungalans they encountered were fearful. In addition to rumors of sumog infestations up and down the coast, many reported seeing bands of goat-men moving north. As yet there had been no gabha attacks on Dungalans, but many had lost farm animals to them.

Hanna and Brie crossed the meandering Tyfed River several times, once by means of an enormous moss-covered tree-trunk bridge. And they passed through the Stags of Menhooley, a cluster of large standing stones atop a flat-topped, grassy mound.

Hanna did not seem concerned that they followed no set course, though she occasionally teased Brie. "I've always had an affectionate spot for the horse Araf," she said, "though I'm not sure I would have chosen her as trailblazer."

"Better Araf than me," muttered Brie. But they both guessed, without speaking it out loud, that it was the fire arrow that led them.

It was twilight, a murky, fog-laden twilight. They made camp in a stand of trees, aged wild oaks with crinkled leaves and fissured bark that had a wizened air of secrecy. Hanna and Brie were both quiet as they ate. The animals were quiet, too, and there was a muffled stillness all around them.

When Brie slept that night, it was deeply.

She was gazing down into a valley. In the center of the peaceful valley lay a lake and from the lake rose the bell tower. The figure of the man was stepping off the surface of the lake onto the grassy turf. He gazed up at Brie and beckoned. *Come.*

Brie awakened and rose, taking care not to disturb Hanna. Quietly she picked up her bow and quiver and began to walk through the sessile oaks. She moved deliberately, silently. After walking some time, she finally arrived at the edge of a bluff, where she could see down into the valley below. The murky predawn light faintly illuminated a tall stone building with a cone-shaped roof rising from a small islet in the lake.

The bell tower, she thought, half certain, half unbelieving.

She started down the slope, her legs knifing through wisps of fog as she descended. The tower rose straight and bare with only a few windows, narrow black rectangles placed irregularly along its length. Brie could see a tall arched entrance door at the base.

As she drew closer, through the drifting fog, Brie could make out the figure of the man standing at the edge of the lake. Just as in her dream, he moved slowly toward her.

Her eyes were fixed on the man's face. But even as other aspects of him became clear—his black tunic and soft gray trousers, the golden sword buckled at his side, even his gold hair—his face remained obscured. At first Brie thought it was the fog, but then she thought something must be wrong with her vision. The harder she tried to focus on his face, the less she could see it, as if spiderwebs were stretched over her eyes. She rubbed them, but the filmy blur remained.

"Welcome." The voice was deep and rich and warm, promising unbounded hospitality: a haven of comfort, ease, and refreshment after a long journey. But there was an undercurrent of something else.... What was it? she wondered. Satisfaction, as though something planned for a long time had come off as expected.

# FIFTEEN

# The Man with No Face

The man's warm, caressing voice wrapped around Brie, drawing her closer. But still his face was blurred, shifting.

"I have waited long," he said, and Brie's hand was enveloped in his. She was being propelled toward the lake. Somehow the man with no face had taken control of her limbs, the effect reminding her of the paralysis caused by a morg's touch, except that this was not a cold, spreading numbness but a hot prickle, as if the blood inside her veins were being heated by a flame. Terror caught at her somewhere deep inside, but she could not stop herself from moving forward.

The benevolent voice said, "Here, let us cross to the bell tower."

Even with the stunned, burning feeling in her limbs, Brie faltered. Perhaps the man with no face could walk on the water, but she could not.

He gave an indulgent laugh. "There is a pathway made of stone just under the water. An underwater wall, if you like, an amusing contrivance wrought by the original owner. I will not let you fall."

And indeed, like a master puppeteer, he guided Brie's feet across the stone pathway. The water came up almost to her knees and was so opaque she could not see her boots. The path had been constructed with a devilish ingenuity, twisting and turning in such a way that, on her own, it would have taken half the day for Brie to navigate it.

Finally they stepped up onto the islet, and the man led her to the tower's door. There were carvings above the arch, faces with protruding eyes and tongues thrusting out, and the surface of the door was covered with runes.

The door was slightly ajar, and the man pushed it open, leading her into a round, dim room lit by flickering lanterns. The man pulled the large door shut behind them, then went around Brie to a spiral stairway. Unaccountably, Brie's legs bore her up the stairs behind him. It was a narrow, claustrophobic, unlit space, barely as wide as her shoulders. Once they were out of sight of the entryway, they moved upward in complete darkness.

They climbed silently, the only sounds their breathing and their feet on the gray stone steps. On and on they climbed. Surely we will soon reach the top, Brie thought. But they did not. Instead they came to a landing, which was lit by lanterns that revealed three closed doors. Even here they did not pause, continuing their ascent of the circular stairway. They passed many such landings and many closed doors. It did not seem possible to Brie that the tower could contain so many.

At last the man stopped, on a landing that had only one door. Unlike the others, this door bore a mosaic inlay of gleaming white and gold tiles. Withdrawing a large golden key from a leather pouch at his waist, the man opened the door.

Inside was a sumptuous, beautiful room, gleaming everywhere with gold: gold brocade curtains, elegant enormous tapestries worked with golden thread, luxurious gold velvet rugs, tables and chairs with ornate gilt legs. A soft warm light glowed from dozens of intricately wrought, gold lanterns. A golden table was spread with plates of biscuits and cakes, and carafes of honey-colored wine.

"Please," the man with the blurred face said, pulling out a chair, "you must be weary after your long journey."

Brie wanted to protest, but even as she tried to form the words, her legs were moving, bearing her across the room to a gold velvet chair with golden legs.

Before she sat, the man took her bow and quiver. "You will not need these." He placed them on a gilt table near the door.

Again she tried to protest and again she could not.

Returning to the table, the man filled two plates with food, poured two golden goblets of the honey-colored wine, and said with a smiling voice, "Do eat. You will find you can move your arms now." The hot prickly feeling suddenly left Brie's arms, though remained elsewhere. But she did not eat.

"Who are you?" Brie asked.

"First we eat, then we will talk." He drank from his goblet and then began to eat. Brie still could not see his face. "I assure you," he said between bites, "none of the food or drink has been tampered with. The wine is an excellent vintage, from the first pressing of Oldyn grapes, sweetened with the purest clover honey in Dungal. You must try it, Brie."

He had used her name.

"Show me your face," she said.

The man let out a sigh, then replied, "Very well." He took a last bite, set down his golden cutlery, and wiped his mouth with a golden napkin. Then he pushed himself a short distance from the table.

Mesmerized, Brie watched the man's face. The features began to resolve into a definite pattern; it was a well-favored face with a strong chin, a prominent nose, high cheekbones, and eyes as blue as the core of a lasan flame. It was the face of a young god. Memory stirred in Brie. She knew him, but she could not recall...

He smiled. "It is such a pleasure to see you again, Breo-Saight. Breo-Saight—it was a name I gave you, do you remember? I little guessed then I was a prophet, as well as a sorcerer."

*"Look, Brie. Your arrow flew higher than an eagle. It almost set those clouds aflame."*

*"Was it a good shot?"*

*"The best yet. I know, I shall give you a new name. To match your prowess. Breo-Saight. Fire arrow."*

*"Fire arrow..."*

*"Yes. And one day it shall be known throughout the land. Breo-Saight." A dazzling grin. Her own eager smile in response.*

"Balor," she said. Her cousin.

He smiled at her. "I enjoyed the year I spent at Dun Slieve. Your father was an adequate teacher for what I required at the time. Of course I was only just discovering the potential in me for other things."

"We never heard from you after you left," Brie heard herself say, her voice childlike.

"Ah, it could not be helped. I came here first, to Dungal. I knew I was ready for instruction of a different kind, to kindle the draoicht in me. I had always heard that Dungal was rich in such people, but as it turned out, none was powerful enough, except the mad ones like Yldir. And they would not help me. So I went to Scath."

"Medb," Brie said softly.

"Indeed. A tactical choice, and a fruitful one as it turned out. But enough. Shall we return to our meal? You haven't yet tried the wine."

Brie's mind whirled.

This man Balor, her cousin, acted as if he had brought her here. And yet she thought the arrow, and Sago, had guided her path. Without thinking, she glanced at the quiver.

His eyes followed her glance. "Ah, yes. I had almost forgotten." Brie's stomach tightened. Again Balor laid down his golden fork. He crossed to Brie's quiver and peered inside. Wrinkling his forehead, he put his hand inside, riffling through the arrows.

Balor made a sound of annoyance. "Where is the arrow?"

Brie kept her voice level. "Arrow?"

"The fire arrow. That I sent the incompetent fool Bricriu to retrieve. I understood you bore it with you."

Brie was silent.

Balor turned the quiver over, dumping its contents onto a gold brocade couch. Brie stared at the dozen or so arrows. They all looked alike. None bore the markings of story bands nor the fletching of goldenhawk feathers.

Balor frowned, then shook his head. He gazed at Brie. She kept her face still, expressionless.

"I wonder what you could have done with it," Balor intoned softly. "Left it with your traveling companion, perhaps. Or hidden it. Ah well, it is immaterial. You do not have it here. And you will not be departing this tower, not at least without me.

"Now, since it is clear you do not intend to break bread with me, we must move on. I have an invasion to prepare and there is more I would have you know of me." He spoke the word *invasion* as another would have said "evening banquet," Brie thought.

"My eyes," his voice commanded. And, though afraid, Brie gazed straight into those blue-flame eyes, and as she watched, one of them, the right one, drained of all color. The blue-flame dissolved and was gone. The eyeball was completely white.

Casually Balor drew out a dark green eye-patch and affixed it over his right, colorless eye.

*An eye-patch*...Brie's mind twitched. But Balor's voice called her back.

"You see me now as I am. The gabha call me Gealacan, or White-eye. It was an unfortunate legacy of my apprenticeship with Medb. I was tending a concoction, an experimental brew Medb had prepared using a flake from the cailceadon. She left the room for several moments and I, believing it would accelerate my education—correctly as it turned out—scooped up a fingerful and put it in my mouth. Unfortunately a drop splashed into my eye, with the result you see now. I also lost a part of my finger." He held up his index finger to illustrate his words; it was indeed cut off at the first joint. "And my tongue was damaged as well, though Medb was kind enough to repair that. My eye she left as it was. Partly as punishment, and partly, I believe, to make us more alike. Or perhaps you are unaware of the paleness of Medb's eyes? She thinks them exceedingly handsome and was quite pleased with my matching eye.

"At any rate Medb's brew did wonders for my draoicht, much more than she knows even now. After all, she lost the cailceadon, but I shall always have a part of it inside me. And to lose a bit of color from one's eye, well, that's hardly an intolerable price to pay."

Brie stared at the eye-patch. The dark green was wrong somehow. It should have been black.

"Ah, you have guessed. I promise this shall be the last of my revelations. I apologize for the melodrama. Had there been time, I would have parceled them out more slowly."

Brie knew before he had finished. Like clay pressed into place by artful human hands, his blurred features resolved into a new face—a coarse, brutish Scathian face wearing a black eye-patch.

"Not my own, of course," Balor said. "But useful for the occasion."

Brie let out a thin cry, pain coiling in her chest like a serpent. It was the face of the third murderer, the last of the three men she had sought.

It had been Balor who, from his horse, had directed the others as they murdered her father.

In an instant she was back in the Ramhar Forest. She could smell her father's blood, could almost feel it wet on her skin, though she watched him die from a distance.

The man with the eye-patch, the face she had memorized and sought for so long—it had been a false face after all.

Rage filmed her vision. She strained against the invisible bonds on her limbs.

"You are angry. I understand," Balor said. "It will pass, in time. And would you indeed kill your own cousin, Breo-Saight? I think not. Killing is not in your nature, though I have been impressed with your skill of late."

Brie flinched. It was as if he sought to own her by their shared darkness. "Why did you kill him?" she whispered.

"It was Medb's directive, to kill off Eirren's heroes, the prime of its manhood. It was a sound plan as far as it went; indeed I have done much the same here in Dungal—sending the moths for Yldir, a stonefish for your Sago—but I like to think I have improved on the design. Sow fear and hunger through a land with killing fish and dry winds and the strength to resist will be removed."

"Did you kill Cuillean, too?"

Balor laughed. It was a delighted, amused laugh, as though the idea was a lovely one and he wished he had thought of it. "No indeed. It is not my place to spread gossip, but it is said that, in my absence, someone answering Cuillean's description is a frequent and much-favored visitor at Medb's fortress in Scath.

"I see it does not surprise you. Of course, you saw him there in the forest, watching. Just as you yourself watched."

He had known she was there. Hatred coursed through Brie's veins like a swollen river overflowing its banks. She wanted to kill Balor, wanted to see him lying dead on his gold velvet rug, blood flowing down his face, like her father....

"Now"—Balor's rich voice broke into her thoughts— "time grows short. And I have a rendezvous with a sea serpent." He smiled to himself, a silken, golden smile.

Brie stared ahead, unseeing.

"Sadly, I cannot take you north with me to marshal my forces. But though I may be gone long, rest assured you shall not lack for food and drink. And when I am done, I shall return for you." He rose, coming up behind her.

Balor put his hand on Brie's neck. She fought back the nausea rising in her throat. Deftly he unclasped the bioran holding her braids in place, then he deliberately, slowly, ran his fingers up her scalp and through her hair, unweaving the plaits. His fingers were like talons.

"My pretty cousin," he said softly. "We shall rule it all, together." His words caressed, beckoned. "This little land, Eirren, and, one day, Scath..."

Abruptly he released her and moved to the door. Picking up her bow and quiver, Balor smiled at Brie. "I shall find a safe place for these before I depart."

Then he was gone. She could hear him lock the door from the outside.

Brie's body snapped and sagged. The hot prickling palsy that had trapped her limbs was gone. Rising from the velvet-and-gold chair, she ran to the door. She twisted the handle, pulling hard. The door didn't move. She strained and tugged, kicked the unrelenting surface, even tried forcing her fingers into the infinitesimal space between door and wall.

Breathing hard, Brie leaned her back against the door and gazed around the room. Then she searched its periphery, lifting tapestries, looking behind gilt-framed paintings. There were no windows and no other doors. She found her bioran on a small gilt table and refastened her hair, her hands shaking slightly.

One thing she discovered in her search was an ornate cupboard that was apparently the source of the food and drink Balor had promised to provide. Inside were stacks of brisgeinlike bars, as well as dried fruit and biscuits. There were three large, long-necked carafes of clear water, and another with honey-colored wine. The cupboard's contents would not sustain a person more than several weeks; Balor must have a way to replenish it, Brie thought.

She had no illusions that she could best Balor when he returned for her, either by outright resistance or by trickery. His power was too immense.

She crossed again to the door and leaned down to examine the keyhole. During the early days of her quest to find her father's killers, before she met up with Collun and Talisen, Brie had encountered a wide assortment of fellow wanderers. One of the more interesting had been a thief named Jinn. At the lodging house of a prosperous smuggler, Jinn had taught Brie the finer points of picking a lock.

She would need something long and pointed. Brie's gaze

fell on a golden lantern. It had a thin handle. Straightened, the handle could make an excellent lock pick. Aided by a golden fork from the table, Brie pried the handle out of the lantern. Then she took up a heavy, shimmering bookend and hammered the handle into a straight line.

Crossing to the door, Brie stuck the point into the lock and wiggled it into the mechanism. Unfortunately the lock bore no resemblance to the one on which the thief had taught her. But finally, just when she was on the verge of giving up, she gave a last frustrated jiggle and turn, and there was a click. The door silently swung open.

"Thank you, Jinn," she breathed.

But Brie couldn't help thinking it had been too easy. And indeed, when she finally stood before the great arched doorway at the bottom of the bell tower, she knew why. There was no way through this door.

She had gone over every inch of the unyielding stone surface. There was no lock. And though she was hardly an expert in such matters, she felt sure it had been sealed by sorcery.

Brie sank to her knees. The great stone cylinder in which she was trapped pressed down on her. For a moment she felt lost, withered by despair. Bleakly she gazed up at the flickering lanterns. She wondered if, like the food in the golden room, the oil in them would be replenished until Balor returned for her. Or perhaps he would not return for her and this bell tower was to be her tomb. And perhaps indeed that would be a better thing; Brie thought of Balor's talon-hand on the nape of her neck.

She put her hands to the sides of her head. "I must find a way out," she murmured.

Windows. She remembered seeing them from the outside, just a few, arranged randomly along the length of the tower. And there were golden tapestries that could be fashioned into a rope of sorts, to climb down. She would search the rooms, one by one, until she found a window.

And perhaps she might even find her bow and quiver. She suddenly remembered the arrows lying on the gold brocade—all alike. Where was the fire arrow? It had been in her quiver when she left the campsite.

Brie ran up the circular stairway, arriving out of breath at the first landing. She approached the nearest of the three doors, then hesitated, an unreasoning fear taking hold of her.

Trying to subdue the dread, she slowly turned the handle, opened the door, and looked in. It was dark inside. Brie returned to the landing and took a lantern off the wall. Holding it in front of her, she entered the room. It appeared to be empty, barren. The walls were of stone, dripping with moisture. She spied a window. But as she started toward it, something beneath her feet made a cracking, splintering sound. She looked down to see that the stone floor was covered with bones.

For a moment she froze, then resolutely made her way across the grisly carpet. As she approached the window she saw that it was heavily barred with iron. She tugged on one of the bars; it was unmoving, set deeply into the stone.

She made her way back to the door, spying rusty iron chains and manacles trailing from the walls. Shutting the door behind her, she had the fleeting thought that, except for luxurious trappings, there was little difference between this room and her golden prison cell.

Brie opened the second door on the landing, expecting it to be another dungeon. Instead she found a lush greenhouse with large, abundant green plants. The floor was covered with a thick layer of moss, and Brie crossed the spongy surface to the vine-choked wall. The air was rich and damp, and she started to sweat. She became aware of a musty, rotting smell. It reminded her of the stench of the cro-olachan vine, the blood-drinking plant she and Collun had once come across in their travels. She peered at the vines closely. They did not appear to be cro-olachan, but she took great care as she poked and pushed through them to see if there was a window. There was none.

And so Brie went through the rooms of the bell tower, one by one, each one stranger and ranker than the last. There was a room crawling with insects—black, brown, green, yellow, and orange. They covered the floor and walls, a moving buzzing mass. To look for a window, Brie had to brush them off the walls, her hand covered with her tunic. They glanced off her face and body, some flying frantically around her head.

Then she came to a room with honey dripping off its walls; and a room furred with spiderwebs, with one enormous spider hanging up in a corner. It seemed to see her when she opened the door and immediately scurried along the wall toward her. She slammed the door shut. The floor of one room was covered with small dead birds that she had to wade through, their little lifeless talons scratching against the stone floor. There was a room of shadow and fog, and a room lit by hundreds of ever-burning candles.

One room Brie could not enter, so oppressive was the evil that pulsed from inside. Strange whispering sounds emanated from within the room's yellow darkness. She was able to cast only the briefest of glances, then she pulled the door shut with a shaking hand. It felt as though the door resisted, as though someone on the other side pulled against her. Sweat stood out on her brow as she ran up the circular stairway to the next landing and the next door.

In the end she found only four windows, each one barred with thick bands of unmoving iron. They were shuttered on the outside as well, so she had been unable to see out.

She returned to the landing of the golden room. At first she had thought the circular stairway ended there, but then she noticed a narrow slit through which she found another stairway, this one a spiral also, but even narrower. She had to ascend sideways, holding the lantern over her head.

After a short time her head and shoulders emerged into a chill, open space. The belfry, she realized, staring up at a massive brooding bell that hung fifty feet above her. The bell was black—a hard dull black—its surface pitted and scored with antiquity. The belfry was wholly still, not a breath of air stirred in the oppressive space, yet there was a soughing, gibbering malevolence, like a living thing, that beat at Brie's skin and eardrums. It came from the bell, with its wide gaping mouth and the clapper hanging mute inside, a great evil teardrop.

Gazing up at the walls above, where the lantern light cast eerie shadows, Brie could see where there had once been louver openings to let out the sound of the bell tolling, but they had been mortared shut. A metal ladder rose along the stone wall to the top of the bell stock, and a thick length of hemp hung alongside the ladder. The thought of that hulking bell actually ringing filled Brie with an unreasoning terror.

More than anything she wanted to get away from the belfry, but, setting the lantern down on the top step of the stairwell, Brie inched over to the bottom of the ladder. She wasn't sure how sturdy the floor of the belfry was; it was roughly constructed of wood planking and loose stone. She hoisted herself onto the ladder. The noise that was no noise grew stronger; her eardrums ached and her skin felt as though things were crawling on it. She climbed the rungs, the metal cold on her hands. When she reached a place where the openings had been mortared, she scratched at the surface with her fingernails. But it was as solid as the rock beside it; no bits of soft debris were loosened by her scratching.

Quickly Brie descended the ladder, grabbed the lantern, and slithered down the narrow stairwell as fast as she could. She walked into the golden room and sank down on gold velvet carpeting, rubbing her arms and face until the crawling feeling left her skin.

Brie bowed her head, closing her eyes. She had searched the bell tower from its foundation to the evil top of it. There was no way out.

## SIXTEEN

# The Bell

If only the fire arrow had not been lost to her. Brie could not fathom where it might be. She summoned a picture of the arrow in her mind. She remembered the oddly comforting sensation of it humming against her fingers, and for a moment she could almost feel it. Suddenly the picture changed subtly. She saw her quiver lying in a murky place and, next to it, her bow. Brie gave a start, opening her eyes. The picture faded. But her eyes felt hot and, as had happened before, she could not see clearly. She sat still, puzzled.

Then her stomach rumbled. Thinking back, Brie realized she had not eaten since the evening meal she shared with Hanna. She had lost track of time, but guessed that had been at least a day ago. She thought about the golden

cupboard with its store of food, then shook her head imperceptibly. Perhaps it would indeed be better to die of hunger and thirst in this prison tower than to live as...

Her mind veered away from Balor. Instead she thought of Collun and a deep yearning took hold of her, so overpowering all else was obliterated. She conjured up an image of Collun, and, strangely, a faint humming vibrated under the skin of her fingers.

Collun sat by a campfire, his face illuminated by the orange glow of the flames. He stared into the fire and his face looked tired.

He looked so real, close even. Her humming fingers lifted as though to touch him. "Collun," Brie breathed.

Suddenly Collun looked up, startled.

Then the picture was gone and her vision blurred.

Sometime later, when she left the golden room, her vision was back to normal. Standing on the landing, she could feel the hulking weight of the bell above her, like a totem of doom, challenging her with its ancient evil.

*The toll of a bell*—a signal, to Hanna or Fara, though what they could do for her, she did not know. She again made her way sideways up the circular stairs. A throbbing, persistent mutter seemed to beat against her as she emerged into the belfry. "At your own peril," it seemed to say. "Pull on the rope and know desolation, despair." Its gaping mouth leered at Brie. She grasped the bottom of the ladder and hoisted herself up.

As she came even with the rope, the throbbing noise in the belfry felt almost like a scream. She put out a hand and grasped the thick hemp. It scratched against her palm, and rotted, ancient bits of it fell away. For a moment she feared the whole thing would disintegrate, but it did not.

She pulled.

The bell swayed, but only an inch or two. She pulled again, harder. It swayed again, farther, but not enough for the clapper to strike the sides.

Trying to lodge her backside into the rungs of the ladder, Brie reached out with her other hand so that both hands grasped the rope. She pulled. Still it wasn't enough. With a muttered curse, she pushed herself off the ladder and dropped down, holding fast to the rotting rope.

As she swung through the air the clapper struck the side. The bell rang. Then the rope snapped and she fell.

Her hands caught at a plank of scaffolding, and she hung there. Hand over hand she made her way toward the ladder.

Meanwhile, the bell continued to toll. And the ringing seemed to gain momentum for, instead of subsiding, the bell tolled louder: *Bong! Bong! Bong!* And the chittering, soughing sound that had been so overwhelming before became a tidal wave, assaulting every nerve of her body.

She reached the ladder and clumsily, desperately slid down it. Then she grabbed the lantern.

Suddenly she noticed that a crack had appeared in the stone wall beside her. Two cracks, then three. And the tower seemed to be swaying. The bell continued to swing violently from side to side. *Bong! Bong! Bong!* The walls of the belfry and the floor beneath her feet shuddered with each *Bong.* Then Brie realized the bell tower was starting to break apart.

Side-slipping down the narrow stairway, she emerged on the landing. Inside the golden room she watched as the golden cupboard toppled over; the carafes broke, spraying water and wine over the golden rug and tapestries. Holding tight to her lantern, Brie plunged down the spiral stairway. Inside the stairway, cracks had begun to appear, and dust sprayed out with each new fissure, clouding the air. Brie's heart drummed as her feet pounded the stone steps. The cracks grew larger, more jagged. Small pieces of rubble littered the steps, and shards of stone pelted her head and shoulders.

She took the steps three at a time. Then, as she leaned into the wall for balance, a whole section fell away, and she tumbled headfirst down the stairs. She landed hard on a landing, stone dust raining down on her. Painfully she pulled herself to her feet. The door nearest her lolled open, its wood splintered. A buzzing, flapping exodus of insects swarmed around her. Screaming, she dived for the stairway.

Broken doors gaped open on all the landings. Once Brie slipped in something viscous and almost collided with the enormous spider; another time she tripped and skidded over bone fragments; she fended off clutching vines and choked on thick, smoky fog.

At last she reached the bottom. She ran to the massive door. Spidery cracks crisscrossed its stone surface, but to her horror the door remained unrelenting, immovable. It would be just her luck, Brie thought, if the whole tower collapsed on top of her, but this door remained standing, permanent until the end of time.

"Help!" Brie shouted.

She could hear nothing over the roar of the collapsing tower and the unceasing *Bong! Bong! Bong!* of the bell. Brie winced as a large chunk of stone struck her on the back.

"Help!" she cried again. Hanna and Fara were out there somewhere, though how they would hear her cries over the sound of the thundering bell she did not know. But she kept calling, until her throat was raw and caked with stone dust.

She paused a moment, leaning her forehead against the cracked stone. And through the deafening tumult she heard a very faint cry.

"Brie!"

She held her breath.

It came again, louder. "Brie, are you there? It's Collun."

At first she did not believe; she thought she must be back in the golden room, dreaming of him. He could not be on the other side of the door. She swallowed hard, then shouted, "Collun?"

"Brie!" It was Collun's voice, and it was real.

The bell seemed to be getting louder. To Brie's aching ears it seemed to say *Doom! Doom! Doom!* Through her fingertips she could feel pounding on the outside of the door, but the door did not give. Part of the ceiling collapsed around her. Honey and warm candle wax dripped from above onto her skin; insects crawled across the floor.

"Collun!" she screamed.

She heard him curse, then came a series of muffled sounds accompanied by the neighing of a horse. A long jagged crack splintered down the length of the door.

Instantly there was a crash, a flash of horse's hooves, and the door before her split in two. Brie pushed through the jagged opening. Collun grabbed her hand, boosting her up onto the back of a horse. Wrapping her hands in the familiar soft white mane, Brie leaned her head alongside the horse's neck and whispered "Ciaran," as the Ellyl horse spun and galloped away.

Ciaran navigated the zigzags of the underwater pathway with ease, and Brie turned to see Collun following on the

Ellyl horse Fiain. Pieces of the tower rained down along their path and suddenly a large chunk of masonry plunged into the water directly in front of Brie and Ciaran, hurtling water into their faces and pulverizing the stone walkway beneath their feet. Without hesitating, Ciaran plunged into the water.

Despite the shock of the cold water, Brie managed to stay on the Ellyl horse. Ciaran headed unerringly for the bank of the lake. Like Fara, Ciaran was as comfortable in water as on land. As the lake grew shallower, Ciaran's hooves found bottom; then they burst out of the water at full speed. Ciaran did not stop until they were far away from the disintegrating tower.

Brie anxiously watched for Collun and Fiain and was relieved to see them emerge, dripping, from the lake.

Fiain cantered to Ciaran's side and they all turned to watch the tower. Unbelievably it still stood, though great chunks were missing. The tower began to list heavily to one side, top-heavy with its great evil load.

Suddenly there was an earsplitting sound, a thunderous crack, and as they watched, riveted, the tower finally collapsed. The bell hit the water with an enormous splash, giving a last deafening *Bong!* as it broke the surface and then sunk. The water roiled and heaved, as if from a mighty wind, and large waves sloshed over the banks of the lake. But the bell tower had vanished completely from sight.

Brie stared at the water. The waves subsided and it was not long before the surface was once again smooth, gleaming like a mirror, revealing nothing.

The fire arrow was gone, buried under tons of stone and

wood, at the bottom of the lake. Brie felt short of breath, almost winded, as from a blow or a loss that could never be repaired.

"Brie?" Collun's voice broke into her grief. Ciaran whickered.

Brie tore her gaze from the lake, unconsciously straightening her back. Suddenly she spotted Fara loping over the grass toward them. Brie quickly dismounted and was almost knocked down by the faol's joyous greeting. Fara's sandpapery tongue left her cheeks wet.

"Where is Hanna?" Brie asked, her eyes darting from the banks of the lake to the bluff and back again. Fara let out a low mournful sound.

"I found a woman, unconscious," Collun interjected, "by the side of the lake, with Fara and two dogs. She..." He paused. "Once I convinced the dogs I could be trusted, I did what I could, that is, until the bell started to toll...I do not know if she will make it."

Brie gave an anguished sound. Urging Fiain forward, Collun quickly led Brie to a small grove of ash trees a short distance from where they had watched the tower collapse. Brie saw Hanna lying still, Jip and Maor huddled beside her.

Bending her ear to Hanna's chest, Brie listened for the older woman's heartbeat. Nothing. Her own heart was pounding, loud, too loud to hear anything. She continued to listen and finally heard a faint thrum, as if from far off. But she could not tell if the sound came only from her desperate need to hear something.

"Hanna," Brie murmured, thinking, She cannot be dead; she must not. In despair Brie lay beside her friend to warm her. She encircled the inert, chilled body with her arms—heart to heart, brow to brow, hand to hand—willing Hanna to breathe.

Then Brie heard a faint noise, like a breath. Brie opened her eyes. She put her hand above Hanna's partly opened mouth. Yes, she could feel a whisper of air.

"Hanna!" Brie cried.

The older woman's eyelids wrinkled, then opened. Brie sat up, taking her friend's cold hand in hers and chafing it gently.

"Thank Amergin," Brie breathed.

Hanna gazed quietly up at her.

Brie could tell Hanna lacked the strength to speak and gave her hand a squeeze. "Rest now," she said.

Night had fallen, and silently Collun set about lighting a fire. He took herbs from the wallet he wore across his chest and made a posset of hyssop and lavender for Hanna. When it was done the older woman obediently drank it, then slept. Brie fell asleep as well, sitting beside Hanna, holding on to her hand.

Brie woke in darkness. For a moment she did not know where she was, thinking herself back in the bell tower. She was very cold and began to shiver uncontrollably. She carefully sat up and wrapped her arms around her knees, trying to stop the shivering.

"Brie?" It was Hanna, and Brie could just make out her figure, lying propped up an arm's length away. She was drinking more of Collun's concoction, holding the cup herself. Collun was leaning forward, poking the fire with a stick. Flames leaped up, illuminating his face.

"I have met Wurme-killer," Hanna said in Eirrenian.

Collun frowned. "Collun," he said. "Are you hungry, Brie?"

"Starving," Brie replied in a hoarse voice.

And though it was the middle of the night, Collun re-heated the water and began mixing up a batch of oatcakes. Brie moved closer to Hanna and to the fire.

"What happened to you, Biri, in the tower?" asked the older woman, gazing critically at Brie.

Brie shook her head, unready to talk of it. "First you," she said.

"There is little enough to tell," responded Hanna. "When I woke and found you gone, the dogs and Fara picked up your scent and followed it down the bluff to the lake. There was a thick mist over it, obscuring the tower, but I guessed this to be the lake we sought.

"Fara was all for swimming right out into that mist, but I didn't like the look of it. So, more fool I, I decided to try to lift the cursed thing. Now fogs, either lifting or causing them, make me dizzy, but this one had my head swirling like the Corryvrecken whirlpool. The harder I tried, the worse the spinning got, until I hardly knew ground from sky. And I realized, just a little too late, that this was no ordinary fog, but a llen dewin, a sorcerer's veil. And an almighty powerful sorcerer's at that. I felt myself being pulled into the vortex, and I could not stop it. That's the last thing I knew. Except for the dogs howling and Fara licking my hand raw with that tongue of hers."

"It was Fara who led me to the lake and to Hanna," interjected Collun, handing Brie an oatcake. He offered her honey, which she refused, and then he sat down to eat an oatcake himself. In the light of the fire, Brie covertly watched Collun. He looked different to her. Taller and leaner. Of course he had gotten older since she had left him at Cuillean's dun. But his gestures were the same. Brie's heart squeezed with some indefinable emotion.

Collun looked up and Brie quickly averted her eyes. Abruptly Collun rose and left the fire, carrying the pan he'd used for cooking.

"I like your friend," came Hanna's voice, drowsy. Soon Brie could hear Hanna's even breathing.

When he returned to the fire, Brie asked Collun if Hanna would be all right now.

"I believe so, though I know little of weather magic. At any rate, sleep will do her good," Collun responded. "It looks as though you could use more rest yourself," he added, gazing down at Brie's haggard face. Suddenly self-conscious, she raised her hand to her matted hair, bits of insect and candle wax still tangled in it.

"Collun, I..."

"Go to sleep, Brie." She could not read his face in the darkness above the fire, but the chill in his voice puzzled her. It was almost enough to keep her from sleep, but not quite. Again she drifted off, to the sounds of Hanna breathing and the firewood settling.

Brie woke early. The sun had dawned bright and it promised to be a warm spring day. Both Collun and Hanna still slept. Brie stood, dug out the remaining sliver of Monodnock's white lilac soap from her pack, and walked to the lake. Fara appeared silently at her side as she gazed out over the smooth mirrored surface. It was as if the bell tower, with its strange rooms and great evil bell, had never even existed. Like the fire arrow, it was gone without so much as a ripple to show for it.

Fara rubbed against Brie's leg, purring. "I know," Brie said, rubbing her thumbs over the tips of her fingers, remembering the tingling feeling of the arrow. "I'll get over it." But she was not sure she ever would.

Quickly Brie washed in the cold water. When she returned to camp she found that Hanna still slept, but Collun had kindled the fire. He was brewing chicory and the familiar smell warmed her. She had not had chicory since leaving Eirren. Collun poured her a cup and she took it gratefully.

"If you had not come, I would have died. Thank you," she said humbly.

"In truth, I did little." Again she heard the chill in his voice.

"Collun...," she began.

"More oatcakes?" He interrupted her.

"Please," for she was still very hungry, though this new tone in Collun's voice distracted her from her rumbling stomach.

Suddenly Brie remembered the dream she had had of Cuillean's dun and the soldier Renin dead. "Did something happen, Collun? At Cuillean's dun?"

Collun's face shifted, his eyes went opaque like teine stones. "Several months after you left, there was an attack, by Scathians and morgs."

"The soldier Renin?"

"Dead." His voice was flat. "You knew?"

"It was a dream I had, but tell me."

"There is not much to tell. They came by sea. We were taken by surprise. Fortunately it was a small band and we managed to fight them off." His jaw had gone rigid. "We buried Renin on that headland overlooking the sea. And over his cairn I pledged that would be the end of it; I would no longer be the bearer of the cailceadon. It has cost too much." Brie knew that Collun was thinking of Crann, the wizard of the trees.

"I journeyed to Temair and gave the trine and stone to Queen Aine and King Gwynn."

Brie knew how much it must have cost Collun to give up his beloved trine.

"They agreed to take it?"

"It was not a choice."

Anger, that was what Brie heard in Collun's voice. A silence grew up between them.

"So, Brie, did you find your revenge?" Collun's eyes were still hard, opaque; and though they were said almost casually, the words were like a knife thrust.

# SEVENTEEN

# Return to Ardara

**B**rie looked down at her hands; they looked dirty and she rubbed at them, though she had just washed them in the lake with Monodnock's soap, two, three times.

"Why did you come here?" she whispered.

Collun turned away. "When I was at the royal dun in Temair, there were visitors, neighbors of your aunt and uncle. They told of your stay at Dun Slieve and of your subsequent departure for the north and the mountains. Then word came of creatures called gabha who had attacked a farmhold along the way into the Blue Stacks. I was concerned and thought to journey there, but was told the mountains were impassable. I spent the winter in Temair with my sister."

"How is Nessa?" asked Brie quickly.

"Well, thank you," he replied politely. The cadence of his voice was stilted, formal, as if she were a stranger with whom he was exchanging pleasantries.

"Near winter's end the Ellyl horse Ciaran came to Temair. Through Fiain she conveyed the message that she believed you to be in danger. Ciaran, Fiain, and I made our way through the Blue Stacks, fending off several goat-men as we went. I had thought to journey to the village of Ardara, where your trail led, but Ciaran pushed us straight north.

"She was unerring, insistent, but I confess I came to feel the whole thing a fool's errand. Then, not long ago, something happened. I was sitting by the campfire when suddenly I heard you calling me. Your voice, clear as a bell, if you will pardon the expression." Brie smiled, but Collun did not smile back.

"It was so real that I actually stood up and looked around the campfire. And then I saw you. Only it wasn't you; that is, your edges were blurry and there was gold around you. And then you were gone, just like that. But for a moment I could see a large tower in the middle of a lake. Then everything faded. I looked at the map of Dungal I had brought with me from Temair. And there was a lake, very near to where we were. It did not take us long to reach the lake and the tower.

"It was Ciaran who led us over that confounded path in the water and Ciaran who broke the door down."

"How?"

"When that big crack appeared, she just flew out with her hooves, right in the center of it. The door split open and there you were.

"What happened to you in the bell tower, Brie?" he asked, and for just a moment she heard an echo of the old gentle voice she remembered so vividly. Strangely her eyes pricked with tears. Running her hand through her wet hair, she answered, making her voice brisk.

"I was a prisoner, a sorcerer's prisoner. Balor is his name. He turns out to be a cousin of mine."

Collun stared at her. "Cousin?"

"It is a long tale; I have not the heart for it now. But Balor is planning to invade and overthrow Dungal, with Eirren not far behind. The people of Dungal must be warned. There may still be time to raise an army." There was color in her cheeks and her hands were clenched.

"I see," said Collun.

"Is Hanna strong enough to travel?"

"I am," the older woman said, coming up behind. "And if what you say is true, we must leave at once." She was pale, but her eyes held strength. "Where is this sorcerer now?" she asked.

"I do not know. North, he said, to marshal his forces."

"He must have a stronghold of some kind. Did he say anything else?"

Brie shook her head. "Wait, yes...He said something about going to meet a sea serpent."

Hanna's eyes darkened with a puzzled expression. "Serpent," she said, musing. "Where is that wizard's map of yours?" she asked abruptly.

Brie handed her Crann's map, with a sidelong glance at Collun.

"I seem to recall hearing of a rock formation, far north, lying off the coast, that bears a resemblance to a wurme or serpent." The older woman ran her finger along the line of Dungal's coast on the map.

"Ah," she breathed. "Carreg-sarff. Here, as I thought." She pointed to a cluster of dots on the map. "Perhaps the villain Balor has chosen Sedd Wydyr as his stronghold."

"Sedd Wydyr?"

"It is an ancient fortress, built by one of Dungal's first queens. She used the native white stone as well as crystal-bearing rocks of far-off Gledna to build her castle. The royal family had considerable draoicht in those days, but it was still a magnificent feat of workmanship. It was said that when the sunlight shone on Sedd Wydyr it glittered so brightly as to bring blindness on those who beheld it. It also went by the name Crystal Castle."

"It sounds like a dwelling that would suit Balor," Brie said dryly.

"I have not traveled that far north so I have not seen Sedd Wydyr, but even if it still stands, it would be in ruins."

"Like your ancient queen, Balor has considerable draoicht," Brie replied. "I am sure he has restored the crystal castle and that it glitters even brighter than before."

Both Hanna's mare and the bay horse Araf had bolted when the bell began to toll, so Hanna rode with Brie on Ciaran. They decided to go directly to Sedd Brennhin, the royal seat of Dungal, to tell Prince Durwydd himself of the threat to Dungal. Hanna had met the prince on several occasions and felt sure of an audience.

But as they began moving up the bluff, away from the lake, Brie felt uneasy, torn. A curious tingling had begun on her hands, not unlike the humming of the fire arrow.

"Bother," Brie muttered. "The arrow is gone," she told herself sternly.

"What?" asked Hanna from behind.

"Nothing," Brie replied. The Ellyl horse hesitated, giving a low whinny.

Suddenly Brie laid her hand on Ciaran's neck. "The lake," she whispered. And the horse wheeled and headed back to the lake.

"Brie?" Collun called after her. But Brie did not hear.

When they reached the lakeshore, Brie dismounted and began walking along the water's edge. Clouds had come up, blanketing the sun. The water was very still. Brie strained to see into it, to see the broken tower and, somewhere among the mountain of jagged stone, the fire arrow. But all she saw was her own face reflected back at her, drawn and desolate. Collun's face appeared beside hers.

"What do you seek, Brie?"

"An arrow."

"Can you not make more arrows?"

"No," Brie said impatiently, eyes focused on the water.

"Son of Cuillean," called Hanna, still astride Ciaran. Collun moved back to Hanna, who spoke to him in a low voice.

Brie paid no attention to them and continued to walk beside the lake, rubbing her tingling hands against the sides of her legs. What did she think she was going to do? Dive in and scavenge among the rubble for an arrow that had no doubt been splintered into a hundred pieces? Or did she think the arrow might miraculously rise to the surface and float across to her? She felt the tingling again and kept walking. She walked until she was more than halfway around the lake. The tingling had grown stronger.

"Uffern," she muttered. The tingling was turning into an unpleasant itching. Suddenly she noticed she was moving away from the lake into the sedges and shrubs. She wasn't quite sure why; there was no path, though perhaps a very faint trace of someone at some time having moved this way before.

She entered a small copse of trees. Inside the grove she discovered a large circular patch where the trees had been cleared away, except for a tall, slender rowan, which stood in the very center. Brie walked up to the tree and stood in front of it, half-expectant. Nothing happened.

Staring at the bark of the tree, looking for something, though she did not know what, she rubbed her stinging hands against her tunic.

"Brie?" Collun called. He had followed and was moving through the trees toward her. Brie silently motioned for him to stop before entering the exposed circle, then she went back to gazing at the tree.

She felt keyed up, irritable. The itching on her hands was now a burning, painful sensation. She kept wanting to rub them against her tunic, but when she did, it hurt. What does this tree have to do with anything? she asked herself crossly.

Then, inconsequently, she had the memory of Aelwyn laying her hands against Monodnock's porth, and she had the sudden urge to do the same to the rowan in front of her. At least it might make the prickling feel better, she thought.

She laid her burning hands on the tree's surface and the next moment she was standing in darkness, her palms resting on something cool and smooth to the touch.

"Uffern," she muttered again. "Now where am I?" Fortunately her pack was on her back, and after fishing out several lasan sticks, she lit one on the rock floor of wherever it was she was standing.

In the dim light she could see she was in some kind of tomb, a passage grave it looked to be, and she was in the vaulted inner room. Her hands had been resting on a marble column carved to resemble a rowan tree. Then she heard a pounding sound and someone faintly calling her name.

She lit another lasan stick and, spotting a torch stuck in a wall sconce, took it down. Quickly she set the torch alight and hurried down the passage that ended in a bolted door. With some effort she lifted the bolt and pushed open the door. Collun stood there, looking startled. Brie could see Hanna behind him, with the two horses.

"What happened, Brie?" Collun asked.

"I don't know. Come in if you like," said Brie, still irritable. She abruptly turned and made her way back down the passageway. Collun followed, while Hanna remained outside with the horses.

The rowan tree column stood in a center chamber, with another chamber on either side of it. The middle chamber was piled high with glimmering ornaments: jeweled boxes from which cascaded gold bracelets, gorgets, arm rings, finger rings, pendants, bead necklaces, and torques. The room to the left was devoted mainly to swords and scabbards, as well as shields, with a few chests holding silver and gold coins, and some with tapestries folded inside; the third chamber consisted mainly of burial urns and pots, as well as more weaponry.

As Collun gazed about in awe, Brie took the torch and began to prowl the chambers, illuminating every dark and cobwebbed corner. Her palms felt as though they were on fire. Finally she found what she sought—her quiver and bow. They were haphazardly propped up against the wall, in the shadow of a large sarcophagus.

Barely able to breathe, Brie pulled the arrows out of the quiver, holding them in her burning hand. She stared down at them, bringing the torch close. They were all arrows she had made: plain, unadorned arrows. A sob caught in her throat. But then one of the arrows blurred. It began to change, metamorphosing with flashes of gold and purple and brown and shimmers of pure light. And, amazingly, there among the other arrows in her hand lay the fire arrow, complete with story bands and goldenhawk fletching. Relief coursed through Brie and her knees almost gave way.

As she straightened, she felt a surge of irrational triumph. The fire arrow had concealed itself from Balor; it had been stronger. If the arrow had been a person, she would have hugged it to her fiercely. As it was, she just gazed down at it, a stupid smile on her face.

"You found what you were seeking?"

She looked up at Collun. "Yes, yes, I did." She saw that Collun was staring at the arrow. "It's, um, a magic arrow. It's sort of done things to me, like, uh, leading me in here, I guess," she said. "And that night by the campfire, when you thought you saw me? Well, I think the arrow did that, even though it was here and I was in the tower..." She trailed off.

"I see, I think." He was eyeing her a little warily.

"Don't look at me like that," she said, sounding cross. "Let us return to Hanna." Brie put the fire arrow back in the quiver and slung it across her back. She noticed that the fiery feeling in her hands had gone.

"Wait," Collun said, looking around the chamber. "I wonder..."

"What?"

"Well, I was just thinking. Perhaps I ought to arm myself," he said offhandedly.

Brie stared at him. The Collun she knew before had disliked weapons of any kind.

"Kled came with me to Temair. He gave me some lessons in swordplay. It helped to pass the winter."

"I see," Brie said.

Collun took the torch from Brie and, lifting it up, scanned the array of swords.

Brie watched him as he moved slowly through the chambers. He lifted an elegant sword with a golden hilt, encased in a golden scabbard. He unsheathed it with a flourish, and the gleaming blade seemed to pulse; rays of gold lit the chamber. Uneasy, he resheathed it.

None of the swords seemed to suit him. Then he crossed to a blade lying on the ground, half obscured by a gilded trunk. He picked it up. It was a plain sword with no carving or precious metal. There was a little nick in the blade near the grip, and faint markings on the blade, but they were too worn down to make out, except for a very dim eight-pointed star. The scabbard was plain dark leather.

"This one looks about right for me," he said. Brie watched as he found a baldric and strapped the sword to his waist. It did look right somehow.

"I'm ready," Collun announced, his voice impersonal again. Brie picked up a small sword for herself, as well as an extra dagger.

When they left Balor's treasure chambers, Brie turned to look at the white marble structure. As she did the marble almost seemed to wrinkle and fold, and spiral shapes began curling across its surface. Then the building evaporated, leaving nothing behind but the single rowan tree in the center of the glade.

The first night of their journey to Sedd Brennhin, as Hanna slumbered and Brie restrung her bow, Collun asked, "So how did you do that, I mean, find the rowan tree and make the passage grave appear?"

Brie shook her head. "The fire arrow must have been working through me somehow. All I knew was that my hands were driving me crazy."

"That's some arrow," Collun said.

"Yes."

A silence grew between them. Then Collun abruptly spoke. "You have never answered the question I asked. Did you find your revenge?"

Brie stared sightlessly down at the bow across her lap. A sudden bright image of the bog and the dying men and the blood on her skin came before her eyes, and she began to tremble. She felt the old shame, as if her skin was fouled with blood that could never be washed off. "I cannot...," she breathed.

He was beside her at once. "Tell me, Brie." She could feel his breath warm on her cheek, and his fingers encircled her wrist.

And she did; she told Collun all of it, as she had told Lom on the deck of the Storm Petrel, only this time she let the tears come and Collun's arms went around her as she wept. Brie thought she had never felt so much of pain and of joy all at the same time.

When Hanna woke in the morning she saw Brie and Collun side by side, sharing a laugh at Fara, who greedily was eating oatcakes as fast as Collun could flip them out of the pan. The older woman smiled to herself, but said nothing of it.

That day as they rode ahead of Collun, Hanna asked Brie, "Who is Balor, this black sheep of your family?"

"He is, uh, was consort to Medb." She cast an uneasy glance back at Collun.

"Does he do her bidding?"

"I do not know, but I believe he plays a lone hand."

"To betray the Queen of Ghosts is perhaps imprudent?"

"Fearless, at any rate. Hanna, Balor killed my father." Hanna reached forward for Brie's hand, holding it hard. "You told Collun?"

"Yes." But the one thing she had not told him was what Balor had said of Collun's father, Cuillean, and his new abode in Scath.

Not being fond of the sea, and perhaps leery of the potential for flood, Prince Durwydd had moved the royal seat of Dungal from its original spot on the coast to a verdant but isolated valley that lay a day's journey from the fishing village of Mira. The old Sedd Brennhin, which Fionna had saved from the great flood and from where she ruled the kingdom of Dungal for many peaceful and prosperous years, lay deserted.

As they journeyed, Hanna told them something of Prince Durwydd. "He has little will for ruling, as I have already told Biri. Indeed it was ill-omened that he should have been the only heir to the throne. His main preoccupations are the stars, their movements and meaning, and Ellylon; he is fascinated by the mysterious kingdom of Tir a Ceol. He has even managed to befriend several Ellylon and, on several occasions, visited the northern reaches of Tir a Ceol with them. To his credit, he keeps several sound advisers around him, but they are not rulers."

It took five days of hard travel to reach Durwydd's fortress. As they entered the valley, Brie spotted a flutter of movement to the north. She was not sure, but thought that just as they entered the valley from the east, a company of men on horseback had left it, heading north. She was too far away to have seen what manner of men they were.

As they came to the dun's entrance, they saw that the portcullis was raised and the large door ajar.

"This bodes ill," said Hanna, peering uneasily about for watchmen or guards. Brie's nose twitched. She smelled goat.

Inside the fortress they found a hideous silence, and the terrible reek of goat-men. The inhabitants of the dun had been slaughtered, and not very long ago. Their bodies lay scattered about the rooms and hallways. Hanna's face was grim, her eyes a burning black.

But as they searched the dun they found no trace of Prince Durwydd, dead or alive. In a corner tower they came across one of his advisers, a grizzled, gray-bearded man called Ralfe, who was sorely injured, yet still alive. He told them that Durwydd, oppressed by his subjects' troubles with drought and sumog, had fled to Tir a Ceol, for a short "vacation," as he called it.

"He left yesterday; today the foul creatures came." Ralfe

shuddered violently. As both Hanna and Collun worked to heal him, Brie gazed around the tower room, at the blood and lifeless bodies. Balor had indeed woven his net wide and strong, she thought.

Eventually Ralfe had fallen into an uneasy slumber, and Collun told them the adviser had a good chance of recovering. Further searching led them to several more survivors of the brutal attack, among them a voluble cook called Iryna, who had hidden in the storeroom at the bottom of the fortress, behind barrels of ale. She had some healing skill, so Collun put her in charge of the wounded. Her son, steady-eyed beyond his young years, had hidden with his mother in the storeroom and turned out to be a capable and energetic helper.

"When he returns, we will tell Prince Durwydd of the gabha," said the son.

"And you must tell him, too," said Brie, "of the powerful sorcerer whose bidding they do. Even as we speak, this sorcerer marshals his forces to invade Dungal. The army must be readied—" She broke off. "*Has* Dungal an army?" asked Brie.

Hanna shook her head. "Not one that is trained or organized. There has been little need of an army in Dungal, not for hundreds of years."

"An army must be mounted now."

"Yes, but—," began Hanna.

"*We* will mount an army. We will start with Ardara and work our way north, to Sedd Wydyr," said Brie decisively. Hanna's black eyes widened; she and Collun exchanged a glance.

"Yes, let us go to Ardara," Hanna agreed.

They traveled swiftly, pushing the Ellyl horses to their limit. They arrived in Ardara spent and exhausted.

Brie and Hanna decided to split up, while Collun waited with the horses on the outskirts of town. Hanna would go to Farmer Garmon and then on to the village, while Brie would head directly for the harbor and to Sago.

Brie hoped to find Lom first. There was much she wanted to explain to him, though she did not know where she would find the words. But when she arrived at the harbor, it was deserted. And, despite the fact that it was a fair day, perfect for fishing, the boats were all pulled up on the sand. She headed into town and found Lom at the Speckled Trout with Jacan and a knot of other fishermen.

They told Brie that the waters around Ardara continued to be infested with sumog. Several more fishermen had been killed when sumog viciously attacked their boats. A small child had even been dragged to his death when he strayed too close to the water's edge. No one would go out on the water now.

When Sago had recovered from the stonefish poison, the old sorcerer had gone out in his boat and a few twinkling lights had been seen. But after the first night there were no more lights, and freak storms had blown up. They found pieces of Sago's boat washed up on shore. A group of villagers had gone to see how the sorcerer fared and found him weak and completely addled. It was as if the loss of his boat had broken the old man. Lom made it a point to go every day to make sure he ate and slept, but said he feared the sorcerer had burned out the last of his sorcery. And the sumog kept ravaging the waters of Ardara.

"I know where sumog come from," Brie said, and then she poured out her tale. All the patrons of the Speckled Trout gathered round to listen. At first her tongue felt like a tangled fishing line, but the words came and the fisherfolk listened. As she spoke, Brie caught a glimpse of the innkeeper on the edges of the group. She suddenly remembered the stonefish the innkeeper had planted in Sago's amhantar and cursed herself for a fool for choosing this place to tell her tale. But there was nothing she could do. The innkeeper said nothing, just listened closely, a scowl on his face.

When Brie was done it was Lom who said quietly, "When do we go north?"

"At dawn tomorrow."

"Where shall we meet?"

"Veena Creek, on the outskirts of town."

Lom turned and faced the Ardarans. "Who will come?"

There were several heartfelt "Ayes!" and a handful of nodding heads.

Then the innkeeper elbowed his way forward, saying, "Fools! Would you put yourselves in the hands of a leannan-shee?!"

Stunned, Brie stared at the innkeeper. Lom, his face red with anger, took a step toward him. Brie opened her mouth to reveal the innkeeper's treachery, but he spoke first. "Think, ye half-wits," he spit out. "Things only began to go bad after the leannan-shee came to Ardara. She's claimed Lom here, and the boy Dil." Jacan held Lom back while the innkeeper continued. "And you've seen how chummy she's been with that feeble-minded, washed-up Sea Dyak sorcerer. No doubt they've been in it together all along."

A restraining hand still on Lom's shoulder, Jacan spoke loudly. "Pay the innkeeper no heed. Dungal is threatened. We must spread the word. Come." Brie had been on the verge of speaking out about the innkeeper's own complicity in the stonefish attack on Sago, but Jacan had linked his arm in hers and was leading a large group of fishermen out of the Speckled Trout. Looking back, she noticed that a handful of villagers stayed behind and were huddled by the ale tap, listening to the innkeeper.

Lom and the others went to spread the word, while Brie headed for Sago's mote.

"The prodigal returns. Sing hey nonny no!"

Sago was sitting on the front step of his mote, a kittiwake on one shoulder and one at his feet. He looked smaller than before and his head was naked, no cap the color of seawater and no hair at all. He smiled when he saw Brie, but did not try to rise. There was a new fragility in him that frightened her.

"Shall we to battle then?" he said, eyes alight. He tried to stand, but fell back, chortling, "You bring the lantern, I'll bring the pole, and we'll have sumog for dinner tonight!"

"Sago, I am sorry about your boat, about Gor-gwynt."

> *"Once there was a little rig;*
> *a seabird taught it how to jig.*
> *It danced all day, it danced all night,"*

Sago intoned with a frenzied grin, "and then it danced right out of sight."

"Sago, I have met Balor."

The sorcerer laid a finger aside his nose, cocking his head to one side. "Balor, Balor. A shining boy, as I recall, an ambitious boy. Ill-pleased when I would not teach him. I could not see it; no, he had no aptitude for fishing."

"We are trying to gather an army, to fight Balor."

*"Four and twenty sailors*
*Went to kill a snail.*
*And a little maid shall lead them,*
*All around the dale,"*

he chanted, throwing a piece of bread in the air. As the kittiwake on his shoulder launched itself into the air to go after it, its talons dug into Sago's thin shoulder and he winced, doubling over.

He straightened with a grimace, and asked, eyes wide, "And when dost the army march? For I shall march with you, oh yes, indeed, I shall."

"You are not well enough, Sago."

"A parrot fish a day keeps the healers away." Sago grinned. "When and where?"

"Dawn tomorrow. Veena Creek," Brie told him reluctantly.

Sago rose, with an effort painful to watch, picked up his amhantar, and slung it over his shoulder. "Time for one last treasure hunt, then." He raised his hand in farewell and slowly headed down toward the sea. He moved like a very old man, tentatively, stiffly. Brie watched him for several moments, then turned and left the beach.

# EIGHTEEN

# Bren-huan

As she made her way back through Ardara, Brie spotted Lom.

"How was Sago?" he asked as they fell into step together.

Brie shook her head. "He says he will journey north with us."

"He has not the strength."

Brie nodded her agreement absently. Then she cleared her throat. "Uh, thank you for sending me Araf. I am afraid she ran off."

"She found her way back to Ardara."

Brie looked surprised.

"Yes, somewhat of a miracle. But Araf is smarter than she appears to be." They exchanged a smile.

Brie took a breath. "Lom, I..."

"No," Lom interrupted, raising a hand. "I know. I knew when you left Ardara. Your way lies somewhere other than a small Dungal fishing village."

Brie was silent for a moment, then, "I wish it were not so."

"I know that as well." He smiled at her. "Perhaps I am like the horse Araf in that way."

Brie laughed with Lom, then her smile faded. "Will they come? The Ardarans?"

Lom shook his head. "I do not know. Some, but there are many who are afraid. And the innkeeper's words will give them a reason to stay."

"The innkeeper serves the sorcerer Balor. He helped to plant the stonefish that sickened Sago."

"I see." Lom looked grim. "Well, there is still time before dawn. I will do what I can do."

Brie slept poorly that night. By the time dawn came she had been awake for some time, having brewed a pan of cyffroi, given both Fiain and Ciaran thorough rubdowns, as well as a hearty breakfast of oats, and even begun work on new arrows for her quiver.

Collun joined her at the fire, and she handed him a cup of cyffroi. He drank it quickly, expressing doubt that he could ever get used to the taste. Veena Creek was low, showing signs of the drought.

Lom was the first to come, with Jacan, Ferg, Hyslin,

and Gwil not far behind. Lom told Brie that his father, Farmer Garmon, had wished to come, but Lotte had begged and pleaded with him to stay, until, unwilling, he capitulated. Hyslin was there to see Gwil off. A large farmer named Huld arrived at the creek, followed by two brothers, both fishermen, who looked alike, lean and small. A boy named Marc, brother to the girl Beith, who loved to tease Ferg, came. Beith was there, too, to see her brother off. There was no laughter in her snapping black eyes this morning. Dil, the boy to whom Brie had given archery lessons, rode up on a dappled pony. He grinned at Brie, holding up his homemade bow. Then a young fisherman with thick eyebrows called Clun came, accompanied by his younger sister, at whom he frequently scowled for coming against his wishes. She was Maire, a tall girl with a stubborn chin. Then Henle arrived, accompanied by five other fishermen.

And after that no one came.

The moments stretched out, taut and uncomfortable; the sun rose higher in the sky. There was little talk. One horse whickered loudly, while another stamped its hoof against the ground. One of the fishermen coughed. Hanna's dog Jip got into a friendly, but vocal, skirmish with another of the villager's dogs. Finally Brie, numb, said, "It appears our..."—she paused—"um, army is complete." They numbered twenty. "There may be more as we head north, but... At any rate, it is not too late to change your mind."

There was an uneasy silence. Brie avoided looking anyone in the eye. The silence remained unbroken. "Very well then." She mounted Ciaran, looking to Lom or Jacan to take the lead.

"Lead us, Biri," came Hanna's voice. Brie thought she heard a muffled "Aye." She hesitated, but then awkwardly moved Ciaran forward, heading north along the creek. Hyslin and Beith stood together forlornly, watching them go.

Brie had not gone more than a hundred yards when she heard Lom's voice call out, "Hold!"

Brie turned to see a lone straggler riding up behind them. It was Sago.

He had found a pony somewhere—an odd-looking beast, tan with a black patch on its forehead and a short white tail that splayed out from the horse's broad hindquarters, almost like the tail feathers of a seabird. Still, it was a solid, sturdy-looking animal, though Sago must have been no more burden than a feather resting atop the pony's saddle.

That night as they made camp Brie noticed Collun and Lom talking together amicably.

Before arriving in Ardara, Brie had told Collun of her friendship with Lom and even of dancing with him on the deck of the Storm Petrel. Collun had listened, saying nothing. But when she first introduced the two, Brie's stomach had been knotted tighter than one of Jacan's halyards. They shook hands and smiled genially, then someone called out to Lom and he left them. Brie had waited, tense.

"Seems a decent fellow," was all Collun said. He had started to walk away, then stopped, adding, "D'you think he'd be willing to teach me to dance as well? Talisen was always telling me I had two left feet, but since it looks as though you'll be leading the next Beltaine dances..." He had grinned at her and Brie grinned back, realizing again how little she knew of this new Collun.

At each village and farmhold the army came to, they

told of the attack on Prince Durwydd's dun and of the enemy who gathered a war host in the north. And at each village they were greeted with a mixture of fear and disbelief. They fared best with the fishing villages, hard hit by the blight of sumog, but still their army remained modest. By the time they had reached the beginning of northern Dungal, they numbered no more than eighty.

It was a small, motley army, but Brie was humbled by them, astonished by their courage and their loyalty. In their turn, the army seemed to regard Brie with an affectionate sort of respect, even awe, that embarrassed her. They had taken to calling her "Bren," which meant "little queen" in Dungalan. Sometimes they added "huan," the Dungal word for sunlight, because of the times the sun reflected off her hair, a blur of gold at the head of the ragtag army. "Brenhuan," they would say, "you shall lead us to victory like our queen Fionna."

Brie demurred with a laugh. "The color of my hair is the only thing I have in common with your queen."

If Brie was the army's "little queen," Lom quickly became the one they turned to when a problem arose, such as when a harness needing mending or for advice on saddle sores or to grumble about empty stomachs. Though the army was not large, it still needed to be fed every day, and Lom was the expert on foraging for food and other supplies. Foraging grew increasingly difficult as they journeyed farther north, where there were fewer villages, but Lom somehow managed. He also, along with Jacan, Hanna, and one of the fishermen, led the army in various training exercises and war games.

Brie usually rode at the head of the army, with Collun at her side. He had refused to let Brie tell the Dungalans that he was Wurme-killer. They had a quarrel about it, Brie arguing that it would do much for the army's morale and Collun adamantly refusing to go along with her wishes.

Collun often slipped to the rear to check on Sago. He and Hanna were using all their combined herb lore in an attempt to boost the sorcerer's failing health. Brie was impressed by Collun's ministrations to the sorcerer, and wondered if perhaps he did it partly because of a certain wizard of the trees whose death he yet felt the sting of.

And, indeed, Sago showed some small improvement. The Sea Dyak sorcerer had brought his amhantar. In it he carried a sliver of wood he said was from his boat, Gor-gwynt, something prickly he told Brie was a dead ghost anemone, a moon shell that he said he'd found on his last treasure hunt, and another small dead fish that looked familiar to Brie, though she could not recall its name. Sago took the moon shell out frequently, running his fingers over the whorled, gleaming surface. The Sea Dyak sorcerer had also brought along some rope and string, and he began fiddling around with the making of a small fishing net. As he rode, his fingers were constantly tying, knotting, and weaving. He was a comical sight, the Sea Dyak sorcerer, bringing up the rear of the army, sitting on his fat little pony, weaving nets and singing nonsense songs.

After several days they came to the town of Cerriw, which Brie remembered as the home place of Aelwyn, the wyll. Aelwyn was at the center of the village, waiting for them. She told Brie that after safely delivering her friend's healthy baby boy, she had made her way, without incident, through the Blue Stacks, reaching home in time for the harvest festival, Cynheafu. The Dungalan army received a warm welcome in Aelwyn's village. Not only were they supplied with fresh provisions, but also a cohort of recruits, twenty strong, including Aelwyn herself.

Brie thanked the wyll, who replied with a shrug, "A favor for a favor." Brie noticed Aelwyn's eyes stray to Collun as he helped a villager load provisions into his saddlebags, and the corners of the wyll's mouth went up, catlike.

Its ranks having swelled to more than a hundred, the army rode north.

When Collun was at the back of the group with Sago and Hanna (and frequently, Brie noticed, Aelwyn as well), Brie usually found herself riding with Maire, the tall girl with the stubborn chin. She was almost the same age as Brie and idolized her, which embarrassed Brie. Maire had snuck off to join the army to get away from an overstrict father, who believed a girl's place was in the home. "He thinks we are good for nothing more than cooking and cleaning and minding children," Maire said, outraged. "I have long begged him to give me a chance on the fishing boat, but he has always refused. Each time I saw you go out on Jacan's boat, I envied you so," the girl confided.

Brie told Maire that her own father had been the opposite, demanding as much from her, or more, as from the boy he wished he had had.

Maire was silent, compassion in her eyes. "Then," she said with a sudden smile, "let us be to each other what our fathers were not. When we return to Ardara I will loan you all my cooking pots."

"Thank you just the same," Brie laughed, "but, if Jacan is willing, you shall have my place on the Storm Petrel."

"Agreed!" Maire replied with enthusiasm.

Brie looked up at the night sky, instinctively seeking the Bootes, seven stars making up a wheel of light. The farther north they went, the clearer and brighter was the wheel. They had left Ardara half a moon cycle ago and were camped by the Burren—a pair of graceful stone bridges beneath which the Tyfed River ran.

Hanna estimated they were a day and a half from Sedd Wydyr, so Brie formed a scouting party, resolving to lead it herself. Hanna and Collun would go with her, as well as Maire and her brother, Clun. Aelwyn, too, had volunteered, with a sideways glance at Collun. Lom would be in charge of the army, and Brie told him that if her party did not return in three days to move ahead without them.

As Brie stared up at the stars, Collun came to sit beside her. He offered a small skin bag. Brie took it and drank; the liquid lit the back of her throat and she began to cough. Collun patted her on the back.

"Sorry. I guess I should have warned you."

"What is it?" Brie sputtered.

"Aelwyn calls it neno. They make it in her village. Have another sip; it grows on you."

Brie tried another, and this time the drink was smoother, though still fiery going down her throat.

"Brie, may I ask you something?"

"Of course."

Collun took the skin bag and swallowed some neno. He cleared his throat. "Do you journey to face the man Balor so that you may complete your revenge?"

Brie was silent. She gazed down at her hands. The silence grew long.

"Brie," Collun commanded.

She looked up at him, meeting his gaze directly. "No."

Collun searched her face

"In the bog..." She halted a moment, then went on. "Well, after the bog I realized it was gone—the hatred—all of it had drained away, like pus from a wound, as if the bog itself swallowed it."

"Then why?" Collun asked simply.

"Why do I journey with the Dungalan army? I have told myself it is because Eirren is in as much danger from Balor as Dungal. But it is not enough. Perhaps it is the arrow that has ensorcelled me or whatever you call it..." She smiled. "Or because of my great-grandmother...It was she who gave my mother the arrow to give to me. Perhaps I am doing Seila's will. I only know it is something I must do."

At dawn, before the scouting party was to depart, Brie went to find Sago. He was sitting peacefully by the river's edge. She was pleased to see a faint color in the sorcerer's cheeks. When he had first ridden up on his fat pony, he had looked more of death than of life, like a horse that had been ridden too long by too harsh a master.

Sago had made a rough fishing pole out of a length of rope attached to a stick. He had caught nothing with his makeshift pole, but there was peace in his face. And, for once, he did not burst into rhyme when Brie sat beside him.

"Look what I found today," he said, setting down his pole. Out of his amhantar he pulled a buckleberry nut, which gleamed a warm brown in his palm. Then he held out his other hand, and nestled in that palm was the moon shell.

"Not so very different after all," he said, tracing the whorls on the surface of each with his finger.

"No," Brie agreed.

"I have missed much," Sago spoke pensively, "being so much of the sea. Now I see why Yldir chose to live out his life in the bog. Oh, yes, I am enjoying this." He gestured at the trees, the river, the grass.

"I am glad, Sago," Brie responded, then added, "I take a scouting party north, but will return soon."

"And then it is off to battle-o, with a hey ho and a nonny nonny no!" He gave her a wink, then picked up his fishing stick and expertly cast the line.

Brie smiled and left him by the river.

The scouting party departed soon after and traveled through the day, moving stealthily and keeping watch for any sign of gabha patrols. They stopped late at night for rest and food, though they did not light a campfire. The others slept, but Brie was restless.

She had been avoiding the fire arrow for the past several days. She did not know if it was her imagination, but lately when she touched the arrow, the fire in her veins raged stronger and her eyesight blurred. And the effects seemed to linger longer. It made her feel more than ever as if the arrow was taking hold of her.

But tonight the urge to hold it was strong. She picked up her quiver and moved away from the campsite. The surface of the arrow was warm, hot even, the heat pulsing against her skin and traveling up her arm. She shut her eyelids against the heat.

Goat-men, a hundred of them, maybe more, marching through the mountains: the Mountains of Marwol, between

Scath and Dungal. And just beyond the mountain pass they approached was the descent into Dungal, the sea glittering beyond. On the edge of the white shoreline lay a lovely sparkling jewel of a fortress. Sedd Wydyr. The crystal castle. Just beyond the bluff on which the fortress stood stretched the line of rocks that looked like a sea serpent.

To the north and the east of the castle was arrayed an army of goat-men, perhaps three times the size of the reinforcements marching toward them.

The pictures faded and Brie slumped against a tree, resting her flaming cheek against the rough bark.

So much for scouting parties, Brie thought dully, the fire still thrumming along her veins. She tried opening her eyes, but as had happened before, her vision was blurred. Breathing deeply, she blindly guided the now-cool fire arrow back into her quiver.

Balor has laid his plans nicely, Brie thought: sending sumog and the dry wind to break the back of the Dungalans' livelihood; then a murderous assault on the royal dun to remove the country's leaders; and finally a large army of killers to overrun the country. What kind of fight would there be left in the people of Dungal after a harsh winter and a summer of starvation and fear, especially with no ruler to rally them? Balor's army would sweep through Dungal like a deadly plague, picking off villages one by one.

And what have we to counter it, she thought, but this tiny patchwork army? It was like constructing a fence of straws to stop a rampaging herd of bulls.

Suddenly she saw him. Balor was seated at a table in a room high up in his crystal castle, looking out over the sea and drinking a liquid the color of rubies from a frosted goblet.

There was a knock, and Balor serenely lowered his glass, welcoming into the room a large goat-man with matted white hair and bulging eyes. The goat-man's face had more of man in it than the other gabha Brie had seen, but he had grotesque corkscrew horns spiraling out of his forehead.

Balor led the goat-man, whom he called Cernu, to a white marble table covered with a map of Dungal. With his finger, Balor traced a route through Dungal. The goat-man listened intently, nodding several times. They spoke for several more minutes, then the goat-man left the room, carrying the map.

Balor strode to the window. Gazing out at the sea, he smiled and lifted the glass to his lips. But suddenly his eyes narrowed and his movement was arrested. He turned his head and seemed to look directly at Brie, an intent, listening expression on his handsome face. He reached up and lifted the eye-patch from his white eye. Brie's breath stopped. Had he seen her? She did not know how these seeings or visions worked. Was it like a mirror that suddenly became a window? Because she saw him, could he now see her? She reached out her hands as if to somehow close the shutters of the window between them.

Balor shook his head with a puzzled frown, replaced his eye-patch, and turned to look back out the window of his crystal castle. Once again he raised the glass to his lips. Then the picture was gone.

In a haze Brie realized the picture had come without her holding the arrow, like the time in the tower when she had seen Collun. Only this picture had been clearer; this time she had even been able to hear the voices, though she could make out only a word here and there. The draoicht the arrow had been kindling in her was strong now. But had Balor seen her?

"Brie?"

She blinked. She could not see.

Collun sat beside her. "What is wrong?"

"The arrow. It, um, does something to my eyes..." She trailed off, then said loudly, "I saw them, Collun. Hundreds of them, goat-men at Sedd Wydyr. And more soon to come, through a mountain pass. We have three days, at most, before they reach Balor's stronghold. And when they do, his army will begin its march."

# NINETEEN

# Fire Rain

Collun was silent. Brie could not see the expression on his face. She blinked rapidly and rubbed her eyes, then stood, putting her hand in front of her. "Uffern!" she cursed. Collun guided her back to the campsite. She could feel Fara against her legs, and as they walked, the blur began to ease. Soon she was able to see clearly again.

Quickly they woke the others and told them what Brie had learned.

"The arrow shows you things that are far away?" asked Maire, her eyes wide.

"Sometimes," Brie replied.

"And you told me there was no draoicht in you," Aelwyn said with her catlike smile.

"It rests in the arrow, not in me," Brie said shortly.

"Do we return to camp?" asked Maire.

"Yes," Brie replied. But she made no move to depart.

"It is too bad you did not consult the arrow before. It would have saved us a trip," grumbled Aelwyn.

"Mmmm," responded Brie, her mind elsewhere. "Aelwyn," she said suddenly, "is there, by chance, a porth near? To Tir a Ceol?"

"Perhaps." The wyll looked sulky.

"Aelwyn!"

"Surely the arrow can tell you where it is," Aelwyn purred.

Brie waited.

"Oh, very well. Yes. And it happens to be quite close."

"Why, Brie?" asked Collun.

"I'm not sure. But I was thinking that if we could get word to Silien..."

"Yes, an Ellylon army!" Collun's eyes lit up.

Hanna spoke, her face serious. "No matter how close your friendship with Prince Silien, it would take much for Ellylon to involve themselves in a matter that does not directly concern them."

"They were prepared to help us when Medb threatened," Collun pointed out.

"There was the cailceadon at stake then. Furthermore, there is no time for an army of sufficient strength to be mustered."

"It is worth trying," stated Brie. "At the very least we could send word to King Midir. After all, Prince Durwydd is a friend to Ellylon."

Hanna snorted. "Midir no doubt has as little respect for

our prince as we do. But...as long as it does not take us far off our path," she agreed.

They made it to the porth by midday. Aelwyn led them to an ancient willow tree on the edge of a still, silvery pond.

The wyll approached the tree, her hands upraised. But there was a sudden wrinkling on the surface of the trunk, accompanied by an almost melodic whispering sound. A person with golden hair emerged from the tree.

It was Silien. Collun let out a glad cry and clasped the Ellyl in a bear hug. Fara wound between Silien's legs, while Brie, too, warmly greeted him.

"We had come in search of you," she said in amazement, "and here you are!"

"I was seeking you as well. Well met, Breo-Saight."

"There is trouble, Silien," she said, after introducing him to the others.

"So I have heard."

"Will King Midir help us?" Brie asked bluntly.

Silien shook his head. "No. My father is preoccupied with cleaning up northern Tir a Ceol. Before the Fire-wurme was destroyed, it wrought havoc in the far northern stretches; the waters were fouled and the land corroded. Further, there has been an infestation of nathrach. They are strange, small snakelike creatures and are quite toxic. We believe they were also let loose from the Cave of Cruachan by Medb. They have been bedeviling small pockets of Tir a Ceol. When I heard the rumors of trouble in Dungal, and that you and Collun might be involved, my father gave me leave to investigate, but he said not to count on him should there be trouble. Our own people must come first."

"Did you travel here alone?" asked Hanna.

"Well, no actually... There was a small band of Ellylon stationed at the porth in the Blue Stack Mountains. I asked for a volunteer, to accompany me north. He seemed enthusiastic at first, though I'm afraid... I'd better fetch him." Silien disappeared back into the tree.

The others were starting to fidget when Silien finally reemerged, followed by none other than the Ellyl Monodnock.

The Ellyl prince looked annoyed, saying, "Please excuse the delay." Monodnock's cheeks were almost as bright a red as his hair and he looked terrified. But when he saw Brie and Aelwyn, he let out a glad cry.

"Fair and tender ladies," he said, drawing himself to his full height, "it is a jubilation to see you once again. And shall I say that I am quite gleaming—no, *blazing*—with honor and privilege to have the opportunity, snatched from me so prematurely when last we met, to serve you on your mighty quest."

"Monodnock, well met," said Brie, biting on her lower lip to keep from laughing. She caught Aelwyn's eye, which flashed back at her merrily. Hanna, Collun, and the brother and sister merely looked astonished.

"Monodnock here keeps straying off; it's almost as if he wished to be elsewhere," Silien said with an ironic tilt to his eyebrows.

"Oh, no, no, no! I was merely performing a close inspection as to the state of the tunnels," blustered the taller Ellyl, running both hands through his spiky hair. "I know King Midir has the highest standards and I—"

"Yes, quite," broke in Silien. "Now, tell me," he asked Brie, "is it true that the gabha are on the move? And that they answer the call of a sorcerer with one eye?"

"He is Balor and he has two eyes, but one is all white. He seeks to overthrow Dungal, as well as Eirren. And ultimately, I believe, even Scath itself."

"He desires to conquer the Queen of Ghosts? This Balor does not lack for ambition," Silien said dryly. "The pass you saw, Brie, describe it to me."

The Ellyl listened intently, then nodded, saying, "Yes, it sounds like Tanniad Pass. Perhaps there is something we can do about the gabha coming from the mountains. Come, we must go quickly."

Silien rode with Collun on Fiain, while Monodnock nervously climbed up behind Brie on Ciaran. Silien led them east into the foothills.

"Excuse me." Monodnock leaned forward to whisper to Brie. "Prince Silien isn't truly planning to engage a host of one hundred gabha?" His voice cracked on the final word. "I mean, I know that the prince's draoicht must be impressive and all. But *one hundred* goat-men?"

"There is always danger when one seeks to defeat evil," Brie replied solemnly.

"Of course," Monodnock said tremulously.

By midnight they had begun the ascent into the northern peaks of the mountains. They rested briefly, then pushed on.

Silien, with his keen Ellyl ears, heard the gabha long before they were visible. The sun was rising as the Ellyl led them up a ridge. They then dismounted and followed Silien to the top of an escarpment. Taking care to keep out of sight, they gazed down into the valley that was Tanniad Pass.

In the distance they could make out the beginning of the column of goat-men Brie had seen winding through the mountains.

"There is a little time yet to prepare," said Silien.

He led them back to the ruins of an ancient stone wall. Giving them all a pleasant nod, he wandered over to a cluster of three larch trees. There he lay down on a mat of pine needles and promptly fell asleep. Fara curled up beside him, in her customary position by his shoulder. Monodnock stared across at the sleeping Ellyl, clutching Brie's arm.

"Don't worry, Monodnock," Brie said. "You know how much, um, energy it takes to work draoicht." She remembered all the times she had seen Silien fall asleep after performing some miraculous feat, although she could not actually recall him napping beforehand. She sent Clun to the crest to keep watch on the goat-men, while the others settled against the stone wall.

"He might have told us what he was planning," grumbled Aelwyn, fiddling with a gemstone on one of her necklaces. Brie noticed that it was a saphir and wondered if it was from the rock Collun had given Aelwyn long ago, when she had told their fortunes.

"Silien has always kept his own council," replied Collun. "But rest assured, if there were something we could be doing, he would have told us."

"I am glad to hear it," responded Aelwyn. "You met the Ellyl on your journey to destroy the wurme, did you not?" she asked, looking up at him with wide amber eyes.

Embarrassed, Collun said, "Well, it was before that. He rescued us from a vine, cro-olachan."

"I have heard of cro-olachan," Aelwyn said with a slight shiver. The saphir at her neck caught the sun.

Brie abruptly rose and moved away. She crossed to Ciaran and Fiain, who were grazing nearby. Hanna followed her.

"Have we done the right thing, coming here?" Brie said to Hanna, running her fingers through Ciaran's mane.

"The Ellyl prince must know what he is doing," Hanna said.

"No doubt," Brie responded. "But it is a risk; perhaps we should have returned to camp instead of..."

"Do not worry, Biri. We shall have our day on the battlefield soon enough."

Brie glanced over at the others. Maire had risen and was walking toward the larches, leaving Collun and Aelwyn alone with Monodnock, who appeared to have dozed off himself.

Hanna followed Brie's gaze, then smiled. "You know, wylls rarely use their own love charms; for some reason they won't work. Wylls have to go to other wylls."

"Hanna! I wasn't even thinking...," Brie protested, very much annoyed.

"No, I know. I just thought you might be interested."

"Well, I'm not."

Almost an hour had passed when Clun scrambled down from his lookout post on the ridge. "The gabha are about to enter the pass," he called as he came.

Silien, who was awake now, rose and looked thoughtfully over at Hanna.

"You are a weather maker?" he asked.

Hanna nodded, her eyes blue.

"Come, Traveler," Silien said. "Together we will make

weather music." He turned and began to climb the escarpment. Hanna followed without hesitation.

The others stood in a knot at the bottom, watching.
They could hear the sounds of distant marching. The goat-
men were approaching Tanniad Pass.

The Ellyl and the Traveler lay on their stomachs, peering into the valley. Then Brie saw Silien gesture to Hanna,
and the older woman rolled over onto her back.

Great billows of gray clouds begin to pile up overhead.
And it was not long before a light drizzle began to fall.
Steadily it grew stronger, until Brie and the others had to
seek shelter under a rocky overhang that jutted from the
side of the ridge. The noise from below grew louder. The
gabha must have entered the pass.

Brie saw that Silien had pulled up into a sitting position,
and she briefly worried that he might be spotted. She could
hear faint singing, that agonizingly beautiful Ellyl music
that reached into one's insides and twisted them, causing
all else to lose meaning. Then came flickerings of heat and
flame that scorched Brie's ears and nose and lips; waves of
heat pulsing against her skin, accompanied by glittering
eruptions of orange and yellow and gold.

The music faded and Brie blinked. She looked out at
the rain and saw that scattered among the raindrops were
quills of flame, no more than a finger long. They flared as
they fell, a blur of yellow, orange, and gold, and when they
hit the ground there was a dazzling burst, then they faded.

Ignoring the fire barbs raining about her, Brie ran out
from under the overhang and up the escarpment to where
Silien sat, cross-legged, his face drained of all color and his
lips bent in a half smile. Hanna lay beside him, her eyes
closed, sneezing violently.

Then Brie looked out and over the ridge into the valley. Unlike the intermittent quills of flame on the ridge, there, just a short distance from her, were sheets upon sheets of fire rain. The rain flames fell, unrelenting, on the goat-men below. It was an overwhelming sight, barely believable, and for a moment Brie felt something like pity for the creatures below.

Screams of agony and the appalling cacophony of goat-men and horses burning alive rose up to them. And Brie watched with a horrible fascination as the fire rain consumed all that it touched. Soon after came the smell, waves and waves of it. Brie's throat closed.

Hanna began to cough uncontrollably, and Brie stooped to her. The older woman had a terrible cold, but more, she had a raging fever and was trembling. Brie helped her up, and together they half slid, half walked down the ridge. Collun passed them, scrambling up to assist Silien, who was already falling asleep, dangerously close to the edge of the ridge.

When Collun came down the slope, carrying a limp Silien in his arms, Monodnock let out a shriek, "The prince is dead! All is lost!"

"Oh, shut up, Monodnock," said Aelwyn.

"He sleeps," explained Brie tersely.

They laid Silien on Fiain's back, where he slumped onto the horse's neck, still fast asleep. They gave Monodnock Hanna's horse to ride, while the shivering older woman rode in front of Brie. She too was bent double, her face pressed into Ciaran's soft mane.

They rode quickly, arriving back at the encampment by nightfall. While Collun and Aelwyn took care of Hanna and the Ellyl prince, Brie had Lom gather the company.

The army let out a cheer when they learned of the successful mission to destroy Balor's reinforcements, but listened soberly as Brie described the forces already arrayed against them.

"We must leave at once," Brie said. "The gabha encampment lies beside a forest. We will set up our camp on the far side of that forest, out of sight of the castle. Our main hope lies in taking the goat-men by surprise. Remember, the gabha are not human," Brie told them. And grimly she described the strength and the bestiality of the goat-men.

Shortly before setting forth for Sedd Wydyr, Brie was stowing something in her pack when she suddenly felt a probing in her mind. She stood straight, terrified. It was like a hand groping about inside her head, the fingers prying. *Balor.* He was looking for her. He knew of her escape from the bell tower; perhaps he knew even what she had done to it. She wondered if he had also learned of Hanna and Silien's fire of rain at Tanniad Pass. She tried to make her mind a blank, but it was impossible. She had an irrational desire to grasp the arrow, thinking it might somehow protect her. Then, abruptly, the probing sensation was gone and her body sagged with relief. Had he found her? There had been no flaring moment of recognition, but she could not be sure.

She took the fire arrow out of her quiver and gazed at it. When she concentrated she was able to see the stories on all the picture bands now, all except one, the one at the bottom.

Ought she to use the fire arrow in battle? Brie wondered. It was a powerful weapon, but she dared not risk losing it or letting it fall to the gabha, or worse, into Balor's hands. An arrow was a good weapon, but it had its limitations. Unlike a sword, once an arrow was wielded, it was gone, difficult to retrieve. No, she would not use the fire arrow in battle. Except on Balor.

But...Brie suddenly smiled. There was another way to use fire and arrows together, and she had the Scathian in the bog to thank for the idea.

Brie sought out Lom and told him. His eyes kindled with interest. "I have heard of such things," he said, then went off to find his best arrowmaker.

As the company headed north, Brie felt that the land under her was shrinking, with the mountains on one side and the sea on the other pressing against each other, compacting and merging. And Hanna told her that at Dungal's tip the land between disappeared entirely and sea waves beat against mountain cliffs. Northern Dungal was a place of rock and water, with the occasional eruption of forest; in places trees were bent almost sideways by the long reach of the sea wind. There were few signs of human habitation. The soil was thin and even where there was turf, the rocks seemed always restless, straining to break through.

The army circled east, away from the coast, and arrived at the far edge of the forest while the sun still shone, though because the days were getting longer it was well past time for the evening meal. Quickly they set up camp and Brie sent scouts ahead. When they returned they reported that it was just as Brie had seen: Beyond the forest lay the gabha encampment, which stretched to the east and north of the fortress Sedd Wydyr. The scouts said there were no sentries and no gabha scouting parties. Brie nodded, unsurprised.

Though she believed Balor was now aware that she had escaped the bell tower, he clearly could not conceive of her being able to mount any kind of threat to him and his plans—not, at least, in such a short time.

Or maybe he could. The thought chilled her. Perhaps he knew of their presence here in the shadow of the forest, and cared not.

That night, after all had eaten, Brie spoke to the army. She laid out the battle plan that she, Collun, Lom, and Hanna had come up with. The company listened soberly. Lom went on to explain in greater detail, and, when he was done, the Dungalans dispersed to make a last check of their gear and to snatch what rest they could. Lom moved among them, checking a bowstring here, the sharpness of a blade there.

Silien still slept, while Hanna had recovered sufficiently to sit up, though she blew her nose frequently and drank great quantities of a healing borage tea Collun had brewed for her.

Monodnock sidled up to Brie as she was checking over her own weapons. "Excuse me, fair lady," he said, his voice ingratiating, "but I wonder if you have given some thought to Prince Silien? It seems to me you will need someone to stay here and watch over him as he sleeps. And much as it pains me to miss even a moment of the glorious battle, I would be willing to volunteer for the assignment; indeed, as a fellow Ellyl, I feel it is my honor-bound duty."

"You are too generous," Brie said dryly. "But perhaps...," she began, thinking to herself it would be better if the Ellyl was kept out of the way during battle.

"That will not be necessary after all, Monodnock," came Silien's voice, "though your offer to sacrifice yourself is most admirable." When he saw Silien standing next to them, awake and alert, Monodnock staggered slightly, clutching at Brie's arm.

"But surely, Prince, you are not up to...," Monodnock stuttered. Stark terror moved across his pale face, and one hand began whipping his orange hair into a forest of spikes.

"When do we face the gabha?" said Silien to Brie, pointedly ignoring Monodnock, who let out a small whimper and quickly withdrew.

"You mustn't tease him," said Brie.

"I shall try to refrain," Silien replied with a slight bow. "As to the battle ahead, I regret having to tell you that my draoicht is inadequate; indeed, I would even say that, for the time being, the fire rain has completely depleted it. However, my sword arm, for what it's worth, is yours."

"We are indebted to you, Silien," Brie responded, "for what you have already done for us and for what you offer now." And she thought back to the Silien who in the old days would not have put himself into any kind of danger for a human. Impulsively, she leaned over and hugged him. Silien looked a little startled, but smiled his half smile.

As Brie worked on making more arrows for her quiver, Hanna told her that Sago now seemed alarmingly incoherent—more addled than she had ever known him to be. So, after filling her quiver, Brie went in search of the Sea Dyak sorcerer. She found him sitting cross-legged against a small willow tree. He looked as ethereal and wraithlike as ever, but, surprisingly, his eyes were alert and he seemed quite peaceful.

He gestured for her to sit beside him. "Tomorrow we hunt together again, yes?"

Sago *was* different, Brie thought, but he was not as Hanna had described. Rather, there was an eerie sort of saneness about him. She noticed he had with him the scrap of fishing net he had been working on throughout the journey, but his fingers were still.

"Brie?"

The girl jumped slightly. She had been so startled by this new, placid Sago, she had forgotten he had asked her a question.

"Well, I would not call it a hunt exactly," Brie replied dryly, thinking of the army camped beside the crystal castle. "But, Sago, I think perhaps it would be best if you stayed here at camp during..."

"The fish is larger, perhaps," the sorcerer said, ignoring her words, "but not so very different. To fight the enemy, then perchance to sleep," Sago intoned, then smiled peacefully, tracing with his fingers the loops of his small net.

"But, Sago...," Brie tried again.

The sorcerer continued to speak, still smiling, a dreamy look in his eyes. "Do you know how I anticipate the after-place will be? Indeed, I am quite sure of it. A large lake, with a blanket of comforting, muffling clouds above, the very lightest of breezes. Ideal fishing weather, of course; fish will be jumping—gray, silver, speckled. Then a small boat, the image of Gor-gwynt, and a supple pole at hand..." A blissful smile played around his mouth.

The place Sago described was more real to him than the forest around them, Brie thought. His weird calmness suddenly frightened her much more than his riddling songs and flights of fancy had ever done. She felt a stab of alarm.

"By the by," the sorcerer continued, his tone suddenly confiding. "There is a boy in the village of Mira, a fishing enthusiast like myself, with unusual fingernails...thumbs to be precise. You catch my meaning, I hope." Brie stared at Sago. "His name is Thom. He lives with his mother, near the sea. You will find him, or the Traveler will." He rummaged in his amhantar. "Ah...and this is for you." He held out his hand, then opened it with a mysterious smile, like a conjurer. In his palm lay the moon shell. "Remember what I told you about moon shells?" he asked, eyes twinkling.

Though she was still uneasy, Brie managed a smile and, nodding, replied, "That you can never have too many." She reached out and took the shell. She put it in a pocket of her tunic. "Thank you, Sago."

"Now," said the sorcerer, "I think I will have a spot of sleep. And you shall see; tomorrow this old sorcerer may still have a few fireworks up his raveled sleeve." He stood, gave Brie a wink, and then disappeared into the darkness.

Brie lay down, sure that she would not sleep. But she came awake with a start, the taste of stale cyffroi in her mouth. Dawn was almost an hour away, she guessed. She stood, stretching, and sniffed the air. An odd, thick-fingered fog had come up, shrouding their camp, but she could see figures moving about, preparing for the day ahead.

Collun had brewed a pan of chicory, saying if it was all the same to her he'd rather have it than cyffroi on this particular morning. As they sat together, sharing the chicory, Brie was reminded of another early morning, off the Isle of Thule. In preparation for meeting the Fire-wurme, Collun had layered himself with padding from head to toe to protect against the corrosive slime that came off the creature's body. He had looked lumpy and faintly absurd, but the padding had saved his life.

Collun was different now: older, leaner, and taller. And the sword lying across his knees, that was new for him. He was peering down, at some indecipherable hatch marks on the flat of the blade. Then he glanced up at her and smiled, and Brie's heart did a quick flutter kick. Nerves, she thought, blushing slightly. She stood.

"Shall we to battle?" Her voice was overloud.

"After you," Collun said politely. He also rose and some-how they managed to bump into each other.

"Sorry," they both mumbled, stepping apart.

"Brie," Collun began.

She turned to him, nervous.

"Well, uh, good luck," he said, giving her an awkward pat on the back.

"And you," she replied stiffly, her heart still making that odd flipping movement. She turned away abruptly and ad-justed her bow.

# TWENTY

## The Battle

**B**rie swung herself onto Ciaran's back. Collun and Fiain came up beside them, and silently they entered the forest, Fara padding alongside. The fog had thickened and it eddied up around Ciaran's chest, making her skittish. The Dungalan army, with its ragtag blend of foot soldiers and those who were mounted, fell in behind them.

"I wonder if your Sea Dyak sorcerer has woven this mist for us," said Collun.

"The only weaving Sago is interested in is that little fishing net of his," Brie replied. And indeed she had seen him not long ago perched on his fat pony. The alarming calmness had gone and he was back to his old self, working on the ragged net and singing of oranges and gooseberries.

She was glad, at least, to see that he had stayed at the rear of the army. Brie noticed that Monodnock had attached himself to Sago, most certainly because of his position at the back.

The company made its way through the woods in the predawn darkness. Brie marveled at how quietly this mass of people, horses, and dogs was able to move through the trees.

When they reached the forest's edge, Brie signaled to the archers to come up along her right side and spread out. Brie could just make out the beginning of the gabha encampment, a cluster of crudely built wooden huts, thatched with straw, scattered among the sedges and shrubs of the fields stretching to the east of Sedd Wydyr. With a satisfied nod, Brie again signaled, this time to the archers who bore the special arrows.

The incendiary arrows flew high, their arcs wavering slightly because of the wad of oil-soaked hemp lodged next to the arrowhead. Some plunged into the ground, igniting the dry grass and scrub; some plummeted down onto the thatched roofs of the gabha huts; one or two even found a sleeping goat-man. Plumes of smoke rose, mingling with the fog, and bursts of fire flared throughout the camp. The goat-horses began a frenzied braying, and there were guttural shouts from gabha throats.

Brie signaled to a man from the village Cerriw, and the melodic, high-pitched notes of a Dungalan war horn sounded.

She and Collun exchanged glances, then Brie laid her hand on Ciaran's neck. They broke forward, the two Ellyl horses neck to neck. Brie could hear the muffled thunder of hooves behind her.

Ciaran was a nose ahead of Fiain as they burst into the gabha camp, trampling flame and sparks under their hooves. A scattering of goat-men came running with snatched-up weapons.

At Brie's unspoken command, Ciaran halted and, digging her knees into the Ellyl horse's back, Brie shot off several arrows in quick succession. Out of the corner of her eye she saw Collun meet the charge of a large goat-man swinging a thick club. And Fara was a whirling mass of claws and teeth and fur.

Brie rained arrows on any goat-man who staggered out of the smoke. Ill-organized and dazed, the creatures were easy targets. Backed up by the Dungalan archers, Brie struck again, and then again. Sweat trickled into her eyes, and her arm began to ache. From beside her, around her, and over her head, arrows flew. Any goat-men that the archers missed were met by Dungalan soldiers with swords and spears.

Bodies lay thick on the ground. Then Brie heard the strident note of another horn; it made a sound different than the Dungalan horn—a raw, jarring series of notes. Ahead of her, a stone's throw away, she saw what looked like two large white corkscrews, spiraling up, splitting the smoke. It was the gabha leader, Cernu. The gabha horn sounded again, and the goat-men fell back, answering the call of their leader.

Dismounting, Brie found Collun in the fog and smoke. He, too, had dismounted. The Ellyl horses were, on their own, doing considerable damage with hooves and teeth to the gabha they met. Collun's sword blade was bloody and he looked pale, but he managed a grin of sorts when he caught sight of Brie. Brie felt something rub against her legs and looked down to see Fara, whose white coat bore streaks of blood.

Before Brie and Collun could exchange a word, the goat-men surged forward. Cernu had organized his forces and they were attacking. Brie and Collun advanced to meet them. The Dungalan horn sounded again, and from then on Brie was surrounded by the feral, snarling faces of goat-men. Her ears rang with a fearful noise—swords clanging, screams of the injured and dying, and the braying of the gabha. She swung her small sword, her mind gone somewhere else. She killed, over and over again, but it did not seem real.

There were only a handful of moments that pierced through the numbness, an occasional vivid glimpse of something familiar and startling, such as Collun's pale set jaw as he wielded the sword he had found in the passage grave; Aelwyn the wyll, small and fierce, her colorful layers of clothing swirling as she laid about her with a shining sharp knife, jewels sparkling in its handle; Silien, the Ellyl prince, nimble and deft, his silver eyes gleaming and the blue-tinged sword he held in his hand flashing; Maire, her face shining with fierce courage, fighting alongside her brother. Brie caught sight of the confused, tremulous look on the boy Dil's face when he felled his first goat-man with an arrow. And Brie saw flames reflected on Jacan's sword and on the swinging blade of a goat-man's ax as the fisherman thrust his blade into the creature's side. She had a moment of horrified disbelief as she saw the Ardaran fisherman Henle fall, his chest slit open by a gabha spear.

Then the goat-men were falling back, and Brie had a brief, flaring sense of hope, but it flickered out when she saw the leader, Cernu, marshaling a fresh legion of gabha troops, directing them to circle the eastern flank of the Dungalan army.

The right side of the company turned to face the on-slaught, and once more Brie was pulled into the vortex of straining bodies and plunging weapons. Her sword was knocked out of her hands by a goat-man with a spiked club. Her wrist went numb and she fumbled for her dagger, ducking the creature's next swing. She darted under his arm and plunged her dagger into the top of his stomach. He fell heavily, blood flowing over Brie's numb wrist. She peered and groped around on the ground, but could not find her sword.

Suddenly she saw Dil. A goat-man twice his size had pinned him to the ground, his fur-matted hands encircling the boy's throat. Like lightning Brie sheathed her dagger and reached for an arrow, but found that her quiver was empty, except for the fire arrow.

For a split second she hesitated, then realized she would not be able to get a clear shot; too many were lurching in and out of the arrow's path. Brie drew her dagger, muttered a curse under her breath, and ran at the goat-man.

She was upon him before he saw her and she sank her knife into his neck. He let out a bray and jerked backward, surprising her. The dagger fell from her hand and she was thrown to the ground, the breath knocked out of her.

Suddenly the goat-man was on top of her and the smell of him was up her nostrils and in her mouth. Her face was buried in the thick foul hair of his chest and she could not breathe. She screamed soundlessly and pushed at the strain-ing body. Then the goat-man abruptly went limp. With a great effort she heaved the inert body off her and lay still a few moments, gasping for breath. Hanna smiled down at her, a bloody blade in her hand. She offered Brie a hand up, giving her back her own dagger, then turned to meet the charge of yet another goat-man.

Somehow Cernu and his army had managed to turn the Dungalans around and were pushing them toward the sea, along the southern edge of the fortress Sedd Wydyr. Behind them, not a hundred yards back, was the white beach. The sun had risen and was now shining in the eyes of the Dungalans.

Then Brie saw Hanna go down, and the goat-man she had been fighting raised his club to crush her head. This time Brie did not hesitate. She quickly reached for the fire arrow. No one was in the way. She nocked the arrow to her bow, but as she pulled it back, the string broke. Brie let out a cry of frustration.

Hanna twisted away from the goat-man's club just in time, but the creature grabbed her by the hair, unsheathing a knife.

Brie grasped the arrow in her hand and sprang toward the goat-man. As she ran she realized this was the second time she had used the fire arrow as a knife and irrationally wondered if the arrow minded.

As if in response the shaft stung her fingers with heat, shocking her a little, but she maintained her grip. The goat-man saw her coming and, still holding Hanna by the hair, threw back his head and brayed.

Brie slashed at him with the fire arrow.

There was a smell of scorched hair, a flash of orange and blue, and the goat-man was looking at his smoldering arm in surprise. He let go of Hanna, who crumpled to the ground, eyes closed. Brie struck again, and again there was the stench of burning animal flesh. The goat-man fell heavily, the hair on his torso aflame, dead before he hit the ground.

Brie's hand smarted, and she briefly glanced down at the webbing of tiny blisters already appearing on her palm. Then she crouched beside Hanna. The older woman had a knife wound in her side, but she was conscious. Quickly Brie pulled her a short distance from the fighting, to a clearing alongside a clump of sea grass.

Spotting Collun, Brie called out to him. He ran up and checked Hanna over, binding her wound. Hanna weakly protested that she was fine, ready to return to battle. Brie shook her head decisively.

Looking out at the ragtag Dungalan army, Brie's heart constricted. They were weakening. Most had borne at least one wound and all were exhausted, their faces pale under the blood and dirt. So far they had lost only a handful of soldiers, but it was only a matter of time, Brie thought, before it would be many more. Her own clothing was soaked with blood, though most of it gabha, and her body ached with fatigue. Ordering the older woman to stay put, she and Collun returned to battle. The sun was directly overhead.

Ciaran and the faol came to Brie. Wearily the girl mounted the Ellyl horse. Ciaran reared, letting out a whinny that sounded like a war cry. Brie heard the words "fire arrow" burn inside her head, and she was not sure if they came from Ciaran or from the arrow itself, but she drew herself up. She grasped the shaft of the fire arrow and held it aloft. It still burned against her hand, but as she held it high the fire arrow began to send out a yellow light, like a sort of beacon.

Then Ciaran plunged into the ranks of the gabha army.

Brie wielded the arrow with a relentless, stupefied violence. The gabha were living creatures to her no more, merely targets to be burned and obliterated. The arrow was practically fused to her hand under a mat of blisters and oozing flesh. She marveled at the strength of the shaft, like a peerless war blade tempered in the finest forge.

The gabha were spooked by the arrow and fell away in droves. And the sight of their Bren-huan wielding the fire arrow gave the Dungalans new heart.

The heat from the arrow seemed to have set Brie's whole body aflame and her arm was desperately tired, yet propelled by flame and pain and sheer stubbornness, she fought on. At one point she remembered dismounting Ciaran, because she noticed a nasty slashing burn across the horse's right flank. Ciaran protested, but Brie ignored her. She sliced and torched with her arrow-sword, while Ciaran and Fara stayed beside her, fighting with their hooves and claws and teeth.

"Brie," she heard through the searing haze of flame and smoke. It was Lom; he had laid a hand on her arm. Brie stared back at Lom, barely recognizing him. Smoldering bodies lay around her in heaps.

" 'Tis time for retreating," Lom said almost gently, his face gaunt with fatigue. "Come." He pulled Brie through the lines, Ciaran following. The sun was low in the gray-orange sky.

Only then did Brie realize that the gabha had retreated. Cernu was marshaling his troops, to reorganize and to calm the goat-men's fear of the maiden bearing fire in her hand.

In a daze Brie followed Lom to the shelter of some ruined buildings that lay at the edge of land and shore, perhaps once a small fishing enclave under the royal protection of Sedd Wydyr. Sea grass and reeds sprouted freely among the stones. Curlews circled above, and the air smelled of salt and seawater. Ghostlike, Brie walked among the Dungalans, searching their faces; she spotted Jacan, Ferg, and Gwil, but not Henle. She saw Maire and her brother, Aelwyn, Sago and Monodnock, Silien, the boy Dil, and finally Collun, crouched beside Hanna. They exchanged a few exhausted words. Hanna reassured Brie that the wound to her side was not serious and told her to tend to her own hurts. Brie nodded and, still dazed, walked to the side of a small stream, which meandered through the ruined buildings on its way to the sea. Fara materialized at her side. Brie washed gabha blood and charred flesh off her skin. Fara rubbed against her legs, lapped at the water briefly, then bounded to Silien, who was distributing bars of brisgein. Next Ciaran came up and drank thirstily. The Ellyl horse raised her head, and for a moment horse and girl stood side by side, Brie's shoulder resting against Ciaran's warm neck.

*There is little left in me, Ciaran,* Brie thought. She had never been so tired.

*More than you think, Breo-Saight,* came the Ellyl horse's response. *And try washing your face. It's a mess,* Ciaran added, looking sideways at Brie.

"Well, pardon me, but you're not exactly spotless yourself," Brie retorted.

Ciaran flicked her tail and went off in search of some brisgein.

Brie crouched down to soak her burnt hand in the cool water. Vaguely she was aware of someone—a fisherman, she thought, because of the indigo jersey and the braided criosanna he wore at his waist—coming to the stream near her. He limped and wore a large handkerchief bandage over half his face; Brie wondered if he had had his battle wound looked at. The sun was setting.

Suddenly the fisherman lunged at her. With a splash, she went sprawling facedown into the water. Before she could react, the man had grabbed the fire arrow out of her quiver. He let out a shriek of pain as the arrow burned his hand, but he was running, desperate, hobbling off on his crippled leg.

With an astonished sense of déjà vu, Brie scrambled up out of the water and took off after Bricriu. He was heading toward the bluff on which Sedd Wydyr stood. Despite her own fatigue, she had begun to gain on him and was sure she would catch him. But then she saw a small door in the side of the bluff, a thick wooden door striped with iron, no doubt with a lock or an iron bar on the inside. Panic rose in her. She did not think she would be able to reach him before he got to the door.

Then a gray blur swept past her. It was Collun astride the horse Fiain.

In moments Collun caught the man. He swung off Fiain, and in an instant his sword was at Bricriu's throat.

"Release the arrow," Collun said. Even from a distance Brie could hear the cold fury in his voice. Bricriu froze.

Her breath coming in gasps, Brie ran up. Neither Collun nor Bricriu moved as she reached them.

"There is very little that keeps me from running this sword through your evil neck, Bricriu," Brie heard Collun say. He pressed the tip of his sword deeper into Bricriu's throat.

The trembling man dropped the arrow onto the ground. Brie darted forward and picked it up. The arrow buzzed against her fingers. But Collun did not lower his sword.

Bricriu sank to his knees, his hollow eyes wild with fear. Then she saw his glance fall on Collun's sword.

"I know your sword, Wurme-killer." The words had come from Bricriu. With a shock Brie realized it was the first time she had heard him talk since being entertained by him in his dun, long ago; his voice was grotesque, a wheezing whisper, sounding as if someone on a previous occasion had run a sword through his voice box.

"My sword?" said Collun, distracted.

"It is fitting that you carry it," Bricriu croaked. Collun looked blank, and Bricriu's wrecked face shifted into a travesty of a smile. "Surely you know? It is Cuillean's, your father's sword. He has no need of it now. In Scath."

Collun went pale.

"Queen Medb gave him his choice of swords."

Collun took a step back, letting his sword drop from Bricriu's throat. In an instant Bricriu made a dash for the door in the bluff, with a frenzied scuttling movement like a wounded crab. Collun did not move, his eyes fixed on the sword. Brie thought to give chase, but Bricriu was already at the door, then through. She could hear the clang as an iron bolt dropped into place.

Brie went to Collun. He could not take his eyes off the blade in his hand.

"Did you know of this? My father and Medb?" Collun asked in a low voice.

Brie nodded reluctantly. "Balor told me."

"Why did you not tell me?"

"I..." Brie trailed off as no words came. Collun gazed at her a moment, then his eyes went back to the sword he held.

"Brie." Collun's voice was almost a whisper. "I could have killed Bricriu."

"I know."

"I looked into his eyes and the memory of all that he did to Nessa, the way he tortured her, starved her, it filled me, until..."

"I know," Brie said again. "But you did not kill him."

There was another silence between them. Then Collun's jaw relaxed a little. "Brie," he said, "the next time I start to lecture about revenge and arrows doubling back, promise you will stop me?"

"I promise." Brie smiled at him.

"Let me see your hand," Collun said. And carefully he applied mallow salve and bound her burnt hand with a length of muslin from his leather wallet.

The Dungalans had lost many. Of those who remained, fully two-thirds were injured, some grievously. And all were exhausted. Brie had assembled Lom, Hanna, Collun, Silien, Aelwyn, and Jacan by the remains of what looked to have been an ancient Sea Dyak sorcerer's mote.

Lom reported that roughly two hundred goat-men, perhaps more, remained. Hanna grimly detailed the state of the Dungalans, the extent of their injuries, how many lay near death and how many were already gone. And Silien, gray-faced with exhaustion, told them his draiocht was still unusable. As the others, bleak but dogged, began to discuss what Cernu's strategy might be, Brie's throat tightened with despair. She had led these people to their deaths, she thought, and suddenly she felt Balor again, inside her mind.

This time, of course, he knew where she was and he was laughing at her.

Anger flared in Brie, and she raised her eyes to the glittering fortress by the sea. Why did he not show himself?

Then, stifling her anger, Brie concentrated on the laughter. There was no trace of cowardice in it, or even a desire to remain unsoiled by the violence below. Indeed, what she sensed from Balor was more a feeling of irrelevance, as if all the mud and sweat and smoke and fear down there on the battlefield had little or nothing to do with him and his plans. It puzzled her. The laughter grew louder, flooding her head. Brie groaned and pressed her fists against her ears.

"Brie?" Collun said, worried. The others were watching her.

"I'm sorry," she replied. "It's nothing." Then, ignoring the ringing in her ears, she said, "Lom, if what you say is true, then the odds are, uh, not exactly even."

"No, they are not," he agreed.

"What say you?" Brie asked those gathered. "Shall we retreat? Or..." She paused.

"Or do we give our lives to put a mighty hole in the villain Balor's invasion?" Hanna said for her, matter-of-factly.

"Flight would sit ill with most in this company," suggested Lom.

"What of Sago?" asked Hanna. "Is he the same?"

Brie nodded grimly. While the Dungalans had been spilling their blood on the battlefield, the Sea Dyak sorcerer had stayed at the edge of the forest, astride his fat pony, weaving that pathetic little fishing net of his. Not surprisingly Monodnock had chosen to stay with the sorcerer.

And before calling this council Brie had sought out Sago. She had found him sitting cross-legged by a heap of rocks. The sorcerer had been unreachable, eyes glazed, nonsense words tumbling out of his mouth; he was lost in madness. As she stared down at him, Brie could not even picture the amazing sorcerer of light who had destroyed the sumog back in Ardara.

"Well, do not forget there is one among us who bears a fire arrow," Lom said, breaking into Brie's thoughts with a tired grin.

"The gabha will find it difficult to forget that," agreed Hanna.

Brie tried to smile, but there was still a buzzing in her ears where Balor's laughter had been, and that puzzle of his indifference.

There was a sudden commotion down near the white stone beach, a shriek that sounded like Monodnock, followed by an eruption of laughter, then a murmuring of voices. Jacan soon appeared, supporting a half-fainting Monodnock. The orange-haired Ellyl had a dusting of some odd white powder on his cheeks. He sneezed loudly.

"I was only seeking to bathe in the sea," Monodnock whined, "when I was suddenly attacked by them."

"By what?" Brie asked.

"Moths, thousands of them," Monodnock sputtered. "Ghost moths!"

Brie stared at him with a faint stirring of alarm.

"Yes," confirmed Jacan in a calm voice. "There are white moths covering the beach. They fly up into your face when you step on the white stones."

Brie abruptly stood and, gesturing for Jacan to join her, began striding toward the shore.

"Has anyone been affected by the moths?" she asked, urgent.

"I am not sure what you mean," Jacan replied thoughtfully, "but no, other than terrifying Monodnock here and making a few men sneeze."

They had arrived at the beach. When she looked closely, Brie could see the scores of moths resting atop the stones. Their wings pulsed, making the beach look like a living thing. She took a step forward and a swarm of them flew up at her face. She hastily stepped backward. She dipped her finger into a trace of white powder left on her sleeve and sniffed it. It made her sneeze violently, but she felt nothing else, certainly nothing resembling the confusion and empty eyes of Yldir. If these were the moths Balor had used, then he must have added his own sorcery to them. Still, to be cautious, she advised the Dungalans to stay off the beach.

Sentries were posted to watch the gabha camp. The mist, which had been burned away by the sun during the day's battle, came up again during the night, ragged and drifting.

It was a queer night, at once edgy and deathly still. The moon hung in the sky like a swollen yellow fruit. Many among the exhausted company slumbered with a deep-reaching exhaustion, but as many could not sleep, tossing restlessly. There were low-pitched murmurings of pain from those whose wounds bit deep, and the soothing voices of those who tended them. Friends walked together, exchanging words unsaid before; one or two found refuge in song, strains of which, elegiac and silvery, wafted over the ruined buildings with the fog.

Brie sat with Collun and Hanna, Fara curled at her side. She had seen Lom a short time ago walk off into the fog with the girl Maire. Though Hanna's side was heavily bandaged, Brie and Collun had long since given up trying to talk her out of fighting on the morrow.

Unless they were attacked first, the Dungalan army would move as soon as the sun rose.

From where she sat, Brie could see Sago, still cross-legged, by the small heap of stones.

Brie suddenly had horrible images of Sago blundering into the thick of battle, mistaking a gabha ax for a leaping silver kingfish. Resolutely she sought out Monodnock. She found him among the trees at the edge of the forest, secretly snacking on sweetmeats he had squirreled away in his pack. She dragged him back to the heap of stones and ordered him to sit on a rock several feet from Sago.

"I have something very important for you to do, Monodnock," Brie said to the apprehensive Ellyl. "Tomorrow morning, when the battle commences, I want you to ensure that Sago stays far away from the fighting. Do you understand, Monodnock? It is very important." Monodnock looked at her for a moment, uncomprehending. Then his face was split by an enormous smile, so unbelieving was he of his good fortune.

"You must stick to the Sea Dyak sorcerer like barnacles to a rock. Will you pledge to do this, Monodnock?" Brie's eyes bored into the Ellyl's.

"Of course, fairest of maidens. Much as I would have it otherwise, I shall keep the ancient sorcerer far, far away from the perilous battle," Monodnock simpered. "In jeopardy of my own life shall I ensure that your directive is followed!"

Brie turned to look at Sago. He was still bent over his webbing of string and hemp, his frail fingers moving slowly. She fervently hoped that when the battle began he would stay right where he was, lost in his private world.

But Sago suddenly raised his head and, with a deranged grin, gave Brie an exaggerated wink. Then he returned to his slow work. Brie felt a little sick. Hanna had dozed off, but Collun had seen the wink and said, as Brie returned to his side, "You are worried about the Sea Dyak sorcerer."

Brie sighed. "Well, if Monodnock has anything to say about it, they will be halfway to Tir a Ceol when the battle starts." Then she said abruptly, "You could return to Eirren, you know."

"I know." Collun calmly drank hot cyffroi.

"Queen Aine and King Gwynn ought to be warned."

"Yes," Collun agreed, his expression unchanged.

"You are not Dungalan," she persisted. "There is no reason for you to give your life."

"No more are...," Collun started to say, then stopped, a thoughtful look on his face.

Brie shook her head, nettled. "I do not know for certain that my great-grandmother was from Dungal."

"I was not thinking of Seila."

"Then...?"

"I was thinking of the Storm Petrel, of your dancing for the first time. And fishing the deep waters; shooting the arrow of binding; and even this cyffroi..." He gestured at the cup in his hand with a grimace.

Brie stared at him for several moments. "It is true," she replied slowly. "I was happy for a time in Ardara. But..." She paused, then said deliberately, "I was happy, too, at Cuillean's dun."

Brie thought Collun's eyes widened, but she could not read his thoughts.

"Brie...," he started.

"Excuse me," came Aelwyn's voice, "but Lom told me to tell you there is movement in the gabha camp." The sun was just rising, and the wyll's amber eyes glittered.

# TWENTY-ONE

# Sago's Net

The battle began, not with a fiery headlong rush into a sleeping enemy camp, but with two armies facing each other across a stretch of turf. One was small, weakened by injury and fatigue, but determined and wildly brave, while the other was enormous and subhuman, led by the cunning intelligence of a monster.

There was an eerie silence as the armies approached each other, no battle horns sounded, no gabha brayed. But then the two armies merged, and the noise grew and swelled as the killing began again.

As before, Brie and Ciaran, with Fara loping at the horse's side, cleaved a burning gash through the gabha ranks, but Brie sensed something different in the goat-men

who engaged her. They seemed bolder, reckless even, and she realized that the gabha general Cernu had devised a new strategy. She found herself being pushed to one side by thick bands of goat-men. The more she hewed down the more did Cernu send to take their place. Brie was fast becoming isolated from the rest of the Dungalan army.

Vainly she tried to move toward her company, but clusters of gabha kept appearing, continually harrying her and Ciaran. Her anger mounted, but with it came some measure of despair. She saw that the Dungalans were being driven back, closer and closer to the white stone beach.

Then she suddenly caught sight of the Sea Dyak sorcerer; the last time she had looked, Sago, with Monodnock huddled beside him, had been seated by the same heap of stones. Now he was mounted on his pony and was riding into the gap between Brie and her army. There was no sign of Monodnock.

The frail sorcerer made a ridiculous, startling sight as he trotted along on the broad-beamed pony with the fish-like tail, and Brie heard a sound like a laugh coming from one of the gabha near her. Sago was singing, a nonsense song no doubt, and in one hand he held his little fishing net. Cursing Monodnock under her breath, Brie furiously slashed at the gabha hemming her in, trying desperately to break through to get to Sago. But by the time Ciaran had broken free, Sago had changed course. He was heading for the bulk of the gabha army, which was inexorably pushing the Dungalans toward the beach.

"Sago!" Brie shouted.

But he did not hear her, or chose not to hear her, and she watched, horrified, as he approached the nearest of the rear guard of the goat-men.

"Faster," she urged Ciaran.

A gabha had spotted Sago and turned to hew him down with an enormous ax. The Sea Dyak sorcerer lifted his paper-thin hand, the hand holding the net, and called out in a surprisingly loud voice, "Heva! Heva! Heva!" Brie recognized the words as the cry of the huer, the Ardaran fisherman whose house overlooked the bay, letting the other fishermen know of the reddening of the sea that meant pilchards in the bay.

The goat-man with the ax paused, surprised by the loudness of Sago's voice perhaps, and Brie watched in amazement as the small, ungainly fishing net in Sago's hand began to widen and spread. There was no light coming from the sorcerer, as it had with the sumog, but his face, which was transformed by an uncanny expression of pleasure, seemed to glow white, almost moonlike. The net, which gave off a faint white glow of its own, stretched and extended over the rear guard of the gabha army. The goat-men gazed up at it in growing wonder and fear. The Dungalans, especially the fishermen among them, had begun moving back, away from the net, the moment they heard "Heva! Heva! Heva!" The fishing net kept spreading, floating impossibly several feet above gabha heads, until most of the goat-man army was under its shadow.

Then the net drifted down, settling on their heads and shoulders and arms. Where it made contact with the furred hide of the gabha, it adhered, as though imbued with some sticky, deadly sort of glue. The strings of the net did not stick to Dungalan skin or hair, and those caught under it were able to burrow their way out between the bodies of the trapped and struggling goat-men. The gabha were panicking, braying loudly.

Then Brie noticed that the creatures were clutching their necks, as though having trouble breathing. Some had fallen to the ground, their limbs stiff and wracked by small jerking movements; gagging, choking noises came from their throats. And, in that moment, Brie suddenly realized what kind of fish it was that she had seen in Sago's amhantar. It was called puffer fish, and Jacan had once told Brie that the puffer fish was the most poisonous of the fish that inhabited the waters by Ardara; he had seen a fellow fisherman die in a matter of minutes, his breath stopped and his body paralyzed, from careless handling of a puffer fish.

Brie suddenly heard a powerful braying, and she spun around to see the goat-man general Cernu, astride a swift goat-horse, bearing down on Sago. He had no weapon in his hands, but before Brie could reach them, Cernu had lowered his spiraling horns and plunged them into Sago's thin chest. The sorcerer was knocked off his mount, falling backward onto the ground, the net dislodged from his hand. Cernu jumped off his steed as well and leaned over Sago. For a horrified moment Brie thought the goat-man would lift the featherlight sorcerer up into the air, impaled on his horns.

But he did not. He turned and faced Brie, an evil grin on his grotesque face, blood dripping from his horns.

"Brie!" came a warning shout from Collun, who had circled around toward her. Before she could react, a terrible pain radiated across her back. Brie toppled off Ciaran onto the ground. A goat-man, one of the band she had been fighting earlier, loomed above her swinging his club. With an agonizing upward lunge, Brie struck with the fire arrow and the creature collapsed.

By the time she turned back, Brie saw that Cernu was locked in hand-to-hand combat with a Dungalan. No, not a Dungalan, she realized with a shock, but Collun.

The gabha general towered above the boy. From somewhere the creature had produced one of those lethal clubs, studded with sharp spikes, and he was swinging it ruthlessly at Collun, who danced just out of reach.

But even as Brie moved toward them she saw Collun take a mighty blow to his head. He collapsed, falling to the ground, and lay there, unmoving.

Letting out a shout of pure rage, Brie charged the gabha general. The fire arrow sang in her blistered hand.

Cernu lowered his horns, brandishing his club at the same time. Brie swerved to the side, then rounded back. But he kept her at bay with his horns and his club. Frustrated, she slashed wildly. She could tell Cernu felt the heat from the arrow, but when she gazed up into his bulging, savage eyes she saw no fear.

Suddenly Brie was terrified, conscious of her puny human frailty. A terrible chill fear flooded her and she cowered back. Cernu let out a bray of victory and pushed forward to deliver a deathblow. Brie watched, hypnotized, as the spiraling horns came down at her.

Then something brushed past her legs, and a snarling whirlwind of fur launched itself at the gabha's haunches. For a moment Cernu was knocked off balance, then he let out an impatient grunt and swung his club at Fara, catching her across the neck. The faol tried to rise, but, stunned, fell back again. The gabha general turned back to Brie, but in that moment she darted under the reach of his horns and thrust the fire arrow up into his bearded chin.

Blood poured down her hand and the giant figure stiffened. The club dropped from his hand. As he fell, Cernu opened his mouth to bray, but all that emerged were flames. He hit the ground with a crash, his head afire.

Brie staggered, almost falling to the ground herself. Anxiously she looked around for Fara. The faol had an ugly gash on her neck but was already on her feet and trotting toward Brie. Together they found Collun. He lay where he had fallen, eyes closed, the side of his head a sticky mass of blood.

Brie was sure he was dead. Trembling, her fingers sought his pulse; she just barely could feel a whispering thrum against her fingertips.

Then she saw Sago on the ground several feet away. He lay on his side, curled up, face peaceful. He might have been sleeping, except for the wide stain of crimson across the front of his tunic. Brie crossed to him and crouched down.

Around them the battle continued to rage. The Dungalans who had crawled out from under Sago's net were now fighting the goat-men who remained. But Brie was unaware of anything save the Sea Dyak sorcerer. His eyes flicked open.

"Hand me my pole," came a faint whisper, light as a puff of air. "Fish are biting." A smile curled his lips. Then his eyes sought Brie's, his thin fingers wrapping around her hand. "Remember the boy Thom. Watch his thumbnails as he grows," he said clearly. Then his eyes closed and he was dead.

"Brie," said Hanna, who stood behind her. "Help me with Collun." And as she and Collun had done for Hanna the day before, Brie and Hanna lifted Collun and carried him to a safe place.

Brie bent anxiously over Collun, her fingers finding his wrist again. "Will he...?" she asked Hanna.

"It is early to say," said Hanna, but she did not look hopeful.

"Stay with him," said Brie. Wearily she once more mounted Ciaran. Because of Sago, more than half the gabha army lay dead, and the rest were in disarray without their leader. But the battle was far from over, and Brie and Ciaran went to rejoin the Dungalan army.

As she rode, Brie heard the high pure call of a battle horn. She looked around, afraid. A small army was emerging from the forest, the sun reflecting off its shields and swords, blinding Brie for a moment. Then she saw the Dungalan standard raised high above them. Brie blinked in amazement. As the army came closer she recognized the man leading it—Ralfe, Prince Durwydd's adviser. The new army merged with the battle-weary old, and soon the remaining goat-men were in full retreat. It was not long before the last of the gabha were fleeing into the foothills.

By early evening the battle was over and the heartbreaking task of finding and burying the dead had begun. Most had lost close friends or family, and there was little of celebration in those who remained. Of the Dungalans who had journeyed from Ardara, fourteen had survived the battle, among them Lom, Jacan, Ferg and Gwil, Maire and her brother, and the boy Dil. Along with Sago and the fisherman Henle, the boy Marc, brother to Beith, had fallen, as had four fishermen.

Monodnock had disappeared, and Brie sent a small search party to look for him. The Ellyl was found in the forest, apparently hiding in a tree. He came down only because he overheard two of the searchers speaking of the enemy's defeat.

He appeared before Brie disheveled and exhausted, twigs sprouting from his orange hair. At first he could not meet her eyes.

"Most gracious and generous maiden," he said, gazing at her left shoulder, "allow me to offer my most heartfelt laudation and homage to your stunning rout of a most fearsome and multitudinous foe." Monodnock's eyes shifted to Brie's forehead. "It was a vast and irreparable disappointment to me that I could not stand shoulder to shoulder with you as you swept aside the evil tide."

"Monodnock...," Brie began, stone-faced.

"And alas, as it turned out, I could not, uh, I was not able to, uh, obey your mandate, wise as it was, or rather, uh, appeared to be..." The Ellyl suddenly brightened. "However, as Sago did mount his steed, I, uh, had a flash, a vision if you will"—Monodnock warmed to his theme, newly confident—"that this ancient man of power had within him one last burst of magnificence and that to hold him back from his heroic errand would be an incalculably grave error."

"I see. And did this 'vision' also tell you not to accompany Sago on his 'heroic errand,'" Brie asked, "in spite of the fact that I had ordered you not to leave his side?"

Monodnock reddened, but blustered on. "Of course, I intended to do as you directed, and was in the process of attempting to procure a steed of my own, when I suddenly sensed that my presence would almost certainly interfere with the, uh, spheres of power encircling the sorcerer. You can see, then, that I did not dare cause any obstruction between him and his desired goat, uh, goal..." Monodnock trailed off. His hair was a spiky jungle and his lanky form trembled with exhaustion from his lengthy vigil in the treetop.

Brie found herself veering between the urge to laugh out loud and the desire to give Monodnock a severe scolding. However, compassion won out, and she sent the Ellyl, sagging with relief, to find a bite to eat.

The Dungalan survivors gathered the slain gabha into large heaps and, as was the Dungalan custom with the remains of an enemy, set the mounds aflame, although as the smell wafted over their camp, Brie rather wished they hadn't. She had had enough burning goat flesh to last a lifetime.

The frayed remnants of Sago's net lay everywhere. Lom saved the largest intact piece he could find to take back to Ardara. The new arrivals listened in amazement to the tale of the Sea Dyak sorcerer's miraculous net.

Prince Durwydd's adviser Ralfe approached Brie as she helped with the digging of a grave, asking for a private moment of her time. As they walked in the direction of the mountains, Ralfe confided in Brie that just prior to the newly mustered army's departure for the north, he had received a message from Prince Durwydd in Tir a Ceol.

"Our prince, in so many words, stated that he was abdicating the throne; that he had chosen to make a life for himself in Tir a Ceol and would not be returning." Brie could see that Ralfe was in the grip of some powerful emotions, and she realized that the strongest was a deep shame for the actions of his prince. "I took it upon myself to delay

imparting this distressing news to anyone until this moment. It was an egregious act of deceit; still, I have no
regrets," he said stoutly. "Furthermore, I now consider myself under arrest for high treason, and do place myself in
your custody."

Brie gaped at the grizzled man. "That's nonsense," she
said bluntly. "You acted in the best interests of your army
and your country."

"Notwithstanding, I did not have the authority to mount
an army..."

Brie waved his words aside. "Tell me, Ralfe, is it not
unusual for Ellylon to allow a human to live with them?"

"Prince Durwydd has royal blood, and the Dungalan
royal family is known to have some amount of draoicht
within them. Perhaps this is why."

"I see."

Between them, Brie and Ralfe agreed that now would
perhaps not be the best time to tell the Dungalans of their
prince's decision.

"What will happen?" Brie asked. "Who will rule in
Durwydd's absence?"

"There is a young cousin, a boy who lives in the village
Pennog. He is young yet to rule," said Ralfe.

"But he will not lack for loyal and farsighted advisers,
of that I am certain," Brie replied with a smile.

❦

Throughout the day, as Brie helped dig graves, kindle
pyres, and—when she got the chance—care for a still unconscious Collun, she often found herself casting uneasy
glances at Sedd Wydyr, which stood glittering against the
blue sky. She knew, as they all knew, that although the

gabha had been defeated, Balor still lived. Even if he did not show himself, he lived.

Lom suggested that Balor must have fled once he saw the battle was lost. Brie said nothing, but she knew that was not true. On the other hand, she could feel no trace of Balor, even when she held the fire arrow and boldly sought him with her mind. All she got was a bad case of blurred vision for her efforts.

"He must have returned to Scath, taking the man Bricriu with him," Hanna suggested, sitting with Brie while she waited for her eyesight to return to normal. Collun lay nearby, his condition unchanged, and Fara was seated beside Brie, trying to dislodge the bandage Hanna had fashioned for the gash on her neck.

Brie shook her head, dissatisfied. "We will have to search Sedd Wydyr," she said.

Leaving Aelwyn to watch over Collun, Brie led the search of the crystal fortress. Using makeshift ladders to scale the outer wall, several Dungalans opened the gate from the inside for the rest of the search party. The inside of the castle was as opulent and shining as the outside, yet it was cold, devoid of any humanity. They searched the entire structure, every room, every twisting corridor, even out through the underground tunnel that exited through the door in the side of the bluff, but they found no trace of life. They did find another tunnel, a long one that led them to an entrance hidden deep in the foothills, and most were satisfied that Balor must have escaped through this route.

But Brie was not. She alone had felt Balor's power and could not conceive of him fleeing in such a way.

They buried Sago where he had fallen on the battle

plain. First, as Hanna and Brie had done for Yldir, they crafted a small boat-shaped casket. They laid the fallen sorcerer in the boat, along with his empty amhantar, a makeshift fishing pole Brie had made, a small piece of the fishing net, and a skin bag of wine. The small piece of wood from the boat Gor-gwynt they placed in his open palm. Someone had gone out on the white stone beach, in spite of the white moths, and found a large smooth rock to use as a memory stone for Sago. As Hanna etched words onto the stone, Brie noticed a number of seabirds clustered overhead, some just hanging there, others gliding in tight circles. When they lowered the boat-casket into the earth, a fisherman from Ardara brought out a small pipe and played a short melody that Brie recognized as one of Sago's favorite nonsense songs, about a whitebelly and a plover. The seabirds above had grown in number, a large hovering cloud of whites and blacks and browns.

As the music ended, the seabirds cried out and then, almost as a solid mass, they flew away.

As the birds disappeared over the sea, Brie heard someone say with a sigh, "With Yldir and Sago gone, I'm thinking that's the last of the Sea Dyak sorcerers."

"Actually, no," Brie found herself saying, "I don't think so."

Several faces turned to her, questioning.

And Brie told them what Sago had said to her about the boy Thom who lived in the town of Mira, and about his thumbnails.

"I know the lad," said a fisherman from Mira in wonderment, "and a fine young fisherman he's already showing himself to be. Father's that proud of him. Wait until he hears of this..."

Because many of the Dungalans were uneasy near the moth-infested white beach, not to mention the looming, empty fortress of Sedd Wydyr, Lom suggested they move camp to their old site on the other side of the forest.

And so they finished their burying and burning and wearily traveled back through the trees, glad to see the last of Sedd Wydyr and its bloodstained battlefield.

The newly arrived Dungalan army had brought with them fresh provisions, and that night Hanna oversaw the cooking of an impressive feast. There was also a new supply of good Dungalan mead, and as the evening wore on the somber mood of the Dungalans began to lighten.

They were just finishing a delicious medlar comfit when a Dungalan who had ridden with the original army rose to his feet, his cup of mead upraised. Brie couldn't remember his name, but she knew he was a fisherman from the small town of Clibden with a boat he called Bream. The flames from the cooking fires lit his face and he called out, loud, "To Bren-huan!" And there came a great yelling and clapping.

Brie blushed. For a mortified moment she was afraid they were going to ask for a speech, but then Hanna stood and added her own toast to that of the fisherman from Clibden. She compared Brie's bravery to that of Queen Fionna and said that when Brie had led them to battle she had looked like a Dungalan war goddess, her braids flying behind her like bolts of golden lightning. When Hanna finished, there were more cheers and cups being refilled. After that came many rounds of toasts to all the many acts of bravery and comradeship during battle. Monodnock tipsily even offered a toast to himself, taking credit for dispatching Sago on his miraculous errand. It was late by the time the assembled companions began drifting off to their bedrolls.

Brie, Hanna, and Silien remained sitting by their campfire, Collun lying an arm's length from them. He was still unconscious, though Hanna said the wound to the side of his head looked better. But she could not say more.

"The truth, Hanna," said Brie, her face intent. "Is Collun going to recover?"

"I wish I had an answer, Biri. But even if his body heals, head wounds are difficult. It may be that his wits will be affected."

Brie's stomach tightened.

"He may be as a child, Biri," Hanna said gently.

Like a kesil, Brie thought, thinking of the handful of wandering wild forest men in Eirren. She stared at Collun's bandaged head. "Can we do nothing? Silien?"

The Ellyl shook his head. "The healing waters of Tir a Ceol cannot help hurts of the mind. I am sorry."

"Biri," Hanna said, her voice brisk, "your hand needs more of that mallow salve." Brie looked down at her blistered, oozing palm, the one that had wielded the fire arrow. The strip of cloth with which Collun had bound her hand had come loose.

Hanna had Collun's wallet of herbs and, with Brie's help, soon had made a small amount of the salve, which she applied to Brie's hand. The salve stung and soothed at the same time. But Brie noticed that Hanna's eyelids were drooping and that Silien had already dozed off.

"Get some sleep, Hanna," Brie said. "I'll watch Collun."

"Only if you promise to wake me in a few hours," Hanna murmured.

Brie brewed a pan of cyffroi, then reached for her bow

with its broken string. She restrung it with a string she had borrowed from one of the Dungalan archers. Her quiver was empty except for the fire arrow; when her hand was better she would make new arrows. Idly, she took out the fire arrow. It hummed lightly against her unburnt hand. Then she looked at the story band at the very bottom of the shaft.

Brie caught her breath. The story band slowly unraveled itself, revealing the story of the Dungalan battle against the gabha. Hypnotized, Brie watched the events unfold in moving, vivid pictures. When she came to the part where Sago was run through by the gabha general's horns, tears welled in her eyes. And when Collun fell, his head crushed, the tears spilled over, wetting her cheeks. Then came the grave digging, the smoke from the pyres and the uneasy waiting by Collun's unconscious body.

"Where is Balor?" Brie whispered through her tears, clutching the arrow.

The white stone beach flashed in front of Brie's eyes, luminous in the moonlight, pulsing faintly.

# TWENTY-TWO

# The Fire Arrow

Brie abruptly stood, then realized she could not see. Stuffing the arrow in her quiver and feeling for her bow, Brie called out softly, "Fara?"

She felt the furry body of the faol brush against her legs. "Guide me, Fara. I cannot see. I wish to find Ciaran, to watch Collun. And then I need to go to the stone beach."

Fara began to move forward and Brie kept near the faol by resting her hand on the animal's back. Fara had long since rid herself of the bandage on her neck and Brie could feel the puckered edges of the faol's wound.

"Brie?" It was Aelwyn's voice.

Brie stopped short, turning her face toward the voice.

"I could not sleep. How is Collun?"

"The same," Brie answered, keeping her voice casual. "Aelwyn, would you do me a favor and sit with him? I, uh, need to look for mallow, in the forest. It's for burn salve..." She trailed off weakly, hoping Aelwyn would not ask questions.

"Yes, of course. But..." There was curiosity in the wyll's voice.

"It should not take long. Thank you." Brie walked forward, her hand still on Fara's back, trying to move with the assurance of one who can see. "To the beach, Fara," Brie whispered.

Brie felt the branches of the trees around her as they entered the forest, but Fara guided her surely, and she did not stumble or fall.

She could tell the moment they emerged from the forest: the moonlight brightening the dimness of her sight, the air on her face, and the strong smell of the sea. They moved quickly across the battlefield, and as they were making their way through the ruins near the shore, Brie's sight began to return. By the time they stepped onto the white stone beach her vision had returned to normal. She could clearly see the moths that swarmed up with each step. There were more than she remembered, and she had to keep waving her hand in front of her face to keep them from lining her lips and closing her nostrils. Fara playfully swatted at a few, but because there were so many she soon tired of the game.

Suddenly unsure, Brie gazed around, still waving away the moths. The moon was so bright that except for the dun color of the sky it might have been day. Brie saw no sign of Balor.

She moved closer to the water and the number of moths began to diminish. Restlessly her eyes scanned the bluff, the glittering fortress, the battlefield, and then the beach and across the sea.

Squinting, she took several steps closer to the water, until it was lapping the tips of her boots. There was a long jagged line of darkness resting on the horizon, a deeper dark than the murky night sky, and Brie stared at it until her eyes hurt. The darkness stretched left and right almost as far as she could see. At first she was puzzled; then vague, uneasy fears began stirring in her.

She stood very still, her body rigid. Fara had seen the darkness, too, and let out a low sound. Together they watched as the darkness grew larger and moved closer.

Boats. Hundreds and hundreds of boats. The swollen moon shone on them as brightly as a sky full of torches. Brie could make out the arching long necks of the prows of long boats with bloodred sails billowing above. They looked like a fleet of winged sea serpents splitting the waves, bearing down on the coast of Dungal.

She had a sudden tingling sensation on the skin of her neck and arms. Someone was nearby. Almost involuntarily Brie looked up, and there, standing at the tip of the bluff above, was Balor. He gazed straight out to sea, at the approaching boats, and he wore golden armor, burnished, dazzling in the full moon. His head was covered by a resplendent war helmet with the guise of a bird of prey rising in radiant gold from his forehead. Because of the way he stood, Brie could see that across the torso of the golden mail was a black tunic. In the center of the tunic, woven of impossibly bright threads, was a goldenhawk.

He did not turn his face toward Brie, but he knew she was there.

Brie looked back at the boats. They had dropped their

sails and were now being rowed. Each boat was crowded with morgs—there were more standing than sitting at the oars—a ghastly silent horde, some hooded, some baring their skeletal heads. She suddenly remembered that the morgs who attacked Collun at Cuillean's dun had come by boat.

Balor must have emptied the island kingdoms of Usna and Uneach, Brie thought as she stared, unbelieving, at the oncoming multitude. Hundreds of boats, perhaps even thousands, each one carrying a hundred morgs. Even if all of Dungal and Eirren combined stood against them, there would still be morgs to spare.

Brie sank to her knees. Fara huddled against her. No wonder the gabha battle had been irrelevant to Balor. *This* was his true army.

Only when she felt a searing on her already burnt hand did Brie realize she was holding the fire arrow. She must have reached for it, unknowing. Hot tears of desolation and loss stung her eyelids. She found herself thinking of the hero Amergin and how he beat the sea back with his fists. And of Fionna, who had emptied herself to keep the sea from overwhelming her people.

But these were morgs in boats, not the sea, and Brie had no draoicht. The fire arrow did, but she could hardly slash and burn her way through such a horde.

She gazed up again at Balor. The moon gleamed on his golden armor like a beacon. He stood unmoving, triumphant. He must have removed his eye-patch, for Brie could see his white eye under the golden beak of his war helmet.

Numbly she rose from her knees, feeling for her bow. She held the arrow a last time. And then, fingers trembling, she nocked it to the bowstring.

She pointed the arrow at Balor, at the goldenhawk on his chest. For my father, she thought.

She pulled the string back. But then, with a sob that tore out of her gut, she swung the bow away and, thinking irrelevantly of the god Nuadha and his magic teka, she fixed her sights on the nearest longboat of morgs, though it lay well beyond the range of an arrow shot. She focused all that was in her, all of her strength, her will, her passion, and her stubbornness, into that banded, mysterious arrow, until she did not know where she began and the arrow ended ... and she *was* the arrow. Before letting the arrow fly, Brie suddenly remembered the nightmare she had had in Ardara, of flames instead of eyes. She felt the heat of the arrow along her jawbone, and it seared against her first and second fingers as she held the nock in place on the string. She had never felt the arrow so hot, hot enough to burn through the bowstring; her muscles contracted and terror threatened to dissolve her will to shoot.

But with a courage she did not know she possessed, her already kindling eyes fixed on the nearest longboat, she released the arrow. As she watched it soar, an unwavering line of brightness against the dun-colored sky, Brie thought to herself what a farcical, ridiculous gesture it had been, to shoot a single arrow at a war host as vast as the sea itself. Her bow collapsed in fragments in her hands, the string burnt through. But the arrow flew higher and higher, soaring over the sea waves, arcing, then gracefully descending, and soundlessly cleaved the surface of the water, leagues short of the longboats. Brie crumpled to the ground, her eyes on fire.

As she pressed her fingers in agony against her eyelids,

Brie felt a great stillness around her, almost as if all sound had been sucked down under the surface of the sea with the arrow. She could not see with her burning eyes, but pictures, vivid and clear, were forming behind the heat. She saw the arrow cleaving the water, then piercing rock and sand and sticking there in the seabed, upright. A fish was swimming by, a yellow parrot fish (one of Sago's favorites, Brie thought foolishly), and, as the arrow came to rest, the fish suddenly startled, darting away in a great hurry. And Brie saw why; the water surrounding the arrow began to move in an unnatural way. It was as if an invisible giant finger had dipped into the water and was spinning it in circles around the fire arrow. The water began to foam, and the churning grew so intense Brie could no longer see the arrow.

And then the pictures behind her eyelids were taking her up above the water and she saw how quickly the under-water upheaval had spread, for the moonlit sea stretching before her was being whipped into a frenzy, like a violent northeastern storm, yet there was not a breath of wind.

The burning in Brie's eye sockets was close to unbear-able, and the pictures began to flicker, filming over from the heat and pain.

But she could hear the churning and the groaning of the sea. Sprays of water hit her body. The waves were growing larger, and blindly she backed away from the shoreline.

Then through the flickering she could dimly make out one giant wave beginning to form. It gathered itself to-gether and rose, monstrous and impossible, into the night sky, blotting out the moon. And defying all reason, the giant spume of water exploded west, away from the beach. It slammed into the Western Sea with a thunderous roaring blast, as if the earth itself had cracked open.

Then the picture flicked off suddenly, leaving only blackness behind Brie's pain-seared eyes. And she heard another sound, cacophonous and enormous: a blend of hissing and screaming from thousands of morg throats. It lasted only a moment; then came silence, save for the sound of the ocean, restless and ever moving, as it settled back into its familiar rhythms.

Brie realized she was drenched with water, as she lay huddled on the beach of stones. The burning in her eyes had lessened somewhat, though she still kept her hands pressed against them, but her body felt broken and lifeless. And, when she removed her hands and opened her eyelids, she could not see. It was a darkness that frightened her; not just a blurred gray, as had happened before, but a complete and utter black.

She was so weak she did not think she had the strength to sit up, but then she felt Fara's wet fur beside her. When she had pulled herself up, Fara climbed into her lap, filling it. Brie laid her face on the animal's haunch, glad for the warmth.

Then she heard a cracking sound, so loud, as of something very large beginning to splinter. A familiar sound, Brie thought. Oh yes, the bell tower. And she knew, without being able to see it, that the sound came from Sedd Wydyr, and that the crystal castle was shattering.

As splinters of glass and rubble began to tumble down onto the bluff and beach, Brie crawled on her hands and knees to get farther away, Fara close beside her. Moths, some with damp wings, fluttered into her face, but she did not stop to brush them away. Somewhere in the dull recesses of her mind, she thought that Balor wasn't going to be pleased. This was the second of his buildings she had somehow managed to wreck.

Then her battered body began to shake. It was not only Balor's buildings she had destroyed.

He was somewhere nearby. She could feel it and had a sudden insane urge to throw herself into the sea, thinking it would be better to get it all over with quickly. But she did not; she just held Fara tightly as she lay curled up on her side, trembling.

And soon the footsteps came, as she had known they would, and she felt Fara being lifted from her arms and flung aside. She heard the faol hit the stones and then she heard no movement at all, except for the whooshing of moths.

Brie sat up, her arms wrapped tightly around her knees.

"It cannot have happened, and yet it has," came Balor's golden voice, thick with rage and incredulity. "I had not thought the old woman's draoicht adequate, and yet her prophecy was true."

"Old woman?" Brie croaked. Somehow she pulled herself to her feet, weak and blind as a newborn kitten still wet from afterbirth.

"A wyll, a hideous crone, misshapen, offensive to the eye. Before I left Dungal and came to Dun Slieve, this wyll told me that a cousin with an arrow of power would destroy me one day. I disbelieved her, but when I came to your father's dun and saw the unkindled skill in you with bow and arrow, I decided it was as well to be cautious. So I made the serving woman of Dun Slieve talk in her sleep and learned of the arrow.

"I tried to take it from you once"—he laughed his rich golden laugh—"but you had it not. Not yet."

And Brie remembered. One rain-soaked night in late spring, she was in her room at Dun Slieve, woken suddenly from sleep with a horrible pain and fear. Her breath had stopped, and a yellow bird was plunging down at her. Balor's tunic. Even then the goldenhawk had been his emblem. So evil, terrifying had it been that she had hidden the memory until it began to come on its own, unbidden, on a rainy night in Cuillean's dun. Or perhaps Balor himself had hidden the memory from her. " 'Cross my heart and then to die/Stick an arrow in my eye.' "

"I almost disposed of you then, and, of course, I should have. But there was an interruption and I did not wish to be discovered, not until I found the arrow." Masha had opened the door, worrying about rain leaking from the ceiling. "It was a mistake, for as it turned out, the arrow concealed itself from me well. It did so again, did it not, in the bell tower?"

Brie nodded, as if in a trance.

"I could have done much with that arrow," Balor said, regret mingling with his rage. She could hear him take several strides away. He must have been looking up at the ruins of Sedd Wydyr, for he said, "That was to be *our* fortress, you know: rulers of a golden kingdom, Balor and consort." The rage broke over his words like a cresting wave, but his voice did not waver.

" 'Cross my heart and then to die...' " The words echoed in Brie's ears, and she saw the plummeting goldenhawk, suffocating, hurting her.

The strip of cloth Collun had used to bind her burnt hand had come loose again and, unthinking, Brie began unwinding it, her blind eyes fixed on the place where Balor's voice had been. She stood sightless before this sorcerer and his staggering rage, with nothing to protect herself. Her pockets were empty, except for the moon shell Sago had given her.

Why does he not move? Brie wondered.

"And now..." Balor's voice was suddenly impatient. The rage could be contained no more.

"What of Bricriu?" The words tumbled out in a feeble effort to distract.

"Bricriu? I saw him scuttling off toward the mountains, toward Medb. The last time he came groveling at Rathcroghan she broke him. I do not care much for his chances with her now." Brie could hear the shrug of indifference in his voice.

Unlike yourself, Brie thought, for she knew, as he knew, he would have little trouble finding favor in Medb's eyes again, with his golden vanity and his seductive power. She slipped her fingers into the pocket that held the moon shell and pulled it out slowly, almost unmindfully. She heard an odd clanking sound, as though Balor were taking off some part of his golden armor.

"Will not Bricriu tell Medb you intended to betray her?" Brie wondered if Balor still had his eye patch off.

"Who do you think Queen Medb will believe?" he replied contemptuously.

You, thought Brie.

"Now..." He moved toward her.

Brie quickly slid the moon shell into the piece of cloth from her hand and, abruptly lifting it above her head as she would a slingshot, she snapped the shell toward where she guessed Balor's head to be.

He screamed: a high-pitched foul noise infused with outrage and disbelief; a rending, piercing scream. And then something heavy knocked against her. She lost her footing and fell to the stones.

Something was lying across Brie's legs. She reached a tentative hand out and found a face, Balor's face. There was a sticky wetness on his cheek and her hand recoiled, but not before feeling the moon shell, which was lodged in his right eye, the white eye.

Quickly, fighting down a violent hysteria, she pulled her legs free of Balor's lifeless body. Half fainting, she tried to crawl away, but her burnt hand stung fiercely and would not bear her weight. She tried crawling on her elbows, but lost all sense of direction. She did not even know she was heading toward the sea until a large wave came up and slammed into her face. Coughing, she started crawling backward, but her arm brushed against something. She reached for it. It was an arrow.

The fire arrow.

She knew what it was from the shape of the arrowhead and the placement of the damp fletching feathers, but there was no humming in her fingers when she held it. Its draoicht was gone.

She knew that she should feel something, that in another lifetime she would have grieved, but her body was too battered, her senses too numb. She just stuck the arrow into the back of her belt and kept crawling.

"Fara," she whispered, but there came no response, just the sound of the waves and the occasional whooshing of moths.

Brie blindly crawled back and forth over the beach until

finally she touched a heap of damp fur and moths flew up in her face in a great rush.

"Fara," she whispered, feeling for a heartbeat. The faol was alive, but unconscious. Brie lay next to her, stroking the fur along her back until she, too, lost consciousness.

⁘

*Above, the summer sun shimmered and before her spread a dappled rainbow of brilliant colors. Collun stood beside her, proud, his hand resting lightly on her arm. "See the dahlias," he said, pointing. "Like gold."*

*"I've never seen larkspur that tall," Brie said in wonder.*

*"Come see the cosmos, and the harebell..."*

*Brie followed Collun through the magnificent garden, the colors and the sun blinding her. "Wait for me," she called after him. He was too far ahead; she lost sight of him in the riot of greens and reds and yellows and blues. "Collun!" she cried.*

⁘

Then Brie woke. She was lying across Ciaran's back, moving through the forest. But she still could not see.

"Ciaran? Where is Fara?"

*Beside us,* came the Ellyl horse's voice, inside Brie's head. *Her leg is broken, but she came and found me. Brought me to you.*

"How...?"

*She dragged you onto my back by the collar.* Ciaran gave a brief whinny-laugh.

"I can't see, Ciaran."

*I know.*

There was silence for several minutes, then, *Brie.*

"Yes?"

*Collun is awake.*

Brie's heart contracted. "Is he...?"

*He is as he was.*

A great exhausted happiness filled Brie, and her sightless eyes pricked with tears of joy.

# TWENTY-THREE

# Leave-taking

The company finally departed the north of Dungal a week later. At their camping place by the forest, they left behind several fresh burial mounds topped with memory stones for those whose battle wounds had finally overtaken them. There was a sense of loss among those who departed, but the enemy had been destroyed and they were returning home.

Collun was still weak but able to ride on his own. Hanna's wound was healing nicely, and Monodnock rode right up at the front of the company telling anyone who would listen of his brilliance in the final battle, as if he himself had woven and wielded the magic fishing net.

Brie wore bandages over her eyes, to give them a chance

to rest and heal. But when she lifted the bandages and looked toward the sun, the blackness was not quite so black. Both Hanna and Aelwyn had said that, with time, her eyesight would return to normal.

Before departing their campsite, Brie had insisted on returning to the beach to give a proper burial to Balor. A handful of companions, including Hanna, Collun, and Silien, accompanied Brie, and despite what she had told them of the size of the morg fleet, they were stunned by the enormous amount of debris that had been washed up on the white stones. Brie listened silently as Collun described the grisly scene to her.

They buried Balor on the bluff, building a small cairn of white stones to mark the place. Hanna found a smooth stone and, though sightless, Brie managed to etch on it the name Balor. The single word and the small heap of stones seemed enough.

At her request the others left her alone at the cairn. She knelt there, thinking of the lifeless body underneath, drained of the power he had once wielded so effortlessly. Balor had taken much from her—her father, her childhood—until finally the balance had come undone. And it had taken the fire arrow and the small shell of a sorcerer to set it right again.

As they crossed the battlefield where so many had fallen, Brie thought of Sago. She tried to summon up a picture of the Sea Dyak sorcerer sitting by his perfect lake, a basket full of fish beside him, a smile on his face, and a riddling song on his lips. For a moment she could make out a hazy image, but it faded quickly.

Brie thought of the vivid pictures the fire arrow had

once shown her. But ever since the arrow had washed up on the beach, emptied of its draoicht, Brie had also felt an emptiness in herself. There was no more tingling on the skin of her fingers, no more dreams or seeings. Whatever draoicht the fire arrow had stirred in her was gone. She felt a grief, akin to losing a close-bound friend, yet it had been an unruly, sometimes uncomfortable friend.

It rained a good deal as the survivors wound their way south, as though making up for the drought of the summer. The army dwindled as the Dungalans returned to their villages and families. Word of the battle and of Balor's defeat spread quickly. By the time they reached Cerriw, Aelwyn's village, the story of Bren-huan and her fire arrow destroying the morg fleet was already known by most of the villagers. The company was given a warm welcome and was urged to stay for feasting and celebration, but they remained only one night; most among them were eager to return to their own families and loved ones.

In Cerriw, Brie took the bandages off her eyes. Her vision was still blurred, but color had returned.

When Aelwyn the wyll bid Collun a lingering, over-enthusiastic good-bye, Brie could see well enough to notice the faint blush in Collun's cheeks. But when she stepped forward to bid her own farewell to the wyll, Aelwyn slipped a small pouch into Brie's hand. The wyll whispered in her ear, "Take these. You don't want to die unwed after all." Inside the pouch was a pair of glittering saphir earrings.

Brie smiled. "Thank you, Aelwyn."

Silien and Monodnock had decided to journey together to Tir a Ceol, though Brie could tell Silien was less than enthusiastic about his companion. Indeed, as they headed off together, Brie overheard Monodnock say, "Perhaps your father might see fit to grant me a posting that is less remote, something closer to the epicenter, if you will, of King Midir's court?"

Silien replied, straight-faced, "Oh, undoubtedly, my father will indeed wish to reward you, Monodnock; for example, he may even place you as one of the leaders of the Ellyl army, to lead Ellyl troops on missions of the utmost danger."

Monodnock paled. "Oh, well, I was not exactly thinking of so great an honor. Indeed, I should be happy with just a modest dwelling, not too terribly far from court..."

"Or perhaps he will make you a spy, sent undercover into Rathcroghan to ferret out Queen Medb's latest plottings. There is no higher honor than the position of spy."

"That would indeed be a great accolade," Monodnock stuttered, his hands frenziedly plucking at his spiky hair, "but the more I think on it, I believe I should miss my little home in the Blue Stack Mountains too much. And indeed, it is an important posting; you never know when the gabha might start stirring up trouble again..."

Brie laughed as the two Ellylon rounded a bend and their voices passed out of hearing.

They left Ralfe at Sedd Brennhin. Though rumors were circulating that Prince Durwydd would no longer rule (this did not appear to be ill news for the majority of Dungalans, who thought a great deal more highly of Ralfe than they did of their prince), the grizzled adviser still held off confirming the news.

"I wish to ensure that the succession goes smoothly," Ralfe explained. "Messengers will be sent at once to the village of Pennog, where Durwydd's royal cousin lives. Indeed, if you stay in Dungal, Bren-huan, I am certain that the boy prince would welcome you as a member of the court."

Brie thanked Ralfe, but told him that she planned to return to her home in Eirren. He nodded his understanding, invited her to the new prince's coronation should she still find herself in Dungal, and wished her luck.

Now why did I say "home," Brie thought wryly as she rode off, when I have nothing of the sort?

*Tir a Ceol,* came Ciaran's voice in her head.

"I'll thank you not to eavesdrop," Brie retorted with a grin. "And last time I looked, Tir a Ceol was *your* home, not mine."

They arrived in Ardara to find that the sumog had vanished, along with the innkeeper of the Speckled Trout. Again they were urged to stay by the grateful villagers, but Brie said they must move on. Despite the warmth of their welcome, she felt uncomfortable in Ardara. It was almost too painful to stay in this place where she did not belong but loved so well. The Storm Petrel lay on the shore, in need of repair after Jacan and Ferg's long absence, and though she would have given much for one last time on its decks, Brie thought it was probably just as well if she didn't return to the sea.

Before they left Ardara, Brie went to Sago's mote with Hanna. The villagers had decided to keep it as it was, a haven for seabirds and a memorial for the fallen Sea Dyak sorcerer.

Someone—Hyslin, no doubt—had tidied up the inside of the mote, and as Brie gazed around at the dim, wavery green interior, sorrow gusted up in her. Hanna put a strong arm around her shoulders. "Why do you not take something of his, as a remembrance?"

Brie gazed around at the shelves full of his sea treasures. She spied a large cluster of moon shells. "You can never have too many moon shells" echoed in her head. She reached out her hand, then hesitated, remembering the feel of the moon shell lodged in Balor's white eye.

"'Oona, moona, mollopy, mite...,'" came Hanna's voice, chanting the counting-out rhyme, "'bimini, jimini, reena...'" Brie smiled and instead remembered the moon shell in Sago's palm as he presented it to her. She picked out a small shell and placed it in her pocket.

As they left the mote, Brie spotted Hela, Lom's boat, out on the water. Lom was at the tiller and Brie could just make out Maire standing near the prow. Brie felt Hanna's eyes on her. "I'm thinking there may be another wedding in Ardara before Cynheafu," Brie said, her voice level.

Brie and Collun traveled with Hanna to the havotty where she was to meet the sheep farmer Tharda. When the time came to say good-bye to Hanna, Brie felt sorrow settle on her like a mantle; it made her feel heavy and stupid, without words. She looked into Hanna's face and saw that the older woman's eyes were a deep, bottomless gray. Tears pricked Brie's eyelids and she looked away. Her glance fell on Collun, who had stepped away while they said their good-byes. He was being butted rather forcefully by a black-faced mountain sheep, who mistook him for a rival, and Collun was unsuccessfully trying to fend the animal off, an aggrieved look on his face. Jip bounded at the sheep on one side, and Fara jostled it from the other side. The hapless sheep began bleating frantically. Brie suddenly smiled.

"Biri," came Hanna's voice. She was holding out a book for Brie. "Take this with you."

"But this is your havotty book," Brie protested, glancing at the title. It was a book about Fionna.

"I do not need it. I have enough books here," she said, gesturing at her head.

"Thank you," said Brie, taking the book. Hanna leaned over and they held each other tightly for a moment. "I will miss you, Hanna."

"And I you," Hanna said gently, releasing Brie. "But you will be back, Bren-huan."

"Perhaps," Brie replied, doubtful.

"No. You *will* return."

"The hiraeth?" Brie asked. She recalled the long-ago conversation with Aelwyn about the heartsickness that exiled Dungalans feel. "Like a knife in the heart," Aelwyn had said.

"Yes, hiraeth, and because you are queen."

Brie smiled. "Little queen. It is just a name, Hanna."

Hanna shook her head, face serious. "No. You are queen. Sago knew. And Yldir. Seila *is* Fionna."

Brie stared at Hanna. "No."

"When Queen Fionna disappeared, she must have gone to Eirren and had a family. There is a story there. When you return, you will tell it to me."

Brie shook her head.

"Yes, Biri," responded Hanna matter-of-factly, "when the time comes, you will return to Dungal, as queen."

As they rode through the foothills of the Blue Stacks, Collun gazed sideways at Brie. "You are quiet. What did the Traveler say to you?"

"Nothing of importance," Brie replied absently. She sifted through Hanna's words with wonder. She had never known the Traveler to tell an untruth. And yet, queen?! It was not possible. She would tell Collun later; perhaps they would laugh over it together at the campfire tonight.

They rode in silence for a time, comfortable, easy in each other's company.

"Where do we go now, Brie?"

"Cuillean's dun?"

"Perhaps," Collun said, but he did not sound enthusiastic.

Brie wondered if he was thinking of Renin's burial mound.

"We could visit Talisen at his bard school," Collun suggested.

"Or Nessa in Temair."

Neither one said anything for several minutes.

*Tir a Ceol,* Brie heard in her head, and laughed.

"What?" asked Collun.

"There is one among us," Brie said, "probably three, who would enjoy a journey to Tir a Ceol."

Fiain let out an enthusiastic whicker, and Fara came loping up next to Ciaran.

"I always said I would return to Tir a Ceol for my father's bow when my journey was done," Brie mused.

"You gave it to the Ellyl Ebba to keep?"

Brie nodded.

"Then let it be Tir a Ceol," responded Collun with a grin. "We can see what torments Silien has devised for Monodnock. And perhaps we could return to Cuillean's dun by harvesttime, not that there will likely be much to harvest..."

They passed a shepherd whose dogs set up a frenzied barking at the sight of the two Ellyl horses and the faol. Waving a greeting, Brie and Collun rode on.

"I was just thinking, Collun, of all the names I have had."

Collun nodded.

"Brie, Breo-Saight, Bren-huan, Breigit, Biri..." She ticked them off on her fingers. " 'Oona, moona, mollopy, mite...' I hardly know which of them I am anymore. Oh well. Perhaps I shall be nameless," she said with a grin. "I am without a home, after all; I might as well be without a name."

Collun was silent and his face was unreadable. Finally he spoke. "Brie is a very good name," he said slowly. "And you shall have a home at Cuillean's dun for as long as you wish."

Brie flushed. "Even if I do overwater the harebell and pull up the sweet william thinking it a weed?"

"Even then," Collun said, his voice level.

Then Ciaran, with an innocent sidelong glance over her shoulder at Brie, suddenly swerved in very close to Fiain. Smiling, Brie reached out her hand and Collun took it in his.